JACKRABBIT MOON

OTHER WORKS BY
SHEILA MCLEOD ARNOPOULOS

Le Fait Anglais au Québec
(with Dominique Clift), Libre Expression, 1979
Translated into English as *The English Fact in Quebec,*
McGill Queen's, 1980

Voices from French Ontario, McGill Queen's, 1982
Translated into French as *Hors du Québec: point de salut?,*
Libre Expression, 1982

Jackrabbit Moon

A novel by

Sheila McLeod Arnopoulos

Ronsdale Press

JACKRABBIT MOON
Copyright © 2000 Sheila McLeod Arnopoulos

RONSDALE PRESS
3350 West 21st Avenue
Vancouver, B.C., Canada
V6S 1G7

Set in Bembo: 11-1/2 pt on 15
Typesetting: Julie Cochrane
Printing: Hignell Printing, Winnipeg, Manitoba
Cover Art: Katharine Dickinson
Cover Design: Julie Cochrane
Author Photo: Jane Lewis

Ronsdale Press wishes to thank the Canada Council for the Arts, the Government of Canada through the Book Publishing Industry Development Program (BPIDP), and the Province of British Columbia through the British Columbia Arts Council for their support of its publishing program.

CANADIAN CATALOGUING IN PUBLICATION DATA

Arnopoulos, Sheila McLeod.
  Jackrabbit moon

  ISBN 0-921870-72-8

  I. Title.
PS8551.R772J32 2000   C813'.54   C99-911224-4
PR9199.3.A63J32 2000

*In memory of my mother's
dedication to youth of many backgrounds,
when in her teen years, as Alix McCaig,
she taught in a one-room schoolhouse
in the Peace River district
of northern Alberta in Canada.*

And though I have the gift of prophecy, and understand all mysteries, and all knowledge; and though I have all faith, so that I could remove mountains, and have not love, I am nothing.

— First Corinthians, *New Testament*

Acknowledgements

~

THIS BOOK COULD not have been written without the friendship and professional support of many people. I am indebted to Catholyn Jansen, Denyse Gerin-Lajoie and Hélène Gagné for their encouragement in the earliest stages. Iris Fitzpatrick Martin was invaluable as a painstaking reader and critic over the long gestation period of the book.

The St. Urbain Street Workshop in Montreal provided an important forum to test ideas and writing. I am particularly grateful for the feedback provided by the late Michael Morais, Jody Freeman, Jim Boothroyd, and the leader of the workshop, Dan Daniels. Daria MonDésire of The Border Writers Group in Vermont was also extremely helpful. At the Breadloaf Writers Conference at Middlebury College, Vermont, novelist Ann Hood gave me constructive criticism at an important juncture as did Carole Levert of Éditions Libre Expression, who is now publishing a French translation of *Jackrabbit Moon*.

In the last stages, Josh Freed, Ingrid Peritz, Claire Helman, Pat

Machin, Linda Ghan, Filippo Salvatore, Joyce Lautens O'Brien, Dusty Vineberg-Solomon as well as Edit Kuper and once again Catholyn Jansen, provided me with fresh perspectives. The late Susan Blaylock, Luis Millan, Linda O'Neill, Brigitte Christopher, Tasos Anastasopoulos and Justin Hayward offered research assistance in a variety of domains. Librarian Susie Breier from Concordia's Vanier Library and Maureen MacCuish of Lonergan College were also very helpful. I would also like to thank Chris Ferguson, Pierre Goldberger, and my cousin Kevin Lee for theological insights and understanding. Tom Puchniak helped with last-minute research and computer problems and gave moral support when it was most needed. Finally, my heartfelt appreciation to editor and publisher Ron Hatch of Ronsdale Press who believed in the project and who provided the kind of editorial support writers in this country dream of finding.

Montreal, 2000.

CONTENTS

~

The Newsroom

Nick and Eileen

On Trial

Prison

Maggie and Nick

The
Newsroom

ONE

~

The Tribune

MAGGIE LEANED BACK in her chair in the newsroom and fiddled with the pins holding her French twist in place. She had been in a rush that morning to get to the final session of the inquest. Home from India for only three days, she was still feeling high after a month in a little village near Bombay where she had written an undercover series about child labour in make-shift factories. But now she had a tough new assignment to think about.

She looked across the maze of computer terminals to the front of the office and saw her friend Alphie in his familiar brown tweed jacket. "Hi," he called out and headed for her desk. Alphie was an old court reporter. Ten years ago when she had first joined the Montreal *Tribune* as a junior reporter on the police desk, he had taken her under his wing and he still liked to play fatherly editor with her. He had tipped off Max to the inquest while she was in India, suggesting her for the job on her return. She liked talking to Alphie but she hoped he wasn't going to take up too much of her time. She had a hot story to write for Max's six o'clock deadline. Early in the news business game she'd learned that you were only as good as your last story. Competition between writers was acute in a large daily and the spectre of failing to produce on an assignment a nightmare.

"How's the baby killers story going?" Alphie asked as he peered into her computer screen. She was leading with Nicholas Mykonos shaking his fist at the coroner and yelling, "We didn't kill our kid," after the coroner had pronounced the couple criminally responsible for the death of their tiny infant. Alphie patted her on the back. "Good lead," he said.

"The details are awful," she told him. "It turns out the poor little baby died after six weeks of complete neglect. It's almost hard to believe. They went out for a fancy dinner and left him home alone with the window wide open — he froze to death."

"What did you really think of the couple?" he asked. Among journalists, the assumption was always that the juice of the story was never in the paper.

"The pair showed no remorse at all. He's a real biker type with a permanent scowl on his face and she looks like a tart. The kid was probably just in the way."

"Now, now," Alphie said. "Watch that you don't get too cranked up over this."

"Cranked up!" Maggie jammed her hands into the pockets of her navy blue linen suit. "The baby's father looked like a Hell's Angel with a giant chip on his shoulder. Real macho in leather and chains with two gold bracelets dangling on his wrist. Probably stolen. He's a break and entry freak. Likes to lift motorcycles. Only twenty, though he looks a lot older. He's already cooled his heels in a bunch of detention centres."

"A chrome pony," Alphie pronounced as he lit a cigarette like Humphrey Bogart in *Casablanca* and watched her from the corner of his eye. "The sort of boy chick certain girls go crazy over," he said as he ran his fingers through his silver-gray hair. He liked to tease her, sometimes calling her the preacher's daughter.

"Don't throw me that crap, Alphie. Any girl with her head screwed on would have to be nuts to get involved with a guy like that."

"And the mother?"

"The mother looked cheap as hell in a tight sweater, no bra, and a short black skirt. A nude dancer. The sort of pavement princess you see hanging around St. Lawrence and St. Catherine."

She paused for a moment. "But underneath all that get-up," she said slowly, "quite beautiful, with lovely strawberry-blond hair that isn't out of a bottle. Clearly terrified of Mykonos. Part way through the inquest she rolled up her sleeve and I saw a giant bruise on her arm. Typical. She's at a shelter." The police radio two desks away suddenly rose in volume and she yelled over it, "The baby's death was obviously *his* fault."

Alphie ambled away when Alice called from the library, "I think I have that reference you were looking for." The coroner in his final statement had compared the Mykonos baby to Petit Penuel, and Maggie had asked Alice for whatever she could dig up on that famous old Quebec story. "I'll bring it right over to you."

In the reference book from the 1940s, Maggie scanned the piece on the child who had been whipped with ropes and made to walk barefoot through a forest in a snowstorm until he froze to death. Given the nature of the story she was covering, the snow angle fit right in. This might well be the beginning of an important inquiry she could take on for the paper, she thought. While she was away, the Mulroney government had announced it would spend forty million dollars to combat rising family violence. A big exposé on child abuse in Montreal could be dynamite.

She had just finished inserting Petit Penuel into her piece when her Aunt Philana called from New York. "Just got your Bombay stories," she said. Maggie had mailed her clippings of the *Tribune* articles she'd filed from Bombay, complete with colour photos. Aunt Philana, who was her mother's younger sister, had inspired Maggie to take journalism at Columbia in New York and they liked to stay in touch.

"You look pretty cute in those balloon pants and that tunic, sewing buttons on jackets. Did you take your own photographer?" her aunt asked.

"No. One of the kids took the pictures."

"You look like a fifteen-year-old school girl. Nobody would ever guess you're thirty-seven. You like going undercover, don't you?"

"Just like you," Maggie replied. None of this was new to her lively Aunt Philana, an anthropology prof at Columbia who had spent years in Borneo and whose idol was Margaret Mead. Her aunt was such a contrast to her mother who had traded the dream of being an actress for the reality of becoming a Presbyterian minister's wife.

"How did you do it this time?" her aunt went on.

"A street worker from Bombay brought me in. The first night in that dusty one-room shack eating rice and beans off a leaf on the dirt floor was really something. There were eight kids and not much to eat. The next day the oldest one, Geeta, helped me dress up in a *salwar kameez* outfit. Then we walked hand in hand to the sweat shop with a gang of urchins." She sighed at the remembrance of the haunted looks in their eyes. "That's when I knew I'd be able to deliver a page one series of pieces. There was so much happening in the factory, no one noticed me."

Maggie looked up and saw Max Cousins, the managing editor, a tall, big-boned, blond Aussie with perpetually tanned skin, signalling her from outside the row of editors' offices that ringed the wide-open newsroom where all the reporters worked. "Got to go," she said. "Glad you liked the pieces. I'm on to something else — something really big here in Montreal."

She stood up and yelled across to Max, "My story will be ready by six." Normally a coroner's inquest wasn't of great interest but she knew this one would lead to a sensational child abuse trial. Max kept waving at her so she hurried over.

Max always wore a suit but he walked like a surfie from Bondi Beach and played it to the hilt. He believed all women were meant to be decorations for the Crocodile Dundee lizard he displayed on the pocket of his jacket. "Listen up, guys," Max called out to all the reporters clacking away at their terminals. "I have some great news! The *London Times* is taking Maggie's series on child labour in India." A thrill went through her, and led by Alphie, there was a round of applause, but she saw signs of annoyance on a few faces.

"And," Max tapped her shoulder and flung her his I'm the king of the beach smile, "we have our final addition to the investigative team." Great. Now it was official. She would be the second woman on the team of five. Each would be given time to develop in-depth assignments for page one and would report directly to him, the whip hand under the editor-in-chief in the newsroom hierarchy. "Okay," he said to everyone. "Back to the shop."

Maggie looked to the middle of the newsroom and saw envy in the eye of Barbara Smith-Jones, a reporter of twenty-seven. The day before, she'd watched Barbara in black body-pants and a revealing red sweater playing up to Max, hoping he'd name *her* to the team.

She glanced up at the award plaques on the wall beside Max's office. Maggie had won two national newspaper prizes, the last for a series on the effects of residential schools on native children. She deserved the spot over Barbara on the team. As she wove her way back to her desk, she imagined winning the enterprise award for her India series.

Journalism was her life. Unlike other reporters who were easily distracted by partners and families, she had the freedom to pour her heart into her work. But now she had no time to waste. She had to send her story to Max who would give it a quick once-over before she gave it to the city desk. Then, at seven, she was meeting with the women's caucus of the Periodical Writers Association to put the final touches to a cultural exchange program between Russian and Canadian women journalists.

～

The next morning, Maggie heard the guys guffaw as soon as she opened the big glass doors at the paper. The first edition of the *Tribune* had just been put to bed and the sub-editors from the city desk were rolling down on the escalator for their first beer of the day in the tavern across the street. As she ascended in the opposite direction, she rummaged in her shoulder bag, pretending to be busy. Passing her on their way down, they reeked of sweat and nicotine.

Reggie Garfield, the chief rewrite man, had probably had the last word on her story on the kid killers. His Zellers shirt showed stains under the arms and outlined his pot belly. "Hey, Maggie!" Reggie called out. He had eyes that went mean whenever she protested the changes he made to her stories.

"What a pile of shit you got out of that one," he bellowed. He stretched out his paw to smack her on the behind but she managed to sidestep him. "Used everything you wrote. Pictures, too," he grinned. "Page one, Baby, above the fold. You actually knocked out Meech lake!"

"Thank you Reg," she said sweetly, but she couldn't help remembering how his wife had called for him the night before, complaining that she had no money to buy milk for the twins. Reggie, it seems, hadn't been home for two days.

In the newsroom, Maggie picked up a copy of the first edition and sat down at her desk. The headline at the top of page one read: *Enfant de la Neige — Another Petit Penuel?* The bold byline, "By Maggie MacKinnan," was underneath. She gazed at the photograph of Mykonos looking like an animal in leather and chains. But the courts would bring him down to size, she thought. And she would be there giving readers of the *Tribune* every chilling detail of the story and watching him bite the dust.

The day was just starting and everyone was checking out whose stories had made the paper and on which page. She read her piece and was furious when she saw that Reggie had made changes to her story that she didn't like, but it was too late to do anything, and it wasn't worth a fight.

She walked to the front of the newsroom to get a coffee. "Right on the mark," said Alphie who was monitoring a couple of young reporters working the police radios. "My sources tell me Max's going to ask you to get cracking on a series on child and wife abuse. It should be another feather in your cap. Right after that, you can cover the trial."

She had worked her way up at the *Tribune* covering the usual beats like City Hall and education, but she had burned for the chance to escape the daily grind ever since she had arrived at the paper at twenty-seven, after writing about refugees for a small New York monthly and sending the *Tribune* freelance pieces. Now that she had been named to the team, her full-time job would be doing investigative assignments for page one. Exactly what she had always dreamed of . . .

～

The telephone calls she received that morning confirmed that the time was ripe for a full probe on abuse. Women from shelters all over the city called to tell her that the *Tribune* should go after violent men like Mykonos. A university researcher praised her for her series on child labour in India. "Extraordinary stories you wrote, but isn't it time you explored what's happening in our own Third World?" Maggie spent the rest of the morning in the library with Alice looking for the latest studies on male violence.

Just after lunch Max stepped up to her desk. "I want to see you in five minutes," he smiled and touched her shoulder in a way that made her flesh creep. He always expected her to act as if she were attracted to him but she refused to do it. She usually wore business suits to avoid being a candidate for the sexual politics around the office but it didn't always work. Screw him, she said to herself.

His feet on the desk, Max was on the phone when she entered his office. She pulled her skirt down over her knees as she sat and waited. Max's nickname around the office was KK for Kangaroo Kutie because of a photo in his office of a bare-breasted girl in a kangaroo costume. Sort of Minoan, Maggie had thought after her initial outrage. KK had paid his dues at a London tabloid. Eventually he had insinuated himself onto a better Fleet Street paper and then moved to Canada. She focused on the hall of fame pinned up behind his desk. A series of black and white photos displayed a preening Max with Margaret Thatcher, Jodi Foster, Meryl Streep and Norman Mailer. His favourite picture, garishly framed, showed him cavorting on a trampoline with Pierre Elliott Trudeau in his younger days at the Montreal Jazz Festival. In his stories he had always gone after the obvious.

"The series on Hitler's private parts starts Saturday," he said into the phone. He was probably talking to the news editor. "Well that's about what it amounts to. Okay? Ciao," and he hung up.

"Shocking. Readers will love it," he said apropos of the series on the more gross elements of Hitler's boudoir life. "My old paper on Fleet Street is running it, too. You should read the stuff."

Max was now keeping track of the Montreal tabs in both of Canada's official languages. "We're in for a fight with the new boys down the block. We'll stay a serious paper but we've got to hold on to every reader. There'll be some changes and you guys have to hold up your end."

He dragged on a cigarette and settled his butt deeper into his leather swivel chair. "Good job you did on the kid killers story. The story's got the whole enchilada — murder, wife-bashing, naked dancing. I liked those details you fished up on that Petit Penuel kid the coroner referred to.

"I want you to cover the trial when it comes up. I was talking about it over lunch with the publisher. The *Daily Sun* will be out by then. We've got to beat them on their own turf. It'll be good having a woman cover this. I know you've never covered the courts, but Alphie will answer any questions.

"In the meantime," he thumped the desk, "zero in on child abuse in the city. And look into wife battering too. Dig up everything you can. This is your first assignment working directly for me. We want you to make a specialty of this, and we'll feature every story."

"Fine," Maggie said. "I know from the phone calls I received this morning that the Mykonos baby death is the ugly tip of an iceberg that we've all refused to look at. My work is cut out for me. I'm dying to get at it," and she stood up to go.

"One last thing. When the trial comes up, our readers should be totally enraged. You understand?"

"Absolutely."

"We're counting on you, Maggie. Let me know as soon as you're ready with your first piece."

~

For the next month, Maggie complied with Max's order and homed in on incidents of child and wife abuse all over the Island of Montreal. She was onto a real social issue story, she felt, where the victims were completely defenceless, and she didn't have to look hard to find material.

"Kids are being brutally knocked around, some of them dying in the most suspicious ways," she told Alphie as she wrote the first of her front-page pieces. "From what I'm hearing from the women's centres, things are much worse than we imagine."

"Watch out you don't get too worked up about all this," Alphie told her. But she ignored his comment and went on. "The statistics on abuse are just a fraction of the reality. Mostly because the women are too terrified to do anything about it. First the guys beat up on their wives, and then they kick around the kids."

As she listened to child protection officers, social workers and policemen talk, she kept thinking of the upcoming trial of Nicholas Mykonos who had now become her own personal symbol of male violence.

In response to her series, women phoned to tell personal stories of physical abuse by their husbands or boyfriends, and sexual violation by fathers, uncles and grandfathers. She had always known these violations were widespread but she found the details deeply troubling.

Many of the callers cried. Feeling part-friend, if only for a short time, Maggie listened to their experiences, their emotional accounts becoming "reaction stories" to the series. Writing relentlessly, she took phone calls on the latest article, wrote some more, and took more calls, but the demand for stories and the whirlwind pace of the newsroom overwhelmed her to the point where she realized — with a jolt — that she had stopped feeling anything for the people she was writing about.

At home, however, in the silence of her apartment, she couldn't escape the images of the victimized. One night she woke up in a sweat thinking about the frozen baby. The trial was now coming up. Was she going to be able to keep on writing about such grim material at this frantic pace?

She had just finished watching the CBC evening news late on a Sunday evening when she heard the familiar honk of a car beneath the window of her second-storey apartment on St. Antoine Street. It was Michael. On his way home to the refugee centre he ran in LaSalle, he sometimes dropped by for a chat.

"C'mon up," she yelled out the window. Although he was a United Church minister now in his late forties, Michael looked more like a 1960s hippie. When she had been at McGill, Michael had been campus chaplain but he had also run a street mission in St. Henri. There, in the heart of the working-class neighbourhood, he had conducted chapel services for troubled kids in an abandoned bar on the canal not far from where she now lived. During her last year at university, she had occasionally played hymns for Michael's services on an old pump organ. He had really wanted someone who could play a guitar, but all he could find was her, Miss Minister's Daughter.

Michael swung in the door wearing an earring that some street kids had given him long ago. In his faded jeans and his pony tail, he looked out-of-place next to the Royal Doulton collection of figurines she had inherited from her mother.

"I'm glad you dropped by," she said as she poured coffee. "I'm absolutely exhausted from all these stories I've been writing, and now this baby trial is a week away. I don't know if I'm up to it." She picked up a pile of newspapers and magazines from a chair, dumped them on the floor, and waved him to sit.

"I've been following your stories," Michael said as he stretched out his legs. "I distinctly remember your inquest piece on the Mykonos case."

"It was hard to miss," Maggie said as she thought about the front-page play in the *Tribune*. She put on a new CD she'd picked up of the McGarrigle Sisters and they talked about the kinds of stories different newspapers choose to play up. After a while Michael came back to the Mykonos case.

"You know," he said looking her straight in the eye, "there's nothing like a motorcycle kid and a nude dancer on welfare to tick off the sort of people who read the *Tribune*. You've got to be careful you don't take some outraged posture on all this. There's always much more than you can ever imagine in all these cases."

Maggie thought for a few minutes about Michael's remark and then watched him finish his coffee. She wanted to talk more, but when the McGarrigle sisters finished their last song he stood up to go. Michael was always in such a hurry. "Stay a little longer," she said. "I have a nice piece of apple pie for you." She had made apple pie the night before for the lunch she always prepared for her father at the manse after the Sunday morning church service and she had saved a piece.

"No, I really must shove off. Tomorrow I'm off to Guatemala to try my luck at a little guerilla work," and he drew his hand across his neck. "Just a short trip this time. I'll be back soon," and he kissed her on both cheeks and went out the door.

After he left, Maggie leaned back against her sofa and felt the emptiness of her apartment. On her living room wall, her mother looked down at her from the portrait done the year she died at thirty-seven. Her father had insisted she hang it in her living room. Her mother was small and delicate like the figurines Maggie had inherited from her but her eyes bled with resentment.

Maggie's eyes swept the bare room that called out for a dining room table. She rarely had visitors, and usually ate meals on her lap. She had, after she had left home, always lived alone. There was little here of her except for some geraniums she grew in the kitchen, her graduation picture from Columbia with her aunt Philana, and a picture of her international folk dance group in Ukrainian dress. She was always too busy to think about shopping for furniture and making her place look like a real home.

~

The next morning back in the newsroom, Michael's advice faded as soon as she saw Max who was all smiles and flattery. "You've done a smashing piece of work. The television and radio publicity on your stuff has been terrific," he told her. "You've finished your series now. Get ready for the trial. Chill out. Take a few days off. Next week will be tough."

She sank down in her chair at her desk with a coffee and thirty seconds later the phone jingled. "I have to talk to someone," a girl said. She had a young voice. "I saw your articles."

"Yes . . ."

The girl leapt right in. "It started when I was three. I had this uncle who was always around. He put me on his knee and he, ah, he pulled it out and I had to . . ." she sobbed.

Maggie tried not to let the horrible details that the girl described register. "Look," she interrupted. "You probably need someone to talk to about all this, someone who can help you. I'm going to give you the name of a really good person. Her name is Esther Sykes. She works at the YWCA helping abused women." Maggie gave her a phone number. "Okay?" she asked, and when she heard the girl reply, she said goodbye and hung up.

She was just getting ready to leave when the phone rang again, but this time it was her father. "I've got tickets for *Manon Lescaut* next Saturday. It'll take your mind off all that dreadful stuff you're writing about."

"Okay," she sighed, and ignored his comment. "I'll be there." She squirmed as she thought of how her father expected her to wear her mother's flowered silk suit when she accompanied him to all the big opera productions, the way her mother had until she grew too ill. "Goodbye, Father. See you soon."

She took a sip of coffee and thought about how much happier her father would have been if she'd chosen some other profession, such as teaching in a private school where she wouldn't have to get her hands dirty. In English Montreal, writing for a newspaper carried a certain glamour, she thought, but nothing like the status in the French community where journalists like René Lévesque or André Laurendeau or Solange Chaput-Rolland went on to become prominent political figures who made history.

In the late afternoon, Maggie left the office to escape the phone and decided to visit a toy store where her mother had taken her as a child. Her cousin Moira's three-year-old son might like a teddy bear. Maggie and Moira, without any siblings of their own, had been brought up almost like sisters. They had gone their own ways and were not close but Maggie liked Moira's children and often babysat.

The toy store was in the Greek neighbourhood on Park Avenue where the air smelled of souvlaki and the grocery stores sold olives in barrels and feta cheese swimming in water. Maggie took her red Innocenti up Côte des Neiges and drove across Mount Royal through the mountain parkland.

Down on Park Avenue, inside the store, rows of teddy bears made her think of the old days when her mother was young and healthy. A darling bear with a blue and white polka dot bow reminded her of the one her mother had given her when she was in kindergarten.

As she was paying for it her stomach tightened. She could hardly believe it. In a corner, Nicholas Mykonos was holding a bear very like the one she had just bought. What was this animal doing out on bail? He had a battered knapsack on his back and looked as though he'd been sleeping in his clothes. She looked again. The same wide shoulders and slim hips she'd seen at the inquest. His face was a rich olive shade. Greek. Yes, this was his district. He and his wife Eileen had lived around the corner on Paros Street.

This was the first time she had seen him up close. A pocket knife hung from his belt. Keeping herself well out of sight, she listened.

"I was awfully sorry to hear about the death of your baby," said the saleswoman. Nick squeezed his eyes shut. "Everything the papers said was wrong," he scowled. "Wrong." The saleswoman said nothing.

"Look. If I give you a dollar now?" he asked, "can I come back and pay the rest later? For old times sake, like?" Maggie wondered what "old times sake" was all about. Could he possibly be a friend of this saleslady? It seemed very unlikely. Mykonos was wearing tight leather pants, perhaps the same ones he'd worn to the coroner's inquest. It was a strange sight, this Hell's Angel look-alike clutching a teddy bear.

"Just a minute, Nick," said the saleswoman, and she vanished into the back. While she was gone, he pushed the bear into his leather jacket and before leaving tried to yank open the drawer of the cash register, but it was locked. Maggie followed him out the door and watched him wind his way through Greek and Hasidic women bargaining over items of clothing at a street sale on Park Avenue. Across the road, Bazouki music rang out from a sidewalk café where some older men were playing chess, and he stopped to look. Someone was singing a Greek melody she recognized from her folk dance group. She stood still and watched him tap his foot to the music. Then she followed as he walked down the street and entered two pool halls where he looked nervously around and then left. Finally he went into a bar where motorcycles were parked outside. Maggie could see there were girls inside and a crowd that would conceal her so she took a chance and went in.

"Like something?" a bartender asked. "I'm waiting for someone," she said. The clientele looked as though they were all members of motorcycle clubs.

She listened to Nick try to strike up a conversation with two men leaning against the bar. "The Cougar Rally still on for next Saturday?" he asked.

"Yeah," said a biker with a cougar tattoo on his arm and a spiky ring on his finger. "But you gotta be a member," and he turned away.

Outside, Nick stroked the body of one of the Harleys, his pants revealing every curve of his body. He had that same scowl on his face.

When he continued walking, she followed him across Mount Royal Avenue to Fletchers Field and started up the rough mountain road filled with joggers, cyclists and families with children.

It was a hot August day and the trek up Mount Royal was long and arduous. She was glad of her sturdy sandals and a full skirt that kept her cool. Nick walked quickly, moving as gracefully as a gymnast. As she pursued him up the rocky mountain road, adrenalin was pumping through her veins. At the top, he stopped for a long while to look at the ducks on Beaver Lake.

Near the water, he sat down with his teddy bear behind some trees in a protected clearing where he silently rocked back and forth like the old women in the nursing home scandal she'd once investigated. For a few minutes he dozed off. Why, she asked herself, was she wasting her afternoon shadowing him like this? The trial hadn't even started and already Mykonos was becoming an obsession. A pang in her stomach reminded her she hadn't had supper and she reached into her purse for a granola bar.

When the sun began to fade, Nick stood up and wandered into the cemetery for the poor, and she followed. She had never been here before. Teetering homemade crosses made of wood, wrought iron and plastic dotted the graves. A few people were still strolling around. He stood solemnly in front of a small wooden grave marker. After a while he left the cemetery but she stayed on by herself. Moving up close to the grave she saw that the paste-and-stick letters read Stephanos Nicholas Mykonos. She sat down on the grass, and for a long time she stared at the teddy bear that lay on the ground . . .

∽

Nick kicked the dirt ahead of him as he walked down the mountain. He looked at his watch. Eight-fifteen. He'd go down to the park near the metro where he and his friend Torchy used to plan their break and entries. Maybe he'd see someone he could hang out with. Later, when the subway shut down, there was a place down the tracks in the tunnel where he could spend the night.

Eileen could have stayed with him after the baby died, he thought. That's when he fuckin' needed her the most, but instead she let those bitches Carmen and Retta drag her off to a shelter. Then without even telling him, she'd arranged the burial. This was the second time he'd visited his son's grave. It was Torchy who had told him where to look.

He kicked a tree hard. He had to face it. Eileen and little Stevie were gone. He had rung the bell of a shelter near Park Avenue a week after she left, thinking maybe she was there, but a policewoman came out and said if he ever showed up again, she'd arrest him. They didn't want guys near the shelter.

Eileen could be anywhere now. Probably with her friend Kelly. The next time he'd see her was at the trial. He breathed in hard through his teeth. The inquest had been bad enough and now he'd have to go through a trial. Alone. He had seen the *Tribune* with his picture on the front page the day after the inquest, and the story was all wrong.

"Wrong, wrong, wrong," he yelled out at the dark. He grabbed his pocket knife from his belt, opened it out, and stabbed the tree hard. Those reporters knew nothing about the life he'd had with Eileen and his baby son. The trial was sure to be worse than the inquest. He had tried his best to explain everything to his lawyer, but she didn't understand either. How could anyone know what had really happened? Even he wasn't sure.

Nick and
Eileen

TWO

~

Birth

"COULD I SEE the brown one with the blue bow?" Nick asked. "No, just a minute. The one right behind it with the red and white polka dots." He wanted a teddy bear for his newborn son. There were so many teddy bears in the toy store. With her long stick, the sales-lady took the bear down. She had a streak of gray across her hair like Mum Evans, his last foster Mum. Grandfather bears with glasses, punk bears with green hair, motorcycle bears, E.T. bears, there was every kind of bear he could possibly imagine. He was finding it hard to concentrate.

A wave of fear swept over him as he thought of the terrifying moment early that morning at the hospital when the baby's head had appeared between Eileen's legs. Holding her hand, he had felt her nails dig into him so hard he had wanted to slap her. He had imag-ined his newborn son looking fresh and cuddly, but the cord was wound around his neck as though he were strangling and his face was bright red. He had dropped Eileen's hand as soon as he saw his son all covered with guck. He had wanted to scream. While the doctor cut the cord, he had stared down at the floor, but then he heard the baby give a little cry, and when he dared to look up, he was amazed at the sight of his beautiful baby son washed clean and lying silently in Eileen's arms with his head on her breast.

Had his own mother held him that way when *he* was born? In his top pocket, he felt the envelope with the note from her. He kept it in a bottom drawer along with other treasures, but on special occasions he put it in his breast pocket. The last time was when he got married. The bus driver had found the note pinned to his diaper. "I love you very much, but your father left, and I can't take care of you. Your name is Nicholas Stephanos Mykonos." The writing was scraggly, as though his mother were shaking when she wrote it. She had left him on the bus from Quebec City to Montreal when he was six weeks old and suffering from pneumonia. He pushed the bear he was holding face down on the table. The saleslady was waiting for him to choose.

He touched a bear with a red nose but it only reminded him of Grandpa O'Brien who belonged to the first family he could remember. Judy had told him the O'Briens had been his eighth foster family. She was the last social worker they assigned to him at Parkway House. She moved to Toronto, but before she left he had sneaked a look into his file.

Nick fondled the ears of a pale blue bear that wore a button saying Love you Forever. "Danny, my, ah, brother gave me one like this," he told the saleslady. He usually said foster brother, but this time he said brother. If Danny had been around, instead of in Victoria at that fancy school Pop forced him to go to, the Evans would have adopted him instead of cousin Luke. Danny would have made sure he stayed. He had overheard Mum plead with Pop to let him stay. "Nick has always been special. We can't just throw him out." She had promised him a big party for his sixteenth birthday, but Mum was afraid of Pop and stood up to him only when Danny was around.

"You'll come on weekends," Mum had said the day before he went to Parkway. He was in the hospital then. It was after he had "roughed off" the motorcycles. They said he was "acting out." She brought oatmeal-raisin cookies and held his hand while they watched television together in the visitors room. He spoke to her on the phone, but he never saw her again and Pop blamed him when she died two months later of breast cancer.

"She got it after you came. You wore her down," Pop said. The bugger refused to let him come to the funeral. "It's a small funeral for family only," he said. Danny flew from Vancouver for it. The next day the two of them went to the cemetery and Nick put yellow roses on her grave. He was never sure how to make Mum happy. She always smiled though when he complimented her on her dinners. All the foster mums loved that.

He had to stop thinking about Grandpa and Mum and Danny, and his real mother, who had never tried to find him. He rolled back his shoulders. He was a father now. He had to be strong. He was having a hard time making up his mind about the bear.

"Who's it for?" the saleslady asked.

"My son. My wife had a baby at five this morning." On his way to the hospital, he'd lift a few flowers for Eileen from the supermarket. It wouldn't be hard to snitch them from there. He'd seen some roses the same colour as her hair.

"A boy!" said the saleslady. "That's wonderful! Your first? It must be your first."

"Yes."

"You look so young," she said.

"Not that young. I'm twenty." He was nineteen but his birthday was coming up soon.

"Well, not *that* old either. You're the same age as my grandson Eddie and he's still living at home. Eddie's working at the back, unpacking dolls for my international doll room," she said. "Maybe you'd like to meet him?"

Nick looked away from her and made a face. "Naw," he said. "I'm in too much of a hurry." He felt like kicking the wall. He wanted the grannie to himself. She touched his shoulder and he felt his guard slip.

"You know?" he said, "you're the first person I've told about my son." He had been dying to tell someone.

"Really?" She paused. "What about your parents? They must know."

"My parents died," he said quickly. "In a plane crash." That was how cousin Luke's parents had died. How do you tell someone your mother left you in the sink of a bus and then disappeared?

"I'm awfully sorry," said the saleslady. "What about your brother?"

"He's out west at university." Which was true. Danny now lived in British Columbia.

Nick looked at the row of bears he'd selected to choose from. He leaned toward the one with the red and white polka dots. Eileen had given him a Valentine's card with one that looked just like that when he was living at Parkway. The only nice thing about Parkway was the baseball park down the street where he and Eileen used to meet. As long as he had Eileen, and now the baby, he'd be all right. "Till death do us part." That was the vow he loved best about the marriage ceremony.

"I'll take this one," he said, choosing the one with the red and white polka dots. The saleslady wrapped up the teddy bear in blue tissue paper and tied it with a big blue bow. When Nick took ten dollars out of his wallet to pay, she told him to put it back.

"It's a present," she smiled. "A grannie present." He could hardly believe it. A grannie present! He didn't know what to say and shuffled his feet. "Come back and show me the baby," she called after him as he left.

～

Holding a bouquet of apricot-coloured roses and his parcel with the blue bow, Nick pushed open the glass doors of the hospital lobby. A loudspeaker called out doctors' names. "Uh, I've come to see my wife," he said to a nurse in front of the elevators. "I forget what floor . . ." After Eileen had given birth, he went to her room, but now he couldn't remember where it was. The smell of disinfectant overpowered him. It reminded him of that day in the hospital when he saw his grandpa O'Brien for the last time. The nurse ignored him, and when the elevator doors opened, everyone got on, but he slid down against the wall and shut his eyes.

A Greek family with bags of food, flowers, and balloons was making a noise and he opened his eyes and stood up. When he and Eileen moved to Paros Street, he started picking up Greek words. His friend Torchy thought maybe Nick's father was a Greek sailor who had met his mother when his ship docked for a few days in Quebec City. "Those guys look for a hit in every port," he said. Torchy hung around the pool hall. Nick knew him from his days at the detention centre.

A man in a white coat passed by. "Do you know what floor new mothers are on?" Nick asked. The man looked at him crossly. "See the information desk," he said, and waved to the other side of the lobby.

Nick lined up at the information desk where a man was talking angrily to a woman in a green uniform. He had his arm around a boy of about ten who was crying. "My son needs to see a doctor," the man said. "Go to the children's hospital," said the receptionist.

When Nick had had to go to the children's hospital at the same age for something minor, Pop brought him in because Mum was away. Nick felt a migraine coming on. Hospitals always threw him into a panic. He never knew why until Judy told him it was because his foster parents were always taking him to a hospital and never coming back. There was a no smoking sign but Nick lit up a cigarette, inhaled furiously, then stubbed out the butt with the heel of his boot.

~

Eileen could have used the phone in the room but decided to use the public telephone in a booth down the hall. She didn't want Nicky to catch her calling Kelly. Her friend Kelly had taken her to a doctor and persuaded her to have her baby in a hospital, not at home with a midwife as Nick wanted. She looked at the clock in the corridor. Kelly *had* to be home. Her shift at Salomé's Salon didn't start until noon. Feeling totally exhausted, she leaned against the wall and starting with 0 punched in the number to Sherbrooke. "This is a collect call," she said to the operator, "from Eileen."

"It's a boy," she told Kelly when she came on.

"Wonderful," Kelly said. "Is he okay? And are you okay?"

"My doctor says the baby is pretty good. A little underweight though." Kelly had warned her not to smoke so much hash. "You'll lose your appetite," she'd told her. Nick wanted company when he smoked. But it wasn't just that. The hash made her forget about all the things that worried her.

"Have you called your mother?" Kelly asked.

"No . . ."

"This might be the time to make up."

Eileen hadn't seen her mother for three years — not since the middle of grade ten when her mother found out what was going on with her stepfather Rube, and threw her out.

"You know how much she hates babies." Lying in bed earlier that morning, when one of the other babies had been crying, Eileen had remembered when she was six how her mother had let her baby sister cry night after night. Then one day the baby was gone and she didn't know why.

Kelly had lived in the apartment directly below Eileen when they were growing up in Verdun and she told Eileen what had happened. Her mother stopped feeding the baby. All she did was drink. Eventually a social worker took Eileen's sister away and placed her in a foster home. Later, the baby was adopted. "The baby'd be twelve now," Eileen said.

"Listen. Forget about that baby sister of yours. At least your mum didn't foster *you* out."

Eileen chewed on her knuckles. "It wasn't because she didn't want to." The night Rube moved in with all his belongings when she was seven, Eileen had opened her bedroom door a crack and listened to them talking in the kitchen. "I'll see if she can live somewhere else," her mother had said. At first Eileen thought it was in response to some demand from Rube, but then she realized it was all her mother's idea. "She's a sweet kid," Rube had said. In spite of what happened later, she still felt touched. After all, he stuck up for her. "Why would you want her to go?" Rube had asked. "I'd miss her if she wasn't around."

"Hey! You still there?" Kelly asked.

"Yeah." Eileen pressed her head against the wall of the phone booth. "If it hadn't been for my stepfather, maybe I'd be dead."

"That slob saved you from being dead?"

Eileen tried to straighten up. "Rube had his nice side," she said. Whenever she was sick, her mother vanished, but Rube was always there. Like that time in grade two when she got chicken pox. For a week her mother was gone — probably to a bar downtown. Rube was the one who found a doctor and took care of her.

"Nice side?" Kelly said. "Is that why starting in grade seven, you wanted to sleep downstairs in my room?"

"Okay, Kelly," Eileen said wearily. "Things changed, but when I was little . . ."

Kelly cut in. "I never believed I'd hear you say a good word about that Hungarian stepfather of yours."

"Look. For two years, Rube paid for my ballet lessons." A very promising student, the ballet mistress had said when she was ten. Eileen steadied herself against the wall. If things had turned out differently, she might have become a dancer with the National Ballet.

"You know. I've never really thanked you," she said. When I had nowhere to go . . ." her voice caught.

"C'mon," Kelly said.

"You were like an older sister to me," Eileen said slowly. "If it hadn't been for you, I wouldn't have finished high school."

When her mother threw her out, Kelly gave Eileen a bed in the apartment she'd taken in lower Notre Dame de Grâce with Betsy and

Marylou and then found her a job at the box factory on weekends so she could pay her way. She had made her lunches and helped her with her French homework. Afterwards, Kelly taught her how to strip so she could get into the Sex Trolley.

"C'mon, Eileen."

"If I hadn't had you I might have jumped in the river. Especially after . . ."

"See what I mean," Kelly barged in. "Your stepfather was poison."

Eileen shifted from one foot to the other. "I should go. In a few minutes they'll bring the baby. Besides, this is costing you money."

"That's okay," Kelly said. "Look. Let *me* call your mother."

"Kelly," Eileen pleaded.

"Okay, okay. But send me a picture of the baby. I don't know when I'll be able to see you. And take care."

～

It was Nick's turn at the information desk. "Next," said the lady in the green uniform.

"Uh, I'm looking for Eileen O'Reilly Mykonos. My wife had a baby this morning."

She leafed through some cards. "Fifth floor. Room 549." He raced over to the elevator. Outside the emergency entrance he saw a broken-down drunk he'd met at the Green Pasture shelter. His head pounded. He had to get Eileen out of this place as quickly as possible. Then he remembered what the nurse had said to him after Eileen gave birth. "In two or three days, you'll have the two of them to yourself. Until then your wife stays here at the hospital." After a few minutes waiting for the elevator, he ran up five flights of stairs and was sweating when he reached the top.

A nurse by the desk in front of the stairs motioned for him to come over.

"I'm looking for room 549. My, ah, wife, had a baby this morning."

"Name?" she said abruptly.

"Eileen O'Reilly Mykonos."

"You're the father?"

He nodded. "Nicholas Mykonos. I was here when she gave birth."

"Could I have some identification?"

He looked down the hall and saw the father of the big Greek family. He felt like asking her whether she'd asked *him* for ID. Did he look too much like a biker? Maybe it was his black leather jacket. He put the roses down on the desk and dug into his back pocket. He pulled out his medicare card, and watched as the nurse checked it against Eileen's name.

"That will be fine, Mr. Mykonos," she said curtly. "Fifth door to your left." Bitch, he said to himself as he walked down the hall.

∽

He put the roses and the teddy bear at the end of the bed, gave Eileen a hug, and drank in the smell on her neck that always reminded him of apples. "Everything okay?" he asked. "You and the baby doing good?"

Eileen smiled. "Pretty good." She was glad to see him.

He wanted her home. He was dying to have sex with her. It had been a whole month since they'd had sex. It was natural he wanted her home, wasn't it? He picked up the roses from the end of the bed. "I brought you these. Smell," he said and wafted them under her nose. "They match your hair."

"Oh Nicky, aren't you a doll."

He took a step back. "I won't ask the nurse for a vase because I want you and the baby home with me right away." Eileen fell back on the pillow and Nick examined her wrist. She was wearing a plastic bracelet with the hospital's name on it. Like they owned her. "The nurse at the desk in front of the elevator actually asked me for ID," he said.

"Yeah?" she said.

"You're feeling okay, aren't you?" He tugged at the plastic wrist band.

"Well, kind of tired." The ID business got her thinking about the break and entries Nick had been doing with Torchy. Practically one a day after he quit his job at the box factory and she gave up working at the nursing home. It was no good selling stolen TVs and VCRs to taxi drivers. One of them was bound to tell the police, but she said nothing.

He sat on the edge of the bed and took her hand. "I'm going to bring you back some clean clothes and some more stuff for the baby. Then we'll leave."

Eileen shut her eyes. She was exhausted and still a little sore. In the hospital she felt safe. The nurses did everything.

"Eileen," he said. "Please Eileen." There were some things she still didn't understand. "I can't stand to have you and the baby here. Tell the nurse you're feeling fine, that you want to go home."

Eileen opened her eyes and looked past him the way her own mother used to do when she wanted Eileen to leave her alone.

"Eileen," he said. "Look at me. Twelve hours in here should be long enough. I'll come back for you in . . ." He looked at his watch. "How about five? That'll give you another five and a half hours. Okay?"

∼

After Nick left, the nurse took the baby back to the nursery. Eileen was just about to doze off when the nurse came in and said, "Eileen, you have another visitor."

Her stepfather Rube walked in the door. Eileen was shocked to see him. "How'd you find out I was here?"

"I listened in," he said, "while a little birdie talked to your mother."

"Kelly?"

He smiled. "No. Irene." Kelly's mother, Irene O'Grady, lived downstairs. Eileen reached for her dressing gown to cover herself up. She thought of asking what her mother's reaction was and then changed her mind.

"I bought you a little something," Rube said. "For when you're gorgeous again." From a plastic bag, he pulled out a short burgundy-coloured suede skirt and a pink angora sweater exactly like the set he'd given her when she was fifteen and he'd taken her to that motel. She sighed.

"Size eight okay?" The set he'd bought back then was size six.

He leaned down to kiss her on the lips and she gave him her cheek. "Look Rube. It's like I told you before. I'm married. And . . ."

"Calm down. I didn't come here to start up anything."

"Let's go down to the nursery. I'll show you the baby. He looks just like Nicky. Dark chestnut hair just like his. Wonderful little black lashes. And deep blue eyes. I told you Nicky was Greek, didn't I?" She could hardly walk she was so tired, but she wanted to get away from the intimacy of the bed. Eventually, when it was nursing time again, a nurse rescued her.

Back in her room, after he'd gone, she couldn't help admiring the skirt and sweater he'd bought her. Just like him to buy her exactly the same outfit she'd worn to that motel! It sort of spoiled it. Still. She was keeping them. They'd look great to come and go from the Sex Trolley if she ever worked there again. She put them at the bottom of her suitcase. If Nicky found them, she'd say they were Kelly's.

～

She snoozed for a while and then hurried to prepare for Nick. A few minutes before seven, she tucked her little Stevie into the pale blue snowsuit Nick had found at a church rummage sale. It was too big but a nice colour.

Nick arrived at seven sharp. "C'mon," he said and lifted his sleeping son out of her arms. Eileen picked up her small suitcase and a large canvas shoulder bag, but she didn't want to leave.

"I'm sorry," one of the nurses suddenly said, her hands across the door. "You can't go home. We'd like to observe the baby a little more." For a moment, Eileen thought Nick was going to blow up at the nurse. He had that wild look in his eyes. "Wait here, please," said the nurse.

Eileen sat on the bed and prayed they'd force her to stay the full three days. A minute later, the nurse came back with a large woman who turned out to be the head nurse. She took the baby from Nick. "I'm sorry, Mr. Mykonos, but your wife and child are staying here for two more days. Those are doctor's orders," she said and she marched out of the nursery with his child.

"Did you tell them you *wanted* to stay?" Nick asked Eileen.

"Nicky, Nicky," she said. Tears spotted her cheeks. "I'm so tired and they take care of everything."

Why couldn't Eileen see how *he* was feeling? "You know why I can't stand this place, don't you?" When he was five, after his appendix operation, he was in a ward just like Eileen's. The other kids had mums and dads who brought presents. All he had was the social worker. For hours he sat by the window hoping to see his grandpa come in the front door.

He drew himself up tall. He had to take charge. After all, he was now a father. "Call me when you and my son can leave. Okay? And remember, he's ours. Not theirs. They don't own him." He leaned over and kissed her. "It'll be nice at home. I promise."

∽

Two days later, Nick marched into the hospital room and picked up his son. "C'mon," he said to Eileen. Before she called Nick, Eileen made sure the head nurse agreed they could leave. She did not want a fight. The nurse who had looked after Eileen from the beginning handed her a standard package filled with formula, diapers and night shirts. Eileen stuffed it into her shoulder bag and on her way out grabbed the roses Nick had brought her.

"In two weeks you'll hear from a nurse from the community health clinic," the nurse whispered, as they walked to the elevator behind Nick and the baby. "Oh good," Eileen said, and then remembered that on Nick's instructions, she had given the hospital a wrong address. However, the phone number was correct. "Think you'll be all right?" the nurse asked.

Nick wheeled around. "She'll be all right," he yelled. "And so will our son." The elevator arrived a second later, and as Nick got on, he gave Eileen the baby, held his hand on the side of the door, and stuck his head out. He wanted to swear at the nurse but thought better of it and instead just glared at her. The door shut and he took his son back from Eileen. In three minutes they'd be out of the place.

THREE

~

Going Home

EILEEN BENT OVER sideways and let her heavy canvas shoulder bag slide into the melting ice in the doorway of the bus shelter on Park Avenue. The shelter was mouldy damp and smelled of pee and thawing dog shit. She placed her wilting roses on the bag and dug her hands into the pockets of her coat. It was a typical March day — bright but chilly. She poked her nose out to see if a bus was coming. She still felt faint. The extra two days in the hospital had made hardly any difference. Wind was blowing straight through a smashed window pane in the shelter and she pulled her arms tightly to her ribs. The coat that Kelly had given her when she went to Sherbrooke wasn't nearly warm enough.

A wave of resentment swept over her as she looked at Nick holding their baby. He didn't need the fur-lined leather jacket and black leather pants he'd bought from the extra money he and Torchy had made lifting TVs. Leaning against the side of the bus shelter, she stared

34

down at the dog shit smeared on her boot and sighed. The smell of souvlaki from the nearby Greek pool room where Nick hung out with Torchy made her feel hungry.

Wavering on the bumpy ice in her spike-heeled boots, she let her mind spin off to last summer when they used to make love on a blanket all night under the trees on Mount Royal. She pulled at the silver heart she always wore around her neck — the first present Nick had ever given her. He'd made the money mowing lawns. "To Eileen, love Nicky," was engraved on the back. Inside he'd put a tiny picture Kelly had taken of them kissing. No one in the whole world had ever loved her the way he did. She lifted her little suitcase off the ground. She didn't want water to seep in and ruin the suede skirt Rube had given her. "Do you think a bus'll come soon?" she asked. Nick didn't answer.

～

Back at the apartment, Nick sat on the floor and rocked back and forth while he listened to Guns and Roses sing "Sweet Child of Mine." The music was very loud. When he wanted to shut out everyone, he put the stereo on full blast. There were no curtains or rugs and the sound bounced off the walls. He knew she had wanted to stay longer in the hospital and he was furious she couldn't understand why he had wanted her out.

When they had entered the apartment he had put his son down on the tweed sofa and now he was whimpering. They had been home half an hour and Eileen still hadn't prepared him for bed. He and Torchy, who had taken a wood-working course, had made a crib for the baby from wood he and Eileen stole one night at a construction site. But the crib sat under the window in the alcove in the hall, empty.

"Eileen," Nick said, turning down the music for a second. "Aren't you going to put the baby in the crib?"

"Later. He's fine where he is." The baby continued to whimper. He turned the knob on the tape deck up as high as it would go with a flick of his wrist that made Eileen flare up inside.

Smoking a cigarette, Eileen slumped at the opposite end of the sofa from the baby. The Madonna poster she'd put up peeled forward at the top and the hole in the plaster on the wall behind showed. From the apartment upstairs came the vibrations of another stereo playing loud rock music.

Over the sounds of the competing stereos, she could hear the steady drone of the garbage truck outside. She got up and looked out into the street from their second floor apartment. The lights on the dirty snow made things look worse than usual. No matter how carefully people wrapped their garbage, animals ripped open the bags. Coming up the walk, she had seen chicken bones, coffee grounds and a used diaper on the gray snow. Near the door in the mud were a couple of condoms.

Safes were not for Nick. The baby was his idea. When Eileen discovered she was pregnant, Kelly offered to take her to a clinic in the east end, but he was so excited about the prospect of having a family of his own she couldn't breathe a word about an abortion. Two weeks before the baby was born, when he was sawing up the boards for the crib, he admitted he'd dreamt of having a baby from the first time they'd had sex together on Mount Royal.

"Stephanos Nicholas," he had said when she told him the results of the pregnancy test. "Stevie for short." After that he always called the baby "him." It never occurred to him that she could have a girl. Two weeks before the baby was born, he'd gone crazy getting things for him. The blue snow suit he'd bought at a church rummage sale but she knew he'd shoplifted the rest. One night after they'd come out of Jake's Ice Cream Parlor he went looking for wood for a crib. He dragged her for blocks to a street where flats were being built. The door of one of them was open and they found a pile of wood on the floor.

"We're coming back at two in the morning," he had announced, "when everyone is asleep." Eileen had been frightened of being caught. He lost his flashlight in the dark but they made it out of there with two armfuls of wood. It reminded her of the wild time they'd had in July when they went to La Ronde after the fireworks and, against all the rules, they took a skinny dip between the islands. Nick loved adventures. No one knew how to have fun the way he did.

Looking out at the patches of dirty snow, she thought about last year's magic summer. She would have to start taking the pill. Maybe Kelly could arrange it. She wanted to throw herself in Nicky's arms and tell him how afraid she was of being a mother but she was afraid he wouldn't understand.

She went down the hall to the bathroom and put her head in her hands. She didn't have to go but sat there a long time. It was cold outside yet the apartment was hot. When the landlord was in, the place was stifling, but when he left he turned off the heat and the place froze.

～

Nick stared at his baby son on the sofa and turned down the music. Cautiously he zipped down the sleeper and slowly lifted him up. Looking straight into his eyes, he smiled. Was this how he had looked as a baby? There had never been any baby pictures. A wave of emotion streamed through him as he imagined being passed from one house to another. Opening his shirt, he pulled the child in close and felt his soft face and hands on his chest. His little Stevie would love him as no one else loved him. He wished he had a mum, a brother or a sister to show him off. His son whimpered a little. Nick rubbed his back, but it didn't help. Suddenly the infant opened his mouth and wailed. Had he done something wrong?

After a few minutes Nick put him down and turned up the music. "Eileen," he called on the way to the bathroom, "the baby's bawling." He pushed the bathroom door open hard with his foot. "What's going on?" he asked. Her eyes were puffy.

"Nothing," she said. "Just going to the bathroom."

"I think you should fix the baby."

Eileen came back in the living room to blaring music that couldn't drown out the screams of her child. He was probably hungry but she didn't feel like breast-feeding him. She ripped open her canvas bag and the teddy bear with the red and white polka dots tumbled to the dusty floor.

Nick picked up the bear and glared at her as she dug to the bottom of the bag and pulled out a bottle of glucose. The nipple on the bottle was moist from the water that had leaked into her bag at the bus shelter. She wiped it quickly on her skirt, and without lifting the baby from the sofa, she tried to stuff it into his mouth but he continued crying.

"Look," Nick shouted. "You don't know what you're doing! Why didn't you put the baby into the crib as soon as we came home? He needed to be in his own bed. The bed *I* made for him." The cries of the baby were driving him wild. "I'm goin' out, and when I get back, I want the baby fed and in his crib." He picked his Walkman up off the floor of the living room and left.

When he came back about half an hour later, the baby was in his crib, asleep. "I have an idea," she said as he came in the door. She lit herself a cigarette and stood up. "I think we should show off our little Stevie to Carmen and Retta." They were the only people she knew who might be interested in seeing their newborn son.

FOUR

~ॐ

A Child is Forever

"THE BABY!" Carmen shrieked so loud a barefoot old woman opened a door one floor up and squinted down over the railing. Another door opened and Eileen saw Retta Van Dam peer out looking like an old hippie. Retta was a director of activities in a nursing home. When Eileen was too pregnant to work at the strip bar, Retta had given her a temporary job at the home. "Eileen's new baby," Carmen called. "Come see."

Inside her apartment, Carmen grabbed Stevie from Nick and walked into the living room with him while Eileen and Nick trailed behind. "He's a beauty, a real beauty," Carmen said. "Such lovely white skin."

Her olive-coloured arms around the baby, Carmen settled into a rocking chair in the living room while Eileen admired the batik curtains over the windows and the fashion posters on the wall. Carmen was wearing flowered pants and a scoop-necked black sweater she'd been given by a guy in the rag trade. From Puerto Rico via New York, Carmen sometimes worked as an assistant dress designer and got clothes for free. How lucky she was, Eileen thought, to have a sister in the west end who could look after her children. In addition to her three children in Montreal, Carmen had a twelve-year-old son in Puerto Rico who often visited, and he was also willing to help out.

"Dustin," Carmen called. "Sophia. Pepé. Come and see Eileen's baby." The three children, aged two, five and six, came out in their pyjamas and crowded around the baby. "Different fathers," she had told Eileen when they first met. Just before the baby was born, she had invited Eileen and Nick to dinner along with Retta. When Nick had been out of the room, Carmen had confided to Eileen and Retta that she was trying to get pregnant. "I really don't care what man as long as he's smart. I'm building up a little United Nations," she had laughed.

She always had a man hanging around. A guy from New York who owned a fur shop sometimes came by with presents. The week before, Eileen had heard her yelling down the stairway at a fellow in a leather jacket. Tall and handsome, he looked Spanish or Italian. "Same time, same place, macho man, and when I say 11:30 I mean 11:30," and she had slammed the door.

Carmen looked down at the baby and sniffed. "You little bugger, I can smell a load of shit. Sophia. You know where the diapers are."

There was a knock at the door and Retta came in. "Can I?" she asked and took the baby from Carmen. "You're so lucky," she said to Eileen. Retta had looked after her sister's kids in Holland but had never had any of her own.

"Looks like you, Nick," Carmen declared. "What are you going to call him?" She looked over at Eileen and then back at Nick who was sitting on the sofa with his thumbs in the waistband of his pants.

"Stephanos Nicholas," he said.

"Stephanos Nicholas?" she raised her eyebrows. "Sounds like you backwards."

"My dad's name was Stephanos Nicholas. It's a Greek custom," Nick said. "A boy is automatically called after his grandpa." He had learned all this in a pool room run by Greeks on Park Avenue. Carmen turned to Eileen who was sitting on the edge of the sofa feeling anxious. "You've got your milk, Eileen?"

"Yes. I guess."

When Sophia arrived with the diaper, Carmen changed him, ordered her kids back to bed and then turned to Eileen. "He's whimpering because he's hungry. You can sit in the rocking chair and feed him." She pulled the rocking chair off to a corner, dimmed the lights, placed Eileen in the chair, and settled the baby in her arms. "It's the most marvellous feeling in the world," she said softly. "I can't get enough of it."

Eileen held the baby but she didn't want to do anything and Carmen slowly unbuttoned her blouse. "You fed him in the hospital? Just shut your eyes," she said, propping up Eileen's breast, "and feel him feed."

Eileen closed her eyes and let the baby suck. After a minute she glanced over at Nick. He was chewing the inside of his lower lip feeling edgy again. Why was he always so angry and demanding? There was only so much she could take of this.

Carmen suddenly stood up, put her hands her pockets and looked around the room. "Shit," she said, "I'm out of fags. Nick," she raised her voice. "Got any?"

Along with a joint, Nick had two in his jacket but Eileen knew he had no intention of giving them to Carmen. They were his last. "Nope," he said.

"I'll treat you to a pack," she said, "just for the occasion, if you'll go down to the corner." She gave him a ten dollar bill and Nick left. "Now that he's out of here," she said to Eileen, "you can enjoy it."

Carmen and Retta pulled their chairs up close to Eileen. As the baby sucked, Eileen felt something awaken in her. A delicious feeling spread through her.

"The other breast now," said Carmen, lifting the baby off one breast and settling him on the other. "It's three minutes on one, three on the other."

Carmen gently pushed the rocker. "If you run out tonight and he's still hungry, I can help out. I've got lots," and she patted her breasts. Eileen had been surprised to see Carmen still breast-feeding her two-year-old.

"Lovely pair, aren't they?" Carmen said to Nick when he came back. Nick said nothing. He didn't count. It was Eileen, his son, and the two broads. He hated feeling like an outsider.

"He's hungry as hell," Retta said. "Good thing. He needs to put on weight." The baby was sucking so strongly Eileen started to feel panicky. In an effort to gain control, she began counting to herself and to her relief the baby fell asleep. Eileen quickly pushed her breasts into her blouse and let the baby drop into a hole in her lap.

"Hey!" Carmen said. "Not that way. Let me take him," and she scooped him up and placed him on her shoulder. "You must be tired. Retta and I will make tea. But for you, madame, first, a big glass of milk. You need energy!" She patted Eileen on the head and sailed off to the kitchen. Eileen watched Carmen step down the hall with the baby stuck to her shoulder like a little monkey.

"Right after tea we're going home," said Nick when Carmen and Retta were in the kitchen. They didn't give a shit about him. "They're too stinkin' bossy."

The phone rang in the hall. "Oh, it's you," Carmen said. There was a long silence as she moved from one foot to another and rolled up her eyes. As Eileen and Nick watched, she made an up-yours sign with her forefinger. Finally she said, "Well, I don't care who you're the father of. You can't come this week."

Back in the living room, she said, "Antonio. Dustin's father." While Retta poured tea, she said, "Antonio beat me up once." She handed Eileen her glass of milk. "He thought he'd get away with it."

Nick knew he was in for another fifteen minutes at least and gave Eileen a look which said, "We are bloody well clearing out of here soon."

"It was all because of what I named my son. I had a crush on Dustin Hoffman and called him Dustin. He wanted me to call him Angel. In Spanish it's Anhel. Here it'd be Angel. Okay back home. But not here.

"In the emergency room I vowed I'd pay him back. No dude was going to beat me up and get away with it." Eileen and Nick sat quietly. "I knew he'd show up. When he came to the door I was ready with a big pot of soup simmering on the stove." The baby bobbed up and down against Carmen's shoulder as she laughed.

"So what happened then?" Eileen asked. She was feeling tired but the story pepped her up.

"He didn't know what hit him. Shit, man! I'll never forget the look on his stupid face." Carmen winked at Retta who probably knew the story, and from behind Nick's back, Eileen saw Retta make an upward motion with her hand to indicate Carmen should hype the story even more.

"He thought he was coming over for you know what," Carmen went on. "And what did he get?" Her voice rose. "Hot chicken soup right in the kisser," and she broke into high-pitched laughter.

Carmen looked at Nick. "Don't think that was all." She leaned across to the sofa and placed Nick's hand on her arm. "Feel," she said and flexed her muscle. Nick quickly withdrew his hand. "I flipped the bastard and he fell down the stairs and broke his leg."

"If you don't mind," Nick said, and he got up and went to the bathroom. The visit wasn't what he had hoped for at all. One day maybe he'd take his son to see the grannie in the teddy bear store. He lit up a joint and quickly inhaled.

While he was gone, Carmen told Eileen and Retta that after Antonio beat her up, she enrolled in a quickie course in self-defence so she would be ready for him.

"I look small," she said, "but now I can throw any dude. When I was a kid in New York, I was beaten up a lot. With some guys, it's beat you, bang you, and leave you! Not any more!"

Carmen had married a Canadian she'd met in the rag trade in New York, but she'd told Eileen she'd divorced him after he'd made her have two abortions. She'd had the kids later by three other guys and refused to marry any of them.

Eileen rubbed the back of her neck.

"That doesn't mean I don't want a little nookie now and then,"

Carmen went on. "I can get horny," she said, "just like anyone." Carmen looked straight at Eileen.

"You've got to keep your fella in his place. Guys are all assholes. What's important," she said, "is to stay in control." She was a single parent and determined to stay that way. "None of this 'till death do us part' for me."

In her late thirties, she reminded Eileen of Hazel-Fleurette, the bar manager at the Sex Trolley — fearless, cocky and capable of handling anything. No one stood in her way.

"If I was ever going to live with anyone," Carmen said, "it would be with a woman. Much easier to get along with, and . . ."

Eileen felt Carmen's eyes on her in a way that made her feel uncomfortable and she quickly looked down. "Never forget," Carmen raised her voice and tapped Eileen's knee, "your little Stevie comes first. If you ever need help I'm here. And so is Retta. Eh Retta?" She nodded. "Guys come and go. A kid like Stevie is forever."

FIVE

∼

Dreams

A FEW DAYS LATER, Eileen woke up to the smell of pancakes and bacon from the kitchen and propped herself up on a pillow. The last time she had smelt pancakes and bacon was in Ile aux Coudres. Sun streamed through the window. She shut her eyes and made herself spin back to the weekend last summer that had brought little Stevie into her life . . .

As the sun came up over the water, Eileen watched the sandpipers on the waves. All she'd ever known was Wellington Street in Verdun, her apartment in Notre Dame de Grâce with Kelly, and the strip bar downtown. This was her first time in the countryside. It was magic.

Lying on the grass listening to the crickets, she could still feel the wildness of their motorcycle ride from Montreal to Baie St. Paul. She knew he was taking her on a daredevil ride just from the way he threw his leg over the seat outside her apartment in N.D.G. At the entrance to the expressway, he stopped for a minute and tightened the strap on her helmet. "Ready for take off?" he smiled.

Nick had never owned a motorcycle but he knew a lot about them. He was always answering ads for second-hand motorcycles and getting the owners to let him take a test-run, after which he'd say he'd have to think about it. Eileen usually went for the ride. It was always exciting.

She started shrieking as soon as they tore through the first underpass on the expressway. "Nicky," she yelled. With inches to spare, he swerved in and around the cars at razor-sharp angles that brought looks of astonishment from the drivers of cars and trucks. The more she yelled, the faster he went, and the more risks he took. Down Highway 40 just before the bridge at Trois Rivières they flew like skiers over a jump. Houses, gas stations, trucks and tractors shot by in a blur. Hanging tight to him, her legs squeezing his thighs, she gasped as he took the corners so low she was just inches from the hot asphalt. The wind sucked out her breath and the fields and sky tilted as though she were doing loops in an airplane.

When they hit the Chemin du Roy next to the river he relaxed and slowed down. At a village they had a picnic lunch and walked down the road from the church square to watch cows graze in a field of wild flowers. Except in movies, she had never seen cows. Nicky lifted her over a fence and he took a picture of her patting one.

Gazing into the sky over the St. Lawrence river, Eileen felt the fresh breeze. Ile aux Coudres was such a change from the smog and dirt of Verdun. Lying there quietly, watching the sun rise over the misty water, she was amazed at the silence. Rube and her mother and everything that had happened on Wellington Street seemed far away . . .

She rubbed her eyes and picked up the tick of the clock in her bedroom on Paros Street, off Park Avenue. It was still March, the tail end of winter, not July on Ile aux Coudres. Stevie was fast asleep in his crib in the alcove of the hall but at any moment he could wake up and holler.

She let herself drift back to last summer when she was in the apartment next to the railway tracks with Kelly, Betsy and Marylou, all of them working at the Sex Trolley. Nick was at the group home in LaSalle. If he followed the rules and worked thirty-five hours a week, he got a weekend pass. He always came up with something special for weekends. He loved surprising her. It was his idea to take a weekend motorcycle trip and camp out at Ile aux Coudres. He got the idea from a guidebook he'd found at the group home. "In the middle of the St. Lawrence river in Charlevoix county," he'd told her. "It's an island full of daisies and wild strawberries." He had worked Thursday and Friday nights free for two weeks at Elmer's Garage in return for a loan of an old Harley Davidson gathering dust in a corner. "The first machine I ever owned," Elmer had said when he asked about it. "Belongs now to my son. He's away for the summer. If you can make it run, you can have it for the weekend." After tinkering with it on a Sunday afternoon, and then consulting a mechanic he had made friends with at a second-hand Harley store, the machine had been ready to go.

∼

Nick did a double flip of another pancake in the frying pan and put it in the oven to stay warm. He liked making pancakes and was proud of how well they always turned out.

Vroomm, vroooooom. Outside on Paros street, Nick thought he heard the rumble of a motorcycle. Couldn't be. Too early in the season for motorcycles. Last summer when he had first seen the 883 Harley-Davidson Sportster at Elmer's, he had thought about swiping it and making it look as though it was someone else. Working there all week washing cars and doing errands, he knew when everyone came and went and where the keys were kept. Figuring out how to lift things — cameras, Walkmans, jeans, leather jackets, even the silver locket for Eileen from Birks — was something so natural he could do it in his sleep. But he hadn't wanted to rip off Elmer because Elmer had given him the first job where he actually made minimum.

Besides, snatching motorcycles was how he had first got into trouble. He had sure learned fast. Who else could have found just the right pipe to snap off the kryptonite lock that fastened the Virago 750 to the fence behind the high school? It had been just after he'd found out Mum and Pop were adopting Luke. About a week after that barbecue when he was fifteen. If cousin Luke's parents hadn't died, they would have adopted him. Maybe he was just kidding himself. Nothing he ever did was right. When he got an A in math, Pop complained about his mark in English. Pop, he suspected, had decided not to sign the final adoption papers long before.

He had been more upset about failing the initiation test to get into the Black Tiger Bike Club than spending three months in the juvie joint. The police caught him in Ste. Thérèse on the way to the headquarters in Ste. Agathe. He had two juvie counts against him by the time he was sixteen, both of them for hustling motorcycles.

But when he met Eileen he decided to stop doing crime. The whole summer, until they got married and moved to Paros Street, he didn't snitch anything. Well, there was the locket, and then the $80 for the ballet tickets, but in a way Marie-Hélène had *given* him the $80. He knew Marie-Hélène because she worked the cash at the gas station near Elmer's garage where he gassed up the Harley. When it was hot, sometimes she came by with lemonades at 25 cents a pop, and he gave her a handful of Smarties.

Eileen had told him the *Romeo and Juliet* ballet was playing at Place des Arts and he knew she was dying to go. She had shown him pictures of herself at twelve in toe shoes wearing a short fluffy skirt. "I've never been to Place des Arts," she had said. "And it's the Kirov Ballet. From Russia!" He didn't even know where Place des Arts was but he had found the number for the box office. His heart had turned over when he found out the tickets were $40 each. But that night, around ten, when everything had been quiet, he had skipped out of the group home and nipped over to the gas station. "Look, Marie-Hélène," he'd said. "I'm in a terrible fix. I need $80 to take my girlfriend Eileen to the ballet tomorrow night. It means a lot for her to go. She used to be a ballet dancer.

"Any way you could just sort of lift the $80, and then when I'm outta sight, ring the bell?" He knew she had an emergency bell that rang 911 if there was any problem. It was a small place with no video camera.

"You know. I could have put a stocking over my face and stuck you up easy, but I wouldn't do that to you." Marie-Hélène had looked around in a way that told him she might actually do it but had taken another minute to think about it. "It's only because you're so cute," she had smiled. "And because it's for a good cause. I'll give it to you in an envelope. Walk out of here like nothing's happened. Three minutes after you're out, I'll ring the bell."

~

"Surprise!" Eileen heard Nick call out from the kitchen. She lifted herself up on her elbows in her bed in the apartment and heard the ballet music from *Romeo and Juliet* playing from the sound system in the living room. Nick had bought her the tape after they had gone to the ballet and just before they went to Ile aux Coudres. Humming the tune from the balcony scene, Nick stood at the door of the bedroom, holding a tray with two breakfasts and a yellow rose. He had been in the choir in school and liked to sing.

"Oh, Nicky," she said. He had the most beautiful blue eyes in the world. He put down the tray, lifted her up in his arms, and danced with her the way he had on Ile aux Coudres when they pretended he was Romeo and she was Juliet. "The only thing that's missing is the flowers in your hair," he said.

After they had breakfast, Nick got into bed with her and lifted their son into the bed between them. He wore a diaper and a white T-shirt with a bear on it. Eileen pulled the baby's feet up into the air and touched his little toes. Their little Stevie was like a doll. "I can't believe you and me made those perfect little toes," she said. "He does look like you. Like Carmen said." She stroked his head, touched the pulsing artery on the crown, and shivered inside. She wished Kelly were still in Montreal. She bowed her head and said a little prayer asking for help to be a good mother.

Nick looked at his wife and son. "Eileen?" he said and grabbed her hand. He wanted to tell her about the priest in the Greek Orthodox church. That morning, when she was still sleeping and the stores weren't open, he'd gone to a church and prayed to God to help him be a good father and a good husband.

Normally, he would never have gone into a church, but the Greek church attracted him, and when he had seen the open door, he had gone in. He had been feeling desperate and had wanted time alone to think about his new family . . .

"Please God, give me the strength," he had prayed. "Don't let me hit her, or the baby. Ever." He had felt a hand on his back, and a priest in a long black robe slipped into the pew beside him.

The priest spoke in Greek but then switched to English. "What is it, son?"

"My wife and I have a new baby."

"That's wonderful."

"I'm no good," Nick had cried.

The priest had led him into a chapel at the side of the church with a painting of the Virgin Mary where Nick spoke of the baby's screams driving him crazy, his worry Eileen might leave him, and his terror of the darkness he sometimes fell into. But he hadn't mentioned his greatest fear — the rages inside him that roared up when he least expected.

"God will take care of you," the priest had said. "God loves you, and he loves your wife, and he loves your baby, and if you and your wife pray to him every day, he will take care of you."

That's what Nick now wanted to tell Eileen. The priest had put his hand on his shoulder. "Every day," the priest had said, "I want you to do one nice thing for your wife and baby. I want you to promise God," and he had asked Nick to drop to the floor. "If you want you can pray to the Holy Virgin."

Nick wasn't Greek Orthodox or even Catholic. He had wanted to pray to the Holy Virgin, but couldn't. "Dear God," Nick had said, kneeling on the red velvet cushions on the floor. The smell of the candles had made him feel he was in a holy place. "If you'll take care of me and protect me, every day I will do one nice thing for Eileen and the baby. I need you God." The priest had put his hand on Nick's head, raised his hand in the air, and said a prayer he couldn't follow. Then he asked his name. Finally he said: "Be with thy servant Nicholas, in Christ's name. Amen."

As he had walked down the steps of the church, Nick thought of what he could do that day to help Eileen. When the baby had cried in the middle of the night, twice he had got up to give him a bottle. Even now the shrieks rang in his ears. Just before he had gone out, Carmen had knocked on the door and he had asked her to change the baby. He'd feed him even if he screamed his head off but there was no way he'd change him. That was women's work. Walking down Park Avenue he had decided to buy some pancake mix at the grocery store and make her a breakfast just like he had in Ile aux Coudres. He hoped she'd like that. He was never sure how to treat her. Never knew what she needed and was always worried she'd find someone who could give her more.

"Eileen," he said again. He wanted to tell her what the priest had said but he couldn't get it out. Instead he told her he loved her, he wanted to take care of her, and he would look for a job. "You know that you and the baby are my first family, don't you?"

As far as Eileen was concerned she had no family either, but he always said it wasn't the same. "You had parents," he said when she compared her life to his. Well, it was true, she hadn't lived in all those foster homes and institutions. Maybe it would have been better if she had. Once she tried to tell him about the time she overheard her mother telling Rube she'd tried to get an abortion and couldn't find anyone to do it. But Nick wouldn't listen. Eileen had no idea who her real father was. When she asked her mother, she said: "None of your business."

"You know what the test is of whether or not you have a family?" Nick was always asking. "It's whether you have a place to go at Christmas." Christmas terrified him, he told her, because that's when he really knew he had no one.

Well, she had no one either. Until she was fifteen, she spent Christmas with her Mum and Rube, and what kind of family was that? After her mother kicked her out, she spent Christmas at the Sex Trolley with all those horny men. When she and Nicky got married, she wanted to tell him what happened with her stepfather but she never did. Her feelings about it were all mixed up.

"In a week or so," Nick said, "I'll go out and find a job. I promise. We can stay on welfare. I'll probably get paid under the table. Even the doughnut places pay under the table."

Eileen wasn't sure he'd stay in a job even if he found one. He'd quit the job she'd helped him get at the box factory on Jean Talon. The second time he quit, just before Christmas, he kept pacing the floor of the apartment until the sound drove her crazy. The only thing that calmed him was rock music. If he'd finished high school, or at least grade nine, he might have become a car mechanic like Georgie.

Georgie had lived at the same group home as Nick. Now he was married, had a two-year-old kid, and a steady job. It was because of him that Nicky got the job at Elmer's. Georgie worked on cars at a place on the Upper Lachine road for a lot more than minimum wage. At the box factory nobody got minimum wage because the boss paid under the table like at the old folks home where she worked when she got too big to nude dance at the Sex Trolley. She sighed. She didn't want to think about it. It took too much energy.

"Work'll go fine," Nick said, "as long as I don't go into one of those things," he said slowly. There was a long silence. Eileen looked at him reproachfully. The Christmas before he had fallen into such a deep depression he didn't get out of bed for a week. It had happened after she had gone out to see her friend Kelly and had been two hours late getting home. These episodes, he told her later, always started with a migraine that sent him spinning. They began when he'd been at the Carstairs Centre before the Evans took him. It was after two guys on the night shift started fooling with him. Later, when he had experienced these dark moods at Parkway, he had asked to go into solitary confinement so no one could bother him. Eventually, he had told her, the blackness always lifted.

"I'm sorry I tried to get you out of the hospital early. You wanted to stay longer, didn't you?" He brushed his fingers across her cheek. "You won't ever leave me, will you, Eileen?"

Eileen nuzzled her face in his neck. She loved the way he smelled. "I love you, Nicky my sweetheart, I promise you I won't ever leave. It's okay about the hospital. But it's true. I wanted to stay. I was so tired."

"Listen," he said. "I'll take care of you and the baby for a whole week. For the whole time you would have liked to stay in the hospital." He squeezed her shoulder. "Okay?"

She hadn't felt so warm towards him since they stole the wood for the crib. "The roses and everything," she said. "It was wonderful."

"I fed the baby twice last night," Nick said proudly, "even though it's your job."

She wished he hadn't said "even though it's your job." It made her feel trapped. She heaved the baby up onto her breast and let herself feel the waves of warmth swelling up within her. Maybe she could enjoy being a mother. She wanted to. Nick watched quietly. Sometimes he used to suck Eileen's nipples himself, imagining *he* was the baby.

Eileen tried to hang on to the waves but they died away. She had woken up feeling good for the first time in weeks with the smell of the pancakes and bacon and the memories of last summer, but now she felt scared. The baby was sucking so furiously she felt as though he might swallow her up. She let him tumble away from her and he began to shriek.

"Maybe I should put him on the other breast," Nick said. He was eager to stop the screams. "You okay? You were breathing awful fast."

"I'm fine." After a while the baby fell asleep and Eileen lay without moving.

Nick reached over and picked up his little son and held him close to him. He was wet and needed a change, but Eileen, he knew, was too exhausted to get up. He went out into the hall, laid him on a table near the crib and removed the wet diaper. Copying what he had seen Eileen do, he sprinkled a little baby powder on his bum, tucked him into a new diaper and put him into his crib in the alcove.

When he came back, Eileen was on her side. He looked at her lying in bed, her breasts bursting, and he wanted her. For a whole month before the baby was born, they had not had any sex and it had driven him crazy. He sat on the bed and ran his fingers across her breasts, then slowly he eased her down on her back and lay on top of her. He loved the feel of her warm body beneath him.

Eileen wanted to have sex with him, now more than ever. She wanted to feel him inside her, and she knew he wanted it too. She had felt exhausted after the baby was born but she was no longer the least bit sore. It had been a fast and easy birth even though at the end it had hurt. The feeling of the baby being born made her want to have Nick throb within her the way he had when they were in Ile aux Coudres.

"Ohh," Eileen mouthed as he entered her and began slowly to move up and down. She felt very moist inside.

Out in the hall, Nick heard his son make a gurgling sound in his crib, and he felt euphoric. He waited until her breath told him she was ready to come and then at just the right moment he let the wave of pleasure totally blanket them. The anxiety he'd been feeling burned off and for a second he felt golden. After a few minutes he buried his head in her breast and began to suck the warm sweet milk. He had sucked her before, but this was different. Her breasts were bigger than ever, and hard. Eileen stirred restlessly. He let go of the nipple and raised his head to look at her. "Please." He shut his eyes. "Just a few more minutes . . ."

SIX

~

Hey Kid

NICK STARED OUT the window of the bus going north on St. Lawrence Boulevard. In his hand was a little ad torn from the Montreal *Tribune:* Pantyhose packers and general work, good salary, it said. He hoped he'd be able to do the work. If necessary, he'd fake it.

"Legendre," the bus driver called out. Sylvana Stockings. There it was. He got off. Outside, across a muddy basement window, was a sheet of paper with some scraggly writing in a bunch of languages. There was nothing in English.

The dark entrance smelled of those chickenshit apartments he'd visited with Eileen in the east end where the rents were cheap. A red arrow scratched on yellowing newspaper pointed down narrow winding wooden stairs. He ducked to avoid hitting the ceiling.

Behind a cracked wood counter, a girl with yellow bleached hair was banging on a machine that looked like an old cash register.

"Worker," she yelled as soon as she saw him and went back to her typing. Nick stood at the counter and drummed his fingers. "Do you mind?" she said.

A few minutes later, a squat man in a short-sleeved shirt and a peaked cap padded out. "You Turkish?" was his first question.

Turkish? Did he look Turkish? "No," Nick said. He thought of saying "I'm Greek," but he couldn't speak Greek. "English," he said.

"English," the man muttered under his breath as though he was disappointed. He smelled of sausages and garlic. "From here, then?" he said.

"Yes," Nick replied.

The man picked up a smoking cigar from a dirty ashtray, jammed it in his mouth, and slowly blew out a puff of smoke while he flipped through some papers on a ring binder. White hair grew out of his ears. He was one of the ugliest bossmen Nick had met in his tramp across the city looking for work.

"Tell Pierre we can do their rush order for next Monday," he told the secretary.

"So?" The boss looked at Nick as though he were a deaf person with a card. What's the use, Nick thought to himself. "Experience?" the man asked.

Nick sucked in air through his teeth. Here it was again. He had to stop himself from hammering his fist on the counter. Experience? How could he have experience? He was only nineteen. They always asked whether he had experience. Harvey's, Wendy's, McDonald's, the 7-11s, all the factories. Shit. Any jerk could do these jobs. Why did they always ask for experience?

The night before, when they were going through the *Tribune,* clipping out classified ads in the help-wanted column, he had told Eileen he'd never snag a job unless he knew someone. That's how he'd picked up his jobs at the garage and the box factory. And that's how she'd swung into the Sex Trolley.

He had really wanted that job flipping hamburgers on Park Avenue close to their apartment. He knew he could do it. "Grade nine?" the manager of the place had asked. Everyone wanted grade nine. "No," he'd had to admit. He had done only some of the exams. He'd started flunking after he had gone into the juvie joint. He'd scored lots of As until grade eight, but after he hijacked those motorcycles, and the Evans had got rid of him, he had never been able to concentrate. "Experience?" He *had* experience, he *knew* how to make hamburgers, but he'd never worked in a fast food place before.

This pantyhose job was the tenth he'd taken a crack at, and that didn't count all the calls he and Eileen had made checking to see if jobs advertised were still available. He sighed.

The man was waiting for an answer. "I worked in a box factory. And a garage."

"I see."

He probably wouldn't bag this job either, he thought. Torchy could drag down $1700 on a drug deal plugging into high schools on the West Island where the kids were in the bucks and could shell out for hash and coke. What was he doing here anyways? He looked through a glass divide and saw four black women in brightly coloured dresses with big asses going by in single file carrying cardboard envelopes.

"Okay," the boss said, giving Nick a last look over. "I'll try you out. It's piecework. You get paid for what you do. Period. Hours are six in the morning to six at night for the next three weeks, including Saturdays, take it or leave it. We have a lot of rush jobs. Take a day off, or come in late, and you're fired. We've got plenty of people who want to work here. You get paid every Friday, but this week because you're new, you get paid only on Saturday." He didn't ask for Nick's name, address or social insurance number, or tell him exactly what he would make. "Come with me," he said.

Nick followed him down some more wooden stairs to a dark basement smelling of oil and dust where rows of machines operated by black women were making white stockings that he assumed would eventually become pantyhose. Piercing lights shone on the contraptions that were clanging so loudly he wanted to cover his ears. Apart from the lights on the machines, the rest of the place was in shadows.

He wove in and around plastic bags, oil drums, discarded tools, lead pipes, tires, greasy rags, puddles of scum, plastic tubing, crunched metal waste baskets, half-filled oil tins, broken jars, upturned chairs and small piles of torn stockings. Finally, in a section separate from the machines, he stopped next to a woman in a lime green top with sequins and open shoes counting and bundling stockings. Stretching back to the wall, in and around the piles of trash, fifteen women crouched over cardboard boxes that served as worktables.

"Watch her," the boss ordered, and disappeared.

Nick stood there, moving from one foot to another, watching the women pulling and bundling from banks of stockings. They looked like mechanical toys.

He glanced around. It was a junk dealer's heaven. Only the junk looked larger than life, like the garbage dump he'd seen on a TV version of the musical *Cats*. Worse than Packabox. He looked up. A black loudspeaker stared down at him. Pipes covered a sooty ceiling, and rows of twisted fluorescent light fixtures dripping with rust hung down on chains.

After fifteen minutes, a foreman in stained pants came by. He led Nick to a furnace room with a broken Coke machine and a filthy sink with a cracked mirror over it. A cat with the bones showing through her ass stood at the entrance. "Put your things here," he said. Coats were piled on the floor over a carpet of newspapers. Nick dropped his leather jacket on top.

The foreman led him back to a corner of the junk yard where the women were counting and bundling the white stockings. From a large cardboard box, he brushed away rags and old tools, threw a greasy cloth on top and emptied out a plastic bag.

"Put two stockings together. You know? For the two legs? In bundles of twelve, elastic ends up, always. You understand? Stuff them back in there," and he pointed to the plastic bag. He gave Nick a squared-off sheet. "Mark the number of dozens you do on this sheet." He talked thickly, like the grumpy East Europeans who bargained for vegetables in the small shops around Victoria and Van Horne where Eileen had wanted them to take an apartment.

After two hours, working as fast as he could, he'd done forty dozen. When the foreman came by, inspecting, he asked what the hourly rate was.

"Not by the hour. By the dozen," the foreman said. "Fifteen cents a dozen. He looked up at Nick. "Slow. You're slow." He glanced over at the women. "They make four dollars hour. Nice." He raised his eyebrows and nodded his head as though it were a fortune.

"Ain't minimum four-fifty?" Nick asked. The foreman looked at him as though this was the first he'd heard of it. Another snake, Nick said to himself.

Later, in the furnace room, leaning against the wall, listening to the women talk to one another in Creole, he ate the lunch Eileen had packed for him. Everyone stood. There wasn't a chair in the dump unless it was busted. No one said a word to him. He could have been a piece of broken machinery.

After lunch he made a point of trying to go faster. He watched the women, trying to keep up to their rhythm. Dump a plastic bag, grab two stockings, elastic ends up, one pair, two pair, three pair, up to twelve, now a dozen, elastic band, done. And again, and again, and again.

How did the women do it anyways? No matter how hard he tried, he couldn't go faster than twenty dozen an hour. A lot of wicked work for only three dollars.

At three o'clock, he felt so restless he wanted to bust out and leave. He looked around. The ladies were still going like machines, their hands flying. Women's work, he said to himself. He was all thumbs. The foreman was nowhere to be seen. The can. He'd go upstairs to the can for a change of scenery.

He trudged up the stairs feeling the way he did a week before Christmas when he quit Packabox. Maybe all he could *ever* do was be on welfare and depend on B&Es. He had to get the welfare cheque in his name. As he rounded the stairs, he heard a woman crying. He stopped for a few seconds, shoulder against the wall. *"Bébé malade, bébé malade,"* she wailed.

"Look here, Blanche. You know the rules," he heard the boss say. "The door is locked until six." His hand cracked down on the counter. "No exceptions." The woman clattered down the stairs in her open-backed shoes. When she reached Nick, she stopped and looked up at him. Her eyes were red and he felt sorry for her. "Would you like me to get you a glass of water? Or maybe a Coke?" He still had a Coke left over from his lunch. She nodded. "In just a few minutes," he said. As he continued up, Nick heard the boss say to the secretary, "Every so often it pays to get one of them stinkin' niggers deported."

◦

At seven that night Eileen stood at the door of the apartment waiting for Nick. She had seen him coming up the walk looking discouraged. "So how did it go?"

He slumped down on the sofa. "Piecework," he said looking out into space. "Two hundred and forty dozen. Only thirty-six dollars."

"Where's Stevie?" he asked.

She waved down the hallway to the crib. She'd had a pain in the back of her neck all day from his shrieking. "He's quiet now but he could start up any time." She wanted Stevie out of her sight. They had no money, but perhaps they could go to a movie, sneak in the side door somewhere.

Nick picked up his child, opened his shirt, lay back on the couch and felt the baby's soft smooth skin against him. He was asleep, exhausted from a bout of yelling, but he snuggled in next to him. After a few minutes, Nick put him back in the crib. He stood and watched him. Then he thought about himself at six weeks in the sink of the bus.

"I'll do it for a few days, but that's it. No matter how fast I go, I can only make $3.00 an hour," he said with a steel edge in his voice that warned Eileen not to push. He was so fed up he didn't even tell her about how they locked the workers in. "It's the shits."

She knew about piecework. Before her job at Packabox, she'd sewed the sleeves of baby clothes for a cent a sleeve in the kitchen of a woman in Pointe St. Charles. When she learned how to go fast, the contractor who picked the stuff up every day lowered the rate.

"I was hoping it'd pay by the hour," she said.

They made love before supper while the baby was still sleeping, and it made him feel more relaxed. Later, while they were eating, he told her about the Haitians, and about the woman called Blanche who had tried to leave early because her baby was sick.

"I should have tried to unlatch the door for her," he said. "There's always a way. She was nice to me. Showed me how to go faster. Just before I left, I heard the assface boss order some of them to stay on," he said. "Till eight. Poor bitches. He's got a gun to their heads. A lot of them are illegals." Torchy had told him about it. "One wrong move, and the hellmaster'll send the police to their doors."

〜

At five o'clock on Friday, after five days of work, Nick stopped the foreman as he was going by on his inspection. "I'm quitting," he said. "I want my pay today. My slips are ready." The foreman frowned. "You've told the boss?"

"No," Nick said. He'd calculated what he'd made. One thousand dozen, and he had the slips to show for it. At fifteen cents a dozen, it came to $150.

"The boss wants everyone here tomorrow. Everyone." He threw up his hands. "We need everyone," he repeated. "We have a big rush for Monday."

"Impossible," Nick said. Eileen had persuaded him to work five days. If it hadn't been for her, he'd have quit after the first day.

"The boss'll be mad."

Nick sucked air in through his teeth and moved back and forth on his running shoes like a boxer. He didn't belong here.

"The deal is you work Saturdays. New workers get paid Saturday the first week. The boss told you that, didn't he?"

"I want my money," Nick said. "Today." He punched a hole in the cardboard work table with his fist.

"Okay," the foreman said. "Give me the slips," and he walked off.

Fifteen minutes before closing, the foreman tapped him on the shoulder. "Hey kid," he said. Hey kid was what everyone called him. He didn't have no name and he didn't push it. At Packabox he didn't have no name either. He was there two months and he never talked to nobody. Never made a friend. If the Indians who worked there had to tell him anything, they called him "hey kid" too, only when they said it, it came out Akid. "He'll give you a $100," the foreman told him.

"One hundred!" Nick felt his blood rise. He wanted to jump at the foreman's throat. "But I did 1,000 dozen. It's on the slips!"

"He has slips now. One hundred," the foreman said, and he lumbered away.

"One hundred!" Nick stood there, paralyzed with rage. He felt like grabbing a lead pipe, tearing up the stairway, and ramming the pipe into the boss's stomach. If they paid minimum wage he'd get $225. That was what he was *really* entitled to. And they were going to give him only $100? He dashed over to the wall and banged his head against the concrete. The blow stunned him for a minute but he was too inflamed to feel it. He stood there mumbling. Cheat him out of all that money? No fuckin' way.

Blanche saw him bang his head and she came over and put her hand on his shoulder. *"Doucement,"* she said. After the foreman came by and told her to get back to her work station, he marched back to the small pile of stockings left on his cardboard box.

His eyes darted around the basement like an animal in a trap. The dusty window at the back. It was always open an inch to let in air. He could open it from the outside. He had it. The perfect crime! And a way to give all those women the biggest laugh of their lives *and* show them how to hit the bossman where he would really feel it.

But at six, at closing time, it took very ounce of control he had not to smash the hellmaster in the nose. He put on a long face and stood silently in line along with the sixty-five women as the boss peeled off the week's take from a thick wad of bills. He had seen pictures of refugees standing in line waiting with bowls for rice. That's what they looked like. There was no way he'd *ever* do this again.

He took his $100 and silently waited with them for the bus. Blanche stood next to him and it made him feel better. "Your baby okay?" he asked. *"Mieux,"* she said. "Better." He smiled to himself when he saw the bossman hoist his fat legs into a large black Buick parked at the side, and he thought of the look that would be on his face when he came down the stairs of the factory the next morning.

~

He got almost as much of a buzz out of Eileen telling him what happened as if he'd been there himself. She saw it all from the coffee shop across the street the following day. At six in the morning sharp, through the open window of the basement, she heard a raving roar. The waitress looked up from the counter, startled. "Holy Jeezus," she said. At first Eileen wanted to leave. What if they figured out who she was? What if the bossman looked through the window and came after her? But Nicky had told her to wait until the factory emptied. "Just wait. OK?" he'd said.

Fifteen minutes later, the women spilled out the front door. As they hit the street, wild laughter soared up into the early morning air. It was now April, and still a little muddy, but some of them tumbled to the grass, rolling from side to side. Eileen knew Nick had played with fire, but she felt a thrill of excitement when she saw the results of what he'd done. It was like something from a movie.

The laughter from the women breezed through the coffee shop and the waitress came and stood at the window. Eileen sat with her finger curled around the handle of her coffee cup, trying to look bored. After a while, a man with a jowly face and a peaked cap lurched out the front door of the factory swinging a lead pipe.

"You crazy dames! You're fired. Fired! All of you." Nobody was listening. "Shuddup! Shudduppppppp!" He whirled around, his face blotchy red, vessels popping on his bald head. "Get off my property." He kicked a few of the women on the grass and stood over them, the pipe raised, but they were laughing too hard to notice. Those standing on the sidewalk, alarmed, pulled their friends up from the grass, and the whole lot, still choking with laughter, wobbled off to the bus stop down the street, away from the boss, where they milled about like Gypsies.

～

The whole thing, Nick told Eileen, was easy. And he could never be caught. No one knew his name, his address or his social insurance number. Only Blanche would suspect, and she would never let on.

After work, he had taken the bus to the subway stop where he had hung around until it got dark, and then he went back. It took him two hours. Luckily there was only one window, and it was at the back, so he was able to turn on the lights and work without being seen. When he was finished, he stood back and admired his work of art.

He had emptied every bag for the Monday morning order, slashed each stocking with his pen knife, tied the ends, and made a long white streamer that he wound in and around the fifty machines, the oil drums, the twisted fluorescent ceiling lights, the furnace, the cardboard boxes, the plastic tubing, and the loudspeaker. He would show the greedy boss it was more profitable to pay the workers than to rip them off. He would give him an assembly line he'd *never* forget. He would sock it to him hard right in his wallet where it would really hurt.

There wasn't a single bit of junk he didn't fit into the tangled mess. Light things, like jars, crunched metal waste baskets, an old phone, small tools, even the tires and the one-legged chairs, he tied on to the white streamer so they looked like weird Christmas tree decorations.

His only witness was the cat who stood at the door of the furnace room and looked on quietly. While he worked, he talked to her. "I bet you never saw such a thing before. Eh, cat?" he said, and patted her from time to time. When he wound the streamer around the furnace, he saw three dead rats.

"You did this?" he asked. "Well, cat, you did good," and he picked up the rats and tied them from their tails across the streamer at the front so they would be the first thing the boss would see when he came in at six the next morning.

While he was doing it, he imagined he was tying the boss, the foreman, and everyone who had called him "hey kid" to a railroad track. When he was finished, the factory looked like something you might find if you sprung open all the doors of a nuthouse late at night and let the psychos loose with rolls of toilet paper. Twice he heard police sirens and worried the place had some kind of alarm system but he was too high to care.

He was going to all this trouble not just for himself but also for Blanche and all the other women who slaved in this junk yard for peanuts. He would show the women that revolt was possible. The last thing he did was to go over to Blanche's work station where he tucked a small tin of Coke into one of her work shoes. That way, she'd know for sure that he was responsible.

Just before he left, he cased the shop for some bucks. There was no sign of a safe, but he found a locked steel box at the back of a cupboard. He used a screwdriver to wedge it open and took out an envelope filled with bills. On the bus home, he counted them. Ninety-seven dollars. Ninety-seven dollars. Nowhere near what he was owed if they'd paid him the minimum wage for all his hours. But he had gotten back and that was all that counted.

SEVEN

~

Taming the Furies

STANDING ON THE rim of the bath tub, Eileen slipped off her wrap-around skirt and turned to the side so she could see how big her stomach looked in the bathroom mirror. Almost back to normal. Pretty good for nearly three weeks after giving birth. She hadn't eaten much, especially toward the end, and now it was paying off. She stepped down to the tile floor, pulled off her T-shirt and bra, threw her hips forward, and squeezed her breasts together hard the way she did on stage. Then she looked down at her nipples. No milk. Finally. She'd had a harder time weaning Nicky than the baby. Nick'd been home a week now. She was almost glad they were so hard up. She needed an excuse to flee the apartment. If she could get her job back at the Sex Trolley, *he* could take care of the baby. Besides, she needed money of her own. She was sick of begging Nick for every dollar she spent. She hated the way he tried to control everything she did. It was no way to live.

Bang, bang, bang. O, my God! Who was that? A shiver ran through her. The police? Had they traced the television set? Her mind raced. She grabbed her skirt and T-shirt, rapidly throwing them on as she ran into the hall. The door was cracking back from the hinges. Trying to stop her hands from shaking, she put on the chain.

"Who is it?" she asked.

"Scratch. Scratch O'Neill." She didn't know whether to be relieved or not. "Open the goddamn door," he said in a low voice.

She opened the door. Scratch was wearing a peaked hat on backwards and looked like a wrestler. He stood close to the chain, his nose almost touching it. "Nick there?" His breath smelled of beer.

"No."

"No?" He wedged a thick running shoe into the opening. "Honestly," she said, but he pressed his toe in further. His shirt was open and she saw a spider tattoo on his chest like the bouncer at the Machete on St. Denis where Kelly had a job until the owner got busted for cocaine dealing and the place closed.

"Listen," he frowned. "He owes me 200 bucks today. And another 400 next week. And that doesn't count the interest." He leaned in further. "That's another 200." His eyes scanned the hall. "I'm coming back in a week." He fixed his eyes to her breasts. "Got that, Popsie?"

"I'll tell him you came," Eileen said, shocked to hear of their huge debt.

"The son of a bitch knows what'll happen if he doesn't deliver," and he stomped off.

She went back to the bathroom, sat cross-legged on the floor and pulled out a large plastic kit from the back of the bathroom cupboard. It fell from her hands to the floor. Nick *knew* Scratch would come. She should have figured something was up when he bought that chain-lock for the door from Canadian Tire and told her to keep it on when he wasn't there. If she wanted, he'd get her a gun. A gun?

"You never know," he'd said. "Lots of people have guns. For security." There was no way she'd ever have a gun in the house. Rube had kept a gun in the hall closet. Late one night, toward the end when he was so angry with her, she went down to the boardwalk and threw it in the river. After that, she'd been scared he'd look for it and blame her.

She zipped open her kit and started talking to herself. She had to forget about Scratch and stick with her decision to go back to her job. She fished down to the bottom of her kit. Shit! A bottle of nail polish had spilled all over her turquoise bikini bottom. She looked at herself in a small hand-mirror. A little pancake would cover up the circles under her eyes. With enough makeup, she could pass. She never got any more than three hours sleep in a row. Felix, she hoped, would take her on. Maybe Hazel-Fleurette could put in a good word for her.

Eileen was humming "Get Outta My Dreams, Get Into My Car" — a favourite of Felix's — when she stopped dead. She could hear Stevie screaming all the way from Carmen's apartment. Even alone in the apartment in the bathroom with the door closed she couldn't get away from her colicky infant. She started to feel dizzy. When she collapsed in the corner grocery, the kid at the cash wanted to call the ambulance, but the owner said, "Forget it. She's probably just on dope." She put her head on the toilet seat and everything went black.

. . . Waaaah, waaaaah. The baby's gummy mouth was wide open and roaring red. She picked up a sock and stuffed it in his mouth. The cries stopped, but he kept convulsing like those market chickens that still shook in plastic bags after they were killed. The creature in her arms soundlessly yelped, his eyes hard black stones. She opened the apartment door and ran with him up the stairway to the garbage chute, pulled the handle, and threw him down. Moans echoed up from the basement. Frozen, her heart in her throat, she listened. Nothing. Back in the apartment, she told Nick she'd woken from a nap, looked in the crib, and he was gone. From the balcony off the living room, someone had crept in and stolen him . . .

The black faint slowly lifted like mist off the river and she raised her head from the toilet seat. Off in the distance, in Carmen's apartment, Stevie was still crying. "God, oh God, help me," she whispered and collapsed on the cold tile. She had seen her mother do it. Her baby sister's little hand had snapped like a twig. She rolled her head from side to side. "Please God, don't let me be like her."

Her forehead bathed in sweat, Eileen splashed cold water on her face and went in to lie on the couch in the living room. She was glad she was alone, Nick out looking at motorcycles, and the baby, mercifully, with Carmen. She dragged heavily on a cigarette and pretended it was hash.

"A child is forever," Carmen said. "In time you'll love him more than anything in the world." Time. Maybe that's all she needed. After half an hour, she stood up and looked out the window. Carmen wasn't so nice to her any more. Maybe she saw her leave the apartment that day when she went to the park by herself leaving Stevie at home alone. She still felt faint. She had to get up her courage to call the Sex Trolley.

The resentment she felt at the thought of Scratch at the door boiled up. Nick could have stayed longer at the stocking factory. Why didn't he? She would *not* live forever on break and entries. She had put up with Packabox for over a year. Even though she cut her hands on the cardboard edges, she had been glad of the work. Without that weekend job Kelly found for her, she'd never have been able to help with the rent and finish her grade eleven. Not that having grade eleven was so great. What kind of job could she get with it?

She went back into the bathroom and pulled on her green halter top. Her white spike heels with the silver bows at the back were in the hall cupboard. She could get by with one pair of shoes and a couple of outfits. She became so absorbed in sorting out her makeup she didn't see Nick standing at the door.

"I've just gotta get a bike," he said, putting his arm around her. He was still thinking about that shiny silver and black Harley he'd had to return. He had followed up on another ad in the motorcycles-for-sale section of the paper and convinced the owner to let him try it out. "I just test-ran an XLH Sportster," he said. The sound of the engine was still in his ears. He had taken the bike up Côte des Neiges Road.

Feeling like a Hell's Angel on an iron horse, he had roared the monster up over Mount Royal. The warm and sunny spring day reminded him that summer was just around the corner. "We could use it to get around on. I could fit out the back with a basket for Stevie."

Eileen said nothing and moved away from him. He owed Scratch $800. Then she remembered the $250 she'd borrowed from Rube before the baby was born, and the welfare cheque wasn't due for two weeks. "I suppose," she said.

Nick couldn't tell Eileen the real reason he had to have the motorcycle. It was the only thing that could kill his rage. When he wheeled the bike out of the laneway, revved up the motor and felt the vibrations, that twisted thing inside him shrank. At 150 kilometres an hour, with the windscream in his ears, it was as though he was coming, blast, blast, blaaaaaast. At the very top of Mount Royal, past the road to the Chalet, bent forward and leaning down for a curve around the white rocks with steel netting, and, oh boy, beautiful, something inside him broke. The Harley coasted all by itself as the view of the Olympic tower and the whole of the city by the river opened up to him.

He was terrified of the rage that flamed up in him. He had hoped his little Stevie would take it away but it was still there. There was no one to confide in. Those shrinks the social workers had made him see had pried at it, but he had never trusted any of them enough to open up. Like everyone else, they were always changing. "A Harley, you know, could be a lot more practical than you think," he said.

Eileen wasn't going to say anything, she was afraid of touching him off, but she hoped he wasn't thinking of stealing one. Even an old second-hand Harley, like the one they rode to Ile aux Coudres, would cost at least $2,000. He could land in jail, the penitentiary even, and then where would she be? Panic ran through her. "It was good you put that chain on the door," she said.

"What?"

"Scratch came." She pulled the cap on and off her lipstick. "He's coming back next Monday. He says you owe him $800, and if you don't pay up, there'll be trouble."

"Scratch came! What the hell did he have to talk to you about that for! That's for me to handle!"

He gave her a resentful look. "I suppose you think I shouldn't have quit the stocking factory."

"No."

"Well," he said, shaking down his gold bracelets to his wrist. "The hell with Scratch. He can wait." Bucks. They always had problems with bucks. "Here," he smiled. "I picked up some macaroni and cheese on a five-finger discount," he said. "From Billy's."

Eileen chewed on her knuckles. They'd been doing too much shoplifting. Kelly warned her against it. She wasn't good at it and despite what Nicky claimed, he wasn't great at it either. They had had a couple of close calls. The stores had notices everywhere that they would prosecute. If you went to court, the judges gave out real sentences now, not just warnings. One of the girls from the Sex Trolley was in Tanguay for stealing Geneva Gin from the liquor store, and it wasn't even for her. Just for a guy she was living with who pimped part-time. She had been too scared to tell the judge she hadn't stolen it for herself.

"I *had* to go to Scratch," Nick said. When the landlord threatened to throw them out before the baby was born, when he didn't have the rent bucks, Torchy had told him about Scratch. Everyone at the pool hall knew him. Most of his customers were on welfare. The only drawback was that he charged thirty per cent interest. For people on welfare that was the going rate. "Try him," Torchy had said, "but pay him on time. Or you'll find yourself with a broken leg."

Nick looked over at Eileen's makeup and strip outfits on the bathroom counter. It was the first time he'd noticed them.

"I was wondering when you'd notice," Eileen said. "I'm calling Hazel-Fleurette. If I can get my job back at the Sex Trolley, maybe I can give you money for Scratch when he comes next Monday."

Nick didn't say anything. If those B&Es with Torchy and Teddy had worked out, he wouldn't be in this jam. He was the man of the house. Bringing home the bread was supposed to be *his* job. "Where's Stevie?" he asked.

"With Carmen," Eileen said. "I needed a small break." He shut his eyes. He couldn't let that snoopy Carmen take over. Now *he'd* have to be in charge. He looked down at the floor. Carmen and Retta had become far too interfering. He'd even stopped saying hello to them on the stairway. But could he take care of a little baby? He'd have to. He had no choice. "Okay," he sighed. "I'll take care of Stevie when you're out." Now he'd have to fit any jobs he did with Torchy and Teddy around Eileen's shift at the Sex Trolley.

"Look," he said. "I have a second-storey job I can do tonight that will bring us a little dough." When he had replaced Teddy one night, delivering pizza on a bicycle, he had seen a VCR, a CD player and a small television in apartment four in a classy building five blocks away. The couple that lived there usually went away on weekends. He'd been watching the apartment. He could unload a VCR fast to a flea market down at the Port where he and Teddy picked up shipments of drugs for the pushers.

He waited until eleven o'clock at night when Eileen and his son were asleep. Then he put his folded-up pillow case which he'd dyed black into one pocket, and his matches, hammer, screwdriver, small flashlight, and his thin black gloves in the other. It was always best not to have any finger-prints on anything. Sometimes he and Teddy just put Scotch-tape on their fingers.

It was the weekend, and he had seen the couple leaving earlier that evening with a suitcase, but just to be sure he went up the stairs of the building and rang the bell. No one answered. In the apartment next door, he heard the phone ring and ring and knew that apartment was empty too. He was in luck. He stuffed some thin matchsticks into the lock of the door, so that when he was inside the apartment he'd hear if the couple returned unexpectedly and tried to open their door. Then he went down the stairs and ran quickly around to the back of the building to the fire escape.

He boosted himself up to the stairs and crept as silently as possible up the steel steps until he reached a window. It was shut tight. He used his small screwdriver to jack up the window. Luckily there was no lock at the top, otherwise he'd have had to use his hammer. In a second he was in. Using his small flashlight, he looked quickly around the living room. There was lots he could take — a small TV, a CD player, and a hi-fi stereo VCR he could pitch for at least $100. He'd priced them in the stores and they were nearly $500. He lifted the VCR off the top of the TV, threw it into his black pillow case and opened the front door. In a second he was down on the street and out. He covered the black pillow case with a large shopping bag he'd left under the apple tree next to the entrance and walked around the corner to his street. Once he'd filed off the serial number he'd be in business.

EIGHT

❦

The Sex Trolley

EILEEN NEARLY fell over on her spike heels as she pulled open the heavy door at the Sex Trolley. It was three in the afternoon. The lunch crowd was gone and except for Hazel-Fleurette at the bar getting ready for the Happy Hour the place was empty.

"Well, well, well. If it ain't Rougette. The new mum." Hazel-F, as the girls called her, gave all the strippers nicknames. Eileen's was Rougette because of her hair. Without her head of apricot cotton-candy hair, Felix would have fired her, Hazel-F had said when she first tried out. Eileen plumped down at a table near the bar and looked at the revolving red velvet divan on stage and the life-size pictures of Felix's favourite strippers. At home, getting ready, she had felt excited about dancing. Now all she could think of was her humiliating debut at the Sex Trolley a year ago. She cringed as she remembered how Felix had held her bikini pants high in the air in the dressing room after her strip and then dropped them on the floor in disgust. "I want performers, not schoolgirls," he had said. "You get one more chance."

If she had followed Kelly's advice, she would have been all right. "The first strip is always hard," Kelly told her. "No matter what, don't look at the guys. Fasten onto something and don't take your eyes off it." Over the bar was a picture of a girl on all fours, lights flickering on and off on her nipples like Christmas tree lights. "Fix on the tits," Kelly had said.

. . . "Do You Think I'm Sexy" was the song by Rod Stewart she was supposed to start to strip to. Under the flashing nipples, Felix had swirled a drink, an impatient look on his face because the song was nearly over and her bikini bottom was still on. Finally, knowing she had to, she had ripped the velcro at the side of her bikini bottom. As it fell, she caught a hard look in the eyes of the men.

They had looked like jungle animals ready to tear at her. She had bent over, knock-kneed and spread her arms in a V across her thighs. A hoot of laughter went up from the back of the bar, and she had scurried off, her bikini still on stage, her spike heels clacking like an eight-year-old in her mother's shoes. Some of the customers had thought it was an act and gave her an extra round of applause as she flew down the steps. It was the clapping that saved her. "I think the guys thought it was cute," Kelly had told her afterward . . .

"Your old regular's still around," Hazel-F said. In her head, Eileen was still running down the steps, but when she heard "old regular," she sat up. "You mean Raghead?"

"*Bien oui.* And does he have money! When he gets going he's like a one-armed bandit spittin' nickels, except they're fivers."

Eileen had almost forgotten about Raghead. He was a Sikh from India who wore a turban. He'd been her best customer. Aside from Colin, really her *only* customer. He always asked her to dance at his table and sometimes bought twenty songs in a row. Whenever he came in, Eileen knew she could leave with at least $100.

Raghead had been at McGill for three years taking a PhD in engineering, and in all that time, he hadn't succeeded in getting a single date, let alone sex. "My turban turns them off," he had told her. It was against his religion to get rid of it. Raghead's hair smelled of fish. Never cut, he'd said, and possibly, Eileen thought, never washed.

Hazel-F had told her that the way to keep a man peeling off fiver after fiver was to keep him telling a new instalment of some sad or exciting tale about himself so he'd have to order another song. Eileen didn't have to encourage Raghead to talk. It was her strawberry blond hair that kept him asking for more and more songs. He told her he could never have imagined all that red hair "there" until he saw her.

"Does he still come Tuesday and Saturday?" Eileen asked. If Raghead came this week, maybe she could have $250 by Monday so Nicky could pay Scratch a chunk of what he owed.

"Twice a week, but not always the same days," Hazel-F said. "Except he's taken. Lolly has him now." Lolly was short for Lolita. She had long blond hair and did a Lolita routine tanning in the sun with lollipops.

Eileen looked up at Felix's gallery of favourites and recognized the tall blond holding the heart-shaped sunglasses. "Oh," she said. The thought of building up new customers was exhausting. Until she had them, she'd get her basic $35 a night which was not much better than sewing baby clothes.

"Come up to the bar," Hazel-F said.

Eileen came forward and sat on a bar stool, her feet searching for a rung.

Hazel-F grabbed her under the chin and looked her face over. "Okay. Now take out a tit and squeeze it for me. C'mon. Felix doesn't want any leaking tits up there. OK," she said, when she saw she was dry. "Now walk back a few feet. Take off your skirt." She turned on some overhead lights, leaned over the bar, and looked her over.

Within easy reach of the new office buildings and consulates, the Sex Trolley was considered one of the more elegant strip bars in Montreal. Felix expected his girls to look and act like starlets. When the girls acquired the least hint of sag, he farmed them out to La Scandale up north where the laws were looser. Like an old-fashioned bordello, Kelly had warned.

Hazel-F dimmed the lights. "I've got to admit. You look terrific. Lovely legs," she said. "Like a real dancer."

Eileen had gone to a lot of trouble to look terrific. "Wow," Nicky had said when she stood in front of him just before she left in a pencil-thin jade leather skirt, green net stockings and a soft coral-coloured blouse that brought out the highlights in her hair. "Like a jazzy Juliet," he said. She hadn't looked like that for months.

The inspection was over. "Just one more thing," Hazel-F said. "No drugs." Felix sold cocaine late at night to regular customers, including two cops who dropped in from time to time after their shift, but he didn't want his girls in a daze. The rule in the dressing room was no sniffing, smoking or mainlining.

Once, at the end of the night shift when no one was around, Eileen had seen a girl jab a needle in her arm. The year before, to help her cut through the stiffness she felt at the beginning of the night, Kelly had given her a little hash, but no one knew about that. She'd taken her out to the laneway behind the building for a few tokes before her first strip.

"So." Hazel-F pulled the laces on her bodice so her breasts puffed up higher and lit a cigarette. Before customers started arriving for Happy Hour, she wanted a little woman talk. She knew Eileen had had a boy and she wanted details on the delivery.

"You nearly had it in the taxi? It was that fast?" Hazel-F then launched into the story of her pregnancy at thirty-eight when she gave up smoking for nine months and lay in bed for the final month just to be sure.

She had been a stripper in Jonquière where clients from Abitibi Price and Alcan supplied her with enough money to put her boy through medical school at McGill University. "I wish I could've had more. You have pictures?" she asked and without waiting for Eileen, rummaged into her shoulder bag under the counter. "Nothing beats having a boy. You'll see. This was Jean-Paul last year." She held up a colour picture of her son in a white lab coat shaking hands with an older man. "He was top of his medical class." She put her pictures back in the envelope and gave Eileen a sympathetic look.

"It's a shame you had to come to work so soon. What's wrong with your husband? Can't he work? I took six months off before I went back. Saved the money myself. My asshole husband was long gone. My mother helped me out. Those first six months with my son were the best I ever had." There was a pause and then she asked: "How's the feeding going?"

"Oh fine. Nicky feeds him when I'm gone, and we have these two neighbours who . . ."

"Similac or Infanlac?" Hazel-F interrupted.

Eileen looked blank. She couldn't remember. Usually Retta bought the formula for her and left it at the front door on the way home from her shift at the nursing home.

Hazel-F was tapping the counter with her finger. Her nails were always painted dark purple. She was about to give her advice about baby food, Eileen could just tell.

"Now infa . . ." She stopped when the door opened and Butch and Gros Bec came in.

"Hi guys!" she bellowed. Eileen was glad Hazel-F had them to think about. They were Felix's assistants and would want a beer before customers started arriving. Butch patrolled the floor and Gros Bec kept an eye on the girls' dressing room, popping in regularly to make sure there were no fights and no drugs.

∾

For the first two nights, Eileen danced on stage and waited on tables but did not get a single request from a man to dance at his table. She was the only one out of twenty girls who went so long without a single request.

Finally, at closing time, Hazel-F took her aside. "Felix's complaining you look dead," she said. "You've got to liven up for the weekend. Sleepwalkers aren't sexy."

Eileen didn't want to tell Hazel-F, but her Stevie was colicky, and she got little sleep. She'd have to try harder.

"Your hair and legs are great, but it's not enough," Hazel-F went on. "For Crissake, flirt. When you're on stage, pick out a guy at the ring and work on him."

She gave her a demonstration on stage. "Roll your body, girl. Like this," and she swung her bulging rear around like the sexy Italian women Eileen had seen going into bars up on Jean Talon when she worked at the box factory.

"Shit, the way you act, you'd think you didn't know what a wing-ding was. You're acting too much like a ballet dancer. Heat 'em up to the point where they'll ask you to dance at their table for one song and then another and another. Make 'em moan."

Hazel-F stood behind Eileen, her warm hands around Eileen's hips, and moved them in circles. There was something soothing about the feeling of Hazel-Fleurette holding her. "Think of a belly dancer," she urged.

Afterwards they went out to Dunn's for a smoked meat and a coffee. Famous for its smoked meat, it was the only place that was open after three in the morning and was even busier than the Sex Trolley at the peak. Hazel-F nodded hello at a lot of people.

After she'd had a couple of cigarettes, Hazel leaned back and said, "You want to know the best moment of a strip? It's when you look into the guy's eyes, and you know the poor john is dreaming of being in bed with you, and his prick is hurtin', and the song comes to an end, and you put on your bikini, coldly, as though you were getting dressed in the morning, and you walk over to the bar, and you can feel his eyes hanging right into the crack of your ass.

"Seriously though, if you play it right, this game could work for you. You've got everything it takes — the body, the hair, and a nice personality, the kind that lots of men warm to. All you need is a little more confidence. What you have to do is get to know the business. When you're older," Hazel went on, "and no longer looking like a teenager, you could get a job like I have, overseeing the bar and assisting the owner." Her eyes flashed with pride. "This job has given me a way to control my own life and to help my son. It's made me independent."

Eileen hadn't thought of making a career in strip bars. It was just a way to make some quick money. She didn't think she'd ever be able to run a bar the way Hazel did, and besides, what kind of independence did Hazel have anyway? She was stuck doing everything exactly the way Felix wanted. If Hazel didn't follow orders, Felix would fire her.

～

The next night in the middle of one of her strips on stage, Eileen saw Raghead and two other Sikhs come in the door. Lolly, Hazel-F had said, wouldn't be coming in. She was in luck. The memory of how she could work Raghead into a trance charged her up — that, and the thought of Scratch at the door in three days demanding $800. There was no way she could have the full amount, but $300 this week, and then another $300 the week after would get Scratch off their backs. Nicky could make enough from a B&E to take care of the interest.

Raghead sat right under the stage and waved gently at her, his bushy eyebrows moving up and down. Admiration shone from his eyes. She looked straight into them. Slowly she felt her body come to life and the cloud of gloom she had been in all week coping with Nick and a screaming baby began to lift.

She ran her hand down the side of her breast and around her thigh. She knew her body was peach-beautiful. She was glamorous Rougette with the mother-of-pearl combs and the green net stockings. Not Juliet in the ballet, as she'd dreamed when she was still at ballet school and nothing had yet happened with Rube. But at least not ordinary Eileen O'Reilly. This was what she had wanted when she sat on the bathroom floor that day looking at her strip outfits. It was what drew her to the Sex Trolley.

She swirled her hips around and forward towards Raghead, the way Hazel-F had showed her, enticing him, curling him in. She could see his three gold rings — sapphire, ruby, and diamond. At the end of the second song, she snapped off her bikini close to his eyes. He leaned back in his chair, his hands folded on his chest, a look of satisfaction on his face. For the whole night she danced at Raghead's table.

"You're doing great," Hazel-F said later, "but spread yourself around a little or you may be sorry. Zero in on some others." Eileen couldn't. Like a junkie, Raghead was asking for song after song. By two in the morning, she had a $100 in bills and a promise he'd return the next night.

~

Getting ready for the busy Saturday night shift, Eileen squeezed onto the bench in front of the mirror where ten girls were putting on final touches of colour under hot makeup lights. Saturday night was special. To make each strip different, everyone had an outfit to go with a unique routine.

Boots was in her cowboy outfit with a leather fringe and a rope at her waist. The only one who had befriended Eileen, Boots had a motor scooter and had given Eileen a lift home after her first night.

"You're looking really pretty," Boots told her. For an Irish look, Eileen had had a tam lined up to go with a shamrock bikini but changed her mind after Raghead showed up. Boots was helping her paste a little rhinestone on the side of her nose so she'd look Indian, when the door to the dressing room flew open.

Through the mirror, Eileen saw Lolly. Their eyes connected and a chill went through her. Hazel-F had said Lolly was off Fridays and Saturdays. The dressing room was noisy but Lolly's voice pierced the air. "You better believe I'm working tonight," and she banged her locker door. The girls at the mirror gave Eileen a quick glance. "What do you expect," Eileen heard someone whisper. "You don't let a money-maker like him just slip through your fingers."

Eileen leaned forward under the mirror and tried to concentrate on lining her eyes. If only Kelly were here. She hated being the newest girl. Boots gave Eileen's knee a squeeze and it made her feel a little better. To avoid Lolly, Eileen tried to escape out into the bar early, but as she opened the door of the dressing room, she felt a hand on her shoulder pulling her back. "Think you can charm him with that little Indian sparkler do you?" Lolly picked the rhinestone off her nose and flicked it off into the air. Gros Bec watched from his stool in the corner, a comic book on his lap. "I heard what happened last night," Lolly said. Eileen felt the girls looking at them from their lockers. "Thought you could grab him away when I was off, eh?"

~

Fifteen minutes later, Felix and his favourite stripper were sitting cosily at the bar talking. The red hearts of Lolly's lollipops, which bobbed at the back of her head like bunny ears, turned ridiculously in the air like windmills. The two of them were sitting next to the slot where Hazel-Fleurette took orders from the girls who served drinks when they weren't on stage or stripping at tables. Eileen could hardly keep track of the drinks for the customers. She brought gin and tonics instead of Harvey Wallbangers to one table and twice made a mistake in change. Already she was six dollars short. "Just play it cool," Boots told her. "Don't let them get to you." But Eileen thought of saying she felt sick and leaving. Raghead, she knew, was coming in with Indian shawls for her to dance in.

~

No one except Boots would believe Lolly deliberately tripped her, so Eileen never told anyone, not even Hazel-F. At one a.m. Eileen was wending her way through a packed crowd trying to balance ten drinks on her tray for a table far from the bar. Lolly slithered through the crowd as Eileen went flying, the drinks dousing the pants of three elegant gentlemen from the German consulate.

For a full minute, Eileen sat on the floor in a dark forest of pant legs and moving feet, hugging her knees. She felt too sick to move.

When she got up, Butch was bowing over the men who were shaking themselves and looking down at the embarrassing patches on their grey flannels.

"Please send us the cleaning bill," Butch said. Felix pressed through from the bar. "I'm so sorry, I'm so sorry," Eileen kept repeating. The three said something about it being time to go anyway and left. She was grateful they didn't put up more of a fuss. Felix gave her a scornful look and Eileen went back to the bar to order ten more drinks out of her own money. She would now be out $50.

꒰

Lolly did everything she could to turn Raghead on, but no matter what she did Raghead kept picking Eileen to dance at his table. He had brought sparkling orange shawls shot with silver for Eileen to dance in and pearl anklets with bells. The more he told her how exquisite she was, the better she danced on stage, and the more she saw other men looking at her.

"You'll make it a lot easier for yourself if you give the eye to a few others," Hazel-F told her.

"How can I?" Eileen asked. Raghead had told her he expected her to be his for the whole night. She didn't know what to do. Every time she danced, he gave her something new to put on, first the shawls, then various bangles and necklaces. "Don't let any of these jerks push you around," Boots told her outside on the street at the end of the night. "Raghead was your client first, wasn't he? Come on," she said, and gave her a lift home.

꒰

Eileen came in Sunday still on a sexual high after the adulation from Raghead. She wanted to walk out with $90 even though she knew it would be a slow night. Scratch was coming the next day and all she had was $210. She needed $300: $200 for last week's instalment, and

$100 toward this week's. And that was a minimum. Raghead had bought sixty songs altogether over Friday and Saturday nights which would have been enough, but she had spent $40 on a pink satin bikini and lost $50 on spilled and wrongly ordered drinks.

She was relieved Felix and Lolly would not be in. "He's taking me to the Beaver Club tomorrow," she'd heard Lolly boast in the dressing room the night before. Boots told Eileen "he" was Felix. "They've been an item for a while," she explained. Hazel-Fleurette was off too. Butch was at the bar in charge of the club. There were only eight girls on.

∽

It was after her first strip that she looked down at the table right under the lights and recognized Colin, the optometrist from St. Lambert who lived with his old mother. He had a rose on the table and a mint patty, her favourite kind of chocolate bar. Unlike all the other guys, Colin looked at her face. Colin was the only one of her customers she had ever met after work. She smiled warmly at him and continued her little routine. At the end she leaned down over his table and looked into his eyes. "Missed you," he said to her.

He looked quickly at her breasts but then he squeezed her hand and gave her the rose. Colin had lonely, washed-out eyes and a caved-in chest, but he had always been nice to her. One time late at night nearly a year before, when Felix had been selling cocaine and the place had been extra dark, she had let him touch one of her breasts. No one saw because they had been at a far table in the corner. He had said her breasts were like china cups, so white next to the freckles in the V of her neck. He had asked her to meet him after, and bought her a rose from a street seller.

Whenever they met she had let him cuddle up to her on a bench in Percy Park, but she stopped meeting him after she and Nicky went to Ile aux Coudres. Each time he had given her $50, and she had used the money to buy the kind of clothes Nicky wanted her to wear. "All

I want to do is hold you in my arms," Colin had said, but she had always felt she was betraying Nick. Once, but only once, they made love in his car. She hadn't meant to, but that night he had talked about growing up as the non-athletic son of the school's hockey coach, a son everyone laughed at because he couldn't skate well enough to make the team. He had seemed so lonely, and without her even realizing, she had let him slip down her skirt and it had happened. After her strip on stage, she went straight over to him. Butch enforced the no talking rule except while serving drinks, or stripping at tables, so she didn't stay long.

"You look lovely," Colin said.

"Thanks," she said, and smiled like a performer. On her wedding band finger, back and forth, she caressed the jade rings Nicky had given her and tossed back her hair.

"So where've you been?" Colin asked when she came back with a beer.

She hesitated a moment and then she told him. "I had a baby."

"Oh," he said. "I thought maybe you'd gotten involved with one of those small dance companies. Remember, like we talked about last year?" The summer before Colin had told her that she shouldn't waste her time at a strip bar. "Why don't you audition for the Eddy Toussaint Ballet, the Ballet Jazz, or maybe even Les Grands Ballets Canadiens," he'd suggested. But she hadn't had the confidence, and by that time Nick was already in her life. "You're going to be regular?" he asked.

"I hope so." She wanted to work every night until Nicky paid off Scratch.

"I've still got the white tutu with the lace top," he said. "I'll make a real dancer of you yet," he smiled. He had bought it from a ballet shop and had given it to her for a routine she did just for him that was more ballet than strip.

Colin must have known she was in financial trouble because now instead of $5 a song, he gave her $20. "Oh my," she said. She knew he wanted her to meet him afterwards. His eyes had that faraway look.

Until Scratch got his $800, maybe she'd have to make an exception, but it would be hard. She belonged to Nicky. He would kill her if he ever found out.

Every day, Nicky was taking care of their little Stevie, the way he promised, going to Mount Royal with him. Eileen saw hardly anything of her son because of the late nights. She fed him before she went to bed and prepared enough bottles for the next twenty-four hours, but sometimes, by the time she got up, Nicky and the baby were already gone.

∼

"I have a surprise for you," Colin said one night after they had walked up to Percy Park from the club. "I'm going to my car. I'll be back in a minute." She had seen Colin twice after hours. Raghead had not been back and she wasn't getting many requests to dance. Between the dances and extra tips and the afters, Colin had given her $100. She was relieved that all Colin wanted to do was cuddle up.

When he came back, he opened his coat and three little spaniel puppies tumbled out. "My dog had puppies," he said. "I thought you might want to see them."

"I had one just like this," Eileen said stooping down and stroking a caramel-coloured one with white spots. "His name was Barnie — short for St. Bernard. You've heard of those dogs who climb mountains to save people? My stepfather gave him to me for my thirteenth birthday. Barnie died when I was fifteen."

Colin picked up the little puppy who was wobbling around on the grass and put it on her lap. Eileen ran her fingers through his fur. "Barnie used to meet me at the school yard every single day after school," she said.

"You can have him if you like," Colin said.

"No." She vowed she'd never have another dog after Barnie died.

"What happened to your dog when you were fifteen?"

"He ran in front of my stepfather's taxi." She wasn't going to tell him the real story. Rube had killed the dog on purpose. She saw him step on the gas when Barnie jumped off the curb in front of Hank's grocery. Barnie slept next to her on the bed and protected her from Rube. The dog knew she needed him. Rube tried to come in twice in the middle of the night but Barnie growled and Rube had to back off. Two nights after Barnie died, Rube came in and made her open her legs. She didn't want to remember the details. Her mother had been in the house but she was too drunk to hear anything. "What we've been doing up to now isn't enough," Rube had said. "You're old enough now for the real thing."

NINE

~

On the Mountain

NICK LAY UNDER a tree, his earphones clamped to his head and listened to Bill Withers sing "Just the Two of Us" on CHOM. At the station break he shoved his earphones back and sat up. "Oh," he said. A little girl with black hair and gold earrings was holding his baby boy. The child looked up at him and smiled. Down the hill towards Beaver Lake a woman in a black kerchief waved. "Rosalia, Rosalia," she called. *"E yiayia mu,"* the child said to Nick and put the baby into Nick's lap.

In a hollow, a baseball throw from where he was sitting, a Greek family was settling in for an all-day picnic. Nick knew the family was Greek. After living for several months in a Greek neighbourhood he now recognized Greek words. *E yiayia mu* meant my grandmother.

There were about twenty-five people and they looked as though they had arrived for a week with their fold-out chairs, picnic baskets and blankets. It was an unusually warm day for April, almost like summer. Everyone was having fun. A little boy was burying his head in the grandmother's black skirt. Older boys were kicking a soccer ball around. A couple of girls were playing hopscotch. And a man with hairy arms and a blue sailor hat plucked at a guitar. Over a huge pit, smoke rose up over two lambs cooking on long wood poles. A teenage boy was coming through the trees with an armload of wood for the fire.

Nick remembered how, when he was in New Brunswick camping with the Evans and the Greggs, he had gathered armfuls of driftwood from the beach for the clam bake. That was the last holiday he had with them. They adopted Luke in the fall. He and Danny made the fire. If it hadn't been for him, Pop would have had to buy the clams. He had dug out more than anyone. The others gave up after half an hour, but Nick took the whole afternoon. Luke, he remembered, didn't lift a finger for that clambake.

Danny didn't like Luke but Luke was Pop's real-blood nephew. "Blood is thicker than water," Torchy told him. "Everyone knows that." Torchy lived with his grandmother on Durocher street. In the end Pop decided everything. That's why Mum didn't visit him at Parkway, but if she had been his real Mum, maybe she would have acted different. She would have made sure he never went to Parkway. Mum had been so proud of him when she saw all the clams in his pails. "Nicky dug up the entire dinner," she told everyone, but Pop wasn't impressed.

The grandmother walked up the hill slowly toward Nick and sat down next to him. Up close, she wasn't that old. It was just that she was all in black. She leaned over the baby and smiled at him.

Nick pulled the baby in close to him. "Mine," he said. The grandma stroked his baby's arms and ran her fingers through Nick's hair. "Maria," the grandmother pointed at herself.

Nick threw back his shoulders. "Nicholas Stephanos. My son is Stephanos Nicholas." Maybe the grandma would recognize the Greek names. "Mykonos," he added.

"Mykonos?" The grandmother lit up. *"Ise elinas?"*

Nick smiled. "Greek? Yeah, I'm Greek."

She said something he didn't understand and gestured for him to come with her to the picnic. While he adjusted his backpack with the baby things, she bent down and picked up Stevie. All the way down the hill, she cooed at him while the little girl held Nick's hand, gaily swinging it.

"Mykonos? Your name is Mykonos?" The man who had been plucking the guitar scratched his head. "Why you no speak Greek?" He talked to him in broken English at a picnic table surrounded by the family who stopped what they were doing to listen. The grandmother changed the baby with a diaper supplied by one of the young women and fed him with a bottle from Nick's backpack.

Nick explained that his father was a Greek sailor who had met his mother in Quebec City, but left before he was born. "My mother died when I was little," he added. He didn't want to say anything about the bus and the note his mother pinned to his diaper.

"You never met your father?" the man with the guitar asked.

"No," Nick said.

Solemnly, as though it were a strange tale, the man, who was called Costa, explained everything in Greek to the women as they prepared the meal. The older children and the men all understood English but the women needed a translation. Afterwards, Nick joined the boys in soccer. They couldn't believe how fast he could run.

That's how it all started. Maybe he was actually related to them, he told Eileen later. There were no Mykonos names in the Montreal and Quebec phone books, because he had checked, but Costa said there was a Mykonos family on the island of Naxos where they all came from.

"You know what Mykonos means?" Costa asked. "No," Nick said. "In Greek it means beautiful." Costa told Nick everyone in Naxos was related. It was a small island and the families dated back to the time of the ancient Greeks. "Before Christ was born," he said. The idea of an island where everyone belonged to a big family was like a dream. Costa showed him a postcard of the place on a mountain sloping down to the Aegean sea where Apollo, the sun god, was born three thousand years ago. "Maybe as beautiful as Ile aux Coudres," Nick told Eileen. "Maybe even more beautiful." Neither of them could imagine anything more beautiful than Ile aux Coudres.

After his day with the Greek family, he was so eager to tell Eileen everything he went out to the bus stop outside the Greek pastry shop on Park Avenue and sat on a bench with Stevie for a whole hour waiting for her to come home from the Sex Trolley. On his head was a blue sailor hat that Costa had given him.

His story was such a breathless jumble Eileen could hardly follow it. Nick told her that the picnic was to celebrate family members who had "name days" in April. Every Greek, he said, was called after a saint. St. Stephen's day was celebrated in April, which was why they made a special fuss over him and the baby. "If there was a Saint Eileen you'd get presents on Saint Eileen day," he said.

At the apartment he had a plate of Greek hors d'oeuvres ready for her on the kitchen table. "They call it *pikilia*," he told her. After they ate, he tumbled her into bed and told her how he turned the lambs on the poles over the fire, helped carve them up, and how, when everyone was seated, Costa asked him to carry a barrel of wine from the car. "They make their own wine," he told her. When Costa lifted Stevie into the baby carrier at the end of the day, he had been a little drunk from it. All through the meal they kept filling his glass. Their parting present to him was the *pikilia* for Eileen.

The last thing Eileen heard after they made love and before she dropped off to sleep, exhausted from her night at the Sex Trolley, was the song Costa played on his guitar for Nick. It was called *"Ehete Ghia"* (Farewell). "I memorized the chorus," Nick said. "I picked up the Greek words easy."

The Greek family invited him to come back the next day for another all-day picnic and Costa explained the history of the song to him. After the Greek revolution against the Turks in 1821, the Turks circled a town called Zaloggo in Souli. They killed the men who were trying to defend the town. At the top of the hill the Greek women and children watched. They knew that the Turks would take them as slaves and began to do a Greek dance where someone always leads. One by one, a new woman leading each time, the wives and children danced off the top of the hill over a cliff to their deaths. The grannie sang the words while Costa played the guitar and Nick sat next to her with Stevie and listened. *Sto vouno den ze to, Psari out' o anthos, Stin ammoudia, Ki Souliotises den, Zonne dihos tin, Elephantheria.* The fish do not live on the mountain, nor the flowers on the sandy shore. Just as the Souli women live not without freedom.

Costa explained that when families leave their villages to come to North America, they feel sad because they are leaving something they love. So they sing this farewell song, especially at family celebrations. After the grandmother sang the various verses, everyone joined in for the chorus. *Ehete ghia vrisoules, Logi vouna rahoules.* I bid farewell to you water-springs, valleys and mountain peaks.

On the second day with the family, the grandmother noticed the birthmark Nick had on his arm. Nick had always thought it was ugly and tried to cover it up. "No, no," Costa said. Translating as the grandmother spoke, Costa explained that in Naxos the Mykonos men were famous. They fought the Turks, he said. All the men had a birthmark like Nick's. The family came from Anatolia. The grandmother traced the wide arc of the birthmark with her finger. "At the top, a Cross," Costa translated. "And at the bottom, a sword."

Nick wasn't sure why the family was being so kind to him. He had never felt he had anything to offer anyone, but this time everything seemed different. They had made him feel special. Maybe he really *was* special.

At the end of the day, Costa told Nick that every morning the grandmother went to Jeanne Mance Park on Park Avenue to play with Rosalia and her four-year-old brother Dimitri while their parents were at work. She invited Nick to bring his baby and join them. Every day for a whole week at the park Nick called her his *yiayia mu* as though she were his very own grannie, and she looked after little Stevie as though the baby were hers too. *Yiayia* took care of everything. After the first day Nick didn't even bring formula.

Nick took Rosalia and Dimitri on the swings and seesaws, helped them build a sand castle, and when they went to the Schubert baths, played tag with them in the pool. Each day he learned new words in Greek. He could say I love you, grandma, my dad is Greek, my son is little Stephanos. He asked the owner of Le Coin Grec around the corner from his apartment on Paros Street how to say, "We will go all together to church on Christmas" and surprised her with it. *"Ne, ne,"* she smiled. *Ne* meant yes. He thought his *yiayia* was very beautiful, like his own *yiayia* might have been. When *yiayia* was really old and couldn't take care of herself, he dreamt that she would come to live with him and Eileen and little Stephanos. Maybe in Naxos.

~

And then it rained for three days. Nick showed up at Jeanne Mance Park every day, figuring she'd come to get him, but she never appeared. When the sun came out, he expected she'd return, but she never did. He didn't even know her last name. Costa had told him, but it was complicated. Theo something. How could he have been so stupid as not to find out where they lived? Maybe his *yiayia* got sick. Could Rosalia's mother have died? Perhaps the father made them move. If they moved, his *yiayia* wouldn't be able to find Jeanne Mance Park by herself.

In his desperation, he went off to the teddy bear store to talk to the saleslady grannie that had given him the teddy bear the day his son was born, but she wasn't there. A guy about his age was in charge, probably her grandson. He looked like a geek. Fat with creased pants.

He didn't know what to do, so he went back up to Mount Royal and sat under the tree where he'd met Rosalia. From his breast pocket he pulled out his two polaroid pictures of the picnic. One showed him next to Costa around a big cake with the family. The other was of him, the baby, and his *yiayia*. He looked closely at her eyes. They were blue like his. Most Greeks had brown eyes, Costa said.

He looked down the hill and picked out the exact place on the walk circling the lake where he first saw her waving, the wind blowing her skirts. He felt a sudden shortness of breath. If he squinted, he could see the burnt logs near the picnic table where he turned the lambs for the roast. If he sat there long enough, maybe the sun would come out, the family would come back, and everything would start over, like a movie you could reel back to the beginning.

But Nick knew they were gone, just like Mum Evans was gone, and his real Mum was gone. He thought of himself at six weeks in the sink of the bus and inside he felt empty. No one had ever cared about him. He slipped his headphones over his ears and cupped his hands over them so they were tight against his head, blocking out the world. He hadn't used his Walkman since the day of the first picnic. *Midnight Oil* was on. He ripped the headphones off his ears and stared down at Beaver Lake, a rage as big as a tornado building up in him. He looked over at the grass beside him. Oh my God! He'd forgotten to bring his son! He'd left little Stevie at home in the crib. How could he have done that! He'd have to go back. He tried to stand up but he felt too dizzy. He clapped his earphones back on and pushed the slider control on the Walkman all the way forward. He clasped his knees and dropped his head. After the sun went down, a policeman who picked him out with a flashlight asked him if anything was wrong.

TEN

~~

Framed and Fired

EILEEN'S HEART seized up when she saw Raghead come in the door. She had tried to arrange her days so they didn't coincide with Lolly's but it wasn't always possible. Tonight they were both on. Eileen knew what she had to do. Even though she still needed money, she would have to act cold to Raghead so that maybe he'd give up on Eileen and ask for Lolly.

She sighed. Scratch was finally paid off, but all they had was the welfare cheque, and Nick was still at her about getting a motorcycle. She'd told him so many times that the motorcycle idea was crazy. Now, just to keep him quiet, she'd said she had come round to the feeling that it might be just as good as a car.

When Raghead sat in Eileen's section, she got another girl to serve his table, but he marched up to Eileen at the bar and asked for the next song. After her first dance at his table, she said, "Couldn't you ask Lolly? The owner prefers it if clients have several favourites."

"The owner?" Raghead said. Butch took a few steps in from the door so he could hear. "I'll ask for the girl of my choice," Raghead said loudly.

Eileen flushed red. "Of course, of course," she said, but he wouldn't let up.

"The owner? You mean that man over there?" and he shot a withering look at Felix at the bar. "If I want you, I *get you*."

"Absolutely." She looked down and saw her breasts were sagging. It happened when she got upset and her back curved and she fell back on her heels. "Always stand straight," Kelly had told her. "Otherwise you look dopey." She straightened up and tried to act normal.

She didn't have her heart in it but she danced most of the night for Raghead. She wished her friend Boots was on so she could ask her what to do.

At midnight Felix called her over to the bar. He was angry and told her to come with him into the dressing room. Without saying a word, he reached up to the top of her locker and ripped off a piece of masking tape. Two pieces of hash were stuck to it. "You know the rules," he said turning it over in his hand.

"But it's not mine," Eileen said. "Honestly."

"You're the only one that uses this locker. Right, Gros Bec?" Gros Bec nodded.

"That's true," she stammered, "but honestly." It wasn't hers, but even if had been, lots of the girls smoked and sniffed. Boots sniffed in the can and so did Lolly. They used two dollar bills.

"You know the rules," he repeated.

It had to have been Lolly. She was just low enough to do something like this. The lockers weren't locked. Anyone could put anything in them when Gros Bec wasn't looking.

Felix looked at her breasts and flicked at the undersides. "Tighten your straps," he said. "You're starting to sag. I'll keep you on the payroll," he said. "But not here. You'll have to go to La Scandale."

"You mean I'm fired?" she said.

"Well. If that's the way you want to look at it, yes."

~

ELEVEN

Running

WAS THAT NICK? From her seat on the bus, waiting to leave for Sherbrooke, Eileen thought she saw him jump off the escalator at the station. When he didn't find her at the laundromat, he'd go to the coffee shop, and then, she just bet, straight to the bus station. Eileen shuddered at what Nick might do if he discovered the phone message was fake. The way she dashed off Jonquière quickly on a piece of grocery bag could alert him. "Throw it down as though the baby were suddenly crying," Carmen had said the day before when they were making Eileen's escape plans. "I'm putting it at the back of your top drawer."

The phone message said Kel, Jonquière, with a phone number. "Maybe he'll be dumb enough to actually go to Jonquière," Carmen had said. Eileen had wanted to remove the note from her drawer before they went to the laundromat but she was afraid Nick would suspect something. If anything was "off," he could tell from her hand-

writing. He had asked her to send him cards after he stopped meeting the Greek grannie, and when they came he'd complained about
the messages. "I want a nice surprise everyday in the mail," he'd said,
but when he opened his first card he had whined that the way she
wrote "I love you" was "wobbly, like you aren't sure." He was right.
She had come to the point where she wasn't sure.

Eileen loved Nick most when he acted like a Hell's Angel. After
they got married, when they walked down Park Avenue past the pool
hall, the guys in chains and leather always looked up in admiration.
Everyone noticed how handsome he was. Even the police showed
respect, especially after he quickly figured out why a cylinder wasn't
firing on one of the cops' bikes. "Just a loose spark plug," he'd said to
the cop and wrenched it tight. Usually they didn't push him around
the way they did Torchy.

But after the baby was born, Nick had changed. And then, after he
stopped seeing the Greek grannie at the park and she lost her job at
the strip bar, he got worse. All day, the two of them were alone
together with Stevie who never stopped crying. Eileen hated it when
Nick clung to her like a four-year-old. That's why she was leaving
him. "Leaving him?" she whispered under her breath. This was the
first time she had actually said the words.

The last passenger was coming down the aisle of the bus. The driver climbed up the stairs of the vehicle and started the motor. Then
he stood up and took off his jacket. Eileen looked at her watch.
"C'mon," she said. At any minute, Nick could burst through the gate
with his hair flying demanding to get on. The driver looked in his
side mirror and started backing up.

She bent over and pretended to tie her shoes. If that really *was*
Nick and he caught a glimpse of her as the bus pulled out, she was
finished. A nun sitting beside her tapped her on the shoulder, "You
okay?" Eileen pulled herself up. "Yes," she said.

She had moved quickly, running all the way from the laundromat
to the subway. While she had been at the laundromat waiting for
Nick to be far enough away, she had wanted to stop everything. No

matter what she did, he'd find her. But she had gone ahead with it.

How could she have faced Carmen and Retta? Carmen, she suspected, wanted the baby to herself for a while. That, more than anything, she thought, was why Carmen came up with the plan. Every time Carmen held Stevie, she gave him her breast, even in front of Nick.

Eileen pressed the button on her seat and closed her eyes once the bus crossed the bridge and Montreal was behind her. Beside her the nun, who wore a black veil and a cross around her neck, was slowly turning the pages of a black book. She had gray hair and a kindly expression. When Eileen climbed on the bus, she had asked if she could sit next to her. It made her feel safe.

Time went by quickly and when she opened her eyes, the bus was passing a sign marked Eastman. "Do you know how far it is to Sherbrooke?" she asked. "Another forty-five minutes," the nun replied. She looked at her watch. By now, Nick would have passed by Carmen's apartment. Eileen could see Carmen standing at the apartment door with a look that said, "just you try, you asshole."

If the washing machine in the building hadn't been broken, the plan would never have worked. "Eileen's not home?" she could hear Carmen saying. "Well she picked up Stevie at four. I have no idea where she'd be now." And she'd have shut the door. "And if Nick hears him cry?" Eileen had asked. "Don't worry, the music will be on. Besides, he never cries when he's with me."

Carmen had figured out every detail, including what to do with the laundry left in the laundromat. "Fill your green bag with rags," she had advised. According to the plan, Eileen and Nick would leave the baby with Carmen and go to the laundromat where Eileen would busy herself with the "laundry" while Nick would as usual visit Torchy at the pool room. As soon as Eileen stuffed the rags in the washer, and Nick was out of sight, she would run to the subway for the bus station.

For Carmen, the plan was simple. Kelly would help Eileen find a job in Sherbrooke, Eileen would send money, and then Carmen would bring Eileen her son. There had been no answer when Eileen had called Kelly from Carmen's apartment but Carmen pushed her into going anyway. "She's probably working, or doing a trick," Carmen had said. "You'll find her."

~

The way Carmen's nostrils flared made Nick stop asking questions when he went to her door. Going down the walk in front of the apartment building he looked up to her window and saw her watching him. "Bitch," he said.

He slipped around the building and sprinted down an alley to Park Avenue and over to the shops. Maybe Eileen was around there. "We could go to the Four Brothers after," Eileen had said on the way to the laundromat. "For macaroni and cheese."

He ran so fast he was unable to swerve around three women coming out of a fruit store. He bashed straight through them and they fell to the ground like sacks of sand. From behind him they yelled at him in broken English.

A hand grabbed his shoulder. Ready to swat whoever it was, he spun around. It was Porky from the police station. He and Torchy called the cop Porky because of his pig eyes. Porky dropped into the pool hall regularly. He believed Nick and Torchy were involved in the theft of television sets from an apartment building on Durocher street. The two of them were look-out boys and received hardly any of the take, but afterwards the police watched their movements even more than the guys who had actually done it. Nick quickly threw his hands up, shook out his pockets and slowly backed up.

"I ain't done nothin'. Honest."

The cop looked down at the old women picking up fruit off the ground.

"So what's your hurry?" Porky moved so close Nick smelled his gum.

"Got to meet my wife."

"Your wife?"

"Got to meet my wife," Nick said through his teeth.

The cop looked into Nick's sunglasses. "Take off those shades." Nick yanked them off and stared down at the sidewalk. The cop moved closer and Nick met his gaze.

"That's better." The cop looked him up and down and then settled on his gold earring. A circle of people gathered around. Nick flicked back his hair and put his hands in the slits of his leather jacket. The cop pushed Nick's shoulder as though it were a plate of rotten food. "Get moving," he said.

When Nick got to the Four Brothers, he ran to the aisle marked pasta but Eileen wasn't there. He tore up and down the aisles, and was about to leave the store when he decided to check the women's washroom down the corridor at the front. Inside, there was no sign of a stroller. He pushed open the door of the first cubicle and a woman with her pants below her knees snatched her purse from the floor and screamed.

"Nothin' to worry about," he said slamming her door and banging the others open with his fist. "I'm looking for my wife," he yelled. The last door was locked. He crouched down. No feet showed. He rolled over on his back, grabbed the bottom of the door, and like a gymnast on a bar, pulled his shoulders in and up. He had to be sure. A young woman in red boots had her feet in the air. She gripped the sides of the toilet. "Sorry sweetheart," he said as he slipped out. The sweep of the washroom took just a few seconds. "You can put your feet down," he called out as he left. Eileen could have left a note in their apartment saying where she was. It made him suspect the worst. That, and the way Carmen looked at him, as though she had him by the balls. Maybe *she* had Stevie. He had listened outside, but heard nothing.

A wave of panic was building up. He had to stay calm. He looked up and down Park Avenue. He looked everywhere — the dollar store, McDonald's, the park, even the dry cleaners where she once took his leather jacket. No one remembered seeing a girl with apricot-coloured hair and blue jeans pushing a baby in a stroller. "She has a silver heart around her neck," he always added.

Nick trudged back again to the laundromat. A different woman was in charge. "A lot of people come here," the woman said. "I don't remember her. These wouldn't be hers would they?" A mound of wet clothes lay on top of one of the washers. "Been here since five o'clock. Looks like rags."

He thought of going to the Sex Trolley but trashed the idea. She'd been fired from the joint. Why would she be there? Still. Maybe she went off to try to get her job back. He went into a phone booth, looked up the number and asked for Hazel.

"This is Nicholas Mykonos. Eileen Mykonos' husband."

"Yes, yes," Hazel–Fleurette said. "You know she doesn't work here no more, don't you?"

"Yes," he said, "but I wondered perhaps if she dropped by, you see, she isn't home, and . . ."

"Look," Hazel said. "This isn't no coffee shop, girls come here to work, not to hang around. Another girl has her job."

"Okay," said Nick, and he hung up.

∽

The longer she was on the bus, the more Eileen felt she should never have confided in Carmen. If she hadn't told her how Nicky had locked her in the closet, Carmen would never have come up with the plan. She told Carmen that just to prove to her that Nicky was as tough as Antonio. She should have known what Carmen's reaction would be.

"You can't put up with that," Carmen had yelled. "If you can't kick the bruiser out, then leave. I'll take the baby." Eileen didn't dare tell Carmen the half of it. She might have grabbed Nick in the hall. Eileen was glad the big bruise she had was on her back and not on her arm.

"You have that look in your eye," Nick had said. "I just know you're thinking of leaving. You have that same look you had before Christmas when you *admitted* you were thinking of leaving me." A day later, when they were in bed, he noticed the bruise and asked her how it happened. She couldn't believe he was asking. "You threw me against the kitchen table," she said. "I never threw you against no kitchen table. You're imagining it."

She leaned back in her seat and shut her eyes. Two guys across the aisle were drinking beer. Empties rattled on the floor. She was glad the nun was next to her. Only three days before, Nick had thrown some empties against the wall. She certainly hadn't imagined *that*. She'd had a hard time cleaning up the splintered glass and the next day Carmen had asked her about "all that crashing."

Eileen shut her eyes and began to relive a night from the past when she was twelve years old on Wellington Street in Verdun . . .

"I make the goddamn money around here," Rube yelled at her mother. "You can bloody well make me dinner when I come home at night. It's 11:30 and I'm hungry." From her room, Eileen saw down to the kitchen. She hated it when her mother got drunk. She put her fingers in her ears but she still heard everything.

"Crack a six-pack *after* you've made my dinner," Rube went on. "I drive a taxi twelve hours a day for you and your kid. I expect some service. And wipe that stupid stare off your face."

Eileen knew exactly what drove Rube crazy about that stare. She always thought her mother reserved it for her. Eileen could never remember her mother looking at her in any other way. Whenever Eileen asked her anything, she always gave her an Oh-God-what-do-I-have-to-be-bothered-with-now look. She never wanted to see her report card, for example, never cared whether she got an A, and always forgot to sign it. So Rube took over. Before he signed the card, he read the marks out loud and made comments about each one.

A spring in the bed creaked and Rube shot an irritated look down the hall. Her mother was humped over the kitchen table, her chin in her hands, surrounded by beer bottles.

"Stand up," he roared. Eileen's mother stood up and bumped back against the refrigerator. She looked at him as though she didn't give a damn. He picked up a beer bottle and raised it in the air over her head. The last time she got drunk, he had threatened her the same way, only then it was because she hadn't ironed his red-checkered shirt.

Eileen sat rigid in her bed, unable to move, her eyes glued to Rube. She didn't feel sorry for her mother, but she was afraid he might go too far. Every time her mother got drunk and forgot his shirt or his supper, he did something worse. The beer bottle still in his hand, Rube raised his leg in the air like a baseball pitcher and threw back his arm. He had a huge square back. There was a tremendous crash as the bottle hit the wall above the stove and splintered into a million pieces over the burners. The blackness in his face deepened. Her mother was still wearing the same empty stare.

"Get that look off your face," he hollered and smacked her with the back of his hand.

"Don't, don't, oh please, Rube, don't," her mother wailed. He was smacking her harder and harder. "Rube, Rube," she cried. When her mother crumpled to the floor, he pulled her up and shook her shoulders. Finally he threw her against the refrigerator.

Eileen leapt out of bed, ran out to the balcony off her room and stood outside in the snow in her nightie. She was too scared to feel cold. A dog barked. Across the lane neighbours were lying on the sofa watching the late-night movie on television. She wrapped her arms around her back and looked up into the sky. Maybe her mother was dead. In the distance, she heard a police siren and imagined cops in the kitchen, asking why she ran to the balcony and did nothing. A door slammed on the street and Eileen recognized the sound of the old Pontiac starting up. There was a rattle he could never fix. It was Rube, taking off.

Surrounded by broken beer bottles, her mother lay on the kitchen floor like a dead dog on the street. Blood poured down the side of her face. A bone stuck out of her arm and vomit streaked her blouse.

If Kelly hadn't come up and banged on the door, Eileen might have left her mother there all night.

The two of them got a wheelbarrow from the shed and took her to the hospital in it. She looked like a picture from the *Bonjour Police* Rube brought home every week. It was two weeks before the black and blue spots disappeared around her eyes and a month before she got the cast off her broken arm, and even longer before the scar on the side of her face faded.

Eileen didn't know why but she was glad Rube beat up her mother. Part of her wanted it to be just her and Rube. Still, she never wanted him to go berserk like that again. She vowed that from then on, she'd make sure he got the two things he wanted — a hot supper when he came off his shift at 10:30 at night, and a freshly ironed shirt each day for the road . . .

Eileen woke up, rubbed her eyes, and looked out the window of the bus. Three nights ago Nicky had broken the bottles but he had never beaten her so badly she had to go to the hospital. Eileen put her head in her hands. After Nick had smashed those bottles, he lay on the floor in the kitchen and sobbed. "You won't leave me, Eileen, will you?" He had looked up at her. "For better or worse. Isn't that what we promised . . . ?"

∿

Nick went back to their apartment to wait for Eileen to come home or phone. In the silence of the living room he lay on the floor feeling too scared to turn on his stereo in case he didn't hear the phone. He fixed on the empty crib in the alcove and gazed off into the darkening hall.

Night was coming. He pulled out the sofa, and got on his knees in behind to make sure the cord for the phone was snapped in properly. He turned the phone over and rubbed his finger over the switch to make sure it was up at loud. This was the third time he'd checked. He held the receiver to his ear. The dial tone was okay but maybe the ring was broken. He opened the phone book. Fire, police, ambulance, hospital, sexual assault, Carrefour intervention suicide, Quebec Poison Control Centre, Lodging centre for Women Victims of Violence. He gave up moving his finger down the page and dialed O.

"It's an emergency," he said. He sounded as though he had laryngitis. He cleared his throat. "It's . . ."

"You'll have to speak louder, sir."

"My phone is broke."

"Call 611," she said and clicked off.

"It's urgent," he told the operator when he called again. "The bell. I think it's broke. It . . ."

"I'll ring," she said. "Please hang up."

He was hoping the bell was broken. At least he'd know why he hadn't heard from her. Thirty seconds later, the operator called him back and he smashed down the receiver.

He fell back on the sofa and looked at his watch. Seven-thirty. His leg trembled. After he stopped going to Jeanne Mance Park to meet his *yiayia*, there wasn't an hour he and Eileen hadn't been in touch. During the last week she was at the Sex Trolley, he made her call him seven times a night.

Nick hadn't talked to her now for nearly five hours. He wanted to crawl under the bed as he had done that time after Christmas when Eileen was late coming home from seeking Kelly and he had thought she was gone forever, but he couldn't. He had to figure out what to do.

~

The constant roll of the wheels of the bus was driving Eileen crazy and she was feeling more and more anxious as she thought about those weird questions Nick had asked. "Is it Rube O'Reilly, or Rube something else?" She didn't know why he wanted to know, so she said Morenovich even though his last name was really Lorenovich. Then he asked for Hazel's last name. "Hazel from the Sex Trolley? I have no idea. We all go by first names. Even Felix is just Felix." After that he insisted she hand over every dollar she made at the Sex Trolley. It was as though he was scared she'd save some and run away. She hated having no money of her own. Carmen had had to give her the money for Sherbrooke.

After she was fired from the Sex Trolley, he made her go to the welfare office to get the cheque in his name. "I'm the head of the family," he said. "The cheque should be in my name." The night after their day at the welfare office, sitting at the kitchen table, he wanted to know how much she loved him. "Enough to buy me a motorcycle?" he asked. How could she ever buy him a motorcycle?

"I hate it when you give me that blank look. I'm asking you." He was talking through his teeth, saying each word slowly. "Do you love me enough to buy me a motorcycle?"

"Gee . . ."

"Would you do a B&E for it?"

"Do a B&E? Well, like, from where?" Maybe he and Torchy had a job they wanted her to help with.

"Well, say, from Elmer's."

Elmer's? He wanted her to help steal a motorcycle for him from Elmer's?

"Of course not Elmer's," he said reading her mind. "You don't know when I'm kidding. I wanted to see how far you'd go for me."

Then he came up close. "You don't love me the way I want. But you're different from the others. You can never leave. No matter where you go, I'll find you. I have the names of everyone you know."

The next night when he went out on a B&E with Torchy, he tied her to a chair with ropes just to make sure she would still be there when he came back. And after that he had locked her in a closet.

～

Nick sat on the edge of the sofa. Eileen was either with Kelly or her mother. Where else could she go with Stevie? He tried Kelly's number in Sherbrooke. No answer. He rummaged through Eileen's top drawer and found a piece of paper that looked as though it had been ripped off a brown paper bag. Kel, Jonquière, and a number scribbled across it. He tried the number but all he got was a message that said, "There is no service at this number." He raced up to the pool hall and asked the bartender where Jonquière was. "Seven hours from here," he said. She couldn't have hitchhiked there with Stevie. And who would have given her the money for the bus? Rube? Wouldn't Eileen have told him if Kelly had moved to Jonquière? It didn't make sense.

He took out his little black book with important names and numbers from the bottom drawer of the bureau. He had never met Eileen's mother or stepfather, but he had to talk to them, and not over the phone. M-O-R-E-N-O-V-I-C-H. He had written it out a couple of weeks before when he'd quizzed her on Rube's name. He ran his finger down the names starting with M-O-R in the phone book. He was trying to remember whether e came before or after i. Moridy, his finger kept going, Mornstein, Morokhovsky, all the way to Morzym. He flipped back. E came first. Morena, Morenvy. Nothing. Morenovich wasn't there. Maybe they didn't have a phone. They lived on Wellington. He couldn't knock on every door. It was a long street. He knew because Pop Evans had had a 7-11 on Church at the corner of Wellington. Shit. He should have asked her what taxi company. He stared at the floor. He had it! O'Grady. Kelly's mother lived on Wellington, downstairs from Eileen's mother and stepfather. His finger travelled down the OGs. Ogleman, Ogorek, O'Gorman. Here it was! O'Grady on Wellington.

At the subway, he jumped over the gate when the ticket man wasn't looking and arrived at the De l'Eglise station in twenty minutes. On a pillar outside on Wellington was a large poster reading "On the Job" by David Fennario. A guy in overalls stopped him. "Tonight in the basement of St. Willibrord's church, we're performing a play of mine. It's for people from around here. You have a job?" he asked Nick.

"Hell no," said Nick. "There are no fuckin' jobs except ones that pay shit."

"Well, this is for you then. It's a play about how tough it can be out there. And it's free," he said. Nick could tell this David Fennario a thing or two, he said to himself as he walked along Wellington. He wondered if he knew what went on at Sylvana Stockings. He smiled to himself as he thought about the way he'd gotten his revenge at the pantyhose factory. What a play that might make! But he couldn't think about that now.

With the address in his hand, he looked up and down Wellington. Eileen had said she had lived in an apartment above a *patates frites* place. He spotted it next to a second-hand store a block from the metro. He went in the building and looked over the six bent mail boxes in the hall. Number six. Lorenovich. L not M. She must have known she was going to take off and she gave him the wrong name on purpose. O'Grady was number four. Carmen was behind this whole thing. Jonquière was probably a phoney number, something Carmen might come up with. The last in the list of emergency numbers he'd looked at in the phone book suddenly came to mind. Lodging Centre for Women Victims of Violence. He leaned his head against the mail boxes . . .

The blank look in Eileen's eyes always warned him her feelings for him were wilting. It was like a stick of dynamite inside him. He hated himself when he hit her, but afterwards she loved him more. A fight always drew them closer together. But now he had gone too far and she was gone. A migraine was starting at the back of his head.

He went slowly up the stairs and stood outside number six. Someone inside belched and he rang the bell. A beer in his hand, Rube opened the door in a faded red T-shirt that only barely covered his belly.

"I'm Eileen's husband," Nick said, "and — "

"Well, well, well." Rube had the chest of a bouncer in a bar. He leaned against the side of the door and looked Nick over.

"I'm looking for Eileen."

"Come in," Rube said.

Eileen wasn't here. He couldn't smell any Blue Grass perfume.

Maybe they'd take him in for the night. They were his in-laws, weren't they? Family. It wasn't his fault he hadn't met Eileen's parents.

"Effie," Rube yelled down to the kitchen. The man had a thick neck like Scratch. From the kitchen, a chair scraped on the floor.

"If it's the Watch Towers, no," she said. As a game, Eileen had once told Nick, Rube occasionally let in women from the Jehovah Witness church. When it was time for them to leave, he'd ask them if they'd like to see a little film of his family.

"Straight from Hungary," he'd say. When he had everything in place, he'd say, "Ready?" like a photographer taking a class picture, and the screen would light up with a rear view shot of a priest, naked, his robes bunched up to his neck, ready to plough straight into a woman. From "Rasputin and his Women," it was a scene from Rube's favourite porn film.

"No. Nothing like that, Effie. It's someone you'll want to meet. C'mon down."

A woman in a faded blue dressing gown with a stain down the front padded down the hall clutching a beer bottle. Her thin mousey hair was mashed flat over her head.

"This is Eileen's husband," Rube said as though he already knew Nick. The woman hung back against a wall and stared down at the jagged nail of her big toe sticking out of her sock.

Rube waved Nick into the living room. "Like a beer?" he asked.

"Yeah, I would."

Rube put his arm around his wife and steered her into the living room. "I'm sure the two of you'll have lots to talk about," he said before he went off to the kitchen. Eileen's mother looked at Nick with no expression at all.

"I have a picture of the baby if you'd like to see it," Nick said. He had one in his back pocket from the picnic with the Greek family on the mountain.

Effie O'Reilly stared into space. Her lower lip was chalky-looking. Drugs, he thought.

"Don't bother to get it out," Eileen's mother said. "I haven't seen

Eileen for four years. Besides, babies all look the same."

"Mind if I go to the toilet?" Nick asked. She made a face, as though he had dropped into a corner grocery and asked to use the bathroom.

"At the end of the hall," she said wearily. "To the right."

He didn't have to go to the bathroom at all. He wanted to look around the apartment to make absolutely sure Eileen wasn't there. He went left instead of right and looked in the bedrooms.

"Looking for something?" Rube said as Nick swung open a closet door.

"Oh," Nick said. "Where's your bathroom?"

"You're at the wrong end of the hall."

In the bathroom, two beer bottles lay on their sides next to an unflushed toilet. He shut the door, flushed the toilet, covered the seat, and inhaled. If she were here, her scent would have lingered. Old shit, ragged towels and stale beer. That was all.

"I thought Eileen might be here," he said when he settled back into the sofa in the living room. You could get better sofas than this at the Salvation Army store. He could feel the springs in the thing. The room smelled of mould and dust. Rube shoved a beer at him across a vinyl coffee table covered with cigarette burns.

"Eileen send you here?" His mother-in-law was coming to life. "Lookin' for free babysittin' I suppose? That would be just like Eileen," she spluttered. "Trying to get somethin' for nothin'."

"Nothing like that," Nick said. "I thought she might have — "

"She better not be lookin' for no free babysittin'."

Nick could see there was no way they'd ever let him stay the night. Besides, Eileen's mother smelled as though she hadn't taken a bath for a while.

Nick turned to Rube. "Kelly's mother lives downstairs, don't she?"

"Mrs. O'Grady?"

Nick nodded.

"Have you seen Irene in the last few days, Effie?" Effie didn't answer.

"Eileen has got to be with Kelly," Nick said. "I can't think of any-where else she'd go."

Rube threw his feet up on the table and took a gulp of beer. "She working?"

"Well, she was working at the Sex Trolley."

"The Sex Trolley?" Rube threw back his head and laughed. "And you think she's with Kelly?"

Effie took her beer down to the kitchen and pulled the door behind her.

The thought of Eileen going off with another guy had never occurred to Nick. He didn't want to think about it. "Yeah. Well. Kel's her best friend, isn't she?" Nick slowly nursed his beer. He wanted to stay as long as possible. Maybe Rube knew something. If she'd bor-rowed money from anyone, it had to have been from him.

After ten minutes Rube stood up, hitched up his pants and walked Nick to the door. He shook his head. "Gorgeous girl, Eileen. With a beautiful girl like that, anything could happen. I wish I could help you, but I got no idea where she'd be."

Nick went down one flight of stairs and then crept back.

"Poor Eileen," he heard Rube say. "She's never going to make it with a guy like that. He's so moody and suspicious. No wonder she took off. But with a newborn baby and no job, how will she ever manage?"

"Well, that's *her* problem. She better not come 'round here lookin' for no babysittin'," Eileen's mother said.

Nick stood out on the street and looked up at the second floor where Kelly's mother lived. A light was on. He went back up the stairs and rang Mrs. O'Grady's bell. A television blared from the other apartment on the landing. The bell was like a fire alarm, echoing into the hall, but there was no answer.

∽

Passing through the little city of Magog on the way to Sherbrooke, Eileen noticed a Greek restaurant. It made her think of the night before with Nick. To distract him, she had made him moussaka but she burned it and had had to make ordinary spaghetti instead. Moussaka became his favourite dish after he met the *yiayia*.

All through dinner he gave her strange looks, as though he were reading her mind. In the living room, before they went to bed, he grabbed her wrist and said, "If you ever leave, I'll find you, no matter where you go."

The nun shut her black book and looked out the window. A small baby was crying at the front of the bus. He was screeching like he would never stop, the way Stevie sometimes did. If the nun hadn't been sitting there, she would have covered her ears. To blot out the anxiety in her chest, she began to count: one, two, three, four . . .

"Poor little thing," the nun said standing up on her toes and looking down the aisle. "Do you have any children?" Eileen meant to say no. Why did she say yes? Now she'd get every one of those questions. "A boy," she said.

The nun looked at her, admiring, her eyes lighting up for the first time. "How old?"

"A little over a month." The baby at the front of the bus was really howling.

"You're not going to be away from him for long, are you?" the nun asked and sat down again.

"I'm not sure what's going to happen." The nun had an accepting look in her eyes that made Eileen want to confide in her. "My baby is with my next-door neighbour. You see . . ." she began.

"And your husband?"

"My husband is driving me crazy," she blurted out. "Sometimes he hits me. He wants to control everything I do." She started to cry. "I, I couldn't stand it so I'm going to try to start another life. But I don't know if I can do it. I have a friend in Sherbrooke who's going to help me. She's helped me before."

"Does your husband have a job?"

"A job? No, not right now. He doesn't even have grade nine. He worked in a factory, but they don't pay and . . ." She couldn't tell her that they'd been living on welfare and B&Es.

"What kind of work can you do?"

"I could work in a restaurant or a bar," she said. She didn't want to tell her she'd been a stripper. "I've had some experience in Montreal."

The nun, who looked about sixty, patted her hand. "Tough," she said. "It can be very hard being a single mother. We see them all the time at the hospital where I work."

"I don't know how this happened to me," Eileen said, horrified at the idea of becoming a single mother. That's the *last* thing she wanted. "I feel so confused. I do love my husband, at least I think I do. He was my very first boyfriend. It's just that he's so angry all the time. Everything was okay until our son was born."

"How are you finding your baby?"

"Colicky. He cries all the time. And I'm always so tired."

"Do you have a family?"

"Not really. My mother doesn't like babies."

"Any nearby friends?"

"Just the next-door neighbour who's looking after Stevie. But she makes me nervous. Sometimes she looks at me funny. Once she touched me in a way I didn't like. You know what I mean? Like she wants to start something?" She wondered if the nun would understand.

"Start something sexual?" the nun asked.

"Yeah . . ." Eileen squirmed at the thought. "She's always giving orders, always at my door telling me what to do. My husband hates her. But she's smart with kids, a lot better than I am, and she's good with my little Stevie."

"I'll give you my phone number," the nun said just before they got into the Sherbrooke station. "If you have any trouble you can call," but Eileen wasn't sure she meant it.

Later, sitting in a strange park as the sun went down, Eileen thought of calling her. It took her an hour to find Kelly's apartment, and when she got there, she discovered Kelly had moved to Magog two days before. The woman in the next apartment gave her the new address. "She has a job at Lulu's Paradise," she said. From a car radio, she thought she heard Tiffany singing "Heaven is a Place on Earth." It was playing at the McDonald's the first night she and Nick met. It was "their song."

The last bus for Magog left just as she entered the station. It was ten o'clock and the waiting room was almost empty. An old man with his fly open was being hustled out. She would have come back earlier, but every time she rose from the bench in the park, her head spun. The next bus was at ten the next morning. She sat down on a bench in the station to wait. She'd had no supper but she wasn't hungry. From around her neck she took off the silver heart Nicky had given her and felt its warmth in her hand. She leaned back against the wall and prayed that Kelly would be in Magog when she arrived.

～

When no one answered at Kelly's mother's apartment downstairs from Eileen's parents, Nick went down Wellington Street. At a phone booth in a video arcade, he called home but there was still no answer. On Church Street next to Notre Dame des Sept Douleurs church, he stared into the 7-11 his foster father had once owned. Looked the same. Pop had liked it when he helped pile the newspapers. That was when he thought he was at the Evans for good. He walked over to Atwater where he could hitchhike onto the expressway for the West Island. Maybe his foster father would take him in for the night. It was a crazy idea. Pop didn't like him, but he went anyway. He had to keep running so he wouldn't do something crazy, like jump off a bridge, or dive from the top floor of a hotel.

It was an hour before he got a hitch on a motorcycle. He knew right away the guy was a fag. He rode a lime green and purple Honda, a piece of Jap scrap that went fast but did not vibrate like a Harley. When they got to the train station near St. John's Road and stopped for a light, Nick suddenly hopped off. "Thanks a lot," he said and ran until he heard the biker speed down the highway. Then he trudged up St. John's Road until he came to the turn-off for Marigold Walk. He hadn't been back for four years. He had forgotten how perfect the houses looked. They were all the same, white with green shutters and tulips in the front. None of the families wanted any of the houses to look different. A year after he came, a Portuguese family moved in and painted their house bright pink. The neighbours made such a fuss that Mr. de Silva repainted the entire thing white.

"Order," his foster father had said. He remembered Pop saying that what he liked about Marigold Walk was that there were no faded work pants hanging from crowded clothes lines or rusty old refrigerators no one ever got round to hauling away from the lanes.

"Nick reminds me of all that," Pop had told Mum just before they decided to adopt cousin Luke. "He's got street kid blood. Reminds me of those kids that used to hang around Wellington after dark, planning the next break and entry. We left Verdun to get away from all that."

The closer Nick got to the house the more nervous he was about ringing the bell, but he'd have to risk it. A cell in a police station would be better than facing his empty apartment. A kid with a ghetto-blaster went by and he listened to Rick Astley singing "Never Gonna Give You Up." There it was, the house where he'd spent most of his life. The yellow tulips in front of the house reminded him of Mum. He and Danny planted them for her the fall before he left. He stood for a few minutes on the step before he rang. Luke answered the door. "Oh, hi," Luke said. "For a moment I didn't recognize you." From behind Luke, Nick saw his foster father. "You in some kind of trouble? Is that why you're here? Go upstairs, Luke, will you?"

The man Nick had always thought of as Pop stepped onto the outside porch and shut the door behind him. Now he reminded him of a cop. "I don't ever want to see you again. You hear? You're not wanted."

"I was just in the district," Nick said, "and I wanted to say hello."

"Well, get out of the district. You don't fit here. You never fit here," and he turned into the house and slammed the door.

His heart pounding, Nick walked slowly down the street. He

should have known. When he reached the train station down at the expressway, he called home, but there was still no answer. Then he called Kelly's mother, told her he was Eileen's husband and he needed Kelly's number.

"She doesn't have a phone number yet. She's just moved to Magog," Mrs. O'Grady said but she didn't have the exact address. "It's across from a restaurant called Couscous Heaven."

For emergencies, Nick had $50 in cash sewn into a hidden pocket in his jeans. It would cover his bus ticket and any eventualities later, but by the time he got downtown the last bus had gone. He started to walk toward the Jacques Cartier Bridge for a hitch, but after he'd walked a few blocks he sat down on a curb. He had no juice left in him. He thought of friends he could call. Teddy, Torchy, perhaps Georgie. But then he'd have to admit that Eileen had left him. He couldn't believe he did it, but when he saw a police car on St. Catherine Street a few blocks from the terminus, he rapped on the window and asked the officer to take him to a shelter for the homeless.

TWELVE

~

Magog

EILEEN HAD MET Kelly's boyfriend Barry at lunch and knew he didn't want her around just by the way he frowned when Kelly said Eileen would be staying until she found work. "She's my best friend," Kelly told Barry in the corridor outside the apartment. "Job or no job, she can stay here." Eileen had been at Kelly's for three days, annoying Barry who often slept there, but she was pleased at the way Kelly stuck up for her.

Eileen had tried the strip bars but no one wanted her and she knew her next step was to look for a waitress job. After Barry left, Kelly gave Eileen a pale blue suit, a white lace blouse and some matching pumps so she could continue the job hunt. "I bought this outfit so I could look for a receptionist job in a hotel around here," Kelly said. "I want to move up in the world. I might take a hotel and restaurant course at night. Lucky you're my size," she added. "You have to look respectable, especially if you want a job in one of the better restaurants. You can't look like an out-of-work strip girl."

Kelly took Eileen to a couple of inns and all the hotels, but it threw her when the maître-d's asked her if she had experience. All she knew was how to serve drinks at the Sex Trolley. "You have to perk up," Kelly told her. "I know you miss Stevie. But don't worry. When you have a job you can go get him."

The thought of being alone with her son terrified Eileen. How would she manage? Who would look after him when she was at work? Kelly might help out at the beginning but she couldn't depend on her friend forever.

Later, when Kelly went off to do some errands, Eileen tried every restaurant and snack bar on Main Street, but when people spoke to her in French, she sometimes got confused. In one of the snack bars, the cashier smacked her palm on the counter and said, "If you can't speak French, don't look for a job in Magog. This is Quebec. *Comprends-tu?* We speak French here." She tried other places afterwards, but her heart wasn't in it.

In one place with a "waitress wanted" sign in the window, the owner asked if she had children. "I have a baby," she said.

"The job is full-time," he said. "How old is your baby?"

"About a month."

"That young? Well, I have someone else in mind," he said.

Eileen ran into Kelly outside the apartment after her unsuccessful afternoon. It was around five o'clock and Kelly was in a rush to get to work. "How'd it go?" she asked.

"Well," Eileen bit her lip, "Not so good."

Kelly patted Eileen on the shoulder. "You'll tell me about it later. Don't worry," she smiled. "You'll find something. You always do, don't you?"

"Only with your help. I'm no good on my own." Kelly had found her the only jobs she'd ever had — first sewing baby clothes, then assembling boxes, and finally stripping at the Sex Trolley. Hooking was the only work no one had helped her find.

It was how she kept paying her share of the food and rent after she cut her hands at the box factory and had to quit. Nicky was the only one who knew. That's how they'd met. He started a conversation with her at McDonald's near Dorchester Square and told her anything was better than hooking. "You're too beautiful for that," he'd said, "besides which, it's dangerous." The next night they had met at an arcade.

Kelly put her hand on Eileen's shoulder. "Listen. I've left a chicken pie in the fridge for supper. Barry's coming back here tonight, so you'll have to sleep in the living room. I've left a sleeping bag out." She put her arm around her. "Don't worry about Barry. When he gets to know you, he'll adore you, just like I do. I meant it when I told him you're staying as long as you like. You love me, you love my best friend, and her baby too. Okay?"

"Yeah, I guess so." Kelly was so sensible, she thought, and so organized, with a boyfriend who actually had a full-time job. Why couldn't she be more like her?

That evening Eileen watched television but kept losing the drift of two different movies she tried to watch. At eleven o'clock she gave up and tried to snuggle into the sleeping bag. To fend off her feelings of loneliness, she put on the radio, but Whitney Houston was singing "Where Do Broken Hearts Go?" and it made her feel worse.

She should never have listened to Carmen. It wasn't going to work for her in Magog. She put her fingers on the silver heart around her neck and felt the warmth of Nicky's arms around her the first time they slept together on Mount Royal.

Without even thinking, she went to the phone and dialled her number in Montreal. There was no answer. It was eleven-thirty. When she worked at the strip bar, Nicky'd be home at that hour, waiting for her to call. She lay face-down on top of her sleeping bag and cried until she fell into a fitful sleep.

She opened her eyes when she heard a noise on the balcony off the living room. A dark shadow moved outside the windows. She clutched the sides of the sleeping bag. Someone was trying to wrench open the door. "Dear God," she whispered. "Let it be him. Please." She looked out and recognized his chestnut hair.

"Nicky. I'm coming." Her fingers fumbled with the lock on the door. "Oh, Nicky," she sobbed. "I'm so glad it's you," and she fell into his arms. I was so scared and lonely. I prayed you'd come. I missed you so much. I called you tonight but no one answered." He didn't say a word. "Talk to me," she cried.

"We're leaving now," he said, and he carried her down the stairs and put her into the front seat of a car. Driving wildly, he raced the car to the beach where he grabbed her hands and held them next to his heart. "It was all my fault," he said.

She breathed a sigh of relief. For a moment she had thought he wanted to throw her in the water.

"I don't know what gets into me. I can't control it. I don't treat you right, Eileen. It's never going to happen again. The first night you were gone, I prayed to God that if he'd bring you back, if I could find you," he panted, "I'd never tie you up, or lock you in the closet, or hit you, or do any of those crazy things."

He rushed around the car, scooped her up in his arms and carried her down near the water. He held her so tightly, his fingers digging into her flesh, that for a moment she was afraid, but when he set her down in the grass and made love to her, she relaxed. She had forgotten how tender he could be.

"Do you love me, Eileen?" he asked.

"You know I do."

"Where's our son?"

"With my parents," she lied. "Well, ah, with Rube. Kelly's mother is helping out." She couldn't tell him the baby was with Carmen.

"Oh," he said. "That's funny."

"Why?"

"Nothin'." He decided not to tell her about his visit to her parents. "Look," he said. "We gotta get back. I have to get the car to Torchy as soon as possible." Torchy had lent Nick a stolen car for the night.

Before they left Magog, while Nick was filling the car with gas, Eileen called Kelly, told her Nick had come for her, and asked her to call Carmen and say that Rube was on his way to get the baby, and she must give him up.

"I can't talk now, Kelly. Just do as I say, okay? It's really important. It wasn't going to work in Magog. I phoned Nicky," she felt she had to lie, "and I asked him to come and get me. I'll speak to you soon." Then she called Rube and asked him to pick up her son from Carmen. "Don't take no for an answer," she told him. "And when we come, let on you've had him for a few days."

As Eileen stepped out of the phone booth for the car, she heard some familiar music. It was the Prokofiev *Romeo and Juliet*. Nick looked at her with a smile on his face. "I brought the tape just for you." They listened to the music quietly together. When he took Eileen to Place des Arts to see the ballet, she had looked like a princess in a long flowered skirt she had borrowed from Kelly. He had felt out of place in his jeans and boots, but everyone had noticed her, and he had been so proud.

As they pulled away, Eileen put her head in Nick's lap and imagined what it might have been like if they were both ballet dancers. After an hour on the road, a motorcycle raced by and Eileen thought about their bike ride to Ile aux Coudres the year before. She wasn't looking forward to going home . . . "How far is it now?" she asked.

"Maybe half an hour." He was frowning. "Looking forward to taking care of Stevie?"

"Oh yes," she said.

"That's good, because I'll be pretty busy. I've got a deal going with Torchy. It'll be good money."

Eileen didn't dare ask about it. Sometimes Scratch hired Nick and Torchy as lookout guys for the "drug stores." Drug stores were what the police called the apartments off Park Avenue where grass, hash and cocaine were sold. Torchy and Nick watched from the sides of the buildings for police. To confuse police, the "drug stores" moved from one apartment building to another. Sometimes Nick picked up packages of dope down at the Old Port for distribution to these floating drug depots. She hated it when he worked for the traffickers. If he were charged and jailed, then she'd be all alone with the baby.

Her breath caught in her throat. All alone with the baby. She knew now why she ran away. She tried to breathe normally. Carmen had convinced her she wanted to flee from Nicky but that wasn't it. "You okay?" Nick leaned over and kissed her. "I guess . . . ," she said.

When they reached the Champlain Bridge, she cuddled up close to him. Maybe when she saw her son, she'd feel like a real mother. Driving down Wellington, Eileen felt her chest tighten. She hadn't been down the street for four years, not since the day her mother had thrown her out. She covered the side of her face with her hand as they got close to the pizza restaurant where her mother worked. "Don't ever get pregnant and expect me to help you," her mother had told her when she was in grade eight and still a virgin. Well, a sort of virgin. "My days of looking after babies are finished," her mother had said. "I won't babysit." It suddenly occurred to Eileen that if her mother found out she'd asked Rube to look after the baby, she might think Rube was the father. She lay back against the seat and tried to hang loose.

Nick passed Notre Dame des Septs Douleurs church and pulled up at the *patates frites* place just past the metro stop. He seemed to know exactly where the apartment was even though this was their first visit. Reading her mind, he said, "I looked up O'Grady in the phone book," he said. "That's how I know where your parents live." Nick took Eileen by the hand and went to the third floor.

"Well, well, well," Rube said when he opened the door. "How's my little sweetheart?" and gave Eileen a hug. "The baby's beautiful." Eileen wished he hadn't said that. It sounded as though he'd just met the baby. And why did he have to call her "my little sweetheart?" That's what he called her after he started going all the way with her.

"Nicky. This is my stepfather, Rube," Eileen said. Nick wondered what was cookin'. Rube and Eileen's mother made out they knew nothing about Eileen or his son when he came three nights before. And why was he pretending they'd never met?

"Kelly's mother gave me a nice little basket for the little one,"

Rube said, leading the two of them into the living room. He lifted the child into his arms and snuggled him into his shoulder. "We've been getting along like a house on fire. I bought him a little music box. He held the baby out to Eileen. "I'm sure he's missed his mother."

Eileen went forward to take Stevie from him, but her arms felt stiff. Stevie began crying the way she remembered her baby sister had cried years before. "Rub his back a little," Rube said. Eileen pulled him close to her, but he wouldn't stop crying. "Unfit," the social worker had said about her mother. Her son hated her. Perhaps, like her mother Effie, she was a monster mother. Maybe that's why Rube beat up her mother. To punish her. On the bookcase near the window was the white New Testament Eileen had been given when she was confirmed at St. Willibrord church. Maybe God wanted Nick to hit her. A wave of nausea swept over her. She shoved the baby at Nick, ran to the bathroom and threw up in the sink.

Rube was standing outside when she opened the door. "C'mon, Eileen, you've gotta relax. Everything's going to be okay." In the living room he sat next to her on the sofa. "Take it easy," he said.

Rube took the baby from Nick and put him in Eileen's arms. Her little Stevie cuddled into her. Maybe she *was* different from her mother. Rube put his arm around Eileen's waist and she felt a surge of warmth toward her child. Everything that had happened between her and Rube after she was twelve vanished from her thoughts and all she could think of was how nice Rube had been to her. In grade two, when he had first arrived, he'd helped her with her homework and had taken her ice skating. Later he paid for her ballet lessons and gave her extra toe shoes. Eileen pulled her son in close to her and looked up at her stepfather. She wanted him to be proud of her. "Eileen," Nick said. "We gotta get home."

THIRTEEN

∿

Carmen

THE NEXT DAY, when Carmen knocked on the door, Eileen knew it was her and rushed to answer but Nick was right behind her. "Oh hi," Carmen said as though nothing had happened. "Can I come in?"

"Sure," Eileen said, but she felt nervous.

Carmen walked to the crib in the alcove and picked up the baby. "Eileen and I have things to do," said Nick, taking his son from Carmen. "Now ain't a good time," and he led her to the door.

"There's something I want to tell you," Nick said after Carmen left. "Don't you dare tell her about the last few days. That's just for us." The phone rang and Nick picked it up. It was Torchy. "An hour from now? Okay. I'll be there."

After Carmen saw Nick go down the street, she went to Eileen's apartment and knocked hard. No one answered so she tried the door and it opened. A pile of rope lay on the living room floor next to an overturned chair. Carmen looked up at the ceiling. For a split second

125

she was afraid Nick had hanged Eileen. But there was no sign of a struggle. The baby whimpered in his crib down the hall. Carmen went down and stroked him. "Anyone home?" she called.

"Carmen," Eileen called. "Is that you?"

"Yeah."

"I'm in the bathroom. Be out in a minute." She was trying on a strip costume. If she couldn't work at the Sex Trolley, she'd try the place Kelly had worked at on St. Hubert Street. She pulled her jeans and T-shirt over a bright pink sequined bikini and came out into the hall.

"What are these?" Carmen pointed to the ropes.

Eileen bit her knuckles. "I know you'll find this hard to understand but I told him to."

"Told him to what?"

She looked down at her feet. "Tie me up. I, ah, told him to tie me to a chair in the living room." She paused. "We used the ropes when we moved."

Carmen gave Eileen a cigarette. "Didn't he tie you up once before?"

Eileen couldn't remember whether she'd told Carmen about that or not. "You see, he had this job with Torchy. There was no way I could come and he was afraid I would take off. I saw it in his eyes."

"Eileen. What are you talking about."

"He was terrified, Carmen. Terrified I would leave when he went out. You don't know that side of him. So I, ah, I *told* him to tie me up. That way he'd be sure I'd be home when he came back. But he couldn't do it. He kept saying no fuckin' way. The first night I was away, he went to the Green Pasture Mission and promised God that if I came back, he'd treat me right."

Down the hall, Stevie whimpered.

"How long will he be gone?" Carmen asked.

"Two hours. Maybe longer. It's a job on the south shore. He's meeting Torchy at the subway station. If it works out, we'll have a pile of money and we can have some fun."

Carmen marched down the hall, took the baby in her arms and held him up in the air. "Missed me, didn't you?" She put the infant to her breast and looked up at Eileen. "If your stepfather hadn't been such a nice guy, I wouldn't have let him take the baby." She had a sly smile on her face Eileen didn't like.

"Rube's okay," Eileen said. She'd never even hinted to Carmen about what happened with Rube. Kelly was the only one who knew everything. Nick suspected something but she'd never outright told him. "You had a father or an uncle or something who tried to mess with you," Nick had asked her that first night in McDonald's. Later, when she tried to tell him, something always held her back.

"Come to my place," Carmen ordered. "We've got to talk. I'll keep track of the time. We'll be able to see him come in. You've got to tell me what happened." At her apartment, Carmen settled herself into the rocking chair with the baby. "Boil some water, would you?"

"Look. I should tell you," Eileen said. "I called him and asked him to come and get me."

Carmen stood up and put her hand on her hip. "You *asked* him to come to get you?"

"The thing was, Kelly didn't want me." That wasn't true. Kelly was prepared to let her stay, but after three days she was dying of loneliness for Nicky. It had nothing to do with her not getting a job.

Carmen raised her eyebrows. "Get the tea, would you." In the kitchen, Eileen thought about how the baby clung to Carmen like *she* was the mother. Nicky had picked it up right away.

Carmen put on some music and they drank tea. "Maybe it was just as well you came back," she said. "A fortune teller I go to predicted that you and I . . ." She stroked the baby's head as he sucked her breast. "You see. You and Nick are going to break up."

"Did the fortune teller say that?" Eileen asked.

"More or less. Tell me. Whose name's on the lease?"

"His."

"And the welfare cheque?"

"His."

Carmen combed her fingers through her long black hair. "The landlord told me this morning he's going to kick you guys out. Nick hasn't paid the rent for three months."

"Three months!" That was hard to believe. Usually the janitor came to the door and she *saw* Nicky give him the money.

"Look," Carmen said. "My lease here is up soon. My sister's going back to Puerto Rico, and she'll let me have her place in the west end for three months. Free. Why don't the two of us make a go of it? I'll look after the kids. Look at the baby, how happy he is with me. You like working, don't you?"

Eileen said nothing.

"I called Hazel this morning and she told me Felix would take you back at the Sex Trolley three nights a week."

"You called Hazel? And Felix's willing to take me back? You mean I'm not fired?"

"I told Hazel the whole story, how miserable you've been with Nick, and she persuaded Felix. It'll work only if you and Nick split."

Eileen was quiet. "Yeah, well . . ."

"Hazel told me Colin's been asking for you. He's the one that used to give you lots of money for after-hours tricks, isn't he?"

Eileen stared at the floor and Carmen put the music up higher. Eileen had told her Colin gave her money when she met him after, but she had never said what they did. Carmen would never have understood the relationship she had with Colin. She had, after all, slept with Colin only once. "Guys are good for the old in-and-out," Carmen was always saying, "but that's about all."

"Why don't you show me what you do at the club? Get back in practice," Carmen said.

"You mean strip? Here?"

"Well, why not? I'll give you a little grass to loosen up." Carmen opened a drawer, rolled a joint and passed it to her. "My kids are off at my sister's. Gives us time for a little fun."

Eileen took a few tokes until her head started to lighten.

"Come on," Carmen said. "Just do a few steps." She put the music up high. Samantha Fox was singing "Touch Me, I Want Your Body."

Eileen started to dance. Carmen waved her head the way Felix used to, as if to say, "now," and she slowly peeled her way down to her sequined strip costume.

"Fantastic," Carmen shrieked when she saw the outfit. "You must have known I was going to ask you to dance. I wouldn't have believed it. No wonder Felix wants you back. Stand on top of the stool and go all the way."

Eileen was glad when the phone rang and she could stop. When Carmen returned, she was dressed again.

"Feeling shy?" Carmen peeled her blouse open so both breasts were exposed, put Eileen's son back on her breast, raised the music and shut her eyes. "I'll just imagine the rest of the strip."

~

Standing outside Carmen's door, Nick heard every word. Torchy hadn't shown up at the south shore subway station so he was back early. When he discovered Eileen and the baby were gone, he went to Carmen's and listened to the conversation.

After Carmen raised the volume on the music and he couldn't hear anymore, he went down the hall to his apartment and pulled out Eileen's outfits from the bottom drawer of the bathroom cupboard.

"Fuck Carmen," he said ripping at the costumes. "Bloody dyke!" But Eileen was no dyke. No way she'd strip for a woman, damn it. Carmen, he thought, wanted everything that belonged to him.

And what was that crack about Colin? When he met Eileen that night in McDonald's, Eileen said she'd never do another trick. "Take this, you twank," he said, cutting the costumes into pieces with his Swiss Army knife. He'd make sure Eileen would never go back to the Sex Trolley or any other rib joint. Nick went out to the balcony, stuffed Eileen's strip clothes into a tin garbage pail and set fire to them.

"Eileen, c'mere," said Carmen. She had parted the curtain and saw

Nick on the balcony dumping items of clothing into a smoking garbage pail.

"Oh my God," Eileen said. "He's home. And he's burning all my strip costumes!"

Nick went into the living room, looked at the ropes and banged the wall with his fists. Eileen had never said "Carmen, I want my husband, not you." He wanted to tie her up. He fell back against the sofa and hung his head to the side. He couldn't tie her up. "If you want her back," Torchy said, "you have to be nice to her." Doing things like that made her run away. Out on the balcony he threw the ropes in the garbage pail and watched them burn.

He had to win her back. He'd take her to dinner and the movies. "Give her a good time," Torchy said. "Take her out." He'd paid Scratch back, and now he could borrow again. Carrying the garbage pail, he went down the backstairs to the basement.

As soon as Eileen heard him bang down to the basement, she stretched out her arms to take the baby from Carmen.

"Why do you want to go back?" Carmen asked. "Now's as good a time to leave as any. Let him stew." She pulled the baby in next to her. "Leave him now."

"I can't."

"Why? You don't *ever* have to go back. You can leave your son here. You don't know how to take care of him, anyway. And don't think people around here haven't noticed."

Eileen wrenched her son away from Carmen. "I belong with Nick," she said and slipped down the hall.

～

"Eileen," Nick called as he blew into the apartment.

"Nick," she said stumbling into the living room. "I was just looking for my strip outfits, and they're gone."

"Gone?"

"Yes."

"Maybe we were robbed. Listen." He put his arms on her shoulders. "I don't want you to see Carmen no more. She's not gonna babysit." He raised his voice. "Got it."

"Okay." Eileen was relieved. It made the whole thing easier. She didn't want to have anything more to do with Carmen and she was glad she would be moving out.

"C'mere," Nick said and pulled her down to the couch. "Anyone ever tell you you're the most beautiful girl in the world?" He slipped a tape into his Walkman and they listened to Tiffany sing "Heaven is a Place on Earth."

"For the next little while," Nick said, "we're going to have some fun. Go out to the movies, maybe even to Chinatown. We might even rent a nice hotel room downtown and get room service."

FOURTEEN

~⌐

Lost Honeymoon

"WE'RE GOING TO work up to a super-special," Nick said over breakfast. His smile reminded Eileen of last summer and a tingle went through her. He reached over and gave her breast a little squeeze. "It'll be a surprise," he said. April 27th, the anniversary of when they first met, was coming up and for a whole week leading up to it he wanted to do something different. If he could make a killing in B&Es over the next week with Torchy and Teddy, maybe he'd have enough to take her to the Four Winds downtown. They could swim in the heated pool on the roof, order food in the middle of the night, make love whenever they felt like it and look out at the lights of the city. Torchy had an uncle who took his girlfriend there. Nick wondered if they could have a room with a view of the cross on Mount Royal.

"Every night," he said, pushing his cereal bowl into the centre of the table and taking both her hands, "we're going somewhere. Just you and me. And then we're going to come home and make love."

132

He lifted up a lock of her hair. It always smelled of fruit blossoms.

Eileen stared down at the table. When they were out, who would look after Stevie? She couldn't ask Carmen, and Nick didn't like Retta either. Out in the alcove, on the window sill above the baby's crib, the music box Rube had given Eileen for Stevie was playing "Let Me Call You Sweetheart." She had wound it up after she fed him.

"The baby'll be okay by himself," Nick said. He patted her hand. He wanted her to himself, the way they were in Ile aux Coudres. He had to bring back that look in those green eyes of hers that matched the jade rings he gave her. No one else — not even Mum Evans — had ever given him that look. If he could bring it back, he'd know she really loved him.

"It'll be awhile before I have the bread for the super-special, but for tonight, how about McDonald's?"

"Okay."

"The one on Peel street?"

She swallowed. How many times had she gone over everything they'd said to each other that first time they'd met on Peel street.

"Hey. You're not going to cry, are you?"

She pulled her stool up close to his and put her head on his shoulder. When he'd come into McDonald's that night, she had been feeling sick. She never told him she had just given an ugly old man a blow job in his car on a side street. She pushed the memory from her head and looked up at him.

"You saved me," she said burying her face in his neck. She didn't want to let herself go over it one more time — it was too horrible to think about — but if Nick hadn't come into her life at that moment, she might have become a full-time hooker suffering from some horrible disease. Or worse.

He hugged her. "Don't think about all that any more. All that matters now is us." He looked at his watch. "Look. I've got to run. Torchy'll be waiting." He went down to the alcove, picked up his son and cradled the baby's face into his neck. Nick had his own family now and no one was ever going to take it away from him. He wrapped the blanket neatly around his son and put him back in his crib. Then he walked Eileen to the door and pressed himself hard against her. "You'll be okay when I'm gone?" She looked a little shaky.

"I'll be all right," she said, even though the idea of the whole day alone with the baby made her feel anxious.

Nick frowned. "If Carmen knocks on the door, don't answer. See you at seven o'clock. Be ready when I get home. Okay?"

Eileen stood at the window and watched Nick as he strode down the walk. No one had shoulders like his. Or such a sexy little bum. As he turned to march down the street, he did a handspring for her and then blew her a kiss.

Just thinking about his smile and their date that night made the morning go well, but after lunch Stevie became restless and cried for two hours. When he finally fell asleep, she checked the bolt on the front door, tried on the one strip outfit Nick hadn't burned and dreamed about going back to work.

At six o'clock, she pulled on the skirt and sweater Nick had lifted from a store downtown and put in the green combs he'd given her to wear with her flowered skirt the night he took her to the ballet. At six-thirty, she fed and changed her son and wound up the music box. When she looked out the living room window at seven and saw Nick coming up the walk, Stevie was fast asleep in the crib. Like an angel. She touched up her make-up in the hall and sprayed a little Blue Grass perfume on her hair.

"What about Stevie?" Eileen asked when Nick came in. "He'll be all right at home," Nick said. "We can't take him to the restaurant." Eileen felt torn between guilt and her desire to be alone with Nick. Then she remembered the time when they went to the welfare office and left him by himself. He'd be okay.

～

For a few days, Eileen managed to get through the loneliness of the day just by dreaming about what she and Nick were going to do in the evening. One night they went to a pizza parlor and afterwards to an arcade. On another, it was a Chinese restaurant followed by a walk along the Old Port. Every night they left the baby alone, but they were never gone for more than three hours and she always made sure she changed and fed him just before they went out.

After the first couple of days, Eileen began to hate the daylight hours. If the sun was up that meant she was home alone with her colicky baby. And with every passing day, Stevie became even more of a colicky baby. She often went to the garage in the basement to get away from him, but she couldn't escape. In the silence, his screams banged around in her head.

In the afternoon, Eileen took to leaving him by himself. Even if she had nothing to buy, she walked along Park Avenue, going from store to store staring vacantly at things on the shelves. First she'd drop into the Greek fish market and look at the squid on display and then she'd peer into a jewellery shop run by a Hasidic man who was always in black. Sometimes she visited the pawn shop. Once she stood outside the Greek Labour Association and debated whether she should go in and ask them to find work — legal work that paid more than minimum wage — for Nick. After a while she just wandered the streets and prayed for the sun to go down so her real life could begin. She never told Nick she was out most of the day alone. If she looked tired, he took her to a movie. Eileen liked going to films because the stories made her forget she was a mother with a small baby to look after.

One day as she trudged up the stairs to her apartment after hours of aimlessly meandering around her neighbourhood, she met Retta. Eileen hadn't seen her for a while because Retta worked all sorts of shifts.

"Oh hi, Retta," Eileen said.

"Don't hi Retta me." The way Retta had her hands on her hips reminded Eileen of the nurse who told Nick off in the hospital.

"Don't you hear your baby crying? He's been crying and crying. Every day, I've seen you going out," and she grabbed her shoulder.

Retta's long gray hair made her look like a witch. "You've been leaving him alone, haven't you?"

Eileen looked straight ahead. She could hear her son crying through the walls. "I've got to go," Eileen said, wrenching her shoulder away.

"I'll say you've got to go," Retta replied.

Eileen unlocked her apartment door and, without bothering to bolt it again, went down to the hall alcove and picked up Stevie. For a moment he stopped crying but as soon as she put him down he started up again. He hadn't been fed or changed for five hours. Eileen got a bottle and sat down with him in a wicker chair next to his crib.

Retta banged so hard against the door, Eileen's hand shook. The baby lost the nipple and he began to shriek. "If you continue to leave your baby alone," Retta opened the door and howled down the hall over the screams of the baby, "I'll go to the police. What you're doing is against the law. You hear?"

The next day right after lunch Eileen heard a note being slipped under her door. It was from Carmen. "I'm home all day if you want to talk," it said. Want to talk, Eileen suspected, meant leave Nick, move in with her, work at the strip bar and give Carmen all her money. No way. She wondered if Carmen had heard Nick yelling at her the night before. He had thrown a chair against the wall and shouted, "You're not the same as you were last summer. It's the way you look at me. It's not the same!"

It was true. She *was* different. The baby was bleeding her dry. She couldn't love Nick the way she wanted to. Maybe that's what had happened to her mother. Was it because of Eileen that her mother didn't give Rube enough attention and that's why her stepfather turned to her? Inside, she felt more in a muddle than ever.

A day later, Eileen found another note from Carmen under her door. It appeared after she'd been wandering the streets for six hours. "I just thought you should know that Retta has gone to the police," the note said. For two days, Eileen stayed home all day, but no matter how often she fed or bathed or changed her son, he cried. To get away from it, she stuffed cotton wool in her ears and lay in bed with the covers over her head, but escape was impossible.

The following night Nick came home and told her he'd "found gold." He gave her a big hug as he blew in the door. "You look as though you need a special treat," he said. "I'm booking us into the Four Winds tomorrow. It's going to be the honeymoon we never had," he said.

Eileen looked off into space.

"The baby'll be fine for one night, won't he?"

"Gee," Eileen said.

"What do you mean, Gee?" The way she said Gee, Nick thought maybe she didn't want to go. This was the surprise he'd promised her. "You prefer to stay here with Stevie instead of being with *me*?" He stalked down the hall to the crib and for a fleeting moment he hated his son. Whatever his baby wanted, he got. Stevie had Eileen to himself all day, tending to his every whim, and now his son was going to take time that belonged to *him*. Nick grabbed both sides of the crib and shook it. The baby screamed and Eileen went down and picked him up. "You see," Nick said. "All he has to do is cry and he gets what he wants."

"Look," Eileen said. "I'll get Rube to take him. Okay? We can't leave him overnight. My stepfather will babysit."

"Well, if you get Rube, make it for three days." He had enough money for three nights at the hotel for a real honeymoon.

The next day she waited until Nick went out before she called her stepfather. "Rube," she said, "could you take the baby for a few days? Nick and I have to go to Sherbrooke." She felt uncomfortable lying to him but she had to come up with a reason he could accept. "We've just got to find work. We can't seem to find anything here. Nick has this friend in Sherbrooke who says he'll help us find something."

"Gee, Eileen, I'd love to. He's such an adorable little fellow. But what'll your mother say?"

"He could sleep in the back room. He wouldn't disturb anyone there." She thought of the evenings when Rube was out in the taxi.

"If you wanted, you could take the baby with you in the taxi. If you had a bottle, he'd be quiet," she said. "Do you still have the basket?"

"Yes." Rube still had the basket and blankets Mrs. O'Grady had lent him when he had taken care of the baby before. He had put them at the back of Eileen's closet where he knew Effie would never look.

"Well. You could put him in that."

"Okay. You know, Eileen, there's nothing I wouldn't do for you."

Rube picked up the baby that afternoon, and that night they went to the Four Winds hotel. Just knowing the baby was with Rube in Verdun and away from the prying eyes and ears of Carmen and Retta allowed her to breathe easier.

∽

Rube spent most of the afternoon holding the baby next to his bare chest. That was the only way he could keep him from crying. Whenever Rube felt the least whimper coming on, he took a bottle, made sure it was warm and gave it to him. Eileen had given him six already prepared bottles plus enough tins of Similac for three days. "The bottles have to be boiled before you put in the milk," Eileen had explained. In addition to the Similac, Eileen had brought Pampers and extra sleepers. "Once you've fed and changed him, you can practically forget about him." Eileen had lied. The baby cried a lot and Rube worried about what Effie was going to say when she came home from the restaurant. Eileen's son had been much calmer the last time he'd looked after him. Whenever there was the least peep out of him, he lifted Stevie out of the basket to make sure he wasn't hungry or wet.

At four o'clock, just when he was getting ready to go out on his taxi shift, Effie came home. "I've got a little surprise for you," Rube said.

"Yeah?"

"We've got a little bundle to look after for a few days."

"A little bundle?"

"Yeah," he said, taking her hand and bringing her down to Eileen's old bedroom.

Right on cue, the baby suddenly started crying. Rube scooped him out of the basket and he calmed down. "Cute isn't he?"

"So Eileen's been here," Effie said. She pushed her elbows hard into her hip bones and clenched her fists. She wanted nothing to do with her daughter's child.

"Eileen and Nick had to go out of town," Rube trailed after her. "They've got a chance for jobs in Sherbrooke. I couldn't say no."

"What's this Eileen and Nick had to go out of town stuff?" Her voice rose. "Knowing her, it's a lie." She stopped in her tracks. "How come you've been in touch with them?" She wheeled around. "I told you she'd come 'round when she wanted a babysitter."

Rube acted as though he didn't hear. "All the bottles are ready. You don't have to do a thing," he said and bobbed the baby up and down. Rube had agreed to babysit partly because Effie had three days off.

"Gee, Effie, why can't we forget about the past. Eileen's a good kid, and . . ." He tried to hand the baby to her, but she turned away. "For Chrissake, he *is* your grandson."

Eileen's mother screwed up her face. "As I said, count me out."

"Okay. I'll take him with me in the taxi. Rube put Stevie on his shoulder with one hand and with the other picked up the basket. Then he went into the kitchen, took two bottles from the refrigerator and stuffed them in a pocket.

"Have my supper ready when I come home, will ya?"

Rube cut his taxi shift short and came home early. It was hard taking customers while he had a crying baby lying in the front seat in a basket. He couldn't feed and cuddle the child *and* drive the car. As it was, he drove practically the whole time with one hand. The other hand he kept stretched out in front of the basket so Stevie wouldn't fall forward in the event of a sudden stop.

When he got home, Effie was asleep, but she'd made him a chicken sandwich. There were ten empty beer bottles on the kitchen counter.

She had fallen off the wagon. The baby was whimpering, so he warmed some milk and fed it to him, but he wouldn't take much. After about ten minutes, Stevie turned his head away and dropped off to sleep.

Two hours later, at midnight, when everyone was sound asleep, including the baby, the phone rang. It had to be an emergency. No one ever called at midnight. Rube lurched out of his room and into the kitchen. It was his sister-in-law in Cornwall, Ontario, about an hour away. His brother George had had another heart attack and was in an intensive care unit in the hospital.

"I'll come right away, Joan," Rube said. "Tell George I'm on my way." George was his only relative. They had both come out together after the Hungarian Revolution in 1956. He had to go.

It was only after he got off the phone that he remembered he had Stevie to worry about. He smacked the side of his head. What awful luck! Effie would have to stay home and look after Stevie by herself. He couldn't ask Effie to come along. She'd never gotten on with Joan or George.

"Effie," he said, waking her. "I've got to go to Cornwall. George has had another heart attack. This could be it. I have to go. You'll look after the baby, won't you? Some bottles are ready in the refrigerator. When you run out, the tins of milk are on the counter. Don't forget to sterilize the bottles. Ask Irene to help you out if you have any trouble."

"Okay, okay," Effie said and turned over. She smelled of beer. He went into the kitchen, washed out the dirty baby bottles, boiled up some water to sterilize them, poured in the milk and put them in the refrigerator. Rube noticed a whole case of beer under the kitchen table. Rube left one bottle for Effie but took the rest with him. He left her no money. He didn't want her buying more booze.

～

Eileen had never been in a place like the Four Winds. In the bathroom they had a little basket with shampoo, perfumed soap and bath bubbles. The first night they swam in the pool under the sky and looked at the stars. Then they had a bubble bath and made love and went to the Chinese restaurant downstairs. When they came back, they smoked some hash and ordered wine and fresh cherries and chocolates which they filled up on until they drifted off to sleep.

In the morning they woke up to the sound of the traffic down below on Sherbrooke street and a waffles and maple syrup breakfast. Nick ordered almost the same breakfast they'd had in Ile aux Coudres the summer before. "A lot more swanky than last year, eh?" he said after the waiter brought the tray.

During the next three days, Eileen and Nick went for walks on the mountain, took rides around Old Montreal in a horse-drawn carriage, and watched fireworks at Man and His World. It was so sunny during the day it reminded them of summer. At night it cooled down, but that didn't stop them from making love in an out-of-the-way spot. On the mountain, it was behind a bush with a view of the cross, and at Man and His World, it was at the same spot as the year before after the fireworks.

When Rube called from Cornwall, Effie's voice was slurred. "When I threw Eileen out four years ago, I never wanted to see her again. And you know how I hate babies. Rube. I wish you hadn't left me with all this."

When he called again, her voice was even more slurred, and she was in a rage. "I'll have you know I'm doing nothin', friggin' nothin' for this screaming kid. I'm not changin' him, or washin' him, or feedin' him. I've put him in a drawer in Eileen's bureau. You took on this job. You can do it!" And she banged down the phone.

Rube immediately called back. "Have you been out drinking, Effie?"

"I can do what I want," she said. And then she began to sob. "If you stay much longer, well, anythin' could happen, and it'll be all your fault."

"Effie. C'mon. You didn't actually put him in a drawer, did you? If you did, take him out," Rube said. "You're doing this to torture me." There was something in Effie's voice that made Rube decide to leave Cornwall immediately and return to Montreal. His brother George was very sick, but he had to make sure Eileen's son was all right. Once Stevie was back with Eileen, he could go back to his brother.

~

When Rube got home from Cornwall, there was no sign of Effie and the kitchen was littered with beer bottles. Half-full baby bottles were in the sink. Off in Eileen's room, he could hear Stevie whimpering. Rube went to him and was shocked at what he saw. He had vomit down his sleepers and was completely soaked. Rube could tell by the state of the diaper and the rash on his bottom that he hadn't been changed the whole time he was away. The excrement was a watery green and smelled foul.

Rube changed and washed the infant and pulled on some clean sleepers. He felt cold. Eileen had brought a blanket for him, but it was on the floor. He went back to the kitchen, washed out a bottle, boiled some water, and when he had sterilized it, opened a tin of Similac and filled it up. To cover the second and third days, Rube had left four tins of Similac for Effie, but none had been opened. Stevie continued to whimper. Rube went back into the room, picked him up and gave him the bottle, but he refused to take it. His eyes were shut and he wouldn't suck. The child's eyes flickered open only once. His little face was the colour of putty and his eyes were dull as stones. Stevie lay there so limply, with such an air of surrender, Rube got the impression that Eileen and Nick's son thought life wasn't worth trying.

Rube sat on the bed with him and talked softly. "Come on little one," he stroked his legs. "Try a little milk. It's nice and warm. Soon you'll be back with your Mum." Stevie sucked for about a minute and then turned his head away. Rube propped him up on his shoulder and rubbed his back until he got a burp. "There," he said. "Wasn't that nice. You've been a good boy." He tried to feed him again, but the child refused.

~

When Rube brought the baby back and Eileen lifted him out of Rube's arms in the taxi, she thought her son looked different but she didn't say anything. She had forgotten how small newborn babies were. She hugged him close to her.

Eileen looked up at Rube. Her stepfather looked ill, as though he'd been up all night. "You okay?" she asked.

"Me?" Rube sighed. "I'm okay. But my brother is sick. I have to go to Cornwall. Actually," he stared down at the wheel of the car. "He's in pretty terrible shape." Rube didn't want Eileen to know that for most of the three days, Effie had been in charge of the baby. Rube looked at the child in Eileen's arms. "He's kind of thin. Perhaps he has a cold. The last time I tried to feed him, he wouldn't take the nipple." Rube kicked a tire. "Perhaps you should take him to the hospital."

Eileen shook her head. Nick hated hospitals. Only in an emergency would she go to the hospital. Her son whimpered in her arms and she was relieved to hear his little voice. She pulled him close to her breast. Eileen took a deep breath. It went through her mind that maybe Rube had gone to Cornwall to see his brother and had left her mother in charge of her son, but she didn't dare ask. "You weren't trying to get hold of me, were you?" Eileen asked.

"Oh no," Rube said. "I didn't know where you were in Sherbrooke. Find any work?" he asked. "No, not really . . ." Eileen replied and wondered whether Rube had figured it out that all she and Nick had wanted to do was get away from the baby for a while.

~

Over the next two days, Eileen felt confused and faint much of the time. She and Nick smoked hash every night and it kept her in a permanent haze. Every day Nick was out until seven at night but she never left the apartment. All she did was stare out the window. Her son wasn't screaming the way he did before. Now he just whimpered like a tiny puppy. Every three hours she tried to feed him but he would suck for a few minutes and then turn his head.

One afternoon there was a knock at the door. It was Carmen. "Eileen," she said, "you look terrible. That bastard you married is killing you. Can't you see it? Leave him and come with me. You'll be a lot happier and so will the baby." She walked down to the crib. "How's he eating? A little thin, don't you think? Perhaps the hospital might suggest something."

The hospital, Eileen said to herself, was out. It wasn't an emergency. After Carmen left, she went down and looked at her child. It was true that he wasn't eating much, but she *was* trying. Was she trying? Sometimes one bottle lasted a whole day. She looked up at the ceiling and went back to the living room and lay down on the couch. She didn't want to think about it.

That evening was the first in a week that Eileen and Nick stayed home. To please Nick, she made an effort and bought eggplant, tomato paste and ground meat for a moussaka.

"You look whacked out," Nick said to her that night. If she looked unhappy and restless, he worried. He was never sure what caused it and was scared she might want to run away again.

"I'm taking you to a very special Greek restaurant tomorrow night. You know what tomorrow is, don't you," he said and he tweaked her nose.

Eileen nodded. Tomorrow, April 27th, was the day they had met. "I remember," she said.

The following evening, on his way home from acting as an earwig for a "drug store," where they were now hustling heroin, he passed a small restaurant on Fairmount with fish-net on the walls and tiny candles at every table. There was a huge map of Greece spread across the window. He looked hard and saw where the island of Naxos was located. It was the island to which he would return one day with Eileen and his son. He went in and made a reservation.

FIFTEEN

~

Snow

EILEEN COULD HARDLY wait for the day to be over, mostly because Stevie never stopped screaming. He was such a pest. On top of
it, the apartment was so hot she could hardly breathe, even though
outside a strong wind was blowing. April had been beautiful and
warm but now the weather was turning nasty and cold. Nick was out
doing another sneak job with Torchy and Teddy, but when he phoned
to check up on her, she knew from the tone of his voice that it hadn't
worked out.

When she got off the phone, feeling hot and irritated, she opened
the window in the living room and the wind knocked a glass off the
table. She didn't realize it had smashed until she cut her foot and had
to look for a needle to remove a sliver of glass.

~

"It's like a fuckin' sauna in here," Nick yelled when he blew in at the end of the day. "And why's the baby hollering? You can hear him all the way out to the street. Will you get dressed. I want to get outta here." As he went down the hall, he grabbed his wailing child and looked at his spoiled brat face. Jesus, he thought, why did he have to be so demanding. Losing control for a second, Nick shook him hard before he put him down. In the crib the baby lay quiet, his back to Nick. The heat of the apartment rose up at him. "Why is it so fuckin' hot in here?" He yanked open the window in the alcove above the baby's crib. "There," he said and walked down the hall. "You ready?" he shouted at Eileen.

"Yes," she said, and hurried down the hall. She was so eager to get out of the apartment she gave her son only a glance. The last time she had tried to feed him, he had whined and turned away. Now he was quiet. As she shut the door, she noticed the open window over the crib but she put it out of her mind and rushed downstairs. The place reeked of gloom.

Nick covered his ears as they flew down the stairs of the apartment.

"Nick," Eileen said. "He stopped crying five minutes ago. Right after you picked him up."

He looked hard at her as though she were accusing him of something. "Sure, sure," he said. "He's like a horn that always gets stuck no matter what you do to it. He could start any minute."

Nick stood in front of the panel of bells and rang each one hard as though he were squashing bugs. Three seconds later a bunch of bells began to ring, and Eileen heard doors opening upstairs.

"C'mon, Nicky," she said, grabbing his hand as though the cops were chasing them. "We have to get out of here." Running, she knew, would calm him down. "C'mon," she said. It was hard to run in the outfit she had on. She was wearing the suede skirt her stepfather had given her and shoes that were a little tight, but she held his hand and kept going. The temperature seemed to have dropped. She needed a coat and all she had on was a sweater. They jogged for fifteen minutes to the restaurant and the mix of the cool air and the warm run gave them a high that made the events of the day pale.

"Before we go in," Nick said, "we've got to have some Lebanese gold." They went into a lane-way, he lit up a joint, and for a few minutes they inhaled some extra-strong hash. By the time they entered the restaurant, his fouled up B&E, the wails of his son, and his fears Eileen might take off on him were gone.

"Nice, isn't it," he said. The restaurant was like another world. Terracotta jugs and small musical instruments hung from the walls and the ceiling was draped in fish net. A waiter sat them down and lit a candle. Above their table stretched a picture of a harbour with boats, small white houses and a church. Another picture showed a field filled with wild flowers. A boy and a girl holding a basket of flowers sat on the back of a donkey.

"Tell me about the pictures," Nick said to the waiter when he arrived with their selection of Greek hors d'oeuvres. Posters were everywhere.

"Many different islands," the waiter said. "Rhodes, Paros, Crete, Mykonos, Naxos, Hydra."

"Naxos?" Nick asked. "Which one is Naxos?"

"That one," he said pointing to the seascape with the boy and girl on the donkey.

"You from there?" Nick wanted to know.

"No. I'm from Crete."

"I have relatives in Naxos," Nick said. "Some day I'm going there with my wife," and he squeezed Eileen's hand.

"You've never met them?" the waiter asked.

"My father was Greek," Nick said. "He died after I was born."

"Oh."

Nick felt the birthmark on his arm that marked him as a member of the Mykonos family. "I have my father's skin," Nick said, "and eyes."

"I couldn't tell him about my mother and everything," Nick said, after the waiter left. "No one likes orphans. Do you think I really look Greek?"

Eileen leaned forward. "Oh yes." Her eyes lingered on the boy and girl sitting on the donkey. The girl had her arms around the boy's waist the way she had when they rode the Harley to Ile aux Coudres. "Your eyes are as blue as the Greek sea," she said.

After hors d'oeuvres with retsina wine, they had kalimari, followed by the special of the night, red snapper. And to end it, a baklava pastry and Greek coffee.

"Medium," Nick said in Greek when the waiter asked him how he wanted his coffee. He had been in a Greek restaurant with his *yiayia*. That's when he learned that Greek coffee was medium sweet, very sweet or not so sweet.

At the end of the meal they leaned back in their chairs and floated. The combination of hash and wine made the world glow. The waiter came by with a complimentary brandy.

They were so absorbed in thinking about what it might be like to actually go to Greece, they were astonished when they stood up to go outside and saw snow coming down. "Holy Christ," Nick said. The wind was blowing so hard they ran the whole way home.

~

As soon as she opened the door to the apartment Eileen saw wind blowing snow straight through the bars of the crib into the hall. Little Stevie had snow on his shoulders. She shut the window, lifted him up, and shook the snow off him. He was very quiet. She took a deep breath. Well, it was better than listening to him cry. She turned off the lights, undressed in the dark and slipped into bed. Nick crawled in next to her.

"Where's the dope?" Eileen asked. "I'd like to get some sleep." Nick rolled a joint and lit it. The effects of the wine, hash and brandy made Eileen's head reel. She felt hot and just a little sick. For an hour she lay half-awake but unable to move.

In the morning, the baby was stirring but not awake. "Let's go out for breakfast," Nick said. Neither of them said a word about their son as they went out. When they got home, they would try to feed him.

~

Like a drowning person, Eileen saw her life pass in front of her when she turned the corner of the street after breakfast and saw the police car in the lane next to the apartment house. Only the nose showed. It was Carmen and Retta standing outside the apartment building, patrolling it like guards, that gave it away.

When they were out, Carmen must have broken into the apartment, found the baby, and called the police. There was a horrible relief in the thing, the way she felt when she lay awake one night and imagined that she and Nick had actually taken an overdose of junk.

She knew the police hadn't come for Nick because of a B&E or his connection with drug dealers. They had come for Eileen and Nicholas Mykonos, parents of their son Stephanos Nicholas Mykonos.

"I think it's all over, Nicky," Eileen said.

"What?" He hadn't seen the police car.

She was glad he hadn't heard and didn't want him to notice. He would think it was for him and tear out, but she knew it was for *them,* and for *her* as much as for *him.* Carmen and Retta were gone when she looked up again but in the apartment building outside their door, two policemen waited for them.

"Eileen O'Reilly Mykonos?"

"Yes," she said.

"Nicholas Mykonos?"

"Yes," Nick replied.

"You are both under arrest in connection with the death of your baby." The police read them their rights and slapped handcuffs on them. As they ushered them down the walk to the car, Eileen turned around and saw Carmen and Retta looking down at them. Carmen flung open the window of her bedroom and screamed down at her: "You see, you silly bitch. If you'd come with me, this wouldn't have happened. Eileen. He turned you into a dog."

On
Trial

SIXTEEN

~

Scoop

MAGGIE SAT IN Jacinthe Beaulieu's office at the court house and waited for the Crown prosecutor to get off the phone. Wiry, with graying short-cropped hair, she looked like a no-nonsense woman, Maggie thought. Maître Beaulieu specialized in cases of child and wife abuse and had agreed to brief Maggie on the trial opening, which was the next day.

On the prosecutor's desk was a framed photograph of a teenage girl in graduation robes and a young woman in a lab coat holding a baby. Dominating the room was a crucifix and a black and white photograph of a French-Canadian family that featured a severe-looking grandmother in a black dress with buttons down the front.

"My grandparents and their twelve children," Maître Beaulieu smiled when she got off the phone. "We were from L'Assomption. My mother," she said, pointing to a little girl in a first communion dress. When Maggie was in grade one, she had envied the Catholic

girls on the block who dressed like doll-brides for their first communion ceremonies.

"My mother married at eighteen and had six children. I'm the
oldest. She wanted me to be a nun like my two aunts but I was too
interested in having a family." The prosecutor looked into Maggie's
eyes. "Children have always been very important to me. I have two . . .
Before she died, my grandmother told me I could become the greatest lawyer in the world. 'But if you have no children,' she said, 'if you
are not a mother, you are nothing.'"

Maggie felt a twinge in her stomach. That's what her father thought,
too. It had been the topic of his last Mother's Day sermon. She turned
toward the photographs on the prosecutor's desk. "Are those your
children?" She wanted to say the right thing. "And what about the
baby boy?"

"My grandson," she beamed. "I always wanted a boy. My daughter
is finishing medical school. Very difficult for young women today. Do
you have children?"

"No." Everyone asked her that. By the age of thirty-seven, no matter what, the world expected you to have children. "I've never been
married."

"Before we start," Maître Beaulieu said, "I'd like to congratulate
you on the articles you did this summer on the abuse of women and
children. It takes a woman to see it clearly. You should win a prize.
The situation is growing more and more alarming. Men are getting
away with murder. The public wants the justice system to do something about it. We have not prosecuted enough cases. And where we
have, we haven't worked hard enough to get convictions."

She waved at a bookshelf filled with bulging file folders and stacks
of newspapers. "Night after night I've been doing research into cases
across the country and in the United States. I'd be happy to show you
some of it, but it's the Mykonos case I'm concerned about now."

She opened a desk drawer and pulled out a file. "I'm going to show
you the pictures. When Homicide came to me and told me what
happened, I wasn't sure, but when I saw the pictures, I knew I had to

prosecute and that the charge would be criminal negligence and manslaughter. The Mykonos/O'Reilly case will be an exemplary case and I shall seek an exemplary sentence," she said giving Maggie the file.

"Mykonos is . . ." she tapped her fingers on her desk. "Well, let's just say I'm not happy he's out on bail. He was an abusive husband all the way. As for the O'Reilly girl, I'm baffled. I can't understand why she didn't take that poor baby to the hospital herself. If she goes on the witness stand, maybe we'll find out."

Maggie looked down at the first picture in the file. The baby looked like something out of a napalmed Vietnamese village. She turned the pictures over one by one. A wave of nausea passed through her. There were about twenty-five in blue frames, fixed up with the same care that would go into baby pictures a mum would show friends and relatives. They had not been available at the inquest.

"Vous comprenez, Mademoiselle MacKinnan?" Shutting the folder quickly, Maggie straightened in her chair and pulled down hard on the sides of her navy jacket. *"Vous comprenez, Mademoiselle MacKinnan?"* The prosecutor had an insistent voice.

"Yes, I see what you mean. Horrifying," she said, and pushed the folder across the desk. "You'll be showing them to the jury?"

"Of course. On the third day of the trial."

"Will the pictures be available to the press?"

"Yes." Maître Beaulieu picked up the file folder and gave it back to Maggie. "You can keep this set. But you may not release them until the jury sees them. The pathologist will testify and then the jury will see them. I can count on you?"

"Absolutely," said Maggie, surprised that the prosecutor would hand them over in advance without her even asking. "Thanks very much. I appreciate this," and she put the file into her briefcase.

"It's the first time I've given a reporter special treatment, but I consider you different. I know you haven't covered courts before, but I can see that for this case, you more than anyone, will understand the issues." The phone rang, and Maître Beaulieu looked toward the door indicating that Maggie should leave. "I'll see you at the trial," she said.

Maggie went down the elevator and over to a brasserie across from the court house to see Alphie. She saw him through the window before she even opened the door. In his usual brown tweed jacket, he was sitting by himself at a small table behind a full glass of beer and two empties.

"Great to see you, Maggie," he said. "Let me treat you to a beer," and he signalled the waiter.

"Could I have a coffee?" Maggie didn't drink on the job. She couldn't get the photographs out of her mind.

"Looking forward to the trial?"

"Yes." She took a sip of coffee. "Max was after me to see the Crown prosecutor before the opening of the trial. Jacinthe Beaulieu. I just did an interview with her."

"Oh," said Alphie. "With her as prosecutor, there'll be lots of fire-works."

Maggie waited a few minutes. "In my briefcase, I have the most awful pictures of the Mykonos baby. She's given them to me. They're the centrepiece of her case and she says I can have them coming off the presses the moment the jury sees them."

"So?" Alphie smiled and gave her a pat on the back. "The sister-hood, I see, is already getting together."

Maggie ignored the remark. "Who can I trust with these pictures? If I give them to Max he might run them right away," she sighed. "But for us to get a real scoop, they should be processed in advance, ready to go to press the moment the jury sees them."

Alphie adjusted his trademark red silk tie and crossed his leg. "Give *me* the pictures and I'll handle it. The moment the jury sees them, you call me at the paper. You'll get the credit. In fact, you can tell Max right now that the Crown's giving you a scoop on some sensational pictures. Tell him he'll have them the moment the jury sees them so he can run a picture on the front page of the afternoon edition.

"We'll be a day ahead of everyone else. Great stuff, Maggie! Your first court case, and you're right up in front. Well," he looked at her affectionately, "you're always ahead of the pack." He lit a cigarette. "Something else. Tell him to assign Gary to do some drawings of the jury. In cases like this, there's always some jury member, usually a middle-aged broad who faints and the judge has to stop for a recess."

"Alphie, do you mind? I am very close to being a middle-aged broad myself."

"You, Maggie? C'mon. You always look so earnest. You've got a teenage bloom in your cheeks despite that severe French knot you insist on wearing." He smiled. "You're still so wet behind the ears, it shows."

"I'll tell Max," she said, getting back to business.

"So?" He put his hand out, expecting the pictures. Maggie took a last sip of coffee. What if something happened to Alphie? She couldn't tell him, but what if he got drunk and left the pictures in a bar?

"The Crown made me promise not to give these to anyone until the jury sees them." The prosecutor had made her promise no such thing but she had to protect herself. She moved uncomfortably in her chair. "How about this? The night before the jury sees them, I'll give them to you. The Crown, I'm sure, will tip me off. The moment the jury *actually* sees them, I'll call you at the paper and you can release them. OK?"

"Okay, m'dear."

Maggie knew that if she gave them to Alphie the night before, he'd work out something with his long-time drinking buddy, Foxy, who worked for the news desk as a copy editor on the graveyard shift. A page could be made up on the sly, ready to go to press the moment she gave the word. Alphie knew the rules. He wouldn't jump the embargo and burn her source. He'd covered courts for as long as she could remember. When she was in high school, dreaming about becoming a journalist, she'd seen his byline. She would have to trust him.

Alphie scribbled three phone numbers on a scrap of paper. "I'll be in the press room across the street," he said, referring to the court house, "or here, or at home. If I'm not at any of these places, you can try the press club," and he took back the paper and added a fourth phone number.

"Thanks," Maggie said and picked up her briefcase. When she got to the door, she turned around, and walked back to the table. "You think it's going to be okay?" She had butterflies in her stomach.

"Good lord, Maggie, you may *look* wet behind the ears, but you're a tough news-hen. A star. That's why that Beaulieu broad gave you the pictures. Don't dilly dally around." He sounded irritated. "I take it you've done an advance piece for our readers?" Maggie nodded. "Go off now and speak to Max."

She walked down Notre Dame Street to Place d'Armes where she sat for a moment in the square on a bench facing Notre Dame Basilica. Every story, she always felt, was a test. What was she worrying about? She already had a scoop. It would be a good story.

She'd speak to Max, and then go off to La Bodega where she sometimes hung out with her friend Michael. He was still away in Guatemala, but it was a cosy place where she could have a coffee and quietly read the papers. She got up and walked quickly across the square and down St. Jacques Street to the *Tribune*. She didn't know why but she thought tonight might be the last night for a long time that she'd be able to sit around and just enjoy herself.

SEVENTEEN

~

The Sisterhood

AT 9:10 IN THE MORNING, twenty minutes before the courts opened, Maggie found the lobby of the Palais de Justice humming with people pacing up and down, buying coffees, reading newspapers and pestering the information desk. Lawyers and other officials swished past her in ceremonial black robes.

The place was as cavernous as a downtown railroad station and as welcoming as an underground garage with its black ceiling and black balconies bearing down from the upper floors. Misery hung in the air. Next to her on the bench, a man had his head in his hands and another stared into space. She touched the wings of the butterfly pin on her lapel. In her ash-gray suit, she fit right in.

In the middle of the lobby, near the escalators up to the criminal trials, about forty people jostled to get a look at the pillar with the day's cases thumb-tacked to it. Maggie stood at the edge of the crowd and watched. Alphie had told her that this was where the lawyers and the crooks check out what's happening in each courtroom and that she could get an idea of what goes on in the court house just by listening in on conversations between lawyers and their clients.

"*Tes antecedents t'ont fucké.* Armed robbery, police threats. *T'es fucké,*" said an overweight and bearded lawyer in a black robe. His client, a man in his early thirties, had an unkempt beard and wore a black leather jacket and jeans. He had just asked his lawyer whether he'd be serving time.

"But those things happened in New Brunswick," he protested. "Now I have a job. I can't take time off. The judge will take that into account, won't he?"

"*Tes antecedents t'ont fucké.* Your past has screwed you," repeated the lawyer. "You're looking at six to seven years. Go upstairs in ten minutes."

The conversation ended and the man in the black leather jacket went back to examining the bulletin board. The crooks, Alphie had said, are always eager to see if they recognize the names of buddies who are facing the same music.

Maggie looked at her watch. Nine-twenty. She should go up to the courtroom. When the escalator reached the fifth floor, she was confronted with dozens of agitated young men in jeans. Some were sitting but most ranged up and down with a coffee in one hand and a cigarette in the other. Many were accompanied by girlfriends. A young woman in a tight leopard-skin sweater and a miniskirt slid by. Cigarette butts were being ground into the black tiled floor and the noise level was brutal.

Walking down the corridor in the midst of this turmoil, Maggie felt a tap on her shoulder. It was Esther Sykes from the Y. Maggie had let all the women from the various organizations who had helped her with her series on child and wife abuse know when the trial was opening. Esther had contacted the women from the shelter that had helped Eileen O'Reilly file for divorce when she finally left her husband.

"I've spoken to a lot of people," Esther screamed above the racket.

She had hair down to her waist and wore an ankle-length dress made of Indian material. "I've called all the women's groups I could, including ones on the West Island." She manoeuvred Maggie into the women's washroom where it was quiet. "I've taken this on as a special project. Eileen has no family she can count on," Esther said. "All she has is her stripper friend Kelly, and from the shelter, Sally who's helping her with the divorce."

"Eileen's lucky to have you," Maggie said. "C'mon, I can't be late." They left the washroom and the two of them walked slowly down the hall. Outside one courtroom three guys in black leather jackets and boots with chains down the sides paced angrily up and down.

"One of those social worker bitches," said one of them as Maggie and Esther approached. Maggie pulled down on the pockets of her suit, knowing the comment was directed at her. One man stepped directly into her path while the other two stood to the side and leered.

"Just ignore them," Esther said guiding her away from them. "A policewoman comes to a program we give to help women deal with animals like that. If you show the slightest fear, you're in trouble."

Alphie had told her the Mykonos/O'Reilly trial and a bikers' murder case would be tried in nearby courtrooms. Two motorcycle clubs were at war. Four bodies tied to cement blocks had been found in the river facing Nun's Island, and two men were on trial for first degree murder. The corridor outside would look like a meeting of the Hell's Angels, he'd said.

Behind her Maggie recognized some voices and turned around. "Oh, hi," she said to three women from a single mothers support group. One of them had given Maggie the names of several women who had been referred by police to shelters for battered women and children.

Outside the courtroom for the Mykonos/O'Reilly trial, a large crowd waited to get in. Maggie recognized people she'd interviewed for her series. Esther went around and talked to them.

Two radio reporters, both of them women, congratulated Maggie on her series on abuse. "I'm so glad I saw your advancer in the *Tribune* yesterday," one of them said. "We intend to give this thing a big play."

Maggie spotted Alphie near the courtroom door with newspapers under his arm. To reach him, she had to push her way through a mob of about twenty shabby men in ragged clothing.

"Who are those guys?" Maggie asked.

Alphie pulled her off to the side. "I forgot to tell you. The carrion crows. They're a good sign. Rather than panhandle or drink in bars, they go to trials. What goes on in this building beats any soap-opera on TV. They always pick the sensational ones. Some of these guys know a lot, but they can be mean. Know what? They're going to be just about the only men at the trial. Not counting the judge, of course. I've never seen so many women waiting to get into a court-room."

He was right, Maggie thought. The Crown prosecutor and the two defence lawyers were women. Plus all the people from the women's organizations wearing clothes that ranged from jeans and leather to sensible suits like hers. Quite a number were carrying lunch bags. "And have you noticed something else?" Alphie frowned. "Practically all the reporters are women."

Maggie scanned the group. "Why do you suppose that is?" she asked, wanting to hear Alphie's response.

"Well. For the same reason, I guess, that you're covering it." He looked down toward the escalators.

"There she is," Alphie announced as though a star had arrived.

Eileen O'Reilly looked pale and crushed, her face the colour of putty and her hair a greasy orange as though it hadn't been washed for a while. She no longer looked like a sexy stripper, Maggie thought. She was accompanied on one side by a young woman in boots with purple bows on the heels, "probably a stripper friend," said Alphie, and on the other by her lawyer, Martine McKenzie, holding her under the elbow.

Eileen stared at the floor, but before she entered the courtroom, she looked up and caught smiles of encouragement on the faces of the women. Her shapeless navy blue dress looked as though it had been bought in a rummage sale, Maggie thought, but it could not conceal the graceful lines of her body.

A few minutes later Jacinthe Beaulieu appeared with two detectives from the Homicide Squad. One was a man, the other a woman with prize-fighter legs. Maître Beaulieu saw Maggie, gave her a blink of recognition, and Alphie squeezed Maggie's shoulder. "You're on," he whispered in her ear.

The crowd was waiting for Nicholas Mykonos. As soon as he stepped off the escalators, the carrion crows began muttering to one another. "Scum," Maggie heard more than one of them say. Mykonos was wearing jeans and a leather jacket and stared straight ahead. His lawyer, Anna Martelli, from Legal Aid, walked beside him, but about two feet away as though she needed to keep her distance.

Mykonos stiffened as soon as he picked up the hostile faces of the crowd. He looked fierce — the look the press photos usually captured — but for a second Maggie saw a look of defeat on his face. A moment later he raised his chin and lowered the lids of his eyes as if to say, Who the hell do you jerks think you are anyway?

After Mykonos went in, the constable opened the door and the people started to enter. "Well," Alphie said. "You're on your own now," and he left. As Maggie entered the courtroom, she felt a rush of apprehension. Nicholas' blue eyes reminded her of someone. Someone she'd known a long time ago.

She pushed the thought out of her mind and chose a place on the right so she could clearly see the two of them in the box for the accused. Every few minutes Eileen's lawyer looked encouragingly at Eileen but Nicholas's lawyer busied herself the entire time with papers.

A clerk dressed in the usual black entered and deposited some books and file folders on the judge's desk. A few minutes later the judge appeared at the door and the clerk stood up. "Silence," he declared, and raised his hands for everyone to stand. "The Superior Court, Criminal Division, presided by Judge Robert St. Onge, is now in session."

The judge turned to a constable at the front to the far right and

asked him to bring in the jury which had been selected the day before. Once the jury members were seated, the clerk asked everyone
else to sit.

The judge cleared his throat and addressed the jury. "There are
certain principles of justice I would like to make clear. First of all, the
accused do not have to prove they are innocent. The burden of proof
is always on the Crown.

"The Crown prosecutor must establish in your minds the guilt of
the accused beyond a reasonable doubt. Keep those words in mind."
He had a harsh rasping Marlon Brando voice, Maggie thought, and
looked hardened into late middle age like the elders in her father's
church.

The judge lifted his eyes from the jury members and surveyed the
row of journalists, lingering, Maggie thought, for a second, on her
face. The *Tribune* had run her picture at the top of her child and wife
abuse series following the inquest on the case.

"You must try this case in accordance with the evidence heard in
this courtroom," he told the jury. "If you have read anything about it
in the newspapers, dismiss that from your mind now. During the
course of the trial, please refrain from reading the papers."

The judge then turned to the court clerk and asked her to read the
charges.

"Eileen O'Reilly and Nicholas Stephanos Mykonos on April 28th,
1988, in the City of Montreal, did unlawfully neglect their child,
Stephanos Nicholas Mykonos, and did unlawfully commit manslaughter. They both plead not guilty."

Prosecutor Jacinthe Beaulieu began by telling the jury they would
hear from two neighbours who broke into the Mykonos apartment
and took the baby to the hospital when the couple went out and left
him alone. In addition, they would hear from the nurse and doctor
who received the dying baby, as well as a child pathologist. She paused
after these remarks and looked into the eyes of each jury member.
"You will also see pictures of the body of the baby. These will be of
more use to you than any number of eye witnesses or medical
reports.

"My first witness," she said, "is Carmen De La Rosa." Maggie had first seen Carmen De La Rosa at the inquest and remembered her clinging pants and the seductive smile she gave the coroner. Now she was more stylish in a Chanel-style suit in forest green suede with a beige silk blouse and matching green boots, but she swung her hips like a seasoned tart looking for a trick. The woman claimed she was thirty-five though Maggie thought she looked closer to forty. Her occupation, she said, was dress designer.

"How do you know Eileen O'Reilly and Nicholas Mykonos?" the Crown prosecutor asked.

"They lived down the hall from me when I was living on Paros Street, in the Greek district," she said. "Now I live in the west end. Frequently they left the baby alone even though I was willing to babysit any time." The women on the jury looked disapproving. Eileen's face was ashen.

"During the last week of the baby's life he cried a great deal. There were three nights when Eileen and Nick and the baby were gone. I don't know where they went. When they came back, I saw them go out, alone. Again. For the whole evening."

"What happened the next day?"

"The next morning I looked out the window and saw them go out again. I opened the door of their apartment with my charge card." Carmen looked coldly at Eileen and went on.

"I saw right away something was very wrong. I grabbed the baby, raced up the stairs with my little boy and knocked on my friend Retta's door. She has a car. I told her we had to take the baby to the hospital."

Carmen De la Rosa slumped down in the witness box and cried on and on.

"I think we should take an adjournment," the judge said. "Perhaps for ten minutes."

Carmen looked up at the judge. "I don't want to take a bloody adjournment," she screeched. "This isn't some show that can be stopped and started. I have to finish telling my story. How can I ever forget?" Maggie could hear her Spanish accent. "Every night I dream about what happened. If only I'd acted sooner. I should have taken the baby to the hospital the night before." She looked at the front row of the jury and stared defiantly into their eyes.

Maître Beaulieu interrupted. "May we go on, your Honour?"

He nodded. "Yes. If the witness can talk, and is willing."

"And at the hospital?" the prosecutor asked.

"There was a little problem at the hospital." De La Rosa was talking softly. She looked at the prosecutor. "You know, Jacinthe, I told you all that business of, you know. About how I said the baby was mine."

"Yours? Tell the jury about that."

"I told the nurse at the desk the baby was mine. I never intended to take that baby back to Eileen and her husband. I was moving to my sister's anyway. I decided I'd go straight there from the hospital. And never," she shrieked at the judge, "never go back to my apartment on Paros Street! That was the only way that baby was going to have a chance."

"Maître Beaulieu," the judge asked. Do you have any more questions?"

"No," she said. There was a brief cross-examination by Eileen's lawyer, but nothing from Nicholas's lawyer, after which the judge adjourned the session for the day.

EIGHTEEN

~e

Exposure

THE FIRST PERSON on the witness stand the next day was a nurse in her early twenties who had received Carmen De La Rosa and her neighbour Retta Van Dam when they arrived in the hospital with the dying baby.

"He had these wounds. And blisters on his little hands and feet. And he was so thin. For a baby of six weeks. He was covered in bed-sores, and excrement." Maggie noticed she was wearing a wedding ring. She looked young, like Eileen, maybe a mother too.

"I knew something was terribly wrong. His sleeper was soaked. He was very cold." The jurors leaned forward. "Mrs. De La Rosa was so, so, upset, and you know. It wasn't even her baby."

Tears came to Eileen's eyes at the remembrance of her son lying in the crib like a wounded bird after she and Nick came home from their anniversary supper. We should have taken Stevie to the hospital as soon as we came home, she thought. Why didn't we?

167

Dr. George Bennett, the doctor who'd examined the baby, went on the stand next. Maggie thought he looked shaken. A man in his mid-thirties, he was also wearing a wedding band and was probably also a father.

"When I first saw him," he said, "he looked dead. His muscles were rigid, and he had dilated pupils. His breathing was shallow. I suspected hypothermia as soon as I saw the wounds and blisters on his hands and feet. These are wounds secondary to freezing."

"Hypothermia?" the Crown asked.

"Yes, hypothermia," he said. "Exposure."

"Exposure?" Maître Beaulieu asked.

"You remember the night of April 27th? It was unusual perhaps for April but that night the baby was probably exposed to snow and wind."

Eileen winced at the thought of Stevie freezing to death. She knew it was cold outside and she could have stopped Nick from raising the window over the crib, but she had done nothing.

"I have to tell you," Dr. Bennett went on. "Even though we live in a cold climate here in Montreal, it's the first neonate I've seen suffering so severely from hypothermia. I've worked in the emergency ward on and off for more than ten years, and I've never seen anything like it.

"His internal body temperature was only 24 degrees centigrade. When an infant is exposed to cold for up to six hours, his body temperature can fall rapidly. I would estimate that this baby was suffering from exposure for a lot longer than that. If the baby had been brought in earlier, we might have been able to save him."

"Was the baby suffering from anything else?" the prosecutor asked.

"Yes. We did an autopsy after he died. He was suffering from bacterial pneumonia."

Nick buried his head in his hands. How could his baby have died of pneumonia? That's what he'd had when his mother left him in that sink on the bus. How could he not have seen?

"He was very thin," the doctor went on. "He was either not being fed, or, it might have been a case of failure to thrive. You know? Where there is a failure of bonding with the mother? The infant, in such a case, eats, but fails to absorb the nutrients."

Eileen dug her hands into her legs until they hurt. It was all her fault, she thought. Nick hated hospitals, but when she saw Stevie wasn't eating, she could have taken him to the hospital when Nick was out with Torchy doing B&Es. Her little son had never had a chance. She felt lost and ashamed.

"Pneumonia and under-nutrition would have made the infant predisposed to hypothermia," said Dr. Bennett. "In temperate climates in very poor countries we sometimes find cases of hypothermia, especially in infants under one month old, but not in advanced countries like Canada. At least, not usually."

"Have you ever seen a baby suffering from hypothermia?" asked the prosecutor.

"Yes. In Ethiopia. I have worked in Ethiopia. That's the only place I've seen a baby looking like that. The Mykonos baby looked like an African famine victim."

Nick shuddered. Like an African famine victim? How could he have been so blind? He wasn't normal. Terrible things happened to all the people he had ever cared about and he never saw.

The doctor went on. "Cases have been documented in underdeveloped countries — in Iraq, India, Uganda, Lebanon, Ethiopia, as I mentioned, and in Israel among the Bedouins in the desert. But I have never seen a case here."

"How long do you estimate that the baby looked emaciated?" the prosecutor asked.

"Maybe three days. Babies with hypothermia are poor feeders. They're inclined to be irritable. But I'm convinced he was fragile at the time he was subjected to all that cold. The charts show the baby was healthy at birth. He was a little underweight perhaps, but healthy."

The courtroom was silent but Maggie felt a ringing in her ears. It was the cars on the Jacques Cartier Bridge. She was standing at the railing. The lips of the judge moved but she heard nothing except the beat of the cars on the concrete. Everyone stood up and filed out. The judge had called a recess. Feeling confused and dazed, she remained alone on the bench at the front where the journalists usually sat. In front of her swung the long black wings of her father's robe, and over the din of the cars his booming voice intoned the prayer of confession and repentance he said every week at the Sunday service.

After a few minutes, the pall around her lifted and Maggie went out into the corridor and wandered down the hall to the escalators. Eileen was being taken care of by her stripper friend Kelly along with Esther Sykes and Sally from the shelter where Eileen had stayed after the baby died, but downstairs in the lobby Nicholas sat by himself on a bench. Three of the old men Maggie recognized as courtroom regulars watched him smoke a cigarette. "Punk," one of them said. She bought a coffee from the mobile canteen and went outside.

~

She got back to the courtroom just in time to pick up the testimony of the pathologist from the coroner's office. "The Mykonos baby died of respiratory arrest and pulmonary haemorrhage. Virtually every organ in the infant's body had started to deteriorate as a result of the hypothermia." He talked of gastrointestinal bleeding, acute renal failure, and pancreatitis.

While he was testifying, he leafed through the colour pictures that Beaulieu had given to Maggie as well as some special lab photos. In a flat monotone for over an hour he analyzed the state of each part of the baby's body as though he were reading from an anatomy book.

As he spoke Maggie felt waves of nausea wash over her and she was afraid she might throw up. In a dream the night before she had watched a teenaged girl in a braid wrap a baby in a linen towel embroidered with blue forget-me-nots. Once again, she heard her father's voice, "We acknowledge and confess our manifold sins which we from time to time have committed . . ."

Slowly, she came to. Where was she? The trial, yes, the trial. Maggie tried to take some notes but gave up. They had left the window open in a snowstorm. She'd focus her story on the testimony from the doctor and nurse and back it with details from the pathologist. She had to concentrate. The judge adjourned the case and Maggie went up to the Crown prosecutor.

"Tomorrow," Maître Beaulieu said, knowing Maggie wanted to know exactly when the jury would see the pictures. "First thing tomorrow."

"Thanks," Maggie said. She was still in a fog but knew exactly what to ask. "By eleven?"

"Oh yes. Possibly even before eleven."

Maggie rushed to a phone booth and called Alphie, first at the pressroom, and then across the street at the bar. The pressure of the deadline and the scoop made her adrenalin flow. "Tomorrow," she told him. "First thing. They can go in the first edition." That, she knew, was what Max would want.

"Can you give them to me right away?" Alphie asked.

"Within half an hour." She hailed a taxi, dashed up the stairs to her apartment, grabbed her briefcase, and took the pictures to him.

"Look," she said. "The Crown said by eleven, probably before." The papers hit the street at eleven, but the deadline for the first edition was six in the morning. A special page would have to be prepared in advance and slotted in when she gave the signal. "I'll call you as soon as the jury sees them. You'll hear from me right after the session opens, before 9:45."

～

The next morning, waiting outside the courtroom, Maggie saw Eileen come off the escalator with a man of about thirty-six. He was tall and gangly with shoulders that hung forward, but he wore a well-cut suit. He looked like a pharmacist or an optician. She watched near the washroom by the escalators as they met Eileen's friend Kelly.

"I'd like you to meet Colin," Eileen said.

"I'm very glad you're here," Kelly said. "Today'll be a hard day for Eileen."

Colin put his arm protectively around Eileen. As the three of them walked toward the courtroom, Nicholas stepped off the escalator. He saw Eileen and stood there for a moment, pain in his eyes. Then he turned and raced down the up-escalator, taking two steps at a time, nearly knocking over a lawyer in a gown.

He tore across the lobby and flew out the front door on Notre Dame Street. Maggie saw the whole thing from the balcony. He returned with just two minutes to spare when everyone was in place, walking down the aisle slowly with a slight swagger.

After the court was called to order, the judge entered and Maître Beaulieu rose to her feet. This was an important moment for her — the crux of her case. "Your Honour, I would like to show the jury the pictures of the Mykonos baby."

Eileen's lawyer was on her feet objecting but before she could get into the substance of her remarks, the judge asked the jury to leave. The photographs weren't relevant, they should not be shown to the jury, Martine McKenzie argued. There was a fierce exchange between her and the Crown prosecutor. Nick's lawyer said nothing.

The judge listened. Maggie worried that Alphie had given the pictures to Max for the first edition without waiting to hear from her, figuring there was no chance of a hitch. It was now 9:50.

"The court will adjourn for five minutes," said the judge. Everyone in the courtroom spilled out into the corridor.

"What do you think he'll do?" Maggie asked a veteran court reporter from *Bonjour Police*.

"The judge will rule in the Crown's favour," he said. "He's Crown-oriented."

"You think so?" she said.

The reporters waited quietly, thinking about their stories and how much they wanted the pictures. A couple of TV reporters asked the Crown for copies, but she said, "No, not until the judge rules on this."

Maggie stood off by herself feeling terrified. Down the hall, Eileen leaned her head against Colin's shoulder. In the courtroom Nicholas sat alone on the bench for the accused.

The judge took over ten minutes to decide. Maggie took a seat at the back so she could slip out in a hurry with the news. Reading from a sheet of paper, he decreed that they were as relevant to this case as a picture of a concrete slab roped to a body dragged up from the bottom of the river in a murder trial and were definitely allowable. He told the constable to fetch the jury members.

"The jury is looking at them," Maggie told Alphie from a pay phone in the corridor. "The presses are already printing them," Alphie interrupted. He had jumped the gun. "On page one above the fold. Everyone's impressed. And you're getting the credit. Goodbye." Maggie held her breath. She'd been very lucky.

When Maggie reappeared, the members of the jury were passing the pictures along the row, one by one. Everyone in the court was studying their faces — the press, the Crown prosecutor, the homicide detectives, the lawyers for the defence, the judge — everyone, that is except Eileen and Nicholas, who kept their heads down.

Every single juror looked outraged, Maggie thought. No one moved, not even the carrion crows. The examination of the pictures took more than half an hour. After twenty minutes, one of the jurors put her head on her knees. A constable hurried over. "I'll be all right," the woman said. "I'll just keep my head on my knees for a minute." The jury foreman finally handed the pictures to the judge, and the reporters shut their notebooks, waiting for the judge to adjourn the court so they could descend on the Crown for the photographs.

Eileen's lawyer was again on her feet. She wanted the judge to put a ban on publication of the pictures. Maggie hadn't counted on that. Why hadn't Alphie warned her about all these possibilities? Panic ran through her. All she needed was to be found in contempt of court. It was too late now to pull the picture. In fifteen minutes, the *Tribune* would be sitting downstairs in the lobby's newspaper dispenser and upstairs in the prosecutors' offices with her story on the front page accompanied by the horrifying picture of the Mykonos baby. She could imagine the headline: *A Montreal Biafran* or something equivalent, courtesy of Reggie.

She shouldn't have been so eager, shouldn't have trusted Alphie. She remembered the judge's remarks to the jury about the press at the beginning of the trial. The judge took his time. Finally, in his nasty Marlon Brando rasp, he said, "I see no reason why I should do that. No." Maggie relaxed. "If the journalists want to publish the pictures, they can."

~

After the court adjourned, Maggie went straight to the washroom on the next floor up and sat in a cubicle for a long time with her head in her hands. It was normal that the *Tribune* had the pictures first, she said to herself. She, after all, was *the* expert on child abuse. But she felt uneasy. She walked to the sink, splashed water on her face, left the washroom and took the escalator down to the main floor.

The crowd from the courtroom had dispersed, but down in the lobby Eileen, accompanied by Colin and Kelly, were looking at the picture of her baby through the window of the dispensing machine for the *Tribune*. The City Edition was already out and for sale. Four of the carrion crows already had copies. In newsprint, the picture looked worse than the original. Reggie had picked up on the famine in the Third World angle. The over-line on her story was: *Only in Ethiopia?* Underneath, in screaming letters, was the headline. *Not Just in the Third World — Now in Montreal!* And next to Maggie's byline was her picture.

From behind Eileen, Nicholas moved forward until he was standing next to her. Eileen looked from the picture, up to Nicholas, and then back to the picture. Tears streamed down her face. "He never looked like that," she paused. "Did he? Oh please, Nicky, tell me he didn't." Nick took her hand. "No. He never looked like that."

"We have to go now," Kelly said to Eileen, pulling her away. "Your lawyer wants to see you." Colin put his arm around Eileen, and they left Nicholas alone in front of the dispensing machine, staring at the story in disbelief.

The old men stood up and advanced toward Nicholas. Maggie turned her back, took the escalator down to the St. Antoine Street side of the courthouse and walked quickly towards the *Tribune*.

She couldn't face the long list of phone calls she knew she'd have waiting for her in the office from outraged readers, nor did she want to file her story from the Palais de Justice pressroom where reporters would try to find out about her inside track to the Crown prosecutor. En route to the office, she took a detour to a secluded Chinese restaurant where she knew she'd meet no one and wrote out her story in longhand. Later, around midnight, when the brass of the paper had gone home, she'd call one of the sub-editors, Foxy perhaps, and modem it to him.

NINETEEN

～

Witness for the…?

THE DEFENCE OPENED after the weekend break with Eileen's lawyer telling the jury she would be bringing in two expert medical witnesses, both of them pediatric specialists. One would talk about the phenomenon of parents who fail to see illness in a child while the other would deal with the "failure-to-thrive," a syndrome mentioned in the evidence for the prosecution. Carmen De La Rosa and Retta Van Dam, the two neighbours who had taken the Mykonos baby to the hospital, would testify about extenuating circumstances in the case of Eileen. A police officer who had been alerted about the case under the youth protection act would also speak.

The first defence witness was a pediatrician from Ottawa who had done research on perception of illness by parents, especially in a first child. "Sometimes," she told the judge, "a baby can become quite thin, but a mother will not notice. If she's dealing with a first baby, she may think the size of the baby is normal."

According to the doctor who had testified for the prosecution, the baby was thin before he suffered from exposure, and afterwards, of course, worse. Maggie saw that Eileen's lawyer wanted an excuse as to why the couple did nothing.

"Tell me," said the judge, "have you seen the pictures?"

"No, I haven't," the witness said. "I drove in from Ottawa this morning, and prior to that I was in Boston giving a lecture."

So she had missed the pictures completely! Eileen's lawyer squirmed in her chair, but Nicholas's lawyer looked unconcerned.

"I'd like you to see the pictures," the judge said. He signalled the court clerk who handed her the collection. The pediatrician looked taken aback as she examined each photograph.

"Well?" the judge asked.

"Yes, well . . ." She seemed to be rethinking everything as she fixed her eyes on the edge of the witness box. "Even a retarded person," she said, under her breath.

"Would you please speak up," the judge said in his raspy voice. "What were you saying? Even a *retarded* person?"

"Yes," she said. "I think that even a retarded person might have known that this baby needed attention."

What material! Maggie thought. The witness for the defence had turned into a witness for the prosecution. As good as the movies! There was a silence. Finally, when Eileen's lawyer, Martine McKenzie did not follow up with a question, the pediatrician said, "The mother must have been under unusual stress."

The Crown prosecutor had no questions and the witness left the courtroom immediately.

The second defence witness was a child psychiatrist, an expert in the failure-to-thrive syndrome alluded to in testimony for the prosecution. She said that the failure-to-thrive syndrome often exhibited itself in infants under the age of nine months in cases where there was a failure to bond with the mother.

Eileen felt troubled when she heard that. She should never have gone out and left the baby alone so much. Only Carmen and Retta knew how many afternoons when Nick was out that she had left Stevie all by himself.

"An infant can become abnormally thin, and not because the mother isn't feeding him," the doctor went on. "The infant takes in the milk, but doesn't absorb the nutrients."

The judge asked the doctor whether she had seen the pictures.

"Yes," she said.

"I'd like you to look at them again."

The clerk handed over the collection to the psychiatrist who could not conceal a look of discomfort at the sight of them. Everyone in the courtroom looked closely at the doctor's expression. After she had finished inspecting the pictures, Eileen's lawyer resumed questioning.

"Under what circumstances would a mother fail to bond with the child? Could you give examples from your research?"

"I've worked a lot with abused women," the psychiatrist said. "Usually the mother has been abused, abused physically and emotionally as a child, and abused in her relationship with her husband."

Eileen looked up at the psychiatrist and felt reassured by her remarks. But how could she just blame Rube and Nick for everything? They'd been nicer to her than anyone. She bit hard on her knuckles. She had to keep remembering what her lawyer kept telling her. It was Nick's fault.

Nick stole a look at Eileen, the only girl he had ever loved. How could it have happened? They all hated him, he thought, and maybe everyone was right.

Maggie looked over at Nicholas. The night before she had heard Kiri Te Kanawa and José Carreras singing "Tonight" from *West Side Story* and for a fleeting moment, she had thought of the springy way he walked. Eileen, she had to admit, looked more like a girl from the National Ballet than a strip-dancer. A beautiful girl. But whoever Eileen's parents were, they weren't at the trial.

Outside the courtroom door, after the testimony, Esther Sykes talked with a cluster of women. "There was that set-back with those doctors, but tomorrow the big guns will be coming out. Eileen will look very different after Carmen takes the stand again along with her neighbour Retta."

After the corridor cleared, Maggie sat down and smoked a ciga-rette. She wasn't really a smoker but from time to time she bought single cigarettes from a 7-11 near her apartment on St. Antoine. A cleaning man with a mop opened the courtroom door and shouted at someone inside. Maggie stood up and looked into the window of the courtroom. The session was over for the day but Mykonos was still sitting in the dock for the accused. "You have to leave," said the cleaner. Nicholas raised his head but didn't move. Not wanting him to see her, Maggie backed away from the window and walked away.

TWENTY

~

In the Shadow
of the Dome

IT WAS SIX O'CLOCK the next night when Maggie's doorbell rang and from her front window on St. Antoine Street she saw Michael. He was just back from Guatemala.

"Like to come for supper at the centre?" he called up. "I've cooked some chili. I have a friend I'd like you to meet."

"Down in a minute," Maggie said. At the residence Michael ran for refugees in LaSalle, she often met interesting people.

"A Franciscan brother is staying with me," Michael explained in the car on the way over to the refugee centre. "He was a prison chaplain in maximum security prisons here in Canada for several years. Now he's working in Central America."

Brother St. John looked down from a ladder as they walked in the door. He was pinning up a colourful tapestry made by Guatemalan school children next to a poster of the slain Nicaraguan bishop, Oscar Romero.

"Just call me Johno," he said. "That's what the kids in Guatemala call me." Johno was wearing pants and a charcoal-coloured sweater. Up there on the ladder, he looked cool and composed but Maggie saw otherwise after dinner when he responded to some questions from her about prisons.

"There's no bigger hell than a maximum security penitentiary," he said. "Awful things go on. Especially for those poor guys in Protection." An anxious look came into Johno's pale blue eyes as he spoke. "I stayed for as long as I could. There are books you can read if you want to know more. Michael tells me you're covering a sensational trial."

"Yes . . ." She was grateful he didn't press her for details.

He paused and looked closely into her eyes. "All those guys. Even those who have committed murder. They all have something good inside, but there's never anyone around them to see it shine." He shook his head. "Most of them have no one. And it's always been that way for them. Know what I mean?" She nodded but said nothing.

"I left after this kid . . . he wasn't much more than twenty-two. I won't go into why he was there. I did my best with him. But I always felt I could have done more. Maybe it was just too late. I've seen things like ground glass in the food and tear gas in the milk. But that wasn't the worst. It was the cries from the cells in the middle of the night. The despair.

"Everyone is part of it. Some guards try to be kind. They're not all brutal. But if the inmates see a screw being nice to anyone. Well. Guys get raped for less. This kid I was telling you about wrapped himself in toilet paper and set fire to himself." He sighed. "I left after he died. I tried to make a difference but in that sort of atmosphere it's almost hopeless. I can do more in Central America."

∼

Two days later at the Sunday morning church service at St. Ninian's, Maggie looked up at her father as he raised his long black-clad arms and pronounced the benediction. His eyes seemed as flat as those of the judge at the trial, she thought, as she felt him stare down at her in the pew. After he pronounced the Amen, she bowed her head and felt the rush of air as he swept down the aisle in his long robes. As usual, he would wait for her to join him at the church door as he greeted parishioners. Afterwards he expected her to make him lunch at the manse.

But Maggie wanted to get back to the McGill library. After she had spoken with Brother St. John about his experiences in penitentiaries, she had pulled out some books on prisons and she wanted to re-examine them. Her daughterly duties, however, would have to come first.

She felt a warm hand on her shoulder and knew it was Maude Wilkins, Maggie's first Sunday School teacher. "Wonderful work you're doing here, supporting your father. It's great the way you come on Saturday nights to make him dinner. He loves to see you. He needs someone to talk to after he's written his sermon. We're very proud of you, dear. When we ask him to dinner, he always says no. Worries he might impose, I suppose."

But that, Maggie thought, wasn't the reason. Her father abhorred the idea of his parishioners peering into his personal life. He knew a lot about *them* while they remained in the dark about *him*. It was how he stayed in control, like a reporter on an interview with someone for a story. Like *her*, she thought with a twinge of conscience.

Moving slowly toward the back of the church, she wove in and out of the parishioners until another old-timer stopped her. It was a friend of her mother who had always run the Christmas pageant. "Horrid stuff you're having to listen to down at the court house," she said. "Your mother would have been very . . ." but Maggie cut her off before she could say more.

～

"Pretty quiet around here now, isn't it," Maggie said as she and her father crossed the lane from St. Ninian's to the manse. The street, she thought, seemed depressingly still. When she was growing up, the neighbourhood had been alive with families.

"So many older people in the congregation now," her father replied. "Not the way it used to be." As a child she had yearned to play Run Sheep Run and roller skate with some of the more adventurous kids on the block but they had shied away from the manse. If occasionally a child had dared to ring their bell, her father would say she was too busy with homework. Mostly though, it was because she had to help her mother.

The Victorian brick houses on the street had at one time looked elegant but she noticed that now the windows with the lace curtains sagged and the wood stairs were chipped. Their neighbourhood was the dividing line between middle-class Notre Dame de Grâce and upper-class Westmount.

She waited patiently while her father fiddled with the key to the heavy oak front door of the manse. At seventy-four, he was no longer agile. The door creaked open and a cloying smell she associated with funeral homes floated out. There were always too many flowers in the house. Every week the women from the auxiliary installed the bouquets from the Sunday services on the ground floor of the manse.

Her father eased himself into a leather armchair in the living room. A heavy-set man with strong legs and wide shoulders, lately he moved as though his joints ached. Not that he would ever complain. He never talked about physical ailments.

Maggie longed to go off to the library but she had to stay and serve her father lunch. On the piecrust table next to her father stood her baptismal photo showing her newborn face almost lost in all those white robes. A small flimsy thing that could easily have been dropped, she thought. It stirred up a murkiness from the past that she was afraid to think about. She looked more closely at her father's wide-open smile in the photo. He seemed boyish and excited, as if he enjoyed being a father, but her mother looked pale, perhaps even then feeling ill.

"I hope you can come to the service tonight to hear the choir sing

'Hail, The Conquering Hero' from Handel's *Judas Maccabaeus*." Her father circled his arm in the air as though he were a conductor. "They took a whole month to rehearse it, till midnight some nights."

"My folkdance group is meeting tonight," she said. "We're preparing for a competition in Boston. And I have work to do." There was only so much time she could spend around the manse and at St. Ninian's.

The centrepiece of his Sunday evening services was always church choral music. While he loved being in the pulpit, he knew almost enough about music to direct the choir and always conferred with the choirmaster on the choice of music.

Her father still gave the impression of vitality, she thought, but now that he had lost most of his jet-black hair, he was really showing his age. "Next month," he said, "the choir will sing the Handel at the Presbyterian Choral Festival."

Presbyterian. Just the sound of the word made her stiffen. With its old-country views on women, sex, and poverty, Presbyterianism was a millstone around her neck. "Anyone who tries can make something of himself," her father had sermonized when she talked to him about poverty in the city. "God helps those who help themselves," he lectured. Calvinist to the core. When she was at McGill, she had once tried to get him to read John Porter's *The Vertical Mosaic* about the relationship between class and ethnicity, but a day later she found it back on her book shelf.

Maybe it was because of Michael that she felt more comfortable with the United Church. She had never told her father how she had played hymns on an old pump organ at Michael's services for wayward youth in the St. Henri bar when she was a student. He would have disapproved.

She sat on the edge of the chintz loveseat that her mother had re-upholstered twenty years ago, just before her death. To bring her samples of material, Maggie had been sent downtown to Marshall's right in the middle of her high-school-leaving exams. Her mother had always favoured deep colours. The room, with its navy-blue velvet curtains, sombre Victorian furniture and wood-panelled walls, resembled pictures she'd seen of drawing rooms in ancestral Scottish castles.

She stood up and turned on the mantlepiece lights. Over the fireplace were family pictures going back three generations. Presbyterian ministers in clerical collars dominated both wings of the family. On her mother's side, the MacDonalds were well-educated Highland Scots, and on her father's, the MacKinnans were poor immigrant Scottish farmers from Ontario.

This front room, so carefully furnished, had been strictly reserved for church elders, the choirmaster and the head of the Sunday School. As a kid she had tired of all the people traipsing through the manse. She couldn't invite a friend in because they might make a mess, while in other homes the children could jump on sofas and leave toys lying around.

"Let's have our tea and sandwiches," her father said, and they went past the dining room and the kitchen to the solarium overlooking the English garden. They never had lunch in the dining room. Her mother had worked hard when she was first married to refinish the mahogany table and had constantly worried about scratches that might ruin its glistening surface. Even now, her father reserved the dining room strictly for Saturday night dinner.

"The garden's never been the same since you left," he said. "Those blue delphinium. They look pretty scraggly." At twelve, when her mother became too sick to tend the garden, Maggie had taken on the chores. A handyman now clipped off the dead flowers and cut the grass but not much more. "The mums and gladioli are still in bloom. Those were your mother's fall favourites."

He pushed his rimless glasses back against the bridge of his nose and tapped the heel of his sturdy black shoe on the polished floor. When her mother died, he had been only fifty-four, and with his wonderful shock of thick black curly hair, still handsome. He could have remarried, she thought. It would have been so much easier for her.

Her grandmother's blue Mikado tea set which was starting to show cracks waited on the round table next to the gnarled pink geraniums and the tin of black Ceylon tea. Little in the house had changed since her mother's death although here and there Maggie had tried to introduce touches of bright colour.

From the refrigerator Maggie took out the sandwiches she had prepared at home that morning in her apartment. Her father helped himself to a cucumber sandwich. "You remember your friend, Victoria Bailey? Wasn't she with you at McGill?" Maggie nodded in reply, even though Victoria had never been much of a friend. "She's been away in the Maritimes. Now she's back and came to see me about getting her son into the confirmation class. She asked about you."

Strange how few female friends she had kept from the old days. Her two closest buddies, in fact, were Alphie and Michael, both of whom were older. How little her father knew about her life.

"I showed her my scrapbook of your front-page stories. She was very impressed." Maggie held back a smile, wondering how many of those pieces her father had actually read.

He lifted a shortbread out of the cookie jar. She often made him shortbread, scones and his favourite pecan squares from a recipe that had been in her mother's family for generations but she rarely ate them herself. Upstairs in her old room, and at her desk at the office, she kept a cache of May Wests. When she worked late at the paper, she relied on the chocolate and cream cakes to keep going.

"I've been reading those articles of yours about that terrible couple that are on trial." He looked at her coldly. "The father sounds like a complete monster. Those were shocking pictures of the frozen baby in the *Tribune*.

"Having a family," he pronounced slowly while tapping his fingers on the table, "having a family," he repeated, "involves sacrifices." His voice rose and he pulled back his shoulders the way he did in the pulpit. "Sacrifices young people aren't prepared to make any more. The selfishness in our society is appalling."

He leaned forward and looked at her so closely she could smell his acrid breath. "In this world, when you have a family, you have to be prepared to give up certain things. Like your mother did. And Moira," he said pointedly.

She tried to hold her hand steady as she poured his tea. Moira, his brother's daughter. Moira, the perfect one. "I'm not out to break any sound barriers," Moira had remarked when Maggie won the Enterprise award for her series on child labour in India. "My family is my enterprise."

She remembered, sadly, how her father, now showing off her articles to all and sundry, had tried to convince her to become a kindergarten teacher after she graduated from McGill. Such a fuss he had put up about her wanting to study journalism. And in New York! "Not what your mother would have wanted," he had said. Thank God for Aunt Philana who had told her not to listen to him. And how free she had felt when at twenty-two she had finally escaped from the manse to go to Columbia.

The chimes of the grandfather clock out in the living room sounding three o'clock reminded Maggie that she could now think of leaving. She drank down her tea and went upstairs to get her purse. She stood at the door of her mother's pale-blue room with the flowered wallpaper and the dried bouquet on the window sill of blue forget-me-nots and white baby's breaths.

Her mother's spirit, she felt, had never left the manse. On the bed lay the flowered silk suit and cross that her father liked Maggie to wear when he took her out to the opera. He hadn't slept in that bed since her mother's diagnosis. The silver compacts along with the comb and brush set sat on her dresser as they always had. Even the Yardley's talcum powder was still there.

In an antique silver frame was a photograph of her mother at eighteen when she had played Ophelia. A month before she died, her mother had shown Maggie reviews of herself playing the role at eighteen with a professional company in Edinburgh where she had been hailed as a promising young actress. "When I met your father, I was rehearsing for Juliet," she had said wistfully.

"I remember how enchanting she was," her Aunt Philana had described to Maggie, "even though I was only twelve at the time. She had real talent but in those days that didn't count. Things were very tough in post-war Scotland. When your father came along, your grandmother said it was time for her to get married." Her aunt, however, had escaped her mother's fate. "Always travelling and never settling down," chided Maggie's father.

Maggie wiped flecks of dust off the frame and looked closer at her mother's face. She had been beautiful, her expression so radiant. Maggie had her pale green eyes and her quick blush when she felt embarrassed. "Your mother had wanted to be part of the world," her aunt had said, "but by the age of twenty-two, she had been pushed into marriage with a thirty-eight-year-old clergyman, and was expecting a baby."

The lively expression in the photograph was so different from the resigned anger in the painting her father had commissioned the year her mother died, at thirty-seven, Maggie's age now. Her father had insisted she hang the portrait in her living room when she got her own place, and she hadn't had the heart to refuse.

Maggie walked into the adjoining room that had been her own bedroom until she graduated from McGill. A picture of James Dean and a poster of a symposium she had organized at McGill on the Russian writer Pushkin still decorated the plain white walls. She opened her top drawer and bit into a half-eaten May West. On her old bookshelf, along with some Russian histories and two different editions of Dostoyevsky's *Crime and Punishment,* stood her collection of the *Anne* books. Actually her favourite Lucy Maud Montgomery character had been Emily who from a young age had known she would be a writer. She sat on the bed for a moment and held *Emily of New Moon.*

"Magdalena," her father shouted up the stairs. He was the only person who called her by her full name. Everyone else called her Maggie. Magdalena, Maggie had discovered when she was twenty-four, was the name of an Italian woman her father had met in Venice the year before he married her mother. He had probably seen his favourite opera, *La Traviata,* first with her. He never talked about his life before he met her mother.

"Yes . . ." she called out. "I'll be down soon." She looked up in the mirror and saw her hair swirling messily around her face. "Too much like a Gypsy," her mother had said whenever she let her hair grow long. "If you want it long, wear it up in a ponytail or a chignon." A Gypsy. Maybe that's what her namesake had looked like. Eight years after her mother died, Maggie found an anguished scribble about the Venetian woman in her mother's secret diary. When Maggie was born, she'd read, her mother had wanted to call her Catherine, but her father had insisted on Magdalena.

Maggie had never told him when she discovered the diary under her mother's mouldering wedding dress in the attic. She had hidden it at the back of her bookcase behind the Anne books where her father would never think to look. Her room was filled with secrets she had never shared with anyone. In a bottom drawer, under an old tartan shawl, was the red mini skirt and white angora sweater her aunt had given her as a fifteenth birthday present. Size eight. Her mother hadn't let her wear it but it still fit. She picked up her purse and walked down the stairs.

"Two Saturdays from now, it's the Inter-Church Choral Competition," her father announced as she moved down the stairs. "I wanted to remind you. I hope you won't be working."

"I have no idea." She steadied herself against the bannister at the bottom of the stairs. She was eager to get outside. "Sorry," she said, "but I really *am* in a hurry." As she stepped out the front door onto the street she breathed in the tart September air. Her father stood at the door of the manse and she felt his gray eyes following her as she climbed into her small red Innocenti and sped off to the library.

∽

The McGill library was open on Sundays and she often went there to leaf through newspapers or explore new subjects. At a table tucked away in the stacks, no one could find her. It was as quiet and serene as Notre Dame Basilica in Old Montreal near the paper.

She trudged up to the third floor of the MacLennan Library to section HV 9500. All the books she had pulled out the afternoon before were still strewn on a large table. She sat down and began combing through them. They had names like *Bricks of Shame, Four Days in Hell, Cruel and Unusual,* and *Love and Rage.* What she learned was something no one covering courts ever talked about. After his "day in court" the next stop for a kid like Nicholas Mykonos would be an inferno. Prison would be hard for Eileen too, but from what Brother St. John had described, nowhere near as frightening.

She forced herself to leaf through the books. It was just as Brother St. John had described. What chilled her most was the plight of the men on the lowest rung of the so-called "scum ladder." Housed in the protection wing of the penitentiaries, these were the inmates convicted of violating women or children. Branded "Judas goats," they frequently died of mysterious causes. She read of men so anxious to escape the demons inside themselves that they committed suicide by hanging themselves with bed sheets. She looked at pictures of solitary confinement cells, guard towers, and killer dogs. But most terrifying of all were the dead looks in the eyes of the inmates in their cells.

The last book she picked up was called *Messalina in Maximum Security.* She glanced briefly at the first-person story of a reckless criminology professor in Manitoba who had fallen in love with an armed robber who had shown literary talent. The book featured a whole series of accounts told by women who on-the-job became fatally attracted to inmates. She kept turning the pages until six in the evening when a security guard tapped her on the shoulder. The library was closing and she had nowhere to go. She didn't want supper. She had bought the *Globe and Mail* and the *New York Times* but she was no longer interested in reading them. Her folk dance group was meeting but she couldn't imagine dancing.

At seven-thirty, there was an organ concert at St. Joseph's Oratory on the other side of the mountain. She climbed McTavish Street and hiked across the mountain to Beaver Lake glittering in the setting sun. The last time she'd seen the lake was when she had followed Nick up to the paupers' cemetery and had watched him place a teddy bear on his baby's grave.

She walked on to Côte des Neiges until she saw the splendid dome of the shrine where thousands went to be healed. The old penitentiaries built in the nineteenth century had domes just like it with cell-blocks branching off the centre like spokes of a wheel so the guards could keep prisoners under constant surveillance. She stared down at the sidewalk. She had to forget about prisons and about the small baby who had died. She was going to St. Joseph's Oratory alone to lose herself in music, to forget . . .

TWENTY-ONE

~⚬~

They Match Her Eyes

THE NEXT EVENING Maggie sat at her computer terminal in the newsroom and without the help of her notebook tried to remember what Carmen had said on the witness stand. Nicholas had tied Eileen up with handcuffs and there was something about a key. She searched through her brief case one more time looking for her notebook. She wanted to get her piece done before Reggie came in. He was on an earlier shift these days. It was six in the evening and only a few reporters were around. She wished Roddie would turn down the police radio. Between that and the constant buzz of the television sets on the copy desk, one tuned to *CBC* and the other to an American news station, the office was never quiet.

Maybe she could do a side-bar on how Nicholas had given Eileen's boyfriend Colin a black eye early that morning. She didn't need her notebook for that. All the details were firmly etched in her mind. Colin had fled the scene with a bleeding nose. It had happened one block from the court house on the grounds behind City Hall. Maggie rested her elbows on her desk and thought some more about what she'd seen that morning before the court opened . . .

Nicholas had looked vulnerable as he watched Eileen cross from the Champs de Mars subway station, her hair blowing in the wind. Eileen had appeared troubled but as soon as she saw Colin's smile she had beamed. Wearing gray flannels and a navy-blue blazer, this new boyfriend of hers had been waiting for her at the foot of the steps to the City Hall grounds. Maggie had stood at the curb a few feet from the steps and watched. When Colin opened his arms and kissed Eileen on the lips, Nicholas ran up and hit him hard with his fists.

"She's still my wife," he had yelled. "Keep your damn hands off her."

"Not for long," Eileen replied. "We're getting divorced!" In the split second Nick took to listen to Eileen, Colin managed to bolt down the street and into the court house. Eileen had followed, and after Nick watched her disappear, he trudged up the hill and sat in the grass. In the background, as he stared vacantly into space, Maggie had noticed how the copper dome of one of the City Hall buildings cast a giant shadow over him . . .

Maggie sat forward in her chair and tried to focus her thoughts but behind her, on the other side of the row of newspaper files that separated the newsroom from the editorial offices, she heard the determined click of high-heeled shoes coming down the corridor. It was Barbara Smith-Jones, probably in another of her tight skirts. Barbara had studied law for two years and was eager to replace Alphie who was preparing to retire from the court beat. About ten years younger than Maggie, and popular with the senior editors, she was now using her police contacts to do special features. "Why don't you try dressing more like Barbara," Alphie had suggested.

Maggie drummed her fingers on the desk. The fight would be a hard story to write. Maybe she wouldn't write it. No one else had seen it. Fights like that were common around the court house, but this one had real news value. News value. She was beginning to hate the word. "Your story has wonderful news value," Max told her after she scooped all the other papers with the Mykonos baby pictures. "Keep up the good work." She got back to thinking about her notebook. She had to get those quotes from the trial *right*. Where *had* she left it?

The washroom on the fifth floor of the court house flashed into her head. Carmen De La Rosa had been in there with Retta Van Dam. She had to have her notebook for the De La Rosa quotes. Maggie stared at the flashing cursor on her computer screen. Now she remembered. She had put her notebook on the floor in the cubicle. She must have left it there. She'd take a chance that the Palais du Justice was open and go back.

"Hey, Maggie," the night city editor yelled as she approached the water cooler on the way out. "When can we expect your story?"

"I have lots of time, don't I?"

"What've you got on the kid killer?"

"Oh," Maggie said. "It seems he sometimes handcuffed his wife when he went out. At least that's . . ." She stopped in mid-sentence and took a drink. "I'll be close to the deadline." She could send in something up until two in the morning when the news editor held his conference about the contents of page one.

On the way out of the building, she saw Cyril Norgate, the editor-in-chief, stepping out of a taxi. Cyril came from Rhodesia and the proprietary look he sometimes gave the inhabitants of the newsroom was what Alphie liked to call "his Rhodesia look." Cyril's right eye was half the size of his left eye and it was always half shut. Later, he was sure to come by her desk snuffling for foul details he could feed on from the trial. When she was doing her series on child abuse, he had hung around every day inquiring about the molestation cases. Now she made a point of looking the other way or cutting him off whenever he came by her desk.

She walked swiftly down St. Jacques Street and tried the doors on all three sides of the court house but they were locked. By now her notebook had probably been swept up by a cleaner and thrown away.

She'd been in this sort of pickle before. It happened when she got preoccupied. She'd have to paraphrase some of the quotes.

She turned west down the street toward the paper and then changed her mind and walked over to the square facing City Hall where she sat on a bench in the square and scribbled what she remembered. From the square she walked down to the water. The river had always held a special attraction for her, especially at night when it felt as peaceful as a cemetery. She'd take the long way back and write the story in her head so that when she returned she could put it quickly into the computer and leave.

Walking along the road next to the water she saw a figure curled up near a big shed that was sometimes used for theatre performances. The sky was black but the street lights were on. Up closer she saw it was just a boy in a leather jacket, maybe a runaway. She froze. The jacket was unmistakable. It had such a quality look that one of the reporters had suggested Mykonos had stolen it. The boy sat up and opened his eyes. It really *was* Nicholas Mykonos. That morning he had moved like a panther but now he had the face of a kindergarten kid. She took a few steps backward. Perhaps he wouldn't recognize her.

"Wait a minute," he said, slowly coming to life. "I've seen you before, haven't I?"

"Yes?" Maggie said.

He stood up and kicked the dirt. "The trial, isn't it? You're one of the reporters, aren't you?" She was always in the front row.

"Yes." He looked so bedraggled. She didn't say anything for a minute. "What are you doing down *here*," she asked.

He threw back his shoulders. "Oh, just wanderin' around." He looked away from her toward the river.

Maggie looked down at the water and then up at the Jacques Cartier Bridge. For years now, she hadn't been able to cross that bridge. If she had to go to the other side of the river, she always took either the Victoria or the Champlain Bridge. "So you're just wandering around," she said. "You have a place to stay?"

He nodded.

She didn't know why she asked — compassion or just journalistic instinct, anything to elicit material — but she found herself saying, "Look, I was just going to get myself something to eat. Have you had supper?"

"Well, no," he admitted. She was the first person who had shown any kindness to him since the trial opened.

"Come on," she said.

She bought Cokes, hot dogs, chips and May Wests in a fast-food place, and they walked up to Place d'Armes in front of Notre Dame church where they sat on a bench. It was cool but still comfortable. She picked a spot close to the street in case she wanted to slip away quickly.

He said almost nothing as they ate and she wondered whether he knew she was the one responsible for the scoop on the pictures. He was so close she could smell the earthiness of him. It was quite dark but she could see the shape of his legs in his jeans.

"It's a nice square, don't you think," Maggie said after a few minutes. It was crass to try to interview him. "Have you ever been here before?"

"Yeah . . ." He was almost sure she was the reporter whose photo appeared over the story about his son looking like an African famine victim. After the picture of Stevie appeared in the *Tribune* he had stopped even glancing at the papers. It was too painful. He waited for a few minutes, not sure whether he should trust her. "I got married here," he finally said.

"You got married in Notre Dame Basilica? Right here in this church?" She looked up at the spires. "It's a very beautiful church. I sometimes go in there."

"Well, not *in* the church, on the steps outside it." He stretched out his legs and caught a whiff of her perfume. He looked up at her. She was prettier than he'd realized and she had a nice smile.

"You want to tell me about it?"

"You mind?" and he fished into his back pocket and pulled out a joint. "I can't talk without it." He lit up, inhaled deeply, and offered her a toke.

Maggie made a sign with her hand to indicate she didn't want any. There had been a lot of drugs around when she was in university in the sixties but she had never tried anything.

Nicholas took another drag and looked sideways at her. Why was she being so nice to him? If he hadn't felt so lonely he might have taken off, but she had bought him supper, and he hated the idea of going back to the Salvation Army. Even if she *had* written those stories that made him look bad, maybe if he flirted with her a little he could win her over. He looked up at her and smiled.

"I'm listening," she said.

"Christmas Eve," he said slowly. "Last Christmas Eve Eileen and I got married outside the Stop for Coffee bus."

"You mean the bus the priest runs for street kids?"

He took another drag. "Yeah," he said. "A chaplain from McGill married us. Doug Foster. He helped me once when I ran away from a group home."

He smoked the joint to the end. Then he began to talk. "Eileen and I had candles. All the kids did. They were like our family." He waited a moment. "Students from McGill played the guitar. Everyone was so," he sighed, "so fuckin' . . . oh, sorry about my language."

"Don't worry about it," Maggie said. "I hear it all the time. Go on." She patted his shoulder.

"It's just, well, they were all so damned nice to us." He waited a few minutes and Maggie felt the weight of the night. "Till death do us part," Nicholas said the words so softly Maggie hardly heard them. Maggie shifted slightly on the bench. Now she knew who Nick reminded her of. It was Andreas. He had the same sparkling blue eyes. She had met Andreas in 1968 on a hike with an adventure club during her first year at McGill University. He was an architecture student. She saw herself now at seventeen in her childish white blouse, red plaid skirt and long braid she wound around her head. Every weekend for three months she went on outings, hoping he'd notice her. It was a way to have some excitement and get away from her father who was always preaching at her about something. Her mother had died the year before and he counted on her to take care of everything. Finally, in February, after cross country skiing, Andreas took her to dinner at the Pam Pam and then back to his apartment in the student ghetto . . .

Nicholas dug into his back pocket and fished out another joint. "Did you have a best man?" Maggie asked, forcing herself to concentrate on Nick's story.

"Yeah," he said. "My brother Danny came for me. Eileen had Kelly."

"Your brother?" Maggie asked.

"Well, my foster brother. He's studying now to be an engineer in Vancouver. He put up my bail," he added.

"Oh . . . ?"

"Danny was in town this summer to see Pop for a few days. My lawyer found him. He hardly ever comes here. Danny told me the bail was money my foster Mum would have wanted me to have . . ." But Pop had made sure he got nothing, he thought to himself.

Maggie waited for him to say more. "You were telling me about the wedding . . ." she finally said.

"Yeah, well, after the ceremony we had hot wine with cinnamon and cake. Kelly, Betsy and Marylou made the cake. They were the girls that took in Eileen after her mother kicked her out."

Maggie thought of asking about that but resisted. She didn't want to sound too much like a reporter on a story even though that's what she was.

"After that we went in for the midnight mass at the Notre Dame church. Later Danny took us to a fancy dinner down near the Old Sailors Church."

This was a whole new side of Mykonos she was seeing. Maggie felt touched by the story and didn't know what to say.

"Did you notice the rings Eileen is wearing?" Nick went on. He had an eagerness to him, a springiness to his body she couldn't help noticing.

"No." She felt flushed.

"Jade. They're real jade. They match her eyes. I gave her the big one when I found out she was pregnant."

"Really."

"It was an engagement ring," he said. "Well, that and a celebration about us having a baby." He stared down at the cobblestones in the square.

"You really wanted the baby?" Maggie rolled out the question slowly. "It wasn't an accident?"

"No accident," he said. He had wanted to ask Eileen to marry him the very night he found out they were having a baby, but he was afraid she'd say no, so he waited until she was five months pregnant and couldn't work any more.

"Where did you get the rings?" Maggie asked.

"Through a friend." The last thing he was going to do was tell this reporter how he picked them up on a break and entry. What a time he'd had hiding the rings from Torchy and Teddy! The deal on all B&Es they did together was that they shared in the haul and no one was allowed to sneak away with nothing. But as soon as he saw those rings in that house with the big white columns in Côte St. Luc, he knew he had to have them. It was as though the rings were made for her.

"They matched her eyes," he said again. He put his head in his hands and Maggie felt a wave of warmth for him ride through her. Help me, she prayed. For a second she wanted to take him in her arms.

"Nicholas." She put a hand on his shoulder. She had to stay in control. "I have to go back to the paper. But if you want me to take you home, I have a car."

"No, it's okay," he said. "I'm with a friend. It's not far from here." If he'd had the nerve, maybe with more shit in his veins, he would have asked if he could sleep at her place. He hated it at the Salvation Army. It reminded him that he had nobody. When it was warm enough, he sometimes slept in Jeanne Mance Park, or in the furnace room of an apartment building on Park Avenue, but he had to have a shower in the morning so he'd look okay at the trial. That's what his lawyer told him. That was the only reason he was staying at the Salvation Army. They gave him a room off by himself and he always came in late so no one had a chance to make any remarks. Even the nobodies, all these broken down guys who could hardly stand up, knew what had happened to his son.

They walked along together on St. Jacques Street.

"You know how I recognized you?" Nicholas said. "Down at the dock?"

Maggie was surprised he had picked her out at all. No one ever noticed her.

"It was your butterfly pin." He put a hand on her shoulder and gently touched its blue and green wings. He smelled her perfume again. "I noticed it the first day of the trial. I figured anyone who wore a pin like that had to be special." He winked at her the way he always had with Judy, his social worker back at Parkway. "Even though you do, well, you *do* look a bit like a social worker."

Maggie thought of Alphie calling her a nun in drag because of her prim suits and Peter Pan collars. "Never mind," she laughed. "People have said worse."

When they got to the front door of the *Tribune,* Maggie didn't know what to say. "See you tomorrow" sounded ridiculous, as though they were going to see each other at some innocuous place, like work, or a soccer game.

"Thanks a lot for supper," he said at the door.

"I hope it was enough," she said. "Look. I have to go." Through the window on the other side, she waved to him.

Upstairs at her desk, she couldn't write a word on either story. She walked to the water cooler and kept drinking water, hoping her head would clear. The look on his face when he talked about his wedding haunted her. He was so alone. The warmth of his hand on her shoulder had quickened something in her, something that as a reporter she had always been taught to suppress. She had trained herself to stay on the margins of life, honing her skills as an observer, always maintaining her distance. And now . . . She pulled down hard on the sides of her skirt.

She tried various leads on both stories, but they were all disjointed, as though they were written by a person who had lost it. Finally, at four in the morning, while the overnight city editor was out for a smoked-meat supper at Dunn's, and the last deadline for her was coming up, she left a note saying there really wasn't much of a story that day.

TWENTY-TWO

~⌒

Carrion

MAGGIE SAT FOR A few minutes on a bench in the lobby of the court house and thought about Nick before she looked at the day's papers for the story she had failed to write. All of them led with Carmen's testimony about how Nicholas tied Eileen to a chair every time he went out. Something about the cast in Carmen's eyes had made Maggie wonder if she had been telling the truth. Carmen had said that twice she'd had to use a credit card to open the door so that she could feed the baby. "I could hear the baby crying. He had roped her across the stomach around the chair. I could have cut the ropes. But it was her wrists. They were locked around the back of the chair with handcuffs. And he had the key."

To avoid the other reporters, she entered the courtroom as the session was about to start and sat at the back. She knew she would be in deep trouble back at the office and didn't want to face anyone. Up in the box for the accused, Nicholas stared into his lap and Maggie

202

thought of Brother St. John's story about the kid he had befriended in the penitentiary. She shut her eyes for a minute. The Crown prosecutor, the judge and the lawyers, all in robes like the ones her father wore at church, now appeared to her as part of an unrelenting black machine. Around her people whispered angrily.

She put her blue notebook beside her on the bench and looked up at the gray windowless walls. It wasn't just the clerics of the court that scared her. It was also the mob. She said the word in her head and shuddered. In front of her rose the face of a beast like a gargoyle on a church. When it was angry, it struck against Hasidic Jews, Haitian taxi drivers, northern Cree and anyone else it thought didn't belong. It rioted in the streets and gazed coldly at mental patients wandering the streets at night.

Maggie felt the buzz of the court regulars around her and then glanced up at the jury. Accountant, construction worker, teacher, dentist, stockbroker, bus driver, hair dresser, hockey coach, student, housewife, waiter, college professor. No two alike, but all eager to convict. She thought of Esther Sykes and the confederacy from the women's centres who had a message for the world.

But she was also part of the mob. More maybe than any of them. She drew in her breath. When the beast tasted blood, it wanted more, and reporters like her with their notebooks and cameras had better deliver more. The entire society, she thought bitterly, needed to find a culprit.

Maggie looked over at Eileen and Nicholas in the dock. Nicholas looked hastily at Eileen, and a flicker of longing passed across his face. Eileen pulled her elbows into her sides. Once, at the end of one of the sessions when they thought no one was watching, Maggie had seen them look at one another as though they longed to hide away together, but that had been before the new boyfriend.

The court clerk came out from the door at the front to the left. "Silence," he declared. Everyone stood. "The Superior Court, Criminal Division, presided by Judge Robert St. Onge, is now in session." Maggie moved quickly up to the second row. Nicholas gave her a nod of recognition and tried to smile. He looked dishevelled. Perhaps he had gone back down to the docks to sleep.

She knew there would be hell to pay for not writing a story. Every day since the beginning of the trial, her stories had played on page one. That morning, from six o'clock on, her phone had kept ringing, but she had ignored it. It was probably Drew Hampden, the news editor. Every morning at six, Maxwell Cousins turned on his radio at home and tuned in to the CJAF news. When he came in, he usually wanted something he'd heard on the radio on the front page. Drew often had an alternative page one ready to go in case Max insisted the paper go with CJAF's version of the day's news. How could she have been so reckless!

Retta Van Dam had just finished being sworn in when Maggie saw Barbara Smith-Jones coming down the aisle. Oh, oh, she thought. Trouble. Barbara squeezed in beside her. "Max wants to see you," Barbara whispered. "Right away."

"I should stay," Maggie said.

"Max's mad as hell. You have to go back right away. He told *me* to cover the trial today."

Maggie hurried out into the corridor but she was eager to hear how Retta would testify so she slipped into a bench at the back of the courtroom. Max could damn well wait.

Eileen's lawyer began by asking Retta what she had observed about the couple. "Mostly what I heard was him screaming at her," she said. "Once in the middle of the night I heard bottles being hurled against the wall. I was afraid for her and the baby. She was good with the baby," she said slowly.

Good with the baby, Eileen said to herself. Well, that was a switch. Anything, she thought, to make Nick look nasty.

A policeman from the station near their home then testified that he had received a complaint from Retta about *Eileen* and had asked the public health clinic attached to a community centre to visit. "I figured the couple would be known to nurses from the clinic who would be paying them routine visits because they had a new baby."

No nurse ever came, Eileen said to herself, because Nick had made her give the hospital a wrong address.

Retta was called back on the stand. "I complained to the police about *Nicholas*," she told the court. "*Not Eileen*. The police got it wrong. Maybe it was my accent," she said.

Eileen took a deep breath when she heard that. Retta and Carmen had no respect for her, she knew, but they hated Nick and would do anything, including lie, to try to put him behind bars.

Why, Maggie asked herself, did the public health clinic not send a nurse — especially after the police asked a nurse to investigate? Such behaviour, she thought, showed negligence on the part of the health clinic and violated the Youth Protection Act.

Later she found out that Eileen's lawyer had wanted to bring the head of the public health clinic to the witness stand, but changed her mind when she found out that in an earlier case the judge had ruled that parents alone are responsible for their children, and that what social services fail to do is irrelevant.

After Retta's testimony, the judge called for a break and Maggie went out in the hall. When Nicholas came out, she went up to him. "Something's wrong at the office. I have to go back."

"Oh," he said. "Thank you for dinner last night."

Behind them, Maggie could see Colin with his arm around Eileen. He had sunglasses on, probably to hide a black eye.

"Look," Maggie said. "If you like, we can meet again in the square in front of the church. How about seven o'clock?" Barbara Smith-Jones was already approaching the two of them as though Nicholas were now her turf. Something told her she'd really screwed up.

"Sure. Seven's fine."

"Don't worry about supper. I'll bring it. Don't say anything about this to anyone. Okay?" Barbara was practically on top of them. "I've got to run."

Back at the paper, Maggie met Dick Stockwell, the city editor, in the hall outside the city room. "You better have a good excuse about why you didn't file a story last night," Dick said to her in his Texas drawl. "Max's in a rage. We're the only paper that doesn't have the story on the Mykonos trial. He wants to see you in his office right away."

As she walked over to Max's office, reporters looked at her as though they already knew something she didn't. No one spoke to her. They just watched as she hovered outside Max's door.

"Come in, Maggie," Max called. He had his feet up on the desk and was talking on the phone but he waved her in. The city's papers were laid out on a table under Max's poster collection. He had added another bare-breasted girl to his assembly. The rabbit in a pink apron on roller skates was new. Enough to send her father on another of his anti-strip tirades. She tried to think up some plausible excuse for why she hadn't written her story. Max didn't stay on the phone long. "Gotta go," he said. "I have some trouble I have to deal with. I'll pick you up at six."

He hung up and went over to his pile of newspapers. They were all open at the Mykonos/O'Reilly trial story. "Look," he said, showing her the *L'Express* piece. "And this from *Bonjour Police,* and this from *Le Journal,* and this," his voice rose, "from the *Daily Sun,*" the new English tabloid paper concentrating on crime. It was giving the *Tribune* a run for its money. He marched over and shut the door.

"What happened to you, Maggie? I know you were at the paper late last night. Why didn't you write anything?"

"Well, the thing was . . ." Maggie stared at the floor. She didn't know what to say. "I didn't think there was much of a story in yesterday's proceedings . . ." That was the usual reason reporters gave for not writing a story.

"Not much of a story!" He pounded his fist on the table. "Not much of a story? Is that why every paper in the city has a piece on page one, and CJAF led with it on the six o'clock news this morning? Maggie," he said, grabbing her shoulder. "This was *your* story. Why do you think you did all those pieces on child abuse over the summer? It was to prepare the readers for this showpiece trial in this city of child abuse. Didn't you tell me the prosecutor said this was going to be an exemplary case, and she'd make sure that, ah, what's his name there?"

"Mykonos. Nicholas Mykonos."

"That Mykonos, that kid killer, would get an exemplary sentence? I've been getting calls from everywhere about the first-rate coverage you've been giving us on these monsters." He dragged on a cigarette. "Not just from Quebec, but from Ontario, Saskatchewan, Vermont.

"Our circulation is going up. We're not going to have to worry about the *Daily Sun* after all, and you're one of the reasons for it. And now you let me down." He stubbed out his cigarette and then went on.

"You've done great stories on all the social issues — natives in residential schools, elderly in nursing homes, kids in sweat shops. Now you're cashing in on the most ghastly abuse of all. And you fold up!"

"Look," Maggie blurted out. "I think that the way I've handled the trial has been out-of-line. The way I scooped everyone with those pictures." She paused. "There was something wrong with it." Something almost pornographic, she thought. She squeezed the fold of the French twist that pulled her hair off her face. She was shocked at herself for losing control, but exhilarated by the freedom she felt speaking her mind.

"I was encouraged," she went on, "to look for the most sensational stuff. By you, Dick, Cyril. 'Paint it red,' you kept telling me. 'Paint it red.'" She tried to keep her voice down. The office partitions didn't go up to the ceiling and the editor-in-chief next door could hear every word. "You see. There's a lot more behind this story. Stuff that isn't coming out at the trial." She caught herself before her voice broke.

"I began to have misgivings. I saw another side of Nick. I overheard things . . . There are so many pressures to stigmatize him. Suppose it isn't even half the story," she raced on. "I won't be a zombie reporter, responsing . . ." Now she couldn't talk straight. "Responding," she corrected herself, "to what we all call news.

"It crucifies people who may be the real victims, who may be more . . ." She thought of what Brother St. John had told her and of the work Michael had done in St. Henri with kids just like Nick. "We can't just be gatherers of carrion. We've got to be human beings too. Don't you think?" Surely in his heart of hearts, he knew what she was talking about.

Suddenly Cyril opened the door and strode into the office. "I'm sorry," he said. "We're taking you off the trial. You're not fit to do it. Barbara Smith-Jones will cover it from now on. I think you need a break from reporting." Maggie looked over at Max. The look on his face said he wouldn't defend her. He lit another cigarette and leaned back in his swivel chair.

The editor-in-chief hung over Max's desk. She'd been avoiding Cyril whenever he came by and now she would pay dearly for it. "We need some more sub-editors, don't we? Isn't that what you've been telling me, Max?" He turned and gave Maggie a disgusted look. "On the overnight," he pronounced like a sentence and marched out. "I guess you'll have to work on the Rim," said Max. "For now anyway you're off the investigative team. We need some help on the graveyard shift."

The graveyard shift? That's where they farmed out washed-up reporters who could edit copy but were considered unfit to meet the public or be seen during regular working hours. No woman at the paper had fallen so low that the editor-in-chief had banished her to the graveyard shift of the Rim.

Max stood up. "Sorry. Until further notice, you're on the midnight-to-eight shift. You can leave. But come back tonight at midnight."

TWENTY-THREE

~

Temptress

MAGGIE WENT back to the court house that afternoon even though Barbara Smith-Jones was now covering the trial. After all, it had started off as her story. She'd do a magazine piece on the story behind the story. Her shift on the graveyard from midnight to eight gave her mornings and afternoons off. Carmen De La Rosa was scheduled to go on the stand again and Maggie didn't want to miss it.

Halfway through Carmen's remarks that afternoon, Maggie wondered whether she really wanted to see Nicholas that evening at Place d'Armes. When he went out, Carmen said, Nick always tied up Eileen. "After he beat her up and locked her in a closet, Eileen begged me to take the baby so she could go away to Magog and look for a job. I don't know how it happened," Carmen said, "but he was able to track her down. He carried her back to Montreal in a stolen car. Whenever Nick needed anything, he —"

The judge interrupted. "Would you please restrict yourself to things you know about firsthand."

Carmen went on. "Then he burned her clothes. When he got her home, he was so intent on making her his complete prisoner, he took out all her clothes and burned them."

"Tell me," Eileen's lawyer said in cross-examination, "did you ever observe any members of Eileen's family visiting Eileen and Nicholas?"

"No," Carmen said.

"Did she ever say anything about going over to her parents' house?"

"No."

"You never met either of Eileen's parents?"

"No."

~

Maggie arrived at the square fifteen minutes early because she wanted to go into the church first but Nick was already there. "There's something I should tell you," Maggie said when she sat down. She thought about how she had led the other reporters on with the abuse stories prior to the trial and after that with the scoop on the pictures. Michael had warned her about the trap she was falling into and she hadn't listened.

"I'm no longer covering the trial. They've put me on a shift from midnight to eight. They need some special editing on something," she lied. "A new girl is now on the court beat and they want her to cover the trial." She realized that if she hadn't accepted Max's assignment to take on the abuse beat and the trial, he would have recruited Barbara, but that, she felt, was no excuse.

"I've decided to do a big magazine piece." Nick wasn't listening but she went on anyway. "My shift ends at eight in the morning so I can still come to the trial. From time to time we can meet. What you tell me I can use as background." She had to find a way to tell this tragic story in a humane way.

Nick nodded. Inside he was burning up. Everyone was listening to Eileen's side of the story. He wanted Maggie to hear his side too. He pulled out a joint and slowly inhaled. But could he trust her? Something about her seemed different. She seemed a bit of a loner, maybe a little like him.

A dam broke inside him and suddenly he started talking. "Carmen was a dyke who wanted to take Eileen away from me," he told her. "She made Eileen dance for her at her apartment," he said, "in one of her strip outfits. I was standing outside Carmen's door and I heard everything.

"Carmen told my wife, my wife," he yelled, "that she should leave *me* and live with *her*. She had it all worked out. Eileen would go out to work, and she would stay home with her three kids, plus my Stevie.

"Carmen didn't like guys. They were just for making babies. But once in the garage she ran her fingers through my hair and said, 'If you get lonely when Eileen's in the hospital you know where you can come.' She liked my blue eyes."

Nick thought about the blue eyes of the *yiayia* from Naxos and rolled another joint. "No one really knows, but if he's still alive I think my father's a fisherman on the island of Naxos in Greece."

"You know," he said, "I think maybe Eileen was tempted. Carmen has this thing. She was a model before she became a dress designer." He stamped his foot on the cobblestones in the square.

"Everyone is fascinated by her. She's like a, a . . . what's the word?"

"Temptress?" Maggie volunteered.

"Yeah, something like that. Even the judge is fascinated by her. Everyone. Even you."

"Me? No, I don't think so." There was something disturbingly perceptive about him.

"Listen. Some of what Carmen said is true. But it's not *all* true. I have handcuffs, but I never used them. I *showed* them to Eileen but that's all. Eileen must have told Carmen I had them, and she made up that story.

"I hope Eileen says tomorrow that I never put her in handcuffs. I never went that far. I think Eileen's afraid of Carmen, maybe even, well I don't know." He ground his teeth.

"Colin," he blurted out, "is the reason I burned her strip outfits. When I was standing outside Carmen's door that day listening, Carmen said Eileen could make extra money here and there with Colin. That meant Eileen was doing tricks with him when I was looking after our son. Shit! Working at the Sex Trolley was okay. But tricks! Carmen was angling to become Eileen's pimp. I *seen* pimps like her when I was on the street." He breathed in heavily.

"I did lock Eileen in the closet once. I tied her up too. I can't tell you why. I'm too ashamed. Eileen knows. Eileen knows everything," he sighed.

"After Mum Evans, there was no one until Eileen, and when she got pregnant I thought that would be the beginning of a dream that would never end. I'd have a family like everyone else.

"My own blood." He moved close to Maggie and searched her eyes. "My own blood. You know what that means?" Except for her Aunt Philana, Maggie felt her own blood had never been there for her either, but she nodded anyway.

"Can you talk to Eileen maybe?" Maggie ventured.

"Talk to her?" he roared. "She's not allowed. Her lawyer has forbidden her to talk to me. I heard Eileen tell Kelly. And Colin! Don't you think he's a prick? Sorry. I didn't mean to use that word in front of you. You know, of course, why he wears those shades."

"No. Why?" Maggie didn't want to let on she'd seen Nick strike Colin.

"I beat him up."

"You beat him up?"

"Don't play that routine with me, pretending this is the first you heard of it." His eyes darted nervously around. "Last night, I remembered you not just from the trial. You were standing right there when I slugged him. I saw the butterfly pin."

The outburst from him both attracted and scared her. Hers had been a world where emotions were never displayed. "You're right," Maggie said. "I did see it. I'm sorry I didn't admit it. Listen. I don't blame you for socking him. I hope he won't lay charges."

"He won't. He's too ashamed to admit he couldn't fight me off."

Maggie had met with Nicholas Mykonos only twice, both for the purposes of a story, but there was something in their exchanges that ... She thought of Andreas when she was seventeen at McGill twenty years ago. After Andreas, there had been no one. The convent look that Alphie saw came from her reluctance to take another chance on a relationship. She would try anything for a story, take all sorts of chances the way she had on the Bombay sweatshop pieces, but on her personal life ...

"Hey!" he said. "You listening?"

Maggie sat up straight. "Oh, yes."

"You just wait." He touched Maggie's wrist. "I bet Eileen won't tell the judge the handcuffs was a lie. Carmen has a line to Eileen's brain, along with Kelly and her lawyer. You see," he said, looking out into the dark, "all those bitches want everyone to think it's completely my fault. Eileen'll listen to anything. If they tell her that's the way it was, that's the way it was." But he knew that wasn't completely true. Eileen was going along with semi-lies to save her skin so she could run off with Colin, that candy-ass boyfriend of hers.

TWENTY-FOUR

~~∾~~

Crow Eyes

HALFWAY THROUGH THE last day of her testimony, Eileen felt like stopping everything and telling the court she was guilty. The old men in rags who sat in the back row of the courtroom knew she was a monster mother, just like her own mother. They called Nick scum, but their crow eyes told her they despised her too.

While she testified she felt the presence of Colin, Kelly, Carmen, Esther and Sally from the shelter. All of them had tried to convince her that Nick had made her too scared to act. She didn't know for sure about the Crown prosecutor. At first she thought that maybe the Crown was on her side but now she couldn't tell.

Her lawyer, Martine, looked hopeful, expecting her to answer the questions they'd gone over the night before, but as Eileen spoke, she felt Nick's eyes on her, and felt tempted to go against Martine's wishes and tell everyone that they were *both* guilty.

At the very end of the testimony Martine drew herself up tall.

"Eileen," she said, "I want you to remember the feelings. I want you to remember the feelings you had when he tied you up."

Her legs felt wobbly. The judge and jury waited for her to speak. She felt the top of her jade ring on the inside of her hand. Nicky still loved her. He had said so many times that he was sorry. A few feet from her, she could feel him breathing. She was still violently attracted to him. "It seems like so long ago," she said in a small voice. "I can't remember."

The judge called for a break, and outside the courtroom Colin was waiting for her with a cup of coffee. What would she have done without Colin? Right after the trial started she had gone down to the Sex Trolley at eight o'clock on a Tuesday evening and had waited in the laneway where no one could see her. Boots had set up the meeting for her. Raghead had liked her too but she could never have depended upon him. She had been lucky Colin had come. She had desperately needed to have someone. The women at the shelter had arranged it so Nicky would be wiped from her life by helping her to get a divorce.

She was staying now with Kelly in a room at the Y, but that couldn't go on. When the trial was over, Colin said he would take her away to Calgary where he knew of a dance studio where she could start over and study jazz ballet. Colin had a cousin in Calgary who wanted him to become a partner in an optometry business. But all that was just a dream. These next few days would probably be her last days of freedom. She would never get off.

She looked at Nicky standing outside the courtroom door watching her and for a second she wanted to throw herself into his arms. Even now she couldn't help remembering their wild motorcycle ride to romantic Ile aux Coudres where their son was conceived . . .

"Your witness," Eileen's lawyer said to the Crown prosecutor back in the courtroom.

"You heard the doctor from the hospital say that the baby must have been in a fragile state before he suffered from exposure. Two days before the baby died, is it true that your baby was not eating?"

the Crown prosecutor asked Eileen.

"Yes it is."

"Why didn't you take him to the hospital?"

Eileen wanted to admit that she'd had lots of opportunities when Nick was out to take Stevie to the hospital, but then she thought of Colin. "Nick wouldn't let me," she said.

"One more thing. Where were you two days before the baby died?"

"We were at the Four Winds Hotel," Eileen said.

"And the baby?"

Eileen had been waiting for this. She had prepared herself and was almost sure Nick would go along with the lie she was going to tell because it would make both of them look better. "We took him with us to the hotel." She felt Nick breathe through his teeth when she said it but she braced herself and went on. "There was a little kitchen with a fridge and a small burner where I could heat up the milk." She couldn't tell anyone, not Kelly, not even her lawyer, that Rube had had the baby. The Crown, maybe even her lawyer, might subpoena Rube.

Eileen hadn't understood why Carmen had never told the court she had met Rube. Maybe she really *had* gone horizontal with Rube and was afraid it would come out. She was relieved Rube hadn't been implicated. He had helped her out when she needed it. If he testified, something might come out about what had gone on between them. If Martine suspected anything, she would hammer him until he confessed. Eileen shuddered at the thought of Colin finding out her stepfather had gone down on her. Colin might believe it was all *her* fault.

At the end of the afternoon's session, Eileen was startled when she saw Rube at the end of the corridor near the escalators. He waved his arm at her and she wanted to go to him. She knew he must be following the trial in the newspapers.

"Colin," she said. "I see an old friend of my stepfather at the end of the hall." She couldn't tell him it was *actually* her stepfather. "I should speak to him. Could we meet across the street at the coffee house in fifteen minutes?"

She was lucky that Kelly had left right after the afternoon session. Kelly hated Rube.

Eileen and Rube went to the court house cafeteria to talk. Walking up the stairs, she remembered that he was the first person to be nice to her. In spite of what happened after, she could never forget that.

"Eileen, sweetheart," were his first words. He looked worried and anxious. "Maybe the whole thing was my fault," he said.

"Your fault. How could it be your fault?"

"Oh, I don't know." He patted her hand.

Rube stood still for a second. He was thinking of what the baby must have suffered during the three days the child had been alone with Effie and wondered whether he should go to Eileen's lawyer and tell her what had happened. "Eileen's mother, the grandmother of the baby," he saw himself telling the judge, "she was the one that looked after little Stevie during those three days."

He remembered how cold it had been when he was in Cornwall. The doctors thought the baby had been suffering from exposure for several days. Maybe it had started with Effie. When the trial opened, Effie went off to Vermont to stay with a cousin in a trailer near the border and told Rube to go to Cornwall in Ontario. She didn't want either of them to be around during the trial.

"I can't talk to you for very long," Eileen said. "I have a new boy-friend. He's an optometrist. You know? Sort of like an eye doctor? He's waiting for me. I'm divorcing Nick," she said. "It'll take another five or six months."

They finished their coffee and walked down to the main door on Notre Dame Street. He stood still for a moment and looked off into the distance before he said goodbye. "Eileen," he said. "I came here to tell you I'm sorry." He made no attempt to touch her the way he did in the past. "Sorry for everything."

TWENTY-FIVE

~

Nick Takes the Stand

MAGGIE RUSHED ACROSS the lobby of the Palais de Justice and up the escalators to the fifth floor. The city editor had asked her to work with a journalism student after her shift ended and it had made her late. When she opened the door of the courtroom, the place was so packed she had to squeeze into the back row next to one of the carrion crows. Nick was staring down at his knees and looked as though he had slept in his clothes.

He had been disappointed yesterday when she had said she couldn't meet him for supper in the square in front of the church. "You're really not free?" he'd asked her after the session. "No," she'd said. Every afternoon after the judge adjourned the court for the day, he asked her whether she could meet him in the usual spot. "I could bring some Chinese food. You liked that, didn't you?" When they met, usually she provided the picnic, but once he surprised her with Chinese spareribs.

She had made a point of seeing him only twice a week. She needed her sleep after her stint on the Rim all night followed by a whole day in court, but she was also struggling to keep the relationship strictly professional. She was frightened of her growing attachment to him. She always scheduled the meeting at Place d'Armes for eight o'clock, four hours before her midnight shift began, and said goodbye at ten so she'd have two hours to type up whatever he told her. The routine of gathering material for a story kept her emotions in check. She never took notes on the spot and worked from memory.

She had emphasized to Nick that their meetings were background for a magazine piece but after a while she stopped asking him direct questions. Often he said he was tired and didn't want to talk, but she knew he wanted to keep seeing her. "All my life I've had to answer questions," he'd said after a few meetings. "When you ask me all those questions, you remind me of my lawyer. I know I'm going to have to go on that witness stand and answer questions from both of them. First Anna, and after that, the bitch with the slitty eyes," which was how he referred to the Crown prosecutor.

The last time they had met, he had said, "Gee, it would be nice if you'd sit with me during the breaks." There were always many recesses every day during the trial. "Sometimes you act as though you hardly know me." It was how she fought to save her objectivity about the story, not to mention appearances.

Maggie watched as Nick's lawyer Anna Martelli leaned over and said something to him. She looked worried. The judge gave her a cue and she stood up. "Nicholas Mykonos will now take the witness stand," she said. Oh no! Maggie said to herself. She had known it would be soon but she had had no idea Nick would be on the stand today. She hadn't realized that Eileen's defence was over. Now that she didn't represent the *Tribune* any more, no one, not even the other reporters, thought she was important enough to be kept informed.

If she had known he was scheduled to testify, she would have tried to see him. Yesterday being Wednesday, she had looked after Moira's children while her cousin took an evening course, but she could have found a replacement.

Standing there now, waiting to be sworn in, Nick looked as shabby as one of the carrion crows. The leather jacket he was wearing was ripped and filthy and he hadn't shaved.

"Name?" the court clerk asked after he'd sworn on the Bible.

"Nicholas Stephanos Mykonos."

"Address?"

He paused. "I don't really have an address."

"Where did you sleep last night?" the judge asked.

"Last night?" Nick asked.

"That's what I said," the judge replied.

"Last night I, ah, slept in the square outside Notre Dame church. There's a flower stand there."

The square outside Notre Dame church! Had he gone there, hoping, somehow, that she'd pass by?

The judge frowned.

"It was nice out so I didn't go to the Salvation Army," he added.

Maggie was amazed he had admitted the Salvation Army was practically his address. He'd told her more than once he'd do almost anything not to sleep in "one of those places." He'd said he was sleeping at the house of a friend from one of the institutions he'd been in.

Anna Martelli started with a question the Crown prosecutor had asked Eileen. "I want you to tell the court what your reaction was when you saw the pictures of your dead baby."

The jury, Maggie thought, looked at him as though he was a liar. He took his time, looking first at the judge, then to the jury, and finally at the Crown prosecutor, focusing on her as though it were *her* question.

"My son never looked like that. Ever. You think we would have left him lying in his crib if he looked like that?" He was talking through his teeth. "No." He raised his voice. "We would have taken him to the hospital."

"Is it true that you would not allow Eileen to take the baby to the hospital?" Maître Martelli asked.

"It's true. I hate hospitals. I can't tell you why. I just do. They're like prisons." He was talking fast now. "I didn't want my son in no prison unless it was absolutely necessary.

"But naturally, if he was really sick. What do you think I am?" He spat the words at her. She was talking like the fuckin' Crown prosecutor. "If he was really sick, naturally we would have taken him to the hospital."

"Is it true or not?"

Nick looked confused. "Not true, I guess."

"You have heard Eileen talk about how you tied her up. Is that true?"

"Yes." He hung his head. "It happened once." There was a murmur throughout the court. Esther Sykes was sitting in front of Maggie. "Once!" she hissed.

Maggie put down her notebook. The night before, babysitting at her cousin Moira's, she had looked at a film on wife abuse that a friend from the church had recorded from an American television program. She had also found some literature on an organization that helps men who abuse their spouses or girlfriends. She learned that many abusive men block the remembrance of beating up their partners.

"Could you tell the court why?" Anna Martelli asked.

A pained look passed across Nick's face. Eileen stared at the floor. Maître Martelli waited.

"I don't remember," he finally said.

Anna Martelli glanced down at some papers in front of her.

"Nick," she said, her expression softening. This was the first time Maggie had seen any sign from her of sympathy towards him. "I want you to tell the court about the day your baby was born."

"The day my son was born?"

She nodded.

Nick looked over at Eileen who was holding her wedding band finger. "It was like it was the day *I* was born," he said softly. Eileen looked quickly at him and then lowered her eyes. "That was the first day in my whole life that, that . . ." He never took his eyes off Eileen. He opened his mouth to form another word but nothing came out.

"Could you speak up, please?" the judge said.

Maggie's hand tensed on the pen she was holding. Nick tried to speak, but all that came out was a small cry like an animal in a trap.

"Would you like to take a recess?" the judge asked.

"Yes. I think so," said Anna Martelli.

Nick's lawyer left the courtroom without saying a word and everyone filed out — the prosecutor, Eileen's lawyer, the press, the spectators, as though it were just a matter of routine. Maggie stood at the back. Nick was holding onto the witness box as though he were frozen there. Alone. Suddenly he covered his head with his arms and sobbed. Apart from the constable at the front, Nick and Maggie were the only two people left in the courtroom.

Maggie went quietly up the aisle and stood behind him. "Nick . . ." she called softly. He was grinding his face into the top of the witness box, his body shaking. She put her hand on his shoulder and he lifted his head and looked at her. "Oh." His head dropped to the side. "I was so afraid you weren't here. I, I was thinking about the bear." His eyes were bloodshot. "In the cemetery . . ."

"Nick," Maggie said. He looked sick, his face puffy, and his hair smelled rank. "Do you want to find a quiet place to talk? For just a few minutes?"

"Okay," he said. He was breathing quickly. Outside the courtroom, a huge crowd milled about.

"Ignore everyone," Maggie said. "We'll go outside for a few minutes away from this mob." Everyone watched as they walked down the corridor. She led him down the escalators, across the lobby, and outside to Notre Dame Street where they found an empty park bench.

Hunched over his knees, he stared down at the sidewalk for several minutes before he spoke. "All those jury people, even my lawyer. They all hate me. I can't talk to them. I can hardly talk to you. Even though . . ." he straightened up and searched her eyes. "Well, I was hoping, hoping that . . ."

Maggie put her hand on his arm. Containing her feelings of tenderness for him was becoming more and more difficult. "Do you want to tell me what happened last night?"

He gazed out into the rush of traffic on the street. "I did finally sleep in the flower shed," he said. "I hung around the square, and then I kept thinking of Eileen and the night we got married. I went to a drug store and grabbed some pills. No one noticed. I went down to that shed on the dock."

He looked up at Maggie. "Where you saw me that time?" He waited a few seconds. "I made myself swallow them. I stood at the edge of the dock. I thought they'd knock me out, and I would just fall in and drown.

"From the first day I met Eileen I dreamed of having a son of my own." He was having trouble talking. "But the pills didn't work. I was sick. I had this awful headache." He held his head. "I still have it. I looked up and saw the bridge. The Jacques Cartier Bridge. It's the one Eileen and I walked over one time after La Ronde. It looked close," he said. "I wanted to jump off it."

Maggie saw herself at the railing of the Jacques Cartier Bridge looking down into the fast flowing current and she shut her eyes. Next to him, Nick felt Maggie shiver. He wanted to hold her close to him, but waited until she was still. He touched her hand. It was ice-cold. "Maggie?" he said, "you okay?" She looked strange. "I'm fine," she said slowly. "Just keep talking."

He paused for a moment before going on. "I ah, I tried old Hannah, but there was no answer." Old Hannah was a Jewish lady who lived close to the Green Pasture Mission. After the inquest, when he was on the street, she had let him sleep a few nights on her back balcony. She loved flowers and told him she wanted a balcony flower box, so one night he went up to some gardens in Westmount and dug up the most beautiful flowers he could find and planted them in a long cardboard box.

"I went back to the square," he continued. "I thought you might be there. Finally," he sighed, "finally, I crawled into the little shack. That's where I slept."

Maggie said nothing for several minutes. She wondered if there was a way for the court to catch a glimpse of the softer and needier Nick.

"Nick," Maggie said. There was urgency in her voice. "The jury should hear what you told me. Let me tell your lawyer what happened. On the witness stand, let her ask you questions. Do you think you could forget everyone in the courtroom and just imagine you're telling *me* the story?"

She spoke quickly. "All the jury wants to know is that you cared about your baby, that no matter what happened, no matter what you did, you cared. C'mon," and she grabbed his hand. "Everyone'll wonder where you are."

Anna Martelli was waiting for the two of them right outside the courtroom, and she didn't look pleased. "Where the hell've you been," she said. The corridor was empty.

"There's something I must tell you," Maggie said quickly, "something I think the jury should hear. Last night he went to a drug store, bought a pack of drugs, and went down to the dock. He swallowed them, hoping that would be the end. He wanted a quick way to drown." Her voice caught on the word drown. "Ask him what *really* happened last night.

"You know that flower kiosk he mentioned? In Place d'Armes? In front of Notre Dame church?" Maître Martelli appeared skeptical, even irritated. Nick stood to the side, looking helpless. "That's close to the spot where he got married. A minister from the travelling bus for homeless kids married Nick and Eileen right outside the bus last Christmas Eve. The place has all sorts of memories."

There was something offensive about talking about Nick in front of him, as though he were an object to be pushed around in a game, but Maggie felt she had no choice. Over the loudspeaker, the court clerk was calling them into the courtroom.

"Maître Anna Martelli. Monsieur Nicholas Mykonos."

"The suicide attempt doesn't sound plausible," Maître Martelli said briskly. "The jury'll think it was concocted as a bid for sympathy."

"The way he told me, I think it's true," Maggie protested. Maître Martelli took Nick aside. "Just answer the questions I put to you, okay? I asked you how you felt the day your baby was born. Try to answer it. All right?"

Back on the stand, Nick answered the questions from his lawyer and later from the Crown prosecutor like a machine responding to another machine, without the least emotion.

When the lawyer asked him again how he felt the day the baby was born, he said, "I was happy," but it sounded dead. His lawyer never asked about the night before. After a few more questions about the day Eileen gave birth, she gave up.

"One last question," she said. "Did you ever get a visit from a public health nurse?"

"No," Nick said. "At least not when I was home."

"You're sure about that?"

"Positive," he said. "I never knew we were supposed to get visits from a public health nurse."

"Your witness," Maître Martelli said, and looked over at the Crown prosecutor.

"The night before the baby died, did you open the window over his crib?" the prosecutor asked.

"Yes, I did," he replied. "The apartment was hot."

"Why did you leave the baby alone?"

"I couldn't see a problem. He was sleeping."

"And when the storm came up?"

"I sort of forgot I'd opened the window," he said.

A disgusted murmur went through the court. "You sort of forgot that you'd opened the window?" she repeated.

"And when you came home?" she went on. "Did you and Eileen sort of forget to feed him?"

"He was quiet. Sleeping. We just went to sleep."

"I see. You just went to sleep." She paused. "Tell me. Did you and Eileen leave the baby alone on other occasions?"

"Yes."

"Why?"

"Like I said, I didn't think there was a problem. Usually he was sleeping."

"Where were you, exactly, during the three days before the baby died?"

"At The Four Winds Hotel."

"And where was the baby?"

Nick ground his teeth for a second as he thought of how Eileen had lied to the prosecutor about how they had had Stevie with them at the hotel. They should have been able to talk about that *together* in advance.

He looked over at Eileen, her eyes fixed to the floor as though she wasn't listening. Her face was white. He wondered if the lie had something to do with Rube. Maybe she didn't want anyone to know that Rube had looked after the baby. He took a deep breath. No matter what her reasons, he had to admit it would make both of them look better if he said they had taken Stevie with them to the hotel.

"We had him with us at the Four Winds," he finally said. "It was the anniversary of when we first met, and we wanted to include our baby in it as well." He wished now that they really *had* taken Stevie with them to the hotel. Eileen looked up at him, relieved, and he thought, grateful.

After the judge adjourned the court, Maggie waited until everyone except Nick cleared out of the courtroom. He sat for a long time in the box for the accused. She knew he hated going down the long corridor through the hostile crowd.

"Tonight?" she asked. There was no way she'd let him spend the evening all by himself. He nodded, and she quickly left the courtroom.

TWENTY-SIX

~

Spanakopita and Retsina
in the Square

SHAKEN BY EVERYTHING that had happened that day, Maggie stared out into the middle of the square waiting for Nick to show up. He was fifteen minutes late. She hoped nothing had happened to him. She looked into the bags of Greek hors d'oeuvres she'd picked up specially for him at a café on Park Avenue. The last time they'd met he'd talked about the first time he'd had Greek food on the mountain with the family from Naxos. The grannie he'd met there had once made him moussaka. He said she'd always called him *Nickakimu,* meaning my little Nicky in Greek. That afternoon, after the case adjourned, she'd found a Greek cookbook in a second-hand book store. One day she'd make a moussaka herself and bring it to him. She lay back against the bench. She'd have to do it quickly. The trial would soon be over.

She looked up at the spires of Notre Dame Basilica and thought of Michael and Brother St. John and their ministry with the neediest of people. They believed in building a community where everyone would have a chance. They were, perhaps, the only *real* Christians she knew. What she'd learned from them seemed far from her experience at St. Ninian's up on the hill where getting ahead and following the rules seemed to be the key virtues.

A few minutes later, she heard steps on the stones directly behind her and felt a warm breeze on her neck. "Hi," Nick said, and he walked around to the front of the bench. He had a grin on his face as though he had succeeded in playing a joke on her. In new black jeans and a fresh blue shirt, he moved lightly from one foot to another. "Watch," he said, and he did a running leap over one of the benches and then a back-flip as though he were on a trampoline.

After what had happened that day in court, Maggie was amazed at his sudden burst of energy. "Wow," she said. "Where did you learn that?"

"The last school I was in. Before I left the Evans in Pierrefonds." He sat down next to her and poked her arm gently with his elbow. His curly shoulder-length hair smelled fresh. "Were you sleeping?"

"Of course not."

"You were. And I woke you up. Didn't I?" Just knowing she'd been there for him that day in the courtroom — in front of everyone — had pulled him out of the migraine he'd been in. He wanted to entertain her, make her stop being so serious. He was in the mood to forget everything and have fun.

"Hey," she said. "You look really nice." With his wide shoulders and slim hips, he really was handsome. This was the first time she'd seen the black jeans.

"You think so?" That afternoon, after the trial, he had lifted them from a discount store on St. Catherine Street when no one was looking. He had seen himself reflected in a store mirror and was shocked at how scruffy he looked in the jeans one of the Salvation Army guys had given him. Afterwards, to forget about the trial, and everything that had happened to him that morning on the witness stand, he had gone to Dorchester Square and smoked up. He was still feeling the effects.

"You know," he said. "You've never told me anything about your life. What do you do on weekends?" He wondered how old she was and whether she had a boyfriend.

"Me . . . ? Oh, work mostly. And I help my father at the church. He's a minister." She realized there wasn't much to say about her personal life. Except for the travelling she sometimes did with her folk dance group and some visits to New York to see her aunt, her private life was almost non-existent. Nick was in trouble, but unlike her, he jumped right into life.

For a while, the two of them sat in silence. "I was just thinking," she said. "The trial may be over soon, and . . ." She put her hands inside the pockets of her navy blue blazer and pulled at the insides with her fingers.

Nick stiffened. "They're gonna find me guilty, eh? Is that what you're trying to say? I'm ready," he said. "If they say guilty, I have my cyanide."

"Are you trying to scare me?" She gave him a quick glance. "You're not *really* going to do something like that, are you?"

"Calm down," he smiled and stretched out his legs. "I was only kidding." He could always get a rise out of her. "I don't have any, but I know where to get some." Two nights ago he had bought some from Teddy but he wasn't going to tell her that. He put his hand on her shoulder. "You were trying to tell me something."

She straightened up. "Look. In case things happen fast. There's something I should tell you. It isn't true that they took me off your trial because they wanted to put me on a special project."

"Oh. Why then?"

"It's hard to explain. I told them I'd done the wrong thing right from the beginning. They wanted me to hype up everything. You know what I mean? They got mad. I just wanted you to know."

Nick thought of the inquest story she'd done and how she had got it all wrong, but she'd been so nice to him, he didn't want to tell her that. It was too painful to read about himself in the papers, so when the trial started he had tried to avoid them, but he knew that the *Tribune* had been the first to run those pictures of his son on the front page.

Maggie glanced at him, and then over at the steps leading up to the church. The scene Nick had painted of his wedding on the church steps in front of the bus for street kids flashed up at her. There was a lot more to say, but she couldn't tell him that she, more than anyone, had made him look like a brute.

"So they took me off it," she went on after a few minutes, "and put the Smith-Jones woman on the story. The bosses told her what they wanted and she's doing it. What I'll do for the magazine piece will be different."

"So you really *don't* think I'm a monster?"

"No."

Nick squeezed his elbows in tight to his waist. He had to tell her now. She was his only ally, but she had to know. If she could still accept him after he told her what he was *really* like, then maybe he'd feel he could trust her.

"Remember right after Carmen testified? That n-night. It was when you br-brought the pizza." He was speaking slowly, trying to force the words out. "I told you there was a reason why I tied up Eileen.

"Because," he had to control his voice, "I *did* tie up Eileen, and I *did* lock her in the closet, and I *did* beat her. When Anna asked me today why, I couldn't tell her." His eyes were wet.

He hung his head. "I'll never stop loving Eileen, and I loved the baby too. The reason isn't a reason. It's no fuckin' reason," and he beat his head with his fist. He looked up into the sky. "Oh God." The breath went out of him and he collapsed over his knees.

Her heart was thumping. She knelt down on the ground in front of him and held his head in her hands. "Nick, oh, Nick, Nick." His breath felt warm on her neck. After a few minutes, he raised his head and she sat back on the bench next to him. "If you can talk it out," she whispered, "maybe it will be better."

"You're gonna hate me," he said.

"No, I won't." She caressed his hand. "Why don't you eat a little?

I brought you something special." She took stuffed vine leaves, black olives and a small cheese pie from a paper bag and placed them in a napkin on his lap.

He gazed down at the food and then up at her. Even though the light was dim, she could see the flashing blue of his eyes. "Spanako-pita," he said. "Just like I used to have with my *yiayia*. You got them specially for me?"

"There's more." Maggie spread some taramasalata and eggplant salad on a slice of Greek bread and handed it to him. Then she pulled out a half bottle of retsina. "Here." He took a few gulps from the bottle but didn't touch the spread of food on his knee.

"C'mon. When did you last eat?"

"Last night."

"Last night?" She remembered about the drugs. "You aren't still feeling sick are you?"

He shook his head and rocked back and forth on his knees. "How come you're so nice to me?"

Maggie said nothing. She didn't know why, but no matter what he'd done, no matter what he was going to tell her, she would still care for him.

She looked up at Notre Dame church and thought of the chapel service Michael ran for the street kids in the abandoned bar. He always ended with First Corinthians 13. "Though I have the gift of prophecy, and understand all mysteries, and all knowledge, and though I have all faith, so that I could remove mountains, and have not love, I am nothing."

"Aren't you going to eat, too?" Nick asked.

She fished into the paper bag and drew out a spanakopita just to keep him company.

"Here," Nick said, "have some wine to go with it."

"I should get out a cup."

"You can drink straight from the bottle the way I did." He handed her the bottle and steadied it for her as she took a few sips.

Slowly, savouring each item, Nick ate the hors d'oeuvres in his lap.

When he was finished he sat with his fingers locked in front of him. "You know," he said, "no one except you thinks I'm worth a damn. Well, maybe Danny too, but that's all."

"Tell me about your foster brother," Maggie said.

"Danny's in India now on a special engineering project. It's part of his university program, and then he's going to take a job there. That's why he's not at the trial.

"My lawyer called Pop Evans because she wanted Danny to testify. I told her Danny was away for good, but she wouldn't listen. She told me Pop said I had bad genes."

Nick turned to Maggie to get her reaction. "She said Pop told Danny and Luke that Mum would have been upset if they came to the trial. I told you about Luke, didn't I?" Maggie nodded.

"Pop, I think, was jealous." Nick thought of the hours Mum had spent with him after school at the piano when he was in grade seven rehearsing his part in the choir. "Pop hated all the attention Mum gave me."

Nick fished into his back pocket and took out a joint. "You don't mind, do you?" He lit it and inhaled deeply. "You want a toke?" he asked.

"No. But go ahead."

"I've got to tell you why I hit her." He shut his eyes. "Oh God, I can still remember that day," he said with such a sigh of despair Maggie didn't know whether she'd be able to endure what he had to tell her.

"I knew Eileen had been talking to Carmen. I saw that thing in her eyes, that thing that told me she wanted to leave. But I can't blame Carmen, because I saw that look early on with Eileen. Guys were always pushing her around. First her stepfather, and then, well, this isn't something she wants anyone to know, but when I met her, she was working the streets. You know what I mean?"

He took another toke, and then another until the weed started taking effect. "I, I told her that I saw it in her eyes, that I knew she was going to leave me." His voice rose. "I told her that wherever she went

I'd hunt her down. If she ever left me I'd find her, and I'd, I'd . . ."

He felt Maggie recoil from him. He had to collect himself. After a few seconds, he sat up and began talking as though he were alone. "I threw her against the wall of the living room. And then I shook her . . . like I think I did the . . ." He was speaking so softly Maggie didn't hear the last few words. She put her hand on his wrist.

"When Eileen opened her eyes," he said quietly, "that look was still there." He twisted his body on the bench. "She was torturing me on purpose. She *knew* what she was doing to me. I wanted to scratch out her eyes. I wanted to burn off all her hair. I wanted to waste her. She knew she was beautiful. I wanted to take it away from her."

He was panting for breath. Maggie sat as still as she could. Afraid. He bent back and stared up into the sky. "Eileen has the most beautiful angel hair in the world. I wanted to make her ugly," he whispered, "make her ugly forever, so that no one else would want her, and she'd be mine always, and I'd never have to worry about her leaving, because she'd have nowhere else to go."

Maggie felt overcome with jealousy of Eileen. Nick reminded her of Heathcliff in *Wuthering Heights*. No one had ever felt such passion for *her*. She stared at the flower stand in the corner of the square and tried to suppress her feelings.

"But I couldn't make her ugly," Nick said softly. He rocked back and forth. "My beautiful Eileen, my beautiful Eileen of the jade rings, the jade rings she never takes off, because," he hesitated a moment, "she still loves me. I know that. Otherwise she'd take those rings off." He stopped talking for a few minutes and then swung around. "When I did those awful things, I was out of control." He dug his fists into his thighs. "Possessed. Afterwards, I was so sorry, oh my God, I was sorry."

He wanted to throw himself into Maggie's arms and cry. "I had to keep her, because I needed her so bad. I hate saying all this. How could I tell that to the judge and the jury and all those people in the court? Can you imagine how I needed her so bad?"

"Yes," Maggie replied.

"I know what you're going to say, because Danny told me, and so did this friend of mine. I had one friend when we were living on Paros Street. Torchy. He's in the joint. The pigs caught him selling coke. I can just hear what you want to say. It was the perfect way to lose her. All the time I was doing it, I knew that." He banged his fist down hard on the bench and shrieked out into the square. "You think I didn't know that?

"I'm scaring you, aren't I? I scare everyone. Even when I'm on the subway, I can see that I scare people. Women don't want to sit next to me. It's as though the monster is staring right out of my eyes." There was a short silence. "That's why I lose everyone. Everyone, everyone, everyone," he screamed out at the dark.

Maggie put her hand on his knee. "I'm okay. I'm not scared," she said, even though she was.

"I knew I might lose her," he said, trying to keep his voice down. "But I did it anyway. I was crazy. Do you understand? I'll die if you don't understand. I told Eileen — well, not quite like I'm telling you — but she didn't understand. It scared her. You're the first person I've told all this to. I had this fire inside me, this fire I couldn't put out." He dropped his head to the side.

"You know," he hesitated, "I used to worry that my son wanted to leave me too. I had this dream. Stevie was leaning out of the baby carriage telling everyone on the street he wanted a new daddy, that he didn't want me. And then I dreamt that a social worker from the hospital came in the middle of the night and took him away.

"Sometimes, when he snuggled into my neck and I felt his lips on me, I imagined he was my real mother, my blood mother, like I was born from." He paused. "But when he cried, I used to get mad. So mad."

Nick panted like a small child who'd been sobbing and couldn't get his breath. After a few minutes he relaxed. "But when my son held me tight, I thought God was on my side. That finally, finally, he'd given me everything he'd taken away when my mother left me on the bus."

"What! You were left on a bus?" What a great detail to include in a story, Maggie thought, and then hated herself for thinking it. "When?" she couldn't refrain from asking. "How old were you?"

"When I was six weeks old, my mother left me on the bus. The bus from Quebec City to Montreal. She left a note on my diaper saying my name was Nicholas Stephanos Mykonos. The bus driver brought me to a hospital. After that it was all foster homes."

"How come that hasn't come up in the trial?" Maggie asked. "Did you tell your lawyer you were left on a bus?"

"I told her my mother died, just like I told you, even though she's probably around somewhere. My real blood mother must know about the trial. If she's alive, how could she not know? And my father. Well, I think he's in Greece."

Nick rolled up his sleeve and showed Maggie his birthmark. "You see this," he said. "The *yiayia* told me it means I come from this special Greek family that fought against the Turks.

"I tried to tell my lawyer everything, but she hates me. She didn't want to take my case. I had a guy at Legal Aid that I was just starting to get along with. He was a bit older than me, maybe twenty-five, but a week before the trial they told me he had to go into the hospital for an operation. That's when Anna took over.

"Today in court, when she asked me why I beat up Eileen, she looked at me the same way as those broads who hang around Eileen. That's why I couldn't answer. She told me she would get a psychiatrist to speak to me, look at all the records, and testify, but nothing's ever happened.

"All the women — the Crown and Eileen's lawyer, the reporters, the dames on the jury. Even my own lawyer. They all think everything's my fault. I don't know what to think about the judge. Maybe he's afraid of the women too."

Maggie's face felt flushed. From her knees a wave of heat rose up through her body and she could feel sweat stinging the back of her neck.

"You don't think I have bad genes, do you?"

"No, Nick. There's no such thing."

"And you don't hate me?"

"Of course not."

"I didn't know whether you'd understand."

"I do," Maggie said. He gently massaged her hand and she felt comforted by it. "More than you can imagine." Through her blouse she could hear the sound of her heart beating. Something tight and constricted within her was opening up.

They sat quietly. Nick was tearing a hole in an armour of loneliness that had been with her for twenty years. Years ago at the bar-chapel Michael ran for street kids in St. Henri, she had sometimes played "Amazing Grace" on the pump organ at the end of each service. Now for the first time, the words of the hymn meant something to her.

Off in the distance, they heard music from the organ in the church and Nick took her elbow and guided her toward it. In a daze — confused about what was happening to her — she walked with him across the square. Approaching the church, she tripped, and the world around her blackened. Nick gathered her up in his arms and carried her up the steps of the Basilica. For a few moments, as she lay cradled against him in the dark, his arms securely around her, she imagined herself as Catherine with Heathcliff on the moors. At the church doors Nick waited; then, like a dancer in a ballet, he lowered her to the ground. She glanced at him, and a shared look of mutual knowing passed between them. Inside the church, listening to the music, they leaned together against a pillar at the back and she felt the heat of his body against her. The music ended and the church emptied. Except for a stand of burning candles, the church was dark. Nick took her hand, chose a candle, lit it, and lifted it to Maggie's face. Then he leaned forward, and with her hand in his, placed it in the candle holder.

TWENTY-SEVEN

~⌒

Magdalena

IT WAS ONE IN the morning and Maggie was on the Rim trying to concentrate on her copy-editing. Two mornings before, after her shift ended, her dentist had pulled a tooth and right after her mouth had gone into a slow burn. This was the first extraction she had ever had. Painkillers hadn't helped and she was feeling nauseated. Anxiety around Nick and the trial, she thought, was wearing her down. She wasn't used to feeling sick. The last time she remembered having anything more than a mild case of flu was when she was eight and a raging fever had kept her in bed for a week. Her father hadn't been sympathetic. "All I need," he'd said, "is two sick women." Her mother had suffered from Hodgkin's Disease.

By that time, Maggie was already making most of the meals. During those gloomy days when her mother was often in bed, her father made her mother's lunch when she was at school, but Maggie left everything ready, usually a can of Campbell's soup, bread, sliced

cheese and apple sauce. Ever since she had become involved with
Nick, she found herself reliving more and more painful memories
from her childhood.

She looked across at the long table facing her where Norrie, Elkins
and Moulder were working at their terminals. A news agency tele-
printer was clattering away, two TVs at different stations were on, and
beyond them the police radio shouted. She'd been working long
enough at a newspaper to take these background noises for granted,
but now they reverberated in her head. She was easily rattled. Her
relationship with Nick now preoccupied her to the point where she
was losing control of some of the routine aspects of her life. The pre-
vious week, she had run out of gas at a busy intersection downtown.

She felt the contours of her swollen cheek and went back to the
story she was editing, but the pain persisted, and she began to cough.
"My God! Maggie," Foxy said. "Your cheek looks like a balloon. If I
didn't know you, I'd wonder if someone hadn't punched you out."

Around two o'clock in the women's washroom she coughed up
green phlegm. Her face was blotchy red like a bag lady who hung
around the subway station near the court house. Splashing water on
her face didn't help. She wound the handle on the paper towel
machine round and round but nothing came out. Her face was dripping. She pulled the end of her blouse out of her skirt and swabbed
her face.

When she got back to her terminal in the newsroom, Foxy was on
the phone placing bets. He always placed his bets on baseball games
after two-thirty in the morning when there was a lull in the editing
and the chief copy editor took a coffee break. After he got off the
phone he gave her a worried look.

"Gee, Maggie. You look as though you've got a terrible fever." He
put his hand on her forehead. It felt like a rough bear paw on her
skin. She liked Foxy, but there was something animal in his touch.
"My God," he said. "You could fry an egg on your forehead. You
were in the washroom a long time. You been smoking up or something?" He looked over at Roddie on the police desk.

Roddie had served his apprenticeship at the paper by being an office boy and supplying grass or hash to recreational drug users in the newsroom. He and one of the other office boys, Larry, who eventually became a Hare Krishna and shaved his head, used to go into Cyril Norgate's office late on Friday afternoons when they knew "Pop Eye" as they called him was out for a drinking lunch and wouldn't be back. They would shut the door, throw their feet up on his desk, and pop pills. Both had a history of trafficking. When Roddie was in grade eleven, he had been the chief drug supplier in one of the West Island high schools.

"I have *not* been smoking up," Maggie said. "Don't be smart."

"You were taking a long time to answer." Foxy believed anyone who was young in the sixties used grass or hash, not to mention a whole lot of volatile concoctions that were getting publicity.

Speaking of substance abuse, she felt like saying, but didn't. Gin, after all, was the reason Foxy was on the Rim, and not in the sports department covering baseball.

"I think we should take your temperature," Foxy said, and he went off to a supplies room in the wing where the photographers developed film. He found a medical kit and brought back a thermometer.

"Here." She put the thermometer in her mouth and after a couple of minutes handed it to him. She stood up to go to the washroom. "Holy moley," said Foxy, "104 degrees." Her head swam. She leaned forward against the desk, grabbed the edge of the work table and tried to steady herself, but it was no use and she collapsed.

She came to on the floor of the elevator where Foxy kneeled over her, his breath heavy with the smell of cigarettes and gin. As the elevator doors opened, he hauled her to her feet, lifted her up around the waist and carried her to the escalator that went down to St. Antoine Street.

Foxy drank more than he ate, which made her think he couldn't lift anything, but he'd picked her up as though she were a small cat. An amateur prize fighter in his day, he still played baseball even though he was over sixty years old. "If you ever want to go to the

Expos," he'd told her, "I can take you for free." In the summer, he often took in a game and then came straight from the stadium to work. She felt sorry for him because he really wanted to write a sports column.

"You okay?" Foxy asked when they got down to the street level. He still had his arm around her waist. She felt too weak to walk by herself. "What's happening?" she asked.

"I'm taking you to the General in my car. You're shaking and going hot and cold. It isn't normal. I didn't want to call an ambulance. They might take you to St. Luc." The St. Luc hospital, situated close to many of the shelters for homeless, was where the emergency room was always overcrowded with transients, drunks and people who picked fights. It was the closest hospital to the *Tribune*.

Foxy left her in the emergency room of the General and the last thing she remembered him saying was, "I'll let your father know you're here." She was only half-conscious when she heard it, otherwise she might have told him to tell no one except her friend Michael. She didn't want to frighten her father.

In a corridor beyond the reception room, she sat waiting to see a doctor. Several patients were in the corridor. One was a girl in her twenties with scratches on her face. She was holding her hand in pain. "He's broken two of your fingers," said a woman next to her. "This time you should lay charges." A man on a stretcher who looked like an Inuit had two black eyes.

Maybe she had pneumonia. A sore mouth couldn't give her fever and chills like this. She hoped they would give her a quick shot of something so she could take a taxi and go home to sleep. It was four in the morning. By nine o'clock, she wanted to be at the court house.

The day before, Maggie had overheard the Crown prosecutor say she would be summing-up today. The defence would do the same and then the judge would give the jury guidelines in preparation for deliberation on the verdict. She had told Nick that no matter what, she'd see him at eight that night in Place d'Armes. Surely they could give her something so she'd be well enough to leave the hospital.

"Miss MacKinnan," a doctor called out, and she went forward.

"I think I might have pneumonia," she told him. "I've been coughing up green stuff and running a high fever." The doctor ordered an X-Ray and after some more waiting in the corridor an orderly wheeled her off to another floor. When she came back, a nurse told her to lie on a cot in an examining room.

"Maggie MacKinnan? From the *Tribune*?" the doctor asked.

"Yes," she said.

"Haven't seen your stuff for a while. Good series you did on wife and child abuse." He took out a little wooden stick and asked her to open her mouth.

"Nasty infection you have there."

"I had a tooth out two days ago. It was my first."

"I see. The X-Ray shows you have pneumonia." He took out his stethoscope and listened to her heart. He looked concerned. "You're aware you have a heart murmur?"

"No."

"Not a big heart murmur, but a murmur just the same. It's not something I want you to worry about. Ever had rheumatic fever?"

"Rheumatic fever? No." He looked at her closely. "Not that I'm aware of."

"Think back. As a child, do you remember ever having a really bad fever?"

"Yes . . . When I was eight I was in bed for a week."

"Do you know if you're allergic to penicillin?"

"No. I don't think so. Why?"

He called a nurse. "We want to put you on an intravenous penicillin treatment," he said. "You have a bad gum infection, and now pneumonia. The infection went from your mouth to your lungs. If we're not careful it could go to your heart." He took her elbow and guided her to a ward with four beds. "You'll be here for at least two days, then at home for a week, resting."

A nurse gave Maggie consent forms to sign and the doctor left the room, but as Maggie put on a hospital gown, she heard him talking outside the door. "She's battling an infection of the heart. Infectious endocarditis," he said.

"Can I make a phone call?" Maggie asked the nurse who was working on the intravenous hookup. "It's quite important." She wanted to ask Michael to go to Place d'Armes that night and tell Nick to come to the hospital.

"No," the nurse said. "Right now we have to hook you up. We're going to move you to a ward upstairs. You can make a phone call from there."

It was five in the morning before she was settled in her ward where she kept slipping in and out of consciousness. In a lucid moment, she grabbed the phone and called Michael's number at the refugee centre.

"Michael? It's Maggie. Oh. I'm so glad to hear your voice. Look. It's kind of an emergency. I'm in the hospital, with an IV in my arm, but I'm okay. Don't worry. They caught whatever it was. A guy from the paper brought me here. Look." She hesitated a moment. "Could you go to Place d'Armes tonight at eight o'clock and, ah, give a message to . . ."

Michael interrupted. "Maggie, I'd do it, but I have a big meeting tonight."

"Well then, could you, ah, go to the Palais de Justice this morning around twelve? When the trial breaks for lunch? I want you to speak to Nicholas Mykonos. Could you bring him to the hospital, say, around five, before your meeting? If you can't make it," she rushed on, not wanting to explain too much, "just send him here on his own.

"I'm on the eleventh floor at the General. I've got to do these interviews now. The trial's coming to an end." She felt exhausted from the conversation and fell back against the pillow. "Can you hear me, Michael?" A nurse came in with a glass of water and some pills. "Yes, Maggie," he said. "You can count on me."

∿

Like a Russian orchestra conductor who did not want to be kept waiting, Maggie's father swept into the room and stood at the end of her bed. "You all right, Magdalena?" Maggie tried to prop herself on her elbows. "Yes," she said. The clock on the wall moved into focus — five o'clock — just about the time Michael might show up with Nick.

Her father rattled the chain of his pocket watch and pulled on his clerical collar. "I know you were so looking forward to the opera." He had tickets coming up for *La Traviata,* the opera he fell in love with the summer he spent in Venice. They had listened together to his recording of Maria Callas singing Violetta at La Scala when she was at the top of her form and before she met Onassis.

She lay back against her pillow and tried not to lose her concentration. Her father kept rattling the chain of his watch and Maggie thought of the sad note her dying mother had written to her Aunt Philana about the Italian Magdalena. "Eli had really wanted to marry this beautiful Venetian woman," her mother had written her aunt, "but she was Catholic and probably too wild to put up with being a minister's wife." Maggie had to put her mother out of her mind. She was still feeling feverish. If Michael and Nick arrived, her father would feel like a complete stranger and might do something rash. He knew who Michael was and couldn't understand why she was friendly with a rabble-rousing minister from a rival church who wore jeans and a ponytail.

He drew himself up and looked at her the way he used to look at her mother, as though it were her fault she was in bed. Sickness terrified him. "I suppose you've been burning the candle at both ends," he said.

"No," she said. "Remember that fever I had when I was in grade three?" Behind his rimless glasses there was no flicker of remembrance. "It was rheumatic fever." She hadn't the energy to tell him about the murmur, the tooth, the pneumonia, and the possible heart infection.

While he gazed out the window she shredded a piece of kleenex she was holding. Even if he asked her to, she wasn't going back to that dark and musty manse when she got out of the hospital. Like always, she'd end up playing housekeeper. From as far back as she could remember, he looked forward to breakfast at eight and tea at four-thirty. "Eugenia," he'd call over the bannister. When her mother hadn't been able to get out of bed, he had asked for Maggie. He had always pretended that nothing was wrong, that the household was absolutely normal.

"I'm feeling awfully tired," she said, pretending to doze.

"I'll read a little," he said, and he pulled out the score for "He, Watching Over Jerusalem" from *Elijah,* the Mendelssohn oratorio he so loved. "I hope the choir will sing this for the Christmas concert," he said.

When he was safely into the music, she pulled open a drawer next to her bed, and searched for her brush, lipstick, and perfume. She didn't want to look bedraggled when Michael and Nick came. The pins in her hair had fallen out. She brushed her hair, fluffed it as much as she could, and let it fall in large curls around her shoulders.

She looked at herself in her mirror. Surprisingly good. She had never worn it down, mostly because when she was a teenager neither her mother nor her father thought it looked right for a minister's daughter. The few times she had ever tried it, when she was living with her aunt in New York and studying journalism at Columbia University, she thought it detracted too much from her look as a serious journalist.

~

A half hour later, the door opened and Nick and Michael walked in. Nick brightened as soon as he saw her. She could tell he liked her hair. Michael was wearing his earring and Nick had on his tattered black leather jacket. Her father put down the score, stood up and looked at them as though they had the wrong room. He glanced quickly at her. In the half hour he'd been reading the score, she'd transformed herself, and he looked puzzled.

"This is Michael," Maggie said brightly to her father. "You remember Michael, don't you Father?"

"Yes, yes," he said looking uneasy.

Michael patted Maggie's arm. "I've got my meeting, and then first thing in the morning I have a plane to catch for Guatemala," he said.

"Things have been pretty rough, eh?" Michael said to Nick. "If you want to stay tonight at our refugee centre just call me or Brother Johno," he said and gave him a card.

"Take care of yourself," he said to Maggie, and he kissed her on the cheek and left.

"And this is Nicholas Stephanos," Maggie said, making sure not to give his last name. Her father would be sure to identify the name Mykonos. She hoped he didn't recognize Nick's face.

Nick stared at his feet. "My father," she said, nodding at him, and then at Nick. She almost forget to mention his title. "Reverend MacKinnan," she added.

"Father," she said. "I have some work I have to do. I'm doing some interviews with Nicholas for a special magazine piece. He's going out of town soon," she said. Why had she said *that*? It was like a premonition he'd be convicted and sent to the penitentiary.

"Work?" He looked at her as though she belonged to him. He had never seen her with her hair down, she realized, not since she was a small child. "Work, Magdalena?"

Nick's eyes widened when her father called her Magdalena. "Yes," she said. "Have you forgotten? I'm a reporter." Some day, if she got a chance, she'd change her byline to Catherine.

"You have to work *now*? Just a few hours ago, didn't you faint in the office? You had to be carried in here." Oh no. Foxy had told him everything. Nick looked anxious and she tried to give him a reassuring smile.

"Look," she said. "I think you should come back later." She couldn't cope with both Nick and her father. "Don't you have an elders meeting tonight? Come back later, after your meeting." She knew he'd never come back. The elders meeting went until eleven o'clock and always tired him. "Or better still, call me. I think that'd be best." Her father went out into the hall without saying a word.

"Nick," she said. "Don't worry about him. In a few minutes, he'll be gone." The patients in the other beds were sitting up straight, watching. Maggie could feel her fever mounting. She lay back against the pillow and turned her head from side to side.

"Are you going to be okay?" Nick asked. "I wouldn't have come. Hospitals give me the creeps. But I thought I might never see you again." Maggie was silent. "The jury is already meeting. Everything finished this afternoon. When I didn't see you this morning, I . . ."

A nurse walked in. "You all right, Miss MacKinnan?"

"Oh yes." Nick turned around and the nurse looked at him as though he were a Hell's Angel. Probably because of the jacket. "I'm fine," she said. "If I need anything I'll ring."

"It's like prison in here," Maggie said to Nick. "They want to control everything. This tube," she said, tapping her left hand. "It's how they tie you down, keep you from moving."

"You won't be in here for long, will you?" Nick asked. The smell of the hospital was triggering bad memories.

"Don't worry. I won't die."

"What's wrong?"

"Some kind of heart infection. And pneumonia. I have pneumonia."

"Pneumonia?" Nick quivered. His son had died of pneumonia and that's what he'd had when his mother left him on the bus.

He pulled a chair up close to the bed and looked into her eyes. "We'll never be able to meet in Place d'Armes again." By tomorrow night he was sure he would be in Villemont waiting to be sentenced. Guys committed suicide to get out of that joint. "It's all over."

Maggie pulled at the covers on the bed. Her face felt on fire. Everything around her swam. She didn't want to think about what might await him in prison.

Nick rummaged in his back pocket. "I wish I could smoke a joint." He stood up and paced up and down. She put out her hand. "Don't. They'll smell it and throw you out."

"You know the worst thing about today?" He sat down and

grabbed her hand. "In court, Eileen wasn't wearing her jade rings. She put her hands up to her face so the jury could see she was really finished with me. Finished." He was quiet for a few minutes. "Everyone feels sorry for Eileen," he said. "Out in the corridor, all those women put their arms around her."

"Nurse!" A woman in another bed was frantically pulling on the call-cord. Nick turned around almost by instinct, sure the woman was calling because she wanted to get rid of him.

"Just forget about the other patients. Imagine they're not here," Maggie said.

Outside the door of her room Maggie could hear her father's voice. "Look. He's bothering her. I don't know who he is. But he must be told to leave." How dare he, Maggie said to herself but she felt helpless. The door opened and the nurse came in. "We have some procedures to do now. I'm afraid, sir, you'll have to leave," and she drew the curtain around Maggie's bed. "I'm sorry sir," she said, ushering Nick out. "Visiting hours are over." She came back and felt for Maggie's pulse.

Outside in the corridor, Maggie could hear her father's voice. "My daughter is very sick. She has a heart infection and you're bothering her. She's in no state to see someone like you."

Maggie wanted to leap out of bed and run out into the hall, but she felt too faint and the nurse still had her hand on her wrist. She could hear Nick talking. He sounded troubled. "I don't believe you," her father said. "That minister doesn't know anything. And he is *not* a friend of hers. She was too sick to call anyone. Can't you see. She can hardly talk. You don't understand. Visitors must be restricted. Do you hear?" His voice rose. "Restricted to fa-mi-ly."

Family! Maggie wanted to shriek at the top of her lungs. Except for her Aunt Philana in New York, as far as she was concerned she had no family. She stopped hearing voices. Nick must have left.

Poor Nick. Tomorrow was going to be one of the worst days of his life. She hoped he'd go to the refugee centre rather than the Salvation Army hostel where the guys were sure to insult him. The mountain was just across the street from the hospital. Maybe he would walk up to Beaver Lake where he first met the grannie from Naxos. She thought of the farewell song that his *yiayia* taught him when they met in Jeanne Mance Park. Once, in the square, Nick had sung it to her.

The door opened and her father pulled open the curtains around Maggie's bed. "I've taken care of everything, Magdalena," he said. "You'll be able to rest now. I've called Moira. She'll bring you a dressing gown so you can look respectable." Respectable, Maggie thought. For years Moira's mother had been on the executive of the women's auxiliary at the hospital and now Moira was a well-known volunteer. It might get around that Maggie, a member of the MacKinnan family, was in the hospital. She clutched a chunk of sheet. Maggie Mac-Kinnan, reporter at the *Tribune,* daughter of Eli Joseph MacKinnan of St. Ninian's Presbyterian church. She had a name to live up to. "Yes, Father," she said.

∽

The next day, Maggie persuaded a patient in her room to lend her a radio with some earphones so she could tune into the radio news every hour. After she got the news on the verdict, she felt like crying. According to the radio report, a murmur of satisfaction went through the courtroom when they heard Nick had been found guilty, but when the jury foreman said that Eileen had been found guilty too, there was a moan of disappointment.

The story was far from over. There was still the pre-sentence hearing and the sentencing. That night, in a fit of anxiety, wondering where Nick was, and how she might get in touch with him, she called Alphie at the press club.

"I thought I would see you today at the trial for the verdict," he said. "The place was packed. Where are you?" An overhead loudspeaker was paging a doctor.

"I'm at the Montreal General Hospital. On an IV. I have a heart infection. Foxy brought me here."

"A heart infection?"

"I don't exactly have it. I'm fighting it. Nothing to worry about."

"Sounds serious."

"Alphie. Once a person is convicted, what then?"

He cleared his throat. "After an accused is convicted, the men go to Villemont and the women go to Tanguay. That's where Nick will be until he's sentenced, and maybe even for a little while after."

Maggie wondered whether Alphie knew how much she had been seeing Nick outside the courtroom for this magazine piece she was trying to pull together.

"Can inmates call from Villemont?" Maggie asked.

"Yes," he said, "but all calls from there have to be collect."

"Collect?"

"Yes. That's the way it works in the joints."

"Okay Alphie, thanks a lot."

"Maggie, I doubt very much that the Montreal General Hospital will take any collect calls. When you get out," he said, "you can visit, but only after the prisoner fills out forms."

"Alphie," she asked. "Could I call you from time to time? I mean, to ask you questions."

"Sure, Maggie," he said, and he hung up.

～

Five days later, when she was home recuperating, and thinking about how she could find enough energy to try to visit Nick, the phone rang. "Nicholas Mykonos calling collect," said the operator. "Do you accept the charges?"

"Yes. Nick? Nick? You okay? I've been so worried about you." There was a long silence. She looked out into the lonely street facing the expressway on the edge of downtown. "Nick . . . ?"

"I was hoping you'd be able to come to visit me," he said.

"I wanted to, but I've been out of the hospital only two days."

"Oh, so that's why you didn't come to the pre-sentence hearing.

If you'd have been there, maybe I would have had the courage to speak. Listen," he said. "I don't have much time. They won't let me talk very long. I'm getting my sentence tomorrow. Will you be able to come? You've got to come."

"Of course." No matter what, she'd have to go.

"Oh no!" Nick suddenly shouted. "They're gonna cut the phone! When can I call? I won't be able to talk to you in court. You still there?"

"Eight tomorrow night. I'll be . . ." but the line snapped before she could finish.

Maggie leaned back against her sofa. From the portrait on her living room wall, her mother looked down at her with displeasure. Her father had wanted Maggie to have the picture along with the Royal Doulton figurines and her mother's prized antique thimble collection. But she couldn't let her mother intrude on her thoughts now. All she could think of was Nick and the magazine piece she would do on the real story behind the Mykonos/O'Reilly trial. Nick had already given her a lot of material but she wasn't ready to write it yet.

∼

The next morning outside the subway stop near the court house, Maggie thought St. Antoine Street looked bleaker than usual with its pawn shops, parking lots and graffiti scrawled on broken walls. It was an overcast November day. The court house down the road looked as dark and foreboding as the mammoth Stalinist buildings in Moscow. In the nearby underground expressway, traffic droned. When she got to the *L'Express* building across from the court house, she stared at the huge printing presses churning out the day's paper. She could already imagine the hyped-up story preparing readers for the sentencing. She turned her back to the windows and watched the traffic. A "Black Maria" pulled into the basement garage at the side of the court house and Maggie thought she saw Nick's face through the bars. He looked scared.

~

On the fifth floor in the corridor outside the courtroom, an eager crowd was already gathering. Maggie watched from a distance. "Still following this thing?" a reporter from a French radio station asked her. Everyone knew she had been taken off the story by the *Tribune*. "I'm doing a magazine piece," Maggie said, even though she hadn't yet lined up the publication.

The carrion crows were out in full force. "No way the stripper and the ice monster are gonna get no piddly sentences," one mumbled. "At least not him." Maggie shuddered as she listened to them talk.

"D'ja see what *Bonjour Police* did last week?" one of them asked a friend. "A full-pager on child abuse. The poor little Mykonos kid looked like an African famine victim. But not so bad as that one in Ontario who died of starvation because the parents fed him apple juice. And then there was the poor little bugger in Saskatchewan they found in the river."

Maggie turned her back and walked away. Eileen and Nick's case, she believed, was different. There was more to their situation than the press had been able to show. But would she ever be able to make readers see all the issues behind this sensational story? Especially when she had been the one who had gone that extra mile to condemn them?

~

In a cell in the basement of the building, Nick hunched over his knees and tried not to remember, but it was coming back again. The feel of the baby's soft face on his neck, the lilac smell of his skin, the tiny ear on his shoulder. Little Stephanos was his blood, Greek blood from the island of Naxos where maybe one day he would find his real father. The sound of water pounded in his ears. He pulled on the St. Nicholas medal the grannie had given him. The last time he'd seen *yiayia* was in Jeanne Mance Park. St. Nicholas was the God of the Sea, she had said.

"Ile aux Coudres," he whispered to himself as though the words might bring everything back and the nightmare would end. He thought of the beautiful shore on the St. Lawrence river where he and Eileen had felt so close and where his son had been conceived. He stared down at the cement floor. A pain shot to his forehead and he sat up. He tried not to think of those horrible pictures and how his little Stevie must have suffered.

A migraine was starting. "Maggie, oh Maggie," he whispered. On the phone last night, it was like she was right there beside him in the square looking up at the church. He rested his cheek against his knee and smelled her perfume. The sight of her in the hospital bed was still fresh in his mind. Her eyes were so beautiful he forgot she was old enough to be his mother. He knew she suspected he might try the cyanide after he got the verdict, and in the hospital her eyes had begged him not to.

~

From the packed corridor outside the courtroom for the Mykonos/ O'Reilly sentencing, an electronic buzzer finally sounded and the crowd pushed in. "They never give these bums enough," said a man who looked like a bouncer. "Been followin' this show from the coroner's inquest," he said loudly. "Let's hope he gets the rope."

Maggie sat down near the front by herself. She took a deep breath. She had to face it. Nick meant a lot more to her than just this story she was trying to put together, and she wasn't sure how or why it had happened. The door opened at the side of the court room and the guards ushered in Nick and Eileen. Nick looked quickly for Maggie. When he saw a smile light up her face he felt encouraged. Nick swung his hips, and Maggie thought of how he'd carried her up the stairs of Notre Dame church. Maybe no one else wanted to see it, but he glowed with a youthful spirit unmatched by anyone in the courtroom. Next to Nick, the journalists looked like dreary bureaucrats.

At two minutes to ten, Maggie heard the hard click of heels coming down the aisle and watched Barbara Smith-Jones in her ever-so-clingy black skirt install herself in the front row. She was now the favourite of Max and the senior managers.

Maggie turned around and saw Alphie in a seat at the back reading a paper. He'd been so helpful, especially on the scoop, even though in the end, it undid her. "If you need me, or want advice, I'm around," he'd told her after she was taken off the story. "I'm like a shrink," he laughed. "I don't talk!" He still had a soft spot for her.

Up at the front, Crown prosecutor Jacinthe Beaulieu, her close-cropped hair streaked with gray, sat ramrod straight. Maggie thought of the special nod Beaulieu had given her the day the trial opened after their deal over the pictures. It was a moment Maggie now wanted to forget. Nick had a faraway look in his eyes. Maybe he was thinking about his lost child. Eileen pressed her hand over her breast, glanced at Nick, but then fixed on her boyfriend Colin in the front row.

～

A door opened at the back of the court and the chief clerk came in. "Superior Court is now in session," he announced. Everyone rose. The judge entered the courtroom as though he was fed up with the whole thing and had better things to think about. Barely looking at the assembled crowd, or the two accused in the box, he began to read the judgment in a brisk monotone.

"At Montreal, on the twenty-eighth of April, 1988, Nicholas Stephanos Mykonos and Eileen O'Reilly did unlawfully cause the death of Stephanos Mykonos by means of an unlawful act, allowing him to die of exposure, committing thereby manslaughter, an indictable offence contrary to articles 219, 220, and 234 of the Criminal Code."

Maggie could hardly bear to listen to the recitation of everything that led up to the baby's death. She watched as Eileen and Nick shrank into their seats in humiliation.

"Neglect," he charged, "is just as serious a form of abuse as situations where children are beaten, raped, or burned. The perpetrators deserve strong punishment." On their bench, Nick and Eileen looked like two birds crushed on the road.

For most of the reading of the judgment, Maggie kept her pen poised over her open note pad, picking up only snatches of it. The judge went on and on. Finally, in the same monotone, and without so much as looking up, he said: "Mr. Mykonos, I condemn you to imprisonment for nine years. Ms. O'Reilly, to a suspended sentence of two years." Maggie shut her eyes and tried to hold back tears. Nick had been right. Everyone hated him.

~

The crowd was angry. "He should have gotten life," said a man next to Maggie with a briefcase on his lap. The judge rose and everyone in the court stood. Maggie seized the back of the bench in front of her and gripped it until her hands hurt. Nick looked beaten. He glanced longingly at Eileen who had freedom and a life to look forward to with this new boyfriend of hers. Colin raced forward and took Eileen's arm while Kelly, Esther, Sally and her lawyer gathered around. "It's all over now," said Martine. "The judge saw that Nick was responsible." Maggie wanted to rush up and squeeze Nick's arm before the guard took him away, but she held back, and then felt guilty for not coming forward.

In the corridor outside, Esther and the women who had championed Eileen during the trial gathered round. Knowing she needed Eileen's story just as much as Nick's if her magazine piece were to stand up, Maggie stood at the edge of the group, but she didn't feel welcome. She watched the Crown prosecutor and the defence lawyers walk down the hall toward the escalators along with the reporters. Led by Barbara Smith-Jones who talked animatedly to Jacinthe Beaulieu, the group poured off the escalator and moved in a scraggly mob across the lobby toward the press room.

Maggie followed alone. In the lobby, a young couple just out of the civil marriage office posed for a picture. The girl wore a waltz-length full-skirted white lace dress but it could not conceal her slightly pro-truding belly. Maggie stood still and watched. A short veil framed a young and pretty face. Seventeen maybe. The same age she'd been in her first year at McGill University. A pain shot through her like an arrow. She didn't want to remember. She leaned back against a pillar until it passed and then made herself push ahead.

～

In the press room reporters and cameramen elbowed one another as they scrambled for quick interviews before deadlines. It was the usual scrum. The star of the day was the Crown prosecutor. "This has been one of the worst cases I've had. You saw the pictures? He did not get life, but he got an exemplary sentence. I'm happy with the suspend-ed sentence for the girl. She had a tough time."

"Look," Maggie said quietly to a Canadian Press reporter. "What I have to say is, well, just for background . . ." She was still in a fog. "I've, ah, been seeing Mykonos for a magazine piece I'm doing, and . . ." She glanced over her shoulder and saw Barbara inch in behind her. "Never mind," she said and stepped out to the lobby.

She left the building and kept walking until she got to Notre Dame church where she sat down in a pew next to some burning candles. The place was empty. The only person who might have un-derstood was Michael. But she had not had the courage to tell even him what she had been going through. She thought once again of the scripture he always read at the chapel services for the street kids. "Though I speak with the tongues of men and of angels, and have not love, I am as sounding brass, or tinkling cymbal."

In the quiet of Notre Dame church, Maggie's thoughts swirled. Other phrases from First Corinthians Thirteen echoed in her head. "Love suffereth long . . . doth not behave itself unseemly . . . rejoiceth not in iniquity, but rejoiceth in the truth . . ." Kneeling, she folded her hands in a prayer-position and gazed up at a stained glass window. Through the glass, as though she were in a cell, and they were looking in at her from the other side, she saw the eyes of the Crown prosecutor. Finally, she saw the pale blue eyes of her mother. She was holding up a linen cloth. A chill went through her. The cloth was lined with blue forget-me-nots.

Prison

TWENTY-EIGHT

The Harley Davidson Special

"THEY GOT OUT through some underground pipes," Nick whispered to Maggie so none of the other inmates in the visitors room could hear. "It all started in the kitchen. On the other side of the road, a chick waited in a car. That's how they got away." He squeezed her arm and winked. "Would you do the same for me?" Knowing how much he liked to kid around, she forced a smile and said, "Well, I'll have to think about it."

The escape news shared the front page with a story she had edited on a rally held in Hungary to commemorate the thirty-third anniversary of the 1956 rebellion against the Soviet Union. She was still editing copy on the graveyard shift at the *Tribune*. She had been visiting Nick twice a week at the Stillpoint maximum security penitentiary where he was serving his sentence in the Protection Unit. He had been there nearly a year. The visits were wearing her down but the world of the penitentiary fascinated her. Guilt, as much as her com-

mitment to writing Nick's story, also kept her going. She was still taking copious notes for a possible magazine piece on his continuing
story. Some day she would write it.

Maggie knew that Nick found life in the slammer a constant tor-
ment, and that he depended upon her visits to take his mind off the
most troubling aspects of it. After the sewer pipe escape, he began
each visit with a question about her latest blueprint for his breakout
from the pen. He expected her to give him something to laugh
about. Her favourite came from Michael Ondaatje's *In the Skin of the
Lion* where an inmate painting the roof of the Kingston penitentiary
doused himself in blue paint, lowered himself down on a pulley, and
blended in so completely with the blue of the sky that he escaped
notice and vanished into the bush.

Nick then came up with the idea of a helicopter she would rent
to swoop onto a roof where inmates sometimes did workouts. The
two of them would fly to Boston, catch a plane for Greece and take
a boat to the island of Naxos. "The perfect jackrabbit," he said.
"Jackrabbit parole" was one of the many jail house expressions for an
escape. "Taking any helicopter lessons?" he'd ask her from time to
time.

"The Harley Davidson Special" was the escape idea he talked about
most. She would buy a motorcycle, he said, which she would hide in
the fields for him to jump on after he catapulted himself over the
barbed wire to the road. Nick could almost imagine her doing it. He
saw a wild streak in her and the idea of himself racing away on a
Harley with her on the back made him smile.

"Look," he said one day, getting just a little too serious for her, "I
want you to read Roger Caron's *Bingo*. It's about a riot and an escape
from the Kingston Pen. It has a map of the underground of the
prison. They're all the same. You could tell me about it." After a dra-
matic "fence parole," he said, they would escape together on a Harley,
Easy Rider style, across the U.S. to California. The story at first made
her nervous but after a while, whenever he talked about the "Harley
Davidson Special," she dreamed of being a free spirit capable of leap-
ing into Nick's wild and explosive world.

Every escape plan had a number. "And we need a code," Nick insisted. The code he devised consisted of words spelled backwards. For example, escape plan four to take place on the tenth would be "four on ten." In code it would become rouf no net. The stories kept his spirits up and gave him a secret game that the two of them could play together. They always talked in whispers because through mikes in the ceiling the guards could plug into conversations in the visitors room.

Like a reporter living every aspect of her story, Maggie became more and more consumed by Nick's world. One Friday night she set off for a biker shop on St. Catherine Street near St. Lawrence where hookers hung around. A pretty girl in black lace stockings with a cigarette hanging from her mouth was standing outside and for a split-second Maggie thought about Eileen.

During the last week of the trial Nick had given Maggie an envelope with his photos, the note from his real mother and the baseball cap his foster brother Danny had given him. She had a picture of Nick that Eileen had taken in Ile aux Coudres showing him next to the motorcycle in tight jeans and an open shirt.

In the window of the motorcycle shop was a beautiful poster of a biker speeding away on a Harley under a brilliant blue sky. Just the thing for Nick, she thought, but inmates weren't allowed to receive posters from visitors. When she tried to bring in a poster in Nick's early days, the guards had told her that only letters no more than eight by ten inches in size were permitted. She bought the poster and came up with a plan to beat the prison rules.

At Rosie's, a corner video store close to her apartment on St. Antoine Street, a community bulletin board was always full of work-wanted notices. The owner was a young black man who knew the neighbourhood. He teamed her up with an old lady called Mrs. Fairly who did portraits of children in the black community.

"Do a drawing of him on the bike just like in the poster and make him look on top of the world," Maggie said to her. Nick looked cocksure in the picture she gave her to copy, not worn and angry the way he had in the newspaper shots, but when Mrs. Fairly saw the photo, she gave Maggie a knowing look. "It happens around here too," she said as she got her brushes ready, "guys getting into trouble." She handed Maggie a tea before she started. "These days, kids have kids far too young. There," she smiled when the painting was done. Nick, Maggie knew, would love it. He looked like a cross between a Cree and a rock star.

That night, home alone in her apartment, Maggie cut up the poster into eight-by-ten inch sheets, scribbled a note on the back of each of them so they appeared to be letters and would "pass," and sent Nick one a day until he had the entire poster. "You can get some tape and put the poster on the wall of your cell," Maggie told him.

Knowing she was treading close to the line, she said, "Tell your friends you've engineered jackrabbits before and that this is your usual jump-away vehicle." Nick never did put it on the wall because he was afraid the head of his cell block would twig to how Maggie was trying to get around the rules, and might cancel her right to visit, but he taped it together and put it away. From time to time, he unrolled it and showed it to other inmates.

TWENTY-NINE

~

Ara and Dio

MAGGIE LEANED back in her chair in the visitors room and stared past Nick's shoulder to a barred room where a guard with a machine gun in his lap caught her eye. Nick had now been in the penitentiary for a year and a half and this was her first visit after she had come back from a two-month leave-of-absence in Scandinavia and Holland. The guard wore a crafty smile and deliberately ran his hand down the side of the gun as though he were caressing the thigh of a woman. Here she was, back again in this gritty underworld that oozed sex and violence. She shifted her gaze quickly to the ash tray in the centre of the visitor's table.

Nick bent forward so his hair grazed Maggie's lips. He knew she loved the sweet smell of his hair so he always washed it just before she came. "Maggie?" He lifted her chin and looked into her green eyes. Were they the same? Still just as steady? He wasn't sure. He was so glad to see her. So relieved. She had sent him a special card from

Europe on his twenty-second birthday but it wasn't the same as having her with him.

He flicked the St. Nicholas medal around his neck. "When I get out," he asked, "you *will* help me find my father in Naxos won't you?" He was daydreaming about his life once he got out of prison. Parole was possible after a third of his sentence.

She stared at the two ginger ales she had brought up with her from the machine. "Did you hear what I said?" he asked. Just before she left for her trip he had talked about the Greek family from Naxos. The story had made her feel guilty because like the *yiayia* he had met on Mount Royal she was vanishing too, taking off to Europe where she didn't have to go.

She wanted to tell him she would help him find his father but she believed that it would only seal a terrifying bond between them that had been building since the end of the trial. She recognized that she was becoming bewitched by all the wild escape talk that came with visiting him in the prison. During the trial, when she had talked with him in the square, they were more alone, but facing him in this room with a machine gun pointing at them pulled her far closer to him.

Across a table in this bleak room filled with other prisoners and their guests, she felt as intimate with him as lovers in bed. He was not just a teenage kid the way he had seemed when he showed off to her in the square doing back flips over the benches. More than ever she saw Nick as a man who might cast a spell over her as Heathcliff had Cathy. It was an hypnotic thought. She looked out the window into the sky and then straightened in her chair. She had to fight her desire to descend into his chaotic world. Her only security blanket was the magazine piece she still talked about writing.

"Give me a cigarette," he said. He would never bum another cigarette from one of the guys. Too risky. "Cute little ass," one of the prison wolves had said to him in the showers. "Sit on me, and I'll give you a pack." He shuddered at the thought. It brought back the nightmare of what had happened to him at Carstairs when he was seven. That's when his headaches began.

He lit two cigarettes and gave her one. All that day, before she came, he had told himself not to blow up at her. When he first saw her, he was too excited about seeing her to be angry, but now the rage that had torn at him all the time she was away surged up. "It was all an excuse," he said, "wasn't it?"

"What was an excuse?" Maggie took one puff of her cigarette and put it on the rim of the ash tray where it slowly burned.

"Don't play dumb with me, Maggie."

"I had to go to Holland for the magazine piece. I want to contrast the Canadian prison system with the best elsewhere." A high security prison outside Amsterdam was like a summer camp compared to Stillpoint and there were no rapes or suicides. Someday, she said to herself, she would comb through all the notes she was taking and write something.

"I needed you here," Nick said. "Not in some faraway place. Things are happening to me in this joint that I don't talk about." He never gave her details, couldn't risk having other inmates overhear, but he thought she knew the dangers of the pen. When he was at Villemont waiting to be sentenced, one of the inmates gave a cell-mate everyone hated the blanket and threatened to do the same to *him*. *Bonjour Police* wrote about it. Later, in the classification centre, when Nick was waiting to be placed after sentencing, a guard had said, "Even in Protection, you won't stand a chance. Inmates don't like your type. The last one was rewarded with a pinebox parole. He was yoked in the yard weight lifting."

Nick pushed her cigarette into the middle of the ashtray and squashed the burning tip of his cigarette into the back of hers until it broke in two. "Fuck the magazine piece," he yelled. Maggie looked up at the loudspeaker. Any loud talk or strange behaviour, and the "big brother" watching them through a video in the ceiling would tell them the visit was over.

"What do I care about all that garbage. If the only reason you're coming to see me is so you can do that goddamn magazine article, get lost."

She had taken a tour of Holland and Scandinavia to study their prison systems but also hoping that the absence might cool things off. When she came back she wanted to concentrate on the interviewing she was supposed to be doing for the article.

"I mean it," he said and seized her wrist. "I have a right to be in a rage. All I have is you," he whispered hoarsely. "Two months is too long for you to be away. Anything could happen to me here." She gave him juice to fend off all the crazies he was holed up with, but how could he tell her that? "I waited for you to say it," he said. "I promised myself I'd forgive you if you did. You never even said you missed me. Not even that." He lifted up one of the ginger ales she'd bought. "And you know I only drink Cokes."

"I thought about you a lot when I was away," she said, "wondering how you were doing." The truth was she had missed him terribly. When she was with him, sometimes she imagined she was eighteen and not going on thirty-nine. He lifted her out of the drab life she lived working on the Rim at night and helping out her father at the church on weekends. "The machine downstairs was out of Cokes," she added.

The door of the visitors room opened and Marlene, the girlfriend of the Van Gogh rapist, came in. She wore tight pants and boots but she had a pink baby face. Marlene had visited the rapist in the Villemont detention centre when Maggie had first been seeing Nick. He had raped several women in Toronto and then in Montreal before the police found him in Rosemount climbing down from the roof onto a balcony. The one thing all the women remembered about him was a huge scar where his ear should have been.

Maggie suddenly remembered Marlene at twilight in a snow bank in front of the detention centre waving at the rapist who was standing in the window ten floors up. Nick had told Maggie no one had ever showed him such love. The rapist had shared a cell with Nick and several other inmates waiting to stand trial or be sentenced.

The girl threw her arms around her boyfriend. Feeling sick with jealousy, Nick pushed away Maggie's hand and stared at Marlene. She was such a knock-out and so sexy. Finally he turned back to Maggie. "You wanted to get away from me, didn't you?"

"No," she said. "That's not true." But it was. At the end of 1991, in a year and a half when one-third of Nick's sentence would be over, he could be out on parole and "in the free." She didn't have to go to Europe or anywhere else for that matter but she kept looking for excuses to get away from him. Three months ago, before her trip to Sweden, she'd said she couldn't come for two weeks because her car had broken down. She remembered the date — March 11, 1990 — the day Lithuania declared its independence from the Soviet Union. She had edited the story.

Next year she wanted to take a leave of absence from the *Tribune* to go to eastern Europe with her dance group for the summer folk dance festival. She was still in touch with Katerina Petrovsky, the Russian journalist from Moscow who had stayed with Maggie on a cultural exchange right after the sentencing. "Lots of freelance work over here for English journalists," Katerina had written. "You're welcome to come any time."

"Maggie?" Nick put his hand over hers. She felt him soften. "Don't worry about Marlene. You have more beautiful eyes." Nick snuggled his hand into hers. "Is it true?" he asked. "Did you really miss me?"

"I did," she said.

"I want to hear you say it." He pulled his chair closer to her and ran his hand down her back to her hips.

"I missed you very much," she said quickly.

From the corner of her eye she saw Marlene hugging her boyfriend. Maggie dug her fingers into her knee. She had to keep reminding herself that Nick was young enough to be her son.

"I've been thinking about Naxos," Maggie said, making herself forget the sight of Marlene. "Tell you what I'll do. I'll read up everything I can — the geography, the history and especially the Greek myth of Dionysus, the god of wine and his beautiful princess Ariadne. Next time I come I'll tell you what I've learned."

The voice over the loudspeaker announced closing time, and they pushed back their chairs and stood up. In three minutes she would have to leave. The other couples were passionately embracing. Nick looked into her eyes, put his hands around her waist and pulled her in so tight his legs were flush against her. Except for the time when he had carried her up the stairs of the church, this was the first time he had held her. He was five nine and she was only five two but they fit well together. She felt a tremor in his hands and took a step back. She dropped her eyes but she knew she wasn't concealing anything.

"You won't do that to me again will you?" He put his hands on his hips.

"What?" Maggie said.

"Leave!" For a second she thought he was ordering her to leave. "Leave," he repeated in a softer voice. "Like Eileen, like the *yiayia,* like all the others."

She realized he was talking about her trip. "I really had to go," she said but her voice lacked conviction.

The loudspeaker announced the end of the visit. She leaned forward and brushed each of his cheeks quickly. The other women were leaving. She could still feel his palms on the small of her back. The part of her that was trying to maintain control rose up out of the swirl in her head. "Saturday," she said. She could come Thursday but it would be too soon. Saturday would be better.

∼

Maggie spent the next two visits telling Nick everything she could about Naxos — the tiny harbours and fishing villages, the olive groves, wild flowers and solitary beaches. Roots, she said to herself. He had to find his roots. Eventually, maybe she *could* help him find his father in Naxos. When she wasn't at the *Tribune* editing copy on the graveyard shift, or visiting Nick at the penitentiary, she was collecting information about the island where Dionysus fell in love with Ariadne.

She worried that the Greek myth was too romantic a story to tell Nick but one day the tale tumbled out.

"Dionysus was the son of Zeus, the king of Mount Olympus but he lost his mother before he was born," Maggie said. Nick frowned. The story, he thought, sounded weird.

"Semele, his mother, was killed by Zeus' wife, Hera who was mad because Zeus fell in love with her. When Semele died, Zeus took Dionysus from her womb and stitched him into his thigh until he was ready to be born."

"Who brought him up?" Nick asked.

"First a beautiful queen took care of him but she died. After that he went to a forest where he was taken care of by nymphs."

"What about what's-her-name?"

"Ariadne was a beautiful princess who had been abandoned by a hero called Theseus who dumped her on the island of Naxos. Dionysus found her there. He had hired some pirates to row him to the island but the pirates turned on him.

"The pirates were going to put Dionysus in chains. But Dionysus had the power to cast spells. Before they could do anything, he changed their oars into serpents. Then he transformed himself into a lion and roared so loudly they jumped overboard and he turned them into fish. Across the sea, lying on the shore waiting for him, was Ariadne." Nick moved closer to Maggie.

"Together," she went on, "they explored Naxos and found Dionysus' parents — his mother Semele who lived in the underworld and his father Zeus who lived at the top of Mount Olympus. Every year the god Hades let Semele out of the underworld to spend time with them."

There was a long silence after she finished. She wondered which was more reckless, telling escape stories, or this seduction tale from Naxos.

"Know what?" Maggie said quickly. "Maybe you really will go to Naxos and find your father."

"What about Ariadne?" Nick asked. "Did she love Dionysus forever?"

"Oh yes. She probably turned into a dull little housewife who cleaned fish."

"I'm sure it wasn't that way at all." He took both her hands in his. "Ara?" he said.

Maggie looked out the window of the visitors room into the night. She loved losing herself in characters like Cathy from *Wuthering Heights,* and now Ariadne from the Greek myth. It was a way to escape the gray cloak of the manse and St. Ninian's church and the drudgery of copy editing from midnight to eight at the paper.

"Magdalena," Nick called out her name in the sing-song nagging way her father had in the hospital.

"Hey," she jerked out of her reverie. "Don't call me that. I don't like it." The last person she wanted was to be reminded of now was her father.

Nick picked up her hand and patted it. "Ara and Dio will send Magdalena and her father away, okay?" Maggie nodded.

"Ara and Dio sounds nice, don't it?" Maggie smiled the smile that only he could bring to her face. During the trial he had watched when she talked to other people. Her face never lit up the way it did when she smiled at *him.* The loudspeaker announced the end of the visit. "Thursday," he said, tilting her chin up so he could look directly into her eyes. "I think Ara should come an extra time this week."

THIRTY

~

Secrets

EVEN THOUGH this was Nick's second summer at the pen, the sweetness in the air often made him think back to the weekend in Ile aux Coudres with Eileen and the night his little Stevie was conceived. But when inmates taunted him with names like snow monster, he had to face how he had lost him. In his heart of hearts, Nick knew he hadn't wanted his son to die. Every night he dreamt about how he would some day have another boy like Stevie. More than anything in the world, he wanted a child.

The soul of his little boy, he was convinced, still lived, just like the souls of saints. In bed at night he talked to him. When the time came, the spirit of his child would float down from heaven and live in a new boy who would never leave him. He imagined them going to hockey games and digging up clams by the sea, just the way he did with his foster brother Danny. His son would grow up making none of his crazy mistakes. He would finish school, get a proper

271

job, and not do crime.

During the day in the penitentiary, when he worked in the laundry loading the washing machines with sheets and towels, he tried to think through what had happened and felt confused. Maggie was the only one who believed he was good. "Everyone has something divine inside," she told him. "The manifestation of the spirit is given to every man . . ." She sometimes used big words and quoted the Bible at him. "That's not me talking," she had said. "That's St. Paul in a letter he sent to the Greeks of Corinth. Someone has to find that spark," she said, and tapped him in the middle of the forehead as though that's where the spark came from. "It's the spark," she smiled and squeezed his hand, "that Ara saw in Dio."

But no matter how often he told himself he hadn't wanted his Stevie to die, he still worried. Maybe he really was a freak. Perhaps that's why his mother left him on the bus. Sometimes Maggie was blind. If he had been good, he would have rushed his son to the hospital as soon as he saw snow on his shoulders. "Penuel the Snow Child," the coroner called his son. He remembered the faces of the jury when they saw the pictures. "Pictures don't lie, Mr. Mykonos," the Crown prosecutor had said.

"I've got to have children, a family of my own," he often told Maggie. He had been in prison for two Christmases now. In a few months, he could be out on day or even weekend passes and then at the three-year mark he could try for parole. He still dreamt of Eileen even though he knew she was married to Colin in Calgary and would never take him back.

One day in the visitors room with Maggie when there was no one around he put his hand over hers and raised a question he'd been wanting to ask for ages. "Maggie," he said. "Do you want to have babies?"

"Why are you asking me that? I . . ." her voice quavered. "I can't."

Her hand went cold and she drew away. "Can't. How do you know?"

"A doctor told me." She had gone only once to a woman gynecologist who had examined her and told her she could never have a child. "Don't ask me that again," she mumbled, suddenly short of breath.

"Why? Something terrible happen to you?" He paused. "You have a baby and give him up?"

Maggie's head swam. A blade of pain went through her. Andreas had been the only boyfriend she'd ever had, if you could call him that. It was a time of her life she had deliberately blotted out. Best to forget.

Nick took her shaking hand and held it. "You going to be okay?" He lifted her chin and looked into her eyes. "You know Maggie, I've always suspected you've been coming here at least partly because of something you've never told me about."

"No, no, Nick. There's nothing. Really."

Later, during the same visit, he asked her about something that had been bothering him since the trial. "Do think it was possible that my son died of something else?"

"What else?"

"I don't know." She'd done interviews with everyone who had had anything to do with his case. He thought perhaps she knew something no one else did.

"Look. I know you didn't want Stevie to die. It was bad you left the window open, terrible you didn't see he was sick, but he died of exposure. That's what the coroner said. You have to forget about it."

"Sometimes," he said, "when I go to bed, I talk to him. I tell him I'm sorry, that I didn't mean it . . ."

~❧

THIRTY-ONE

The Red Suede Skirt

MAGGIE REALIZED how grim it had become for Nick at the penitentiary when she gave a ride one night to the girlfriend of a prisoner
who told her the other inmates refused to let Nick play baseball.

"Why?" Maggie asked.

"He's one of those, isn't he?" Adele replied.

"It was an accident," Maggie answered. "The inmates would have
heard about him in the newspapers where everything was sensation-
alized. That's how they sell papers. You should know that." It had
been more than two years since the trial but she couldn't shake her
feelings of guilt.

Maggie wanted to ask Adele what her boyfriend was in for but she
knew better. Asking about convictions was touchy. Some of the men
were in for killing their wives. Among prisoners it was all right to
murder your wife but to neglect a child until he died made an inmate
an untouchable. Even the policemen serving time were treated bet-

ter, though if there was one kind of inmate other prisoners hated, it was "a pig."

"Here in Protection," Nick had once told her, "everyone is scum and I'm at the very bottom."

"I'm sure you're not," she had said. "You're always exaggerating."

"You don't understand. There are things I don't tell you. You're the only one who believes I have something good inside. You and my case officer."

The contempt for Nick was so widespread that some of the women who visited looked the other way when they saw Maggie come into the waiting room where they lined up to be searched.

Adele sometimes walked with her from the building to the parking lot after a visit, but only because Maggie always offered her a ride home. It was a way of gathering information about life in the prison.

Adele, who always had a cigarette in her hand, seemed to be about the same age as Maggie. She usually wore tight leopard skin pants, a slinky brown sweater, spike heels and lots of eye makeup. It took her two hours to get to the penitentiary and she could get there only by hitchhiking part of the way.

"I met Jacques through his cousin at the pencil factory where I work," she told Maggie after some casual questioning. "He showed me a picture and asked me if I'd like to write to him." The man had fox-like features and scary, penetrating eyes, Maggie thought. "It was love at first sight," Adele said. "For a while, we were just pen pals, but after a month, he asked me to go on his visitors list."

Always the interviewer on the lookout for details about the joint, Maggie grilled Adele about her life with Jacques, but after a few rides home from the penitentiary Adele finally asked Maggie some questions. "How long have you known your guy?" she wanted to know.

"Oh," Maggie said. "It's sort of hard to explain." Her voice quavered unexpectedly. "I met Nick when he was on trial. I started off preparing a magazine piece about his case. Now I'm doing something on prisons. I work at night at the *Tribune* as an editor, but I also do research."

Adele gave her a strange look and then said, "I thought he was your boyfriend." Maggie let the comment pass and then said, "Well, as you know, things can get complicated."

"At first I thought you were a social worker," Adele commented. "Jacques said the guys thought you were a minister's wife or maybe even a minister. They always talk about the visitors."

Oh no, Maggie said to herself. Not a minister's wife! Anything but that. "I guess I have an image problem," she said to Adele and asked her to light her a cigarette. "The last thing I want to look like is a minister's wife. My father is a minister."

There was a pecking order in prison, Maggie slowly learned, and the appearance of the women who visited was part of the prisoner's scorecard. The Van Gogh rapist, for example, inspired respect because of the devotion of his bombshell girlfriend Marlene with her mass of curly blond hair. Everyone, including Nick, looked up when Marlene stepped into the visitors room. The man had raped a whole household once but he had a gorgeous girl who visited often.

One day while Marlene was visiting Nick slouched back in his chair and said, "Tell me. Don't you have something to wear except these suits you always come in? From now on, I want you to wear something else when you come here. You look like a *liberian*." He pronounced it with only one *r*, but she didn't bother to correct him.

A librarian? Since when had he ever been in a library? Another prisoner, maybe Adele's Jacques, must have suggested it.

Nick shot an admiring glance at Marlene in her tight black jeans, cowboy boots and a T-shirt that looked as though she had nothing underneath and Maggie felt herself wince with envy.

"This gray suit you always wear with the little white blouse makes you look like a nun." He grabbed Maggie's hand and lowered his voice.

"You've got to learn how to dress. Get some black leather pants, a black angora sweater with a V-neck, and a red scarf that ties at the side.

"In that outfit you'll look *better* than Marlene. C'mon," he smiled at her and brushed her cheek with his fingers. "I want you to look pretty."

That evening, driving home from the penitentiary, she told herself she'd look like a nun if she wanted, but later that night, when she went off with the sub-editors to an all-night eatery that also sold magazines, she leafed through some publications to see what female rock artists and biker girls were wearing. The idea of letting go, of taking on a new persona, suddenly seemed irresistible.

At three o'clock the next afternoon, despite her misgivings, she was outside a leather store on St. Lawrence Boulevard in a part of town she never went to. On one side of the store was a sex shop with revolting gear in the window, and on the other, an arcade where men were watching peep shows. She went in and combed through the racks along with two girls in crotch-tight jeans and orange and green hair. A man behind the cash gave her a strange look. In her plain brown pant suit from Holt Renfrew's and her small clutch bag, she knew she looked like an unlikely buyer of leather.

"Can I help?" asked a roving salesman.

"I'm looking for some black leather pants." What the hell, she thought. If she was going to continue visiting Nick, she would have to look the part.

"For yourself?"

"Yes."

He looked her over and picked out a size eight. They cost $150, way more than she would normally pay for pants. It was all part of the research, she told herself, but she knew there was a lot more to it than that.

"You want a top too?"

"You have any black angora?" He gave her two sweaters and she tried on one with a V-neck. In the dressing room mirror she observed herself with the eyes of a reporter and was amazed at how sexy she looked. The pants were just as snug as Marlene's. She could almost pass. She swivelled to the side, threw out her hips and immediately thought of Eileen at the Sex Trolley.

"How are they?" the man called out.

"Fine," Maggie said, a thrill running through her. "I'm taking them." She peeled them off quickly. Her father would be shocked. And so would Moira. But no one at St. Ninian's or the *Trib* would ever see her dressed like this. Two doors down she was delighted to find shiny knee-high black boots. When she pulled them on, she felt like a teenager.

⁓

That night, twenty minutes before she was due to visit Nick at the penitentiary, she changed out of her gray suit in the women's washroom of a McDonald's about a mile from Stillpoint.

Waiting at the counter for a coffee next to a highschool girl in a miniskirt, she thought of how she had felt on her fifteenth birthday when her aunt from New York sent her the red suede miniskirt, white boots and white sweater. A party was out of the question that year because her mother was too sick. The birthday supper with her parents was over at six after her mother took her pills. Her father was already in his study working on his Sunday sermon when the doorbell rang.

A special courier was at the door with a big box from her Aunt Philana in New York. She went into her room and opened it. Along with the outfit was *Seventeen* magazine with a famous teenage model on the cover in the same outfit. A card said, "Come to New York and we'll go shopping together!"

Maggie had been dying to buy something like this but had never had the nerve. "You have to set an example," her mother would say. "After all, dear, you are a minister's daughter." She put on the outfit and went into her mother's room. "Mum," she called out. Her mother opened her eyes and tried to prop herself up on her elbows. "Look what Aunt Phil sent me?" and she twirled around. Her mother put on her glasses and her normally vacant eyes came to life.

"Take that outfit off," she ordered, her eyes narrowing. "I don't ever want to see you in that again."

"But Aunt Phil . . ." Maggie protested.

"Aunt Phil has no taste. Take it off before your father sees you."

Sitting in a booth, drinking her McDonald's coffee, Maggie thought of her mother's girlhood dream of being an actress and how it had been snatched away from her for good after Maggie was born. Perhaps the onset of Hodgkin's Disease had actually started right after the shock of giving birth. She had wanted to be on the stage, not a minister's wife and a mother. Maggie wondered what her mum would think of her now, all costumed-up as a gangster's moll . . .

~

"You look terrific," Nick said when he came into the visitors room at the penitentiary. He flicked the red scarf at her neck. "You even remembered that." Two inmates looked at her admiringly. One made a little O with his thumb and forefinger as if to say, First-rate, buddy, you're really scoring on this one, but Maggie wondered whether he was making fun. From the neck up, she knew she still looked like a *liberian* or a social worker — not a popular item at the pen.

"Come close," Nick said. Her heart leapt to her mouth as he ran his hand down her back to her hips. "You look really great," he smiled. "But next time, put on eye makeup. You have such beautiful green eyes. And do something about your hair. I forgot to mention that. Take out the pins."

"Take out the pins? I've always worn my hair up."

"C'mon," he winked. "You look good with it down," and thought about how great her hair had looked when she was in the hospital. He put his warm fingers deep into her hair and she felt goosebumps rise on her arms as the pins clattered to the floor of the visitors room. Maggie looked up nervously at the video camera in the wall and quickly picked up the pins. "Stop acting nervous," he said as he looked her over. "Your hair looks as though you just got out of bed," he smiled. "But it's better than the *liberian* look. For next week make it look like Madonna's."

~

Two days later in her own neighbourhood, Maggie found herself in front of a hairdressing salon that featured a photo of a girl with a cluster of curly blond hair. She hadn't been to a hairdresser in two years. When her hair got too long, she took some kitchen scissors and cut off the ends.

"You want a cut and set?" asked the receptionist at the desk.

"Well, I think so but I have to talk to someone first."

"Katie," the receptionist called, and a woman of about twenty-five appeared.

Maggie pulled out the pins from her hair. "Could you cut my hair and give me a perm or something? I want my hair to look something like the photo in the window."

"Yeah. Sure." The hairdresser felt her hair. "It's nice and thick."

"I want it to look sort of wild," Maggie said.

"You want me to do it now?"

"Yes." It was two in the afternoon. Her shift didn't start until midnight. "Just one thing, though. I know it sounds crazy, but I want the wild look just for special occasions. Could you leave it long enough so that I can still wear it up?"

By four o'clock, when it was cut, lightly permed and blow-dried, Maggie couldn't believe how bouncy and carefree she looked.

"You look fabulous," Katie told her. "You going to a party or something?"

Maggie nodded. "Sort of."

"You need some eye makeup. Go next door and get some blue eyeliner and black mascara and I'll put it on for you."

In a phone booth outside on the street, she called the penitentiary for an appointment at seven o'clock. It would be a surprise. Nick wasn't expecting her. From the drug store, she got eyeliner and mascara and went back to the salon and Katie dressed up her eyes.

"Thanks a lot," Maggie said.

"A pleasure," the hairdresser said.

If she rushed, she could go to the manse and get the outfit Aunt Phil had given her. She had always been a size eight. It would still fit. Her father would be at the church until six. She didn't want him to see her hair. In the back seat of her car, along with a number of unpaid parking tickets and her shiny black boots, she had a kerchief to cover her hair just in case.

When she arrived at the manse up on the hill, she saw a light on in the living room, heard the final notes of Vivaldi's *Gloria* playing on the stereo and realized her father was home. She threw the kerchief over her head and decided to make a run for it. She braced herself for the musty smell of the house as she swung open the heavy oak door with the brass knocker. "Oh, hi," she said to her father who was sprawled out in his leather chair next to the grandfather clock in the living room. "Just in time for dinner," he replied.

"I can't," she said. "I'm working. I left a book here and I have to pick it up." She rushed upstairs to her room to retrieve the red suede skirt and white sweater from her bottom drawer. She caught a glimpse of herself in her bra and panties as she stepped out of her gray tweed skirt and jacket. Nice and slim, she thought.

She pulled on the skirt and sweater. They were just a little snug. She took a full minute to look at herself in the mirror. Under her thin white sweater her breasts looked full and round, almost naked, she thought. She threw her gray skirt and jacket on top so her father wouldn't notice anything and went out into the hall.

For a second she leaned against the wall. The upstairs always reeked of floor wax. The cleaning woman must have just been here. She could smell the sweat along with the cleaning fluid. The smell of clean had always been stifling. "Cleanliness is next to godliness," her mother used to say, and her father was still trying to keep up the tradition.

She walked past her father's beige study which was dominated by a massive, worn desk, his framed college degrees and a stereo system which now had extra speakers downstairs in the living room. When he wanted to escape from his work at the church, he often listened to big choral pieces. After her mother died he sometimes invited prospective brides and grooms into his study to listen to possible wedding music on his stereo.

Before she went downstairs she stood for a moment at the entrance to her mother's room. The flowered silk suit that her father had always asked her to wear when he took her out to the opera was, as always, on the bed. She went into the room and threw it in the cupboard. "Father. It's over," she said under her breath. She would never again wear that suit.

"*La Bohème* is next week," her father declared as she stepped into the kitchen to say goodbye. He was awkwardly beating up some eggs for an omelette. "Not working, I hope."

"No, no." Her graveyard shift editing copy on the Rim never interfered with his precious opera evenings the way it had when she was a star reporter. "I'm an editor now," she had told him a long time ago, "handling the Eastern European stories." It sounded a lot better than it was. It was two years now since she'd had a piece in the *Trib* and he'd never quizzed her about it. Just as well . . .

Laid out on the kitchen counter was a glossy colour page from the McGill alumnae magazine announcing a guided opera tour of Italy in January. "Oh Father," she said suddenly excited at the thought of him going off and doing something on his own. From the living room stereo speakers the opening bars of *La Traviata* floated into the kitchen. "You aren't thinking of going off to Italy, are you?"

"Not really. . . ." He stood still for a moment and looked out the window and she noticed a rare sparkle in his eyes. "I was just dreaming a little . . ."

Next to the magazine was a folder from the Thomas More Institute. She opened it up and noticed an announcement for a "great books of Italy" course. Something new was going on with him, she thought. Something good.

"I think it would be great if you went on that trip," she jumped in. "Think about taking it." She took her father's hand and held it for a minute. Normally, they never touched but something inside her was loosening up, probably, she thought, because of Nick.

"You knew people in Venice, didn't you, before you met Mum?" She was venturing into taboo territory but she didn't care. "Maybe you'd like to look up some old friends from your youth." Her father lowered his eyes and nodded, almost mechanically, she thought. "*La Bohème* next week will be a real treat," she said trying to fill in the silence. "See you soon," and she left.

Once again, en route to the prison, she stopped at McDonald's to remove her gray suit. Later, she would change back into it for her shift in the newsroom. All she could think of as she spun toward the penitentiary in her red Innocenti was how Nick would react to her new look.

When she checked in, the usual guard didn't recognize her and made her show ID. "It's my hair," she said. "It's different." She felt self-conscious. Two women she had seen before were laughing in the waiting room. Maybe she looked ridiculous. The guard gave her a locker key. For a brief moment, while she was taking off her watch and putting her purse in the locker, as visitors always had to do, she was seized with a dark sense of foreboding. Nick had quickened something inside her that was spinning beyond her control . . .

Upstairs in the visitors room, waiting for Nick to appear, she looked down at her tight red miniskirt and her sleek black boots and thought again of Eileen. She was now front and centre of the story she was covering. *Covering?* She was not covering anything. Like an addict hooked on a drug, she felt herself slipping into a dark nebula. The door opened behind her and Adele sat down at table E beside her. *"Très belle,"* she mouthed the words at her and pointed to her hair. Maggie took a deep breath. A door clanged shut and Nick thumped up the metal stairs. For a moment he didn't recognize her. He stood with his back to the door scanning the room. But he knew what table she'd be at. Table F. She had been assigned the last one. Adele gave her a shot of confidence she desperately needed and Maggie smiled as Nick swung over to her.

"You look wonderful," he said. His presence next to her blanked out the world and she felt her body tingle. "Stand up. Oh my God. Legs too. The boots are beautiful." The other inmates were watching. He took both her hands, shut his eyes, and while everyone watched, gave her a French kiss that sent an electric current through her. She felt his warm legs press into her. Relaxing completely into him, for a second she imagined they were alone under the stars in some faraway Greek island. "Ara and Dio," he said and his warm lips grazed her neck. "That's what we really are now." She looked up into his blue eyes and then put her forehead on his chest. He lifted up her chin and smiled. "Ara and Dio. More than ever before. Sounds nice? Don't it?"

~

After she agreed to dress the way he wanted, Nick tried to find a way to control every aspect of her life, and to Maggie's distress, she allowed it to happen. Working the graveyard shift from midnight to eight in the morning left her free to visit almost any time because visiting hours were evenings and weekends. But then the news editor changed her shift from four to midnight. That meant that she could see Nick only on weekends. It was better for her, but not for Nick.

"Change your shift," he demanded. He put up such a fuss that she told the news editor she had to help her father in the evenings, and got her shift changed back. Nick also wanted to control the days she visited, when she would take his collect calls, and who she saw after work. She never mentioned the suppers she sometimes had with her friend Michael at the refugee centre even though Michael had been especially nice to him at the hospital the night before the verdict and had invited him to stay at the centre. Just thinking about Michael gave Maggie an idea. Now that Michael was working with street kids who lived in LaSalle around the refugee centre, maybe she could ask him to go on Nick's visitors list. He might be the perfect visitor for Nick. Get her off the hook. Later, she said to herself. Perhaps he could fill in for her the next time she went away.

~

"Have I ever told you about the third eye?" Nick asked her one night.

"Third eye?" Maggie asked nervously.

"Yeah. We got this spy network. Works good." He leaned back in his chair and put his thumbs in his pocket. "We caught one of the girls cheating." Maggie didn't say anything. "You won't be seeing *her* around for a while. She has her leg in a cast."

Maggie was anxious and knew it showed. He could read her like a book. Let him think whatever he liked, but there was no way she was giving up the few friends she had, her folk dancing, or her courses in Russian language and literature. She had to remember that. *Remember that,* she told herself.

"The network makes sure wives and girlfriends are faithful," Nick went on. "They can always catch out a lie."

∿

A few nights later, at three in the morning, Alphie asked Maggie to join him for a drink during her dinner break on the graveyard shift. "It's time we had a little talk," he said after he'd spoken to the news editor about a feature interview he'd promised on the freelance activities of Canada's last hangman.

"Maggie," he said as they settled into a smoked meat sandwich at Dunn's downtown, "What are you still doing on the Rim? It's a big waste of your talent to be sitting around with Foxy and the boys editing copy. It's been two whole years since that famous trial you got so hopped up about. Why don't you come up with some fresh story ideas and get out of there?"

"Alphie, I don't know what to say. I was going to do this magazine piece. You know? On Nick? It still makes me boil the way I listened to what Max wanted on that story. I wanted to write about what had *really* happened to Nick. Make it up to him. There was a big hole in everyone's coverage. Mine especially . . . ."

"Well, why haven't you written it?"

Maggie stared blankly into her coffee. "Very hard to talk about. I sort of lost my objectivity . . ." She gazed up at him, "but it wasn't just that."

"You're not still seeing him, I hope," Alphie asked.

Maggie nodded. She thought of how simple her life had been before she met Nick.

"I figured as much. I knew a young lawyer who got caught up in something like this. She worked for legal aid. But you?" He leaned forward. "Such a sensible girl? And a minister's daughter?"

"I'm fed up being a minister's daughter. It's a terrible burden. Worse than taking care of my mother when I was still in elementary school. And who wants to be a sensible girl? Sensible girls have boring little workaday lives in gray apartments." Was being top-of-the-heap in a big newsroom with a tyrant like Max who was mostly interested in the bottom line worth it anyway? She closed her eyes for a moment and thought of the feeling of Nick's warm palms on the small of her back . . . How could she ever give that up?

"Start thinking of a way to leave town," Alphie counselled.

"Well," she said slowly. "I'm studying Russian, polishing it up. I could always go to Russia and freelance. Lots of stories over there now." Alphie's eyes brightened as he waited for her to say more. He was pushing her to protect herself, she realized, to think of her future.

"Remember that week I spent after the trial talking to the journalists in St. Petersburg and Moscow about investigative reporting? I have contacts over there now that I can stay with. It's been a dream of mine ever since to spend some time in St. Petersburg."

"Splendid. By the way isn't that where Dostoyevsky wrote *Crime and Punishment*? You might try some kind of Montreal version," he laughed. "It would probably make a good read." She thought of telling him how she was dressing up as a gangster's moll, playing undercover reporter at the pen, but decided against it. He would tell her she was playing with fire.

He scrutinized her face. "You're looking good though," he smiled. "Not so mousey."

"Really . . . ?" The clothes she wore to the office weren't any different. And at the *Trib* she still wore her hair up. Maybe she looked turned on. When she was at the penitentiary she certain felt turned on. She tried to imagine the look on Alphie's face at the sight of her at the prison in her black leather pants and her hair all wild.

"But you needn't take it too far," Alphie said. "There are certain women who get juiced up by outlaws. You have to watch it or you'll turn into a prisoner yourself. You have to learn how to survive. You can't just run with your feelings."

"Well . . ." she replied. Maybe she already was a prisoner. But for how long could she stay on the sidelines of life, always keeping a safe distance from people? Had she used reporting, she asked herself, the way her father used his ministry, to live vicariously? She wished she could explore some of this with Alphie or maybe Michael but she didn't have the courage.

"What you need is a nice boyfriend," Alphie said. "A nice ordinary boyfriend, somebody maybe in the news or literary business." Maggie looked out into space and Alphie put his hand on her shoulder. "Stay in touch," he said. "If things get rough you can always call." He tipped up her chin and looked into her eyes. "Just don't wait until everything goes too far."

THIRTY-TWO

~~~

In the Hole

NICK STARED FROM his cell into the shadowy corridor and out a small window into the prison courtyard where he watched the sky above the razor wire on the wall slowly go black. How many more times would the sky brighten and fade before she came again? Maggie saw him only once a week now, sometimes less. He could feel her trying to withdraw from him. To while away the hours he watched television. During the day he worked on the assembly line stitching jeans, but nothing he did could stop the fog that was starting to close in on him.

"Program," she had said last night when she came to visit. "Television program, not television pogrom." "I've always said pogrom," he told her, "and I'm not starting now to say p-r-o-g-r-a-m." He spelled it out just to prove he knew how to spell. Right after that she insisted on telling me about the pogroms of Russia.

"I don't want to hear no more about fuckin' Russia." He had been

so mad he had grabbed her wrist and twisted it. He was tired of listening to her talk about what was happening on the other side of the
world. He banged his fists against the wall of his cell. It was all because
of those stupid courses she insisted on taking that she couldn't come
to visit more than once a week. At least that's what she said. His mind
streaked back to last night.

"You're not thinking of going over there, are you?" he had asked.
He knew from the news that there was a lot happening in Eastern
Europe.

"No," she had said, but there was something in her eyes he hadn't
liked. She sometimes talked about foreign correspondents and how
they had to learn other languages.

"Can you really speak Russian?"

"Yes. Now I could do quite complicated interviews in Russian."

"Interviews! The only place you'd do interviews in Russian is in
Russia. You *are* thinking of going over there. Aren't you?"

"If I go over there, it wouldn't be for long, but anyway I'm not
planning anything like that."

"I catch you every time. You *are* planning something like that.
When are you going to finish those courses?"

"In a few months."

She would finish just when he would be applying for parole, he
thought, and pretty well sure of getting it. If she was still studying,
she'd have to stay in Montreal, but if she was finished, maybe the
Tribune might send her away.

She must have known what he was thinking because she said,
"Don't fret about the *Tribune* ever sending me anywhere. I'm on the
shelf. They figure they're doing me a favour letting me work the
graveyard shift on the Rim. Don't you remember? They took me off
the trial because they thought I was doing a shitty job."

He didn't like it when she swore. "I can use those words," he'd told
her, "but not you."

He went back to thinking about those long waits between her visits. "Dallas" was on tonight which meant it was Saturday. He had six

more evenings till she came. Every time they opened the bolts of the cellblock, he put a mark on the back wall of his cage with chalk. When the marks got near the end, he knew he was close to a visit. As soon as the guard came to get him for the visit, he'd rub off everything with the back of his hand.

It would be an eternity before she came. The fog was taking over, laying him lower and lower. When he felt the poison flowing through him, sucking blood from him like a vampire, he'd dream she was right beside him, warm liquid from her filling him up. But that worked only in dreams. He tried imagining it now but it wouldn't work. She was the only one who looked at him as though he were special. Everyone else thought he was trash.

He went through the list of people who had hated him. The nurse in the hospital, the police, the coroner, the reporters, the screws, the Crown, the judge, the jury, even the canaries and the tree jumpers in the Protection block. Everywhere in the joint, they whispered "ice monster" until he didn't know whether it was real or in his head. It came over shower stalls, behind mops, on the way to the visitors room. Even out in the iron pile where he lifted weights. Fast as a bullet, they slipped it to him, usually in English, sometimes in French, once in Greek. He could never get away from it.

Once late at night he sat bolt upright in bed, as though he'd been woken by a cold wind. Wailing through the cell block like a ghost, a voice cried out, "the ice monster is among us." More voices replied. "We've got to waste him." At first he thought it was a dream but in the morning on the assembly line he knew from the way they handed him the cardboard boxes that it came from the guys in his own cell block. When he didn't hear the words, he saw it glowering in their eyes.

If Maggie came three times a week, he could hang on in between, but once a week wasn't enough. He remembered the softness of her hand in his from last night and felt better, but down the cell block someone screamed, and he lost it. He was spinning out of control. He banged his fists against the wall. The first two times it had happened, they had let him go to the hospital, but the white shirt in charge of his cellblock had said he was looking for special treatment and the next time he could go to the hole. The pain in his head was unbearable. It always started with a migraine that split his brain in half.

"Take me to the hole. I've gotta go to the hole." He could hardly say the words he was so short of breath. When they brought his dinner, he'd tell the screw to get his case officer. "Don. Take me to the hole, take me to the hole," he wailed. Don looked at him as if he were crazy when he arrived at his cell. No one ever asked to go to the hole. "You've gotta let me go," he pleaded. He couldn't let the guys see him fall apart.

⁓

Before they shut the door to the hole, he threw out the roll of toilet paper. Two weeks ago, a guy in the hole — maybe this very hole — stood on toilet paper rolls and, using his pants, hung himself from the grating over the window. He wanted nothing in the cell. He wasn't eating so he didn't need the bucket, but they wouldn't take it out. The pen wasn't punishment enough so God was giving him the worst time he could, the whole cell block on top of him, flattening him. Now in the hole where no one could see him, he breathed slowly, exhausted, but always awake enough to feel the heaviness in his chest.

"Maggie, Maggie," he cried into the night. "Ara, Ara." If he could breathe in her perfume, maybe she could give him the juice that would return him to life. Sometimes he heard rasping sobs that sounded as though they came from an old man. Was that him? Or someone else? His sense of smell was gone, but he knew it was mealtime when he heard the rats' nails on the dirt. He never knew when day became night. In the hole, the tiny barred window to the sky was so covered with snow it was always dark, like the Arctic in winter.

Days and days went by. Finally a man in a stiff coat shone a bright light in his eyes and pulled up his lashes, but the flame inside his heart was so low he couldn't talk. Even when he shone the light, everything was black. He heard grave voices around him and picked up a terrible smell. He was like the girl who lay in a coma for years. On TV, she stared up at the ceiling while they stood at the end of her bed and argued about whether or not they should cut the cord.

He tried to sit up and concentrate, but all he felt was a terrible wave of gloom, of half remembered things that made him want to tell them to cut the cord. He heard his baby shrieking. It was so real he put his hands over his ears. "He died of exposure," Maggie kept telling him. "Why do you keep asking whether he might have died of something else?" In the visitors room, she had squeezed his hand, looked up at him with such trusting eyes. He took his hands off his ears and pounded a clenched fist into the palm of his hand. "Only a Greek boy with roots that go back into eternity could have lashes like yours," she'd said.

~

"You have a visitor," the screw said through the tiny bars in the door. He knew how long he'd been in the hole because he counted the times he heard "you have a visitor." Three times. She was still coming. He'd been in here for three weeks. When he was at the bottom of the pit nobody could help him. Only her. And maybe not even her. He had tried to tell her it was because she was there only once a week, across a table, where all they could do was hold hands. In between he couldn't keep the fuckin' flame going. The three times it had happened, it had usually been on a Tuesday half way between the visits.

But when he was out on parole and in the free it would never happen again because she'd be there all the time. Like Ariadne and Dionysus. Maybe they *would* go to Naxos together to find his family as she had promised. "I'm good at research," she boasted. "I can find anything." With her, he could do anything, go anywhere. The tornado had been tearing his brain for three weeks. Maybe he deserved it. But three weeks! Wasn't that enough? Dear God, he prayed and gazed up at the hole above him where on the other side there were dawns and twilights and the bright light of the sun. I need her, and you know I need her. So don't let me down.

THIRTY-THREE

❧

Hockey

A FEW WEEKS LATER, it seemed to Maggie that life for Nick was almost back to normal at the penitentiary. He was out of the hole and working every morning packing jeans.

"I have some news for you," he said one day in an upbeat tone of voice. "I've met a guy in here who's willing to give me lessons in Greek conversation. I'm Greek," he said, "and I want to speak *my* language, hook up with people from *my* country. Stavro and I are doing a little deal," he said proudly. "Free cigarettes from me in exchange for a half-hour a day of lessons. Not bad eh?"

"That's great Nick." This was the first thing he had initiated on his own and it was wonderful that he had found a friend. The prison hadn't ground out his spirit the way it had other prisoners, she thought with relief. Now when he came into the visitors room to see her, he was light on his feet and his eyes glowed.

Those evening picnics during the trial when he'd done back flips for her over the park benches in Place d'Armes seemed like yester-day, but one-third of his sentence was nearly over, and his request for parole would be coming up soon. She had to help him think about what sort of work he could do when he got out. Learning Greek cer-tainly wouldn't help with that.

～

Sitting across from her in the visitors room a few weeks later, Nick folded his arms and smiled. Her green eyes still shone for him. She belonged to him, like Ara belonged to Dio. As he reached out to take her hand, Maggie scraped her chair along the floor. Oh no, he said to himself. Not another lecture.

"You know you have a lot of talent, Nick, don't you," she said. There she was again. That teacher side of her that dropped over her like a baggy dress. He felt a sharp knot in his stomach. When she got that look, the leather pants he made her wear were nothing but dress-up. He hated it when she went on about the jobs she thought he could do.

Just for her he was now taking two grade nine courses by corre-spondence. "If you get your grade nine," she'd said, "then you can say you've finished junior high." One of the courses was in maths and he nearly gave up on it. She'd said that if he ever wanted to be a motor-cycle mechanic, the maths would come in handy.

He'd love that but it seemed impossible. He already knew how to fix lots of things on a motorcycle. It came sort of natural, but with a prison record, who would hire him? Besides, he had no experience working in a bike shop. He'd never be able to do it.

"Look, Maggie. Quit going at me all the time, will ya?" He brought his fist down so hard on the table Maggie jumped. "When I get out of here, I'll go on welfare like the other guys."

"Welfare! You don't have to go on welfare!"

"Look," he said. "What do you know about the real world? You have degrees. You've got no idea what it's like looking in the papers for work and getting no for an answer when you show up. You've applied for only two jobs in your whole life, and you admitted you had a contact for both. You're a big shot in this city."

Not any more, she thought. As Alphie had warned her, she had allowed something uncontrollable to take possession of her. Nick took her hand and as she looked up into his blue eyes she shivered as she recognized the chord he had struck inside her that she could not resist.

"I'm a nobody," Nick went on. "After spending time in the joint, there will be absolutely no contacts around for me."

Maggie looked out the window of the visitors room at the March dusting of snow on the trees from the tail end of winter. Last night, she'd been at the Forum for a hockey game with Moira and her husband and all the time she was there, she'd thought of Nick, and how quick he'd be on the ice. If she could get him to excel at something, it might teach him discipline. Hockey, she thought, might be it. Maybe he could work as a hockey coach for kids. If he could master something practical, the rest would follow.

"I was just wondering," she said, trying to sound casual. "Do you know how to play hockey?"

"Yes," he said slowly and sighed. "I played in Pierrefonds. Danny taught me. I was the fastest skater on the team and scored more than anyone."

"Really?" she said. "You never told me about that." He didn't want to tell her he had quit after he'd had a fight with the coach who insisted he take his turn as goalie. Team sports were not for him. That's why he liked gymnastics. He could do it alone.

"What do you do during your free time on weekends?" she pressed on, "besides learning how to swear in Greek. After all, you're not working, and . . ."

"I lie in my cell," he said and deliberately changed the subject, but a couple of minutes later she came back to it.

"Tell me. Do they have a rink here? Do the inmates ever play hockey? Out in the courtyard maybe?"

"Are you trying to tell me I should play hockey?" He breathed through his teeth. "Here in the pen?"

"Well, why not?"

"Why not?" It was as though he'd stepped on a high voltage wire. "Why not?" he yelled so loud the inmates and visitors at the other tables looked up. He grabbed her arm and turned it until she winced. "I could get yoked out there. You understand?"

Maggie pulled away from him but tried not to show anything. She knew he was at the bottom of the pecking order in the prison, but surely he would be safe out there in broad daylight playing hockey. "Nick. I'm sorry. Okay? I'm sorry."

"You think I'm paranoid, I know, I can see it in your eyes. You're so damn naive, jeezus, so goddamn naive." He let go of her arm and grabbed the brown plastic ashtray on the table and scrunched it up in his hand until it snapped in half. Everyone in the visitors room stopped talking. The snap had been like the crack of a gun.

"You don't understand nothin', Maggie, nothin'." She was always wanting him to do things he could never fuckin' do. Before they moved Stavro to medium security, he wanted to concentrate on learning Greek with his friend, but that wasn't good enough for her. Her idea about hockey made him want to hit her.

Hit her! Hit her! Hit her! He was getting out of control again. If only he could ride off in a Harley for a while. "Maggie," he said. "I can't live up to what you want me to be. Don't you see?" He leaned forward and looked into her eyes. "I'm no good for you." The rage inside him scared him. He had twisted her arm until it hurt. He looked quickly to the floor. "You gotta watch it," he said. "Sometimes I think I should tell you to stop comin' here. I could ruin your life."

∽

"Maggie, it's for you," Foxy said. Someone was calling her on the night news editor's phone.

"For me?" she said. It was one in the morning, a couple of nights later. It couldn't be about a story, because she wasn't reporting any more.

"It's Adele," the caller said. "I'm sorry to call you at the office, I couldn't find your home number. Then I remembered you worked at night. This is the fourth number I've called."

For a moment Maggie didn't pick up exactly who it was. She was still thinking of the story she was editing on Ukraine's desire for independence from the U.S.S.R.

"Oh hi," she said, suddenly remembering Adele from prison. "I haven't seen you for ages. Is something wrong?"

"Yeah. Sort of. Jacques doesn't know I'm telling you this. Don't tell your friend how you heard it."

She hardly knew Adele even though she sometimes gave her a lift from the prison. She wished she weren't taking this call where Foxy and possibly others on the Rim could hear.

"There's something I think you should know," Adele said. Maggie could hear a lot of commotion in the background. It sounded like a bar.

Foxy tapped her on the shoulder. "Don't be long," he said. She knew he was expecting a call from the composing room.

"Adele," Maggie said, "I think we should meet. You know what I mean?"

"I can't. A friend is waiting for me in the car. I'm going away for two weeks."

"Okay. Tell me quickly." She swung around in her chair away from Foxy.

"Your friend Nick . . ."

"Yes . . ."

"I don't know how to say it. Jacques told me tonight. He's in the hospital. *Violé.*" She said the word in French.

"Raped?" Maggie whispered.

"Yes. Last night. And it wasn't just one."

Maggie cupped her hand over her mouth. "He's not seriously hurt, is he?" The phone shook in her hand. "Listen. Thanks for calling.

Adele. I'm going to give you my number at home. Call me when you come back. Leave a message if I'm not there." Foxy tapped her on the shoulder. "I have to go. I'm tying up the boss's phone." She hung up.

"I'm going home, Foxy," she said, slowly standing. "I'm not feeling well." For two hours, too dazed to think, she sat on a cold bench in the dark of the square facing Notre Dame church waiting for the sun to come up. When the doors opened, she knelt at the back and wept.

~

Maggie knew not to go up to the penitentiary until Nick was ready to see her. He would need a few days alone to heal. She'd wait two days for him to call, then, no matter what, she'd show up. Now, more than ever, she had to stand by him.

Two days later, en route to the pen, Maggie opened the door of Rosie's on St. Antoine to return a video she'd borrowed the night before. Left to her own devices, she would have let the video sit around on top of her television set collecting a fine until the store called. She had done it to please her cousin Moira who was trying to help Maggie get her life in order.

After Hydro Quebec cut her electricity, Moira took over paying for the utilities and asked Maggie to give her a cheque to cover them. But Moira couldn't pick up after her totally. Maggie had overdue books from various libraries on her desk, and in the bathroom under the sink were second, maybe third notices, possibly summons, for parking tickets. She had stopped opening envelopes from City Hall. As far as she was concerned, paying fines for parking tickets was a low priority. The worst that could happen would be a bailiff at the door, and she'd worry about that when it happened.

"You could end up with a Denver boot," Moira had warned. She thought about the tangle of bureaucracy she'd have to face to organize removal of a Denver boot. She couldn't function without her car. How would she get to the penitentiary? It was an hour and a half away by public transportation and the provincial busses didn't run all the time. She couldn't tell Moira about that. Moira knew nothing about Nick. The horror of the gang rape completely preoccupied her but she had no one she felt comfortable enough with to share it. She knew what Alphie would say, and Michael was in Guatemala.

She selected another video for later that night when she came back from the penitentiary. Nick hadn't called, but she'd phoned Stillpoint and made an appointment for a visit that evening. She *had* to see him. The morning after Adele rang she had phoned his case officer and left a message but he hadn't returned the call. The lack of communication from the penitentiary scared her.

Maggie stepped out onto the slippery sidewalk from the video store and looked over to the spot where she'd parked her car. Where was her red Innocenti? She'd left it right at the corner of St. Antoine in front of the subway station. It was gone. A burnt orange Buick with fins, circa 1955, was in its place. Three tall youths in charcoal stove-pipe pants wearing earrings and dark glasses were looking down the hill and laughing. She raced over to the curb and looked down the incline.

"Oh my God," she cried. The car had rolled backwards down the hill and crashed into a street light in front of some rickety rooming houses. She hurried down the hill. The car could have burst through one of those flimsy doors and killed someone. She must have left it in neutral. How could she have been so unhinged as to leave the car in neutral on a hill? *Criminal negligence,* she could hear the prosecutor saying, and she saw herself in prison serving a manslaughter term for killing an old lady who had opened her front door at the wrong moment and been mowed down by her car.

She stared at a twelve-inch gash on the back of her car and a smashed tail light. She was losing her ability to cope with everyday life, becoming like Nick. Whether he was living with Eileen, or on the street after Stevie died, or in prison, something was always going wrong. Sometimes she wondered whether Nick was passing into her like blood through an umbilical chord. One crazy move, that's all it took — one crazy move, like not putting her Innocenti in gear — and she could be in Superior court on the fifth floor of the Palais de Justice just as he had been. She looked around to see if there were any police cars on the street. The cops often cruised in her district, especially near the subway station.

She had to get to the penitentiary. Nick would now be expecting her. She climbed into the car and started the engine. The wheels spun on some ice and her car wouldn't move. Except for the youths up the hill, the street was deserted. In the extreme cold under the street lights, the big orange Buick and the houses with tar paper fronts looked unreal. She pushed on the accelerator gently, the way Michael had taught her, but the car wouldn't budge.

The penitentiary was seventy kilometres away. She could always take a taxi but she didn't have enough money in her purse. Crying and in a panic, she ran up to the orange Buick where the three youths in warm leather jackets were standing. As she approached, she slowed down. Covered in metal, with studs on their boots, chains around their necks and spiked bracelets at their wrists, they looked at her coldly.

"I'm in an awful jam," she said, looking down the hill helplessly. "Do you think you could give me a push?" The three exchanged looks. "Maybe," one of them said slowly, pulling himself away from the orange car like a cat stretching.

She stood there with her coat half open, hands in her pockets, teeth chattering. Ignoring her, they started to kid around amongst themselves. After a few minutes, Maggie started walking toward a phone booth outside the subway station.

"How much?" one called out.

She turned around. She could hardly move her lips she was so cold. "Twenty dollars?" It was all she had.

A quick push from the boys and she was speeding along the expressway toward the highway to the north. She stayed in the middle lane to avoid being seen by the provincial police who patrolled the expressways.

She already had ten demerit points for going through a red light in a snow storm and for not stopping at several STOP signs in Westmount. She worried the police would penalize her now for her smashed back light. Two more demerit points and she'd lose her licence. With three different highways and then a special side road to get to the penitentiary, she had to keep track of the exits. All she could think of was the fact that Nick had been raped. Rape! Nothing could have been worse.

~

"We're going to let you visit him in the hospital," the guard said when she checked in. "I've called an escort guard. We're making a big exception." They were afraid of suicide, Maggie thought.

The security woman with the peroxide hair was looking through a barred window into the locker area. She reminded Maggie of the 300-pound Gestapo lady in Lina Wertmuller's *Seven Beauties*. This time she administered only a routine check, up the sides of the legs, the insides of the arms and the bra straps.

She counted the number of steel barred doors they went through as she followed the escort guard. There was still that little part of her that believed she might do a book on prisons. There was a thudding clang as each one closed behind them. No escape was possible through here. There were too many doors. Fifteen. Exactly Nick's age when the Evans threw him out.

They walked outside through a huge walled area with rolls of barbed wire, towers manned by guards with machine guns and kennels filled with vicious barking dogs. "Trained to kill," the guard said to her as they passed within inches of them. In the distance, looking like discarded auto parts, weight lifting equipment sat in a field covered with melting snow. Nick had used them until his lift partner started talking about what a great little ass he had.

The only cheery note was the hockey rink where a game was in progress. Listening to the puck knocking on the wooden sideboards and the swish of the skates on the ice made her want to cry. She walked slowly, ignoring the guard, her eyes on the skaters as they tore down the ice. She had watched the Canadiens playing the Boston Bruins last night on TV and had thought of what a different life Nick might have had if he could have stayed in Pierrefonds with the Evans and played hockey for the high-school team.

Under the glare of the searchlights from the towers, Maggie stood with the guard at the door to the penitentiary. A guard with a machine gun slung over his shoulder opened the triple doors of the stone fortress containing the cell blocks. He was short and square with thick black suspenders and black laced boots. As soon as he saw her, a grin spread across his face. She pulled her coat tight over her black angora sweater. Two other guards, also toting machine guns, watched.

The escort guard muttered something to the gate-keeper who said, "Okay. *Correc.*"

"This way," he said to Maggie. She followed slightly behind him as he led her from the foyer into an enormous oval-shaped cavern with three tiers of cells ringed by a network of bars crawling up to a dome with a skylight at the top. On the second level, a thick cord of inmates, their hands tightly gripping the bars, glared down at her in silence. She could feel the tautness in their legs. A glob of spit flew down and hit her forehead.

"They know we're going to the hospital where Mykonos is," the guard said. She tried to act as though nothing had happened, but when the spit on her forehead moved down to the bridge of her nose, she wiped it off with the back of her hand. Something in her died a little as she felt their hatred for him pelting her like stones. She was ashamed at how little she had understood his terror of the prison. But if the inmates thought they could harm her, they were mistaken. The reporter part of her, the cold observer, took it all in like a tape recorder. They were all nothing more than material. The crooked corridor leading to the hospital was dark and dank, moisture coming up through the loose floor boards. The smell of excrement hung in the air. Naked light bulbs revealed paint the colour of dark urine peeling off the walls. At the end she could see a small light in a nurse's office.

∽

In the semi-dark outside some hospital cells that were smaller than a dining room table, she sat in a small waiting room. Through the latticework of bars on the window, the rays from the circling search lights on the snow gave the room an eerie brightness. Pipes cracked and scratched. Probably rats. Nick lined the base of his cell with cardboard to try to keep them out but his Greek friend Stavro, he had told her, made one of them into a pet and trained it to deliver messages. She heard the dogs in the courtyard barking, and in the distance, from another place in the prison compound, racking sobs. She put her elbows on her knees and covered her ears. They reminded her of the cries of grief of a Palestinian she'd interviewed in a Beirut camp after losing his son in an explosion.

A door clanged from down the hall and the guard ushered Nick into the room. Pulling out a huge steel key from a chain at the back of his pants, the guard locked them in and sat in a chair outside. Nick's eyes were black and blue and he looked devastated. He turned his head away from her.

"Tell me what happened," she said.

He put his head in his hands and sobbed. "Oh Maggie," he said. "It was terrible. Five of them." He shifted uncomfortably on the bench. "The thing I feared most."

"Where?" she asked.

"Behind the hockey rink."

A tremor went through her. "You went out to play *hockey?*"

"Yes."

"Oh no," she cried. "Oh Nick." She threw her arms around him. He did it for her and he was raped. Even a simple pleasure like playing hockey for fun wasn't possible. She knew he could never tell her the details, never tell her how he had been unable to defend himself. She held him close to her and he sobbed in her arms.

How could she ever make it up to him! She'd pull every string she could to get him out of the penitentiary and into minimum security. She'd use the Prisoners' Rights Association, the church committee on prisoners, a contact she had in the solicitor-general's office in Ottawa — everyone she could think of to get him out of this inferno. He pulled back and stared into her eyes. There wasn't much light in the room. "Maggie," he said, his eyes fixed to hers. "Hold me, please."

She took him in her arms and rocked him like a child. For months she'd known that this was what he wanted but she'd never been able to do it. The visitors room was too much like a fishbowl, and besides the intimacy scared her. He began to sob the way he had on the witness stand at the trial.

"Nick, Nick," she said, rocking him. Clinging to her, his head close to her breast, he tried to talk. "Inside I feel so small. I have no juice. I need juice or I'm going to die." She could hear his heart beating. "When I get out, you'll still see me?"

"Yes."

"You won't leave me?"

"No."

"Madame MacKinnan, Madame MacKinnan." It was the guard knocking on the bars, the big steel key in his hand. "I've got to take you back."

She pulled Nick from the bench and put her hands on his shoulders. "Just because of this, well, it doesn't mean you couldn't still be a . . ."

"Shit Maggie," he smiled. "You go on like a stuck record." She would never let up. Still, she cared, and that was all that mattered.

"Madame MacKinnan." It was the guard again. He had opened the gate and there was another guard waiting to take Nick back to his hospital cell.

"Hug me," he said to her. "Just one more time."

He watched her as she disappeared down the hall. She was his Ariadne. And his Semele. He leaned back against the wall and imagined he was still in her arms.

Maggie
and Nick

THIRTY-FOUR

~

The Red Scarf

MAGGIE STILL HAD a half an hour before he phoned. She stared at her agenda, open at Thursday, November 14. *Nick, 8 p.m.,* she had written. She flipped to Saturday. *Nine a.m. halfway house* was written in small print. Sunday said *back at 6 p.m.* She picked up a white file card and wrote *My boss will fire me if I don't.* No matter what he said, the answer had to be no. She glanced at the kitchen clock. A couple of motorcycles whizzed by. "How about renting a motorcycle for the weekend? Wouldn't that be great," Nick had said the last time she had seen him. She was wavering already. She turned the file card over and wrote in capitals so the words would jump out at her. 1. BAD NEWS, 2. CAN'T SPEND THE WEEKEND, 3. MUST GO TO NEW YORK, 4. NO CHOICE, 5. MY BOSS WILL FIRE ME. She looked at how she'd written boss, the s's backwards, the way Nick would write them. The card looked as though it had been written by a mental patient.

She wandered into the living room and looked down to St. Antoine Street. A man of about thirty in jeans and a leather jacket had his hand in a garbage bin. A small backpack with a broken strap hung from his belt. She snapped off the light so he couldn't see her if he turned around. For a few minutes she sat in the dark gazing into the black cavern that stretched as far as she could see under the expressway on the other side of the street. The arching lights on top reminded her of the rows of steel beams that lit up the desert of asphalt and barbed wire around every prison Nick had been in. Wind was churning up loose debris, hurling it into the gloom. She shut her curtains and switched on the light.

She should have said *no* two weeks ago when his case officer called. Nick would be staying at a halfway house for the weekend, he'd said, only a few kilometres from her. "Yes, oh yes, I'd be glad to help with Nick's pre-parole program." Nick's first time out *would* be hard, she had agreed. After everything he'd gone through. A little paranoid? Yes, she knew about that. She had talked quickly. Not to worry, she'd keep him busy, take care of him.

"Ice monster in halfway house in LaSalle." She could see the headline already in *Bonjour Police*. It had taken a number of months to get him out of maximum security — most of the summer in fact — but now everything was moving far too quickly. First the minimum security prison, now a weekend a month, and as soon as he got full parole, a halfway house only a few kilometres from her with no bars at all. Everything had moved swiftly after she had gone to the church committee on justice. A gang rape, she'd told them, and Corrections Canada had done nothing to protect him. She'd primed the committee with shocking details and rehearsed their interview with the warden. "At the very end, don't forget to drop the name of the justice reporter at the *Globe and Mail*."

One month later, the warden moved Nick from Stillpoint to the minimum security prison at St. Bartholomew. Even Nick couldn't believe it. She walked into the kitchen. Two minutes to eight. Maybe she could wait until Saturday morning and fake being sick. No, she couldn't do that. He'd drag her out. Here in the quiet of her apartment, away from Nick, she could take this decision and stick to it, but if she waited until she saw him, he would overwhelm her and she might agree to anything. She could not take the risk.

∽

"Midnight Oil," Nick said as soon as she picked up the phone, "at the Spectrum. That's what I want to do Saturday night. Go out and get the tickets. I've made a list of everything I want to do. Le Chateau for some new jeans, Harvey's for a hamburger, the Majestic Arcade for some fun on the machines, the Peel Pub for a beer and Jake's Ice Cream." He was running out of breath. "Maybe we could go to a shopping mall and then climb the mountain to the cross. And I want to try the swings in Jeanne Mance Park where I used to meet my *yiayia*. And now, about the motorcycle . . ." That morning, in the for sale column of a newspaper, he'd looked up the listing for second-hand motorcycles.

"Nick," she said, breaking in. In no time, she realized, she'd be sucked into his chaotic world. In the prison he was contained but on the street she'd be completely at his mercy, as Eileen had been.

"I've got an idea," he went on. He had the ad in front of him: "*Harley Davidson '69 FL full chrome, rebuilt, stroked*. It's 7,000 dollars. A fantastic piece of machinery. I want you to call and make an appointment. We could take it out on a trial run the way I used to with Eileen." Some day, he said to himself, he would find himself a job as a bike mechanic. He'd show Maggie he could make something of himself.

"Nick, I have bad news," she leapt in. "I can't spend the weekend with you. I have to go to New York. My boss insists. It's a seminar at Columbia's journalism school."

"Wait a minute . . ." He was thinking about how much fun they'd have on the Harley. "You're telling me — what?"

"It just came up. I just got off the phone with my boss. I can hardly believe it myself, but . . ."

"Well you just call that dude right back and tell him you've got other plans."

"Nick, I can't."

"Do it." In the silence she could hear him breathing through his teeth. She looked down at the words on her card.

"He'll fire me if I don't go."

"You won't call him? Give *me* his number and *I'll* call him." She cringed, imagining Max getting a collect call at the paper from the St. Bartholomew prison.

"Give me his number."

"He's unlisted."

"No one is gonna ruin my first weekend out. Give me his name. I'll call him tomorrow. I can find the fuckin' number in the phone book." He laughed bitterly. "I'm not stupid. You think I'm stupid, don't you?"

"You can't call my boss." Before he could go on, she said, "Okay. Pat Barrett." Barrett was a shortened version of the director at a journalism school in Ontario. "But you won't get him," she added. "He called from New York."

"You think I believe that! Called from New York! A semar in Columbia! I bet there is no semar!"

"Seminar," she said.

"Seminar. Semar. I knew it! You've been planning to get out of this ever since my case officer called you. I saw it in your eyes when you came to visit. You want me to stay behind bars, don't you?"

"Nick. Don't say that. My boss will fire me if . . ."

"Who cares if he fires you? What's a job? Nothin'. Nothin' next to this weekend."

All that mattered to him, she thought, was his thirst of the moment and he would do anything to quench it, whether her life stood in his way or not.

"You could get another job," he yelled.

"Look, Nick . . ." They were worlds apart. She looked futilely at her cue cards.

"Look, Nick, look, Nick," he mimicked. "I trusted you. I didn't want to believe it. I spent the whole week making you a present. I'll give you a present you'll never forget!" And he banged the phone down in her ear.

She immediately phoned her Aunt Philana to see if she could in fact go to New York, but she was away at a conference. Not knowing what to do, Maggie left her apartment and walked aimlessly along St. Antoine Street. When she came to the Salvation Army Hostel, she trudged up Guy and along St. Catherine Street to The Main. A fight was going on outside a bar on the corner and she crossed the street. By the time she reached Roy Street, she was too cold to walk and she lurched into La Cabane where she could stare into space without anyone bothering her. Bryan Adams was singing "Can't Stop This Thing We Started." She felt guilty. It reminded her of the excitement in Nick's voice when he talked about going to Midnight Oil.

When La Cabane closed, it was raining but she hardly noticed it and went up the street to Lux which was open all night. It was already four in the morning. She was lucky she didn't have to work that night. Before the sun came up, she climbed into a taxi for Dunn's where she had an early breakfast with a cheery crowd of night cleaners from the sky scrapers on René Lévesque Boulevard. When she and her colleagues from the Rim went there for supper at three in the morning, she often talked to them. But now she lowered her head, ate her scrambled eggs and tried to ignore the rain that had seeped into her clothing. More than anything, a weekend alone with Nick would make her confront everything she had refused to face for more than twenty years. She couldn't do it.

～

Two days later, early on Saturday morning, Maggie stumbled down the stairs of her apartment with a green garbage bag of laundry slung over her shoulder. She went out for breakfast and spent the rest of the morning at a laundromat far from her house. A *Tribune* sat on a bench with a front-page story she had edited on Yeltsin's plan for econom-ic liberalization of Russia. Maggie caught a glimpse of herself in a mirror looking like a school marm and looked away. She tried not to think of what Nick might be doing at the halfway house as she leafed through the pages of a tattered magazine someone had left on the floor.

At noon she went to a book store on Duluth Street where she knew the owner and could get a coffee but the sign said "Closed for Book Fair." It was cold and her pumps were too tight. She walked a half a block and rang Alphie's bell. Maybe she could talk to him. He came to the door in his pyjamas.

"Hi Maggie," he said. "Isn't it sort of early? I've ah, got a visitor." He looked her over. "Anything wrong?"

"No, nothing." Maggie backed down the steps. "I'm sorry. I was at the book store and . . ."

"Bloody cold," he said, his eyes only half open, and he shut the door.

She went up Park to the Rialto Repertory Theatre. A lopsided sign on a string said *East of Eden* at 5, 7, 9; *The Rocky Horror Picture Show* was showing at midnight. She drove back down Park to La Bodega to read the Saturday papers but she was feeling too sad to concentrate.

At one o'clock, she started dropping in on acquaintances. She was passing by, had a call to make and no quarter. "Could she? Just for a minute?" She went from Montreal West to Henri Julien in the east, and then over to Berlioz in the middle of the river on Nun's Island where her Russian professor lived, and finally to Pointe Claire to see her folk dance partner. Michael would understand but there was too much to explain, too much to confess.

As the sun was going down, she slipped into Notre Dame Basilica at Place d'Armes. The five o'clock mass was coming to an end. She lingered in the church until the priest snuffed out the candles and turned off the lights. Outside, Place d'Armes was sad and deserted. She wasn't due at her cousin's for supper until seven so, to kill time,

she went to the Pique Assiette restaurant up near the Forum for a
pineapple juice.

~

At first Nick was shocked at the way she looked in that old gray suit
of hers and her hair pinned back like a social worker. It reminded him
of when he first met her. He hitched where he could, and where he
couldn't, he pulled open a door and said, "Please, it's an emergency,
you have to take me." The drivers took him, never realizing they were
simply following her red Innocenti. He could always see it because
one of the tail lights was smashed. When it got dark, it was like following a motorcycle.

By the end of the day, he had a blueprint of her life and the
addresses of people she had never told him about all over the island
of Montreal. It was a wild trek around the city, past things he hadn't
seen for years, like the Champlain bridge, the oil refineries and the
Humpty Dumpty factory out past Lachine. The last time he'd been
out on the West Island expressway was after Eileen took off for
Magog and he'd hitched a motorcycle ride to the Evans when he
couldn't face his empty apartment.

Around six o'clock, when Maggie went into an Indian restaurant
near the Forum and opened a book, he went down St. Catherine
Street. He was in a rage at the way she had lied to him. He kicked a
stone ahead of him as he walked. A knife shop two blocks down had
a huge Swiss army knife in the window. He watched the knives, each
more than a foot long, open slowly, one by one, ending finally with
the scissors. He went inside. Four knives in shiny red casings lay on
the counter near the door. While the salesman was busy at the other
end, he dropped one into his pocket and slipped out. He dashed to
Fort Street, down the tunnel under the expressway and over to the
lane behind her apartment on St. Antoine. Up a flight at the back, a
flick of the knife at the side of the window across the fire escape and
he was in.

He could smell her perfume as soon as he entered her bedroom. He opened her cupboard. There it was, the red scarf, on a hanger. He plucked it off, buried his face in it and stuffed it in his pocket. He'd been thinking of that red scarf ever since he'd ripped up her picture. He had to have it. He ran his hand down the black kid pants and caressed the black angora sweater. From her bureau, he picked up her butterfly pin and put it in his pocket.

He walked downstairs to the living room and sat in the big armchair in the dark. The kitchen clock said 6:45. He would stay until she came back. A few minutes later, the phone rang and he ran into the kitchen. On the answering machine he heard: "It's Moira. You there? Billy and the twins are looking forward to seeing you. After supper we'll watch a video. I've made up a bed."

Nick switched on a light in the kitchen. A leather address book lay next to the phone. He leafed through the pages looking for Moira. Under B, he finally found Moira and Cliff Brett on Grand Boulevard. He looked up Brett in the phone book to get the exact address. "Shit," he said and sank into the chair at the kitchen table.

He looked around the room. Above the phone, stuck to the wall with scotch tape, was a picture of her with a bunch of people. She looked younger then. He ripped it off the wall and turned it over. He glanced at the back but couldn't understand the writing. It must have been when she had been in Russia. He picked up a pack of matches by the stove, lit a corner of the picture with his lighter, and watched it burn. He felt his back pocket for the red scarf and went out the front door, not caring who saw him.

∼

In front of a large brick house on Grand Boulevard, Nick leaned against her Innocenti and stared at her through an enormous picture window framed with dark green curtains. Maggie had her foot curled under her on a flowered sofa. He hardly recognized her. She was watching television with her cousin. Family photographs in silver frames stood on a shiny table near a couch. Next to the fireplace was a grandfather clock. The living room, he thought, looked like a Christmas card. It was everything he'd always wanted and would never have.

Maggie was talking to her cousin, throwing her hands in the air and laughing. Nick pulled out his Swiss army knife, squatted down in front of the tire and jabbed the blade into the rubber. He shut his eyes and concentrated on her the way he did when they threw him in the hole naked and he wanted to feel her arms around him. When the blade was in up to the shaft, he twisted it, and then listened as the air slowly hissed out. Everything was still. He opened his eyes and straightened up. She was still laughing.

A man was coming down the street. Nick folded the blade and hurried north toward the railway tracks. The leatherette jacket he'd bought from another prisoner to impress her wasn't warm. He hadn't been this cold since he was living under the porch near the river the winter before he'd met Eileen. The wind was whipping his pants like sheets on a clothesline. He came back on the other side of the street and climbed into the centre of a thick cedar hedge in front of her cousin's place. He cut some branches close to the ground and made himself a refuge where he could watch her. He looked at his watch. Eight o'clock. If they'd been together, the way they were supposed to be, they'd be sitting in their seats at the Spectrum waiting for Midnight Oil.

He pulled out the red scarf, breathed her in and drifted off. He cradled into her silky breast, soft as yellow rose petals and sucked. Harder, and more, oh more, he had to have more. Warmth spread through him and he sighed but it lasted only a second and the thirst was back. He opened his mouth wider.

When it began to rain and the water dripped off the oily leaves onto his coat, he pushed away some branches and looked across the street. A little boy was lying in Maggie's arms watching television. She held him close the way Nick had always wanted to be held. Then she stood up and lifted him up in the air so his legs flew back and he began to laugh. How could she!

Nick dropped down to the stumps on the damp earth and moaned the way he did when he hid in the shed after he found out Mum and Pop Evans were adopting Luke. It began to snow. He let the wet flakes plaster down his hair and soak into his clothing. Finally he stumbled out of the hedge and lay face down on the grass until he was covered in white.

~

The next day, back on St. Antoine Street, as she hung up her clothes, Maggie noticed her red silk scarf was gone. It had been on the neck of the hanger with the leather pants and the black angora sweater. He loved knotting it in different places around her neck. The first thing he did when he sat down with her in the visitors room was to tie her scarf.

Six o'clock. The bells from the old church were ringing. She breathed a sigh of relief. Now he would be back at St. Bartholomew. Someone from the halfway house would have delivered him. She emptied out his treasures from the envelope he'd given her before the trial ended and spotted the picture the *Tribune* used when he was three. During the trial, she had traced the picture of him on a swing back to the "Wednesday's Child" feature seventeen years before in the Living Section. "This little boy has never had a home. His mother left him on a bus after he was born. He has been in foster homes ever since. If he doesn't find permanent parents, he could end up in a prison or a mental hospital."

She went back to her cupboard and inspected every hanger. Her red scarf couldn't just vanish. She looked around the room. Nothing else was amiss. She checked the back door off the fire escape and it was locked.

When the doorbell rang, she looked through the peep-hole, saw it was Nick, and opened the door as though she'd been expecting him all along. He was wearing an Expo's baseball cap on backwards. Nick shut the door, slid the bolt into place, and from his pocket, slowly drew out the red scarf.

"How'd you get that?" she asked. From the other pocket, he pulled out his Swiss army knife and opened a blade. "Fits right into your back window," he said. "Sit down," he said, mockingly, playing host. "I won't be goin' for a while, so you might as well sit down."

He waved her into the living room over to an arm chair where she sat down like a child on the edge of the seat. He drew a dining room chair up close to her. From his back pocket he pulled out a little black book. "I think it was between the Indian restaurant on St. Catherine, and let's see, Moira and Cliff," he frowned, "on Grand."

Maggie's stomach fluttered. The hole in her tire must have been his doing. Cliff had changed it for her. He ran his index finger down the page of his notebook. She could see everything written neatly in straight columns with numbers and streets. He licked his finger, flipped over one page, then another. "Or perhaps it was between La Bodega on Park and that place on Victoria."

"Aren't you supposed to be back?" she asked.

"Back? Who says I'm goin' back? Oh yes." He smiled, as though he just remembered something. "I found this." From the breast pocket of his shirt, he drew out the white card he'd found in her address book. "Let me read it: one, bad news; two, can't spend the weekend; three, must go to New York; four, no choice; five, boss will fire me."

Maggie clutched the arms of the chair and through her blouse heard the sound of her heart beating.

"Now listen to me," he said. "I want you to get out of that ugly nun's skirt you've got on. Didn't I tell you to *burn* that skirt?" He raised his voice. "And why are you wearing your hair in that stupid bun?" He pulled the pins out of her hair.

"I want you to go to your bedroom and put on your black kid pants, your boots, your black angora sweater and your eye makeup." She felt the eyes of her mother bore into her back from the portrait on the wall as the two of them walked upstairs. He leaned against her bedroom wall and smoked a cigarette as he watched her pull on the sleek black leather pants under her skirt.

In the bathroom, he watched her put on her mascara. "And eyeliner, more eyeliner. Where's your perfume?" She sprayed on some White Jasmine and fluffed her hair. Then she slipped off the skirt. The social worker look was gone. Nick thought she looked just as good as one of the biker girls in *Easy Rider* magazine. He took her hand, dragging her like a doll back to the living room where he sat her in an armchair.

"Just one more thing," he said, and he pulled the red scarf slowly out of his pocket. "I want to remember you exactly the way you were." He tied the scarf loosely at her neck and looked her over. "You think I don't have the nerve, don't you? There's something you don't understand." He cleared his throat. "I don't care if I get life."

He took the two ends of the scarf and slowly pulled them. "Nick," she pleaded. His hands shook. Suddenly, he leapt across the room, grabbed the photo of Moira's twins off the table, smashed the glass and tore up the picture. For a moment he didn't know what to do. He stood in the centre of the room, nervously scanning it as though he were on a B&E. Then he flung himself at her cherry-wood cabinet in the corner, shattering the glass and doors. The fifteen Royal Doulton figurines sitting on the shelves rattled to the floor.

Maggie ran to a far corner of the living room where she cowered as he fired each of the figurines against the wall. Rosemary of the sapphire blue eyes, Marilyn with her fan, May in her red cape, Dorothy making lace, Susan holding a cat, Sally, with the green bonnet. Her mother had given her Sally just before she died. Lisa, Diana, Maureen, Meg, and Florence. She had lived with them all her life. Rolling towards her foot she saw the head of Jemma, her mother's favourite. A rose ribbon still tied her chestnut hair but her delicate nose was gone. Old Biddy Penny Farthing with the balloons was the last one to go. Nick coiled back like a baseball pitcher and shot her through the kitchen window.

Maggie squeezed into a corner as he grabbed a cabinet containing her mother's antique thimble collection. He ripped off the door at the hinges, swept the thimbles out of the shelves and ground his heel on each one. He finished the hutch by punching his arm through the back and heaving it against the wall. The room lay in shadows, the few lamps she had, knocked over. Only the tiny light over the oil painting of her mother was still on.

"Oh Nick." Maggie didn't dare look up. Standing on a chair, Nick ripped at the canvas painting of her mother with his Swiss army knife tearing it into strips that could never be stitched together. There was a second of silence as he stepped off the chair. He was breathing hard. Finally, he hurled himself against the wall in a series of bursts, his head cracking the plaster until he fell back into the dark room in the midst of the rubble.

For a few moments, there was no sound, just the wind blowing through the gaping hole in the window. Maggie lay crumpled against the wall, weak with exhaustion, as though *she* were the one who had destroyed her mother's porcelain menagerie. Her eyes were dry as sand. Once she had dreamt of smashing them herself. Now Nick had done it for her. A cold wind blew over her and she was shocked at her feeling of gratitude.

Maggie reached out into the dark and felt for Nick. He crawled over to her sobbing the way he had at the trial. "Why Maggie. Why, why? I need you so much." He buried his head in her breast. "I need you so much, and you want to go away. Like all the others . . ." She took him in her arms and they lay together on the floor, the broken figurines and pieces of wood crunching beneath them. Sweat soaked through his shirt. After a few seconds, he fell asleep. As though he had always been hers, she held him tight and rocked him. When she felt him stir, she stroked his cheeks. "They'll be looking for you," she said. "I've got to take you back. I'll call the chaplain, tell him my car broke down. He'll call the warden, and fix it up."

THIRTY-FIVE

~

Toujours Gai

LEANING AGAINST the kitchen counter waiting for Reverend Macauley to come on the phone, Maggie could hear harsh voices echoing in the hallway of the prison.

"It's Control you've got to call," Nick said. "Not the Rev. Why're you calling *him*?"

"I'd sooner speak to him," she said.

"It's urgent," she said in a piping voice when yet another official came on the line. She was getting transferred all over the prison looking for the chaplain.

While she waited for the guards to find him, she watched Nick play with his baseball hat. He must have bought it yesterday. Probably it reminded him of the one Danny gave him before his foster parents sent him away. She stared down at the floor. What she had done was unforgivable. She had been crueller than any of them.

When the prison chaplain finally came on the line, he was cold as sleet and he didn't believe the excuse about the car. "Please bring him back, immediately, Miss MacKinnan, by 7:30." He had always called her Maggie but now it was Miss MacKinnan.

"It won't take even an hour. I can . . ." The phone went dead in mid-sentence. "Reverend Macauley?" She rested her head against the kitchen cupboard.

"So?" Nick asked.

"He's going to call Control," she said.

"Now we can relax," Nick said jumping up and opening the re-frigerator.

"Relax?" Her voice was a croak. "We can't relax. We've got to go."

Nick snapped open a Labatt 50. She kept a few at the back of the refrigerator for Michael when he was in town.

"Just this." He raised his glass and smiled as though the evening were just beginning. "Okay? Then we'll go."

While he sipped, she cut a bouquet of orange petunias spilling over her shiny copper pots hanging from the beams in the ceiling and put them in a glass. "We've got to go," she said as soon as he finished.

She yanked her jacket from the coat stand in the hall and nearly tripped over a piece of broken figurine. Aunt Phil was right about the menagerie. Her father should never have forced it on her. The light over her mother was out. This was the first time her mother's eyes hadn't followed her as she left the house.

As they went down the winding metal steps she heard something drop down through the slats. She had forgotten to zip up her purse and everything rattled down: lipsticks, perfume, cheque books, address books, her licence, her ID for the paper, a reporter's note-book, and her wallet.

"My keys," she moaned after they'd scooped up everything. "Where are my keys?" Her house and car keys were all on one ring. They spent fifteen minutes going up and down the stairway feeling every step, then patting the ground underneath. "What am I going to do?" she said sitting on the bottom rung in the dark next to Nick. The air was a lot warmer than the day before, more like early

October than mid-November. A neighbour was burning leaves. The moon was rising. Nick sat close to her and she could feel his warmth. The two of them looked out at her red Innocenti in the lane.

"If it were a Harley, I could hot-wire it," he said. "You got another set somewhere?"

She suddenly felt so weary she could hardly move. "In my top drawer."

"Bedroom?"

"Uh huh."

He looked up to the third floor at the window he had wedged open the day before with his Swiss army knife. "Shit," he said, feeling the side pocket of his jeans. "I don't have my knife." It was lying on the carpet in the rubble under the painting of her mother.

He raced up the stairs to the top storey of the building. The bedroom window lay three feet away from the landing. He jumped over like a cat and eased the window panel open. "Smart eh?" he yelled down. Maggie looked up at him from the grass underneath.

"Watch," he said. Gripping the window ledge with his hands, he slowly dropped down his legs.

"Nick. Nick! What are you doing?" If he fell, he could kill himself like that guy had at the Villemont detention centre where Nick was placed after his conviction.

"Watch!" He shrieked crazily and swung his legs from side to side like a trapeze artist. He wiggled his behind but she was too petrified to laugh. With a gymnast's grace, he lifted his body up by his arms, hoisted himself to the sill, and slid in through the window. In fifteen seconds he opened the door off the landing. Chin bobbing from side to side, his baseball hat cocked just so, he held the keys in the air like a prize.

In the car, she tried to rush. It was already seven. As they rolled up the ramp from Mountain Street just past the Salvation Army men's hostel, she stepped on the gas. A few seconds onto the Decarie expressway, the speedometer was at 140 kilometres per hour. She crossed over double lines passing trucks that usually intimidated her and

honked at cars too close to the middle line. Drivers gave her angry
looks. She didn't care. She had to get him back fast. In her rear-view
mirror she spotted a provincial police patrol car and slowed down, but
when it passed she brought the needle back to 140.

Nick turned on the radio, moved the dial to some rock music, and
played it full blast. As they came close to the Jean Talon exit, he lowered it and said, "Turn off here."

"Here?" she yelled over the music. "It's not the way."

"Turn off here," he said. He was going to grab the wheel, so she
swerved into the right lane and turned off. When they reached the
four-way traffic light at De la Savane, he said, "Okay. Right."

"Nick, where're we going?"

"You'll see." He was smiling. "Drive to Park Avenue."

"Park Avenue?"

"Your car broke down again. Okay? That's what you'll tell the guys
at Control."

"They'll never believe it!"

"Don't worry," he said rubbing her leg. "You worry all the time.
Everything's gonna turn out beautiful." He tweaked her ear. "You'll
see."

She drove where he asked knowing there was nothing else to do.
She wondered what she'd do if he said, Drive to Vancouver, or Drive
to Mexico City.

"Beautiful," he said massaging her leg. He was looking out the
window as though he'd just arrived in Disney World's Magic King-
dom.

"Here," he said. "Park right here." They were in front of Jake's, a
hang-out for teenagers on Park Avenue where he once took Eileen.
"I'm taking you for a sundae." With a flourish, he fished a ten dollar
bill out of his back pocket. "I put it aside. Especially for this.
Remember? We were going to go to have a super-duper chocolate
marshmallow sundae?"

She switched off the motor and turned to him. He put his hands
tightly around her waist and gave her a look that said you're mine and

I'm in charge. He tousled her hair. "I forgot to tell you," he said as he stepped out. "Your hair looks great." She'd had another permanent and when it was brushed up her hair was a wavy mane. As they skipped up the stairs, he lifted her off her feet and a thrill went through her.

As a teenager she had never gone to places like Jake's. They ordered a sundae with two spoons and shared it, their heads touching as they ate. About half way through, she decided there was no point worrying about the next ten minutes or the next half hour.

"Could we have a second one?" he called to the girl behind the cash. The place was filled with young couples on Sunday evening dates, giggling and holding hands. He was acting as though they had the whole evening. He put a coin into the juke box in their booth and they listened to Paula Abdul singing "Opposites Attract."

When the second sundae came, he slouched back and watched her eating, a grin on his face. "Like it?" She knew he wanted to give her a good time. He took the maraschino cherry he'd saved from the first sundae and threw it into his mouth. "Delicious," he said. "But I'm sure yours is better." She blushed, stunned that he was flirting with her in a teenage hangout while the guards at Control counted the minutes he was AWOL. She wondered whether she looked old. Everyone else was his age and younger.

Outside on Park Avenue her red Innocenti was boxed in between a shiny black Cadillac and a beat-up Trans AM that had moved in behind her. She had barely two inches to manoeuvre. He turned the radio on loud. "I'll direct you," he said rolling down the window and jumping out of the car. Standing on the sidewalk, bouncing on his toes, he suddenly did a couple of backflips and then threw himself into breakdancing the way she'd seen young blacks do on the streets of New York. He knew how to make her laugh, despite herself.

"Toujours gai," she said to herself as she leaned on the wheel. No matter what kind of a scrape she was in, that's what Mahitabel always said. Years before, in New York, Maggie had discovered Mahitabel in a book called *Archie and Mahitabel*. Archie was a cockroach who wrote a column in the *New York Daily News* under the byline of Don

Marquis during the days of speak-easies. Archie's best pal was Mahitabel, a bohemian alley cat who lived on the edge and was always having romantic adventures.

"C'mon Maggie," Nick yelled. Over the music howling out the window, he barked instructions. She went back and forth until her arms ached from turning the wheel and her leg shook from clutching in and out. She was still smiling from the sight of him turning back-springs. Finally he raised both arms in the air like a ground technician to a pilot on a runway. "Okay. Now. You have just enough room."

She shot forward, her tires squealing to a stop smack in the middle of the road. She turned the wheel to the right and without thinking went into reverse. She let out the clutch, stamped on the accelerator and the car jumped backward into the side of the Cadillac. The music drowned out the crash but she felt it at the pit of her stomach.

Nick held his sides and laughed. He looked up and saw a car he recognized cross Park Avenue. "Move over, fast," he said and slipped into the driver's seat. He clutched up like a racing car driver and they roared down a side-street, rock music streaming into the night. A few minutes later, they were on the expressway. *Toujours gai,* Maggie repeated to herself. This was better than any of Mahitabel's adventures. She was amazed at how much she relished this devil-may-care caper.

"I think the Cadillac belongs to Long John," Nick said. "I'd love to see Long John when he gets a look at his crunched-up machine."

"Who's Long John?"

"A drug dealer from around there. A big one. He drinks across the street from Jake's in Benji's Pool Room."

"You don't suppose anyone saw, do you?"

"Naw. The street was bare." He patted her shoulder as though he'd taken care of everything. "C'mere," he said and put his arm around her. Still driving, he ran his hand up and down her arm. Maggie forgot Reverend Macauley, the guys waiting for him at Control, and the smashed Cadillac.

"Maggie," he said as they got closer to the exit off the highway.

328 ■ *Jackrabbit Moon*

"How about tonight for 'tool shed'?" Tool shed was the code word for the "jackrabbit parole" they'd concocted for the minimum security prison. Every time she visited they added some crazy new embellishment to the escape plan.

"A full moon's the worst time," she said. "Besides, I don't have my cow costumes." In one of their many renditions, they escaped by trotting through a farmer's field in brown and white cow costumes. He laughed and hugged her.

About a kilometre down the winding country road leading to the prison turn-off, she felt him tense up. He turned the music off and stopped by the side of the road. "We're getting too close," he said. "You've got to drive. But first, I gotta get something straight." He put his hands on her shoulders. "Look at me." He scanned her face. "Back at your place there." He paused. "You weren't afraid I was going to kill you, were you?"

"No," she said after the shortest silence.

"All I wanted to do was scare you. It was just because I was so fuckin' mad. I still can't believe you finked out on me with that lie." He clamped his hands on his knees, gripping them until the rage passed. "I dreamt about this weekend for weeks. Weeks." His voice caught. "Maggie. Why did you say you had to go to New York?"

She didn't answer.

"Maggie?"

"Yes?" she said looking out the windshield.

He ran his fingers into her hair and held her head with both hands. "You know that if anything ever happened, I'd lay down my life for you, don't you?" She lowered her eyes. "Don't you?"

"I know," she said. If they ever faced guns on an escape, he'd lay himself across her, take the bullets instead of her, he'd told her. He'd rather be dead than lose her. He took her hand and entwined his fingers in hers as if sealing a bond between them. "I know," she repeated softly. She was so wrapped in his aura that she couldn't think of anything except him.

Nick walked around to the other side of the car and as she slipped into the driver's seat he pushed the button of her tape deck.

"All the beautiful sounds of the world in a single word, Maria, Maria, Maria." José Carreras was singing "Maria" from *West Side Story*. Nick turned the sound up to the sky. He had taped the album from the radio and knew every word. Both of them did. He leaned back against the head-rest and let the music flow through him.

The first few bars of the chorus of "Maria," was the signal for the "tool shed" escape plan. "When you whistle the music to go with those three words," he'd always remind her at the end of each visit, "I'll jump down from my window into the yard." He had a room on the second floor of the building.

She swung into the road to the sprawling prison complex that included maximum, medium and minimum security prisons. Moving down the tarmac, she saw the guards with machine guns walking along the walls between towers, but Nick hardly noticed. "Say it loud and it's music playing," Nick sang with the lustiness of an Italian tenor. He had always liked to sing. "Say it soft and it's almost like praying."

Nick signalled her to pull up on the shoulder and he took her in his arms and passionately kissed her. Suddenly a light zoomed in on them from her window and she turned around. Quickly rolling down her window, she clicked off the tape. A man in a green patrol truck stared down at her.

"I'm returning Nick Mykonos," she said. "They're expecting me. I had an accident. That's why we're late." The driver looked suspicious. "Maggie MacKinnan," she said. "I'm on his visitors list." The man was frowning. She spelled out Nick's name. The driver radioed the information to Control at the minimum security building. "Okay," he said.

The patrol truck followed them as they drove in. Just before Nick got out, he embraced her and whispered in her ear. "Tool shed. Tool shed. Moccab at onze." He leapt out of the car and held the door open a second. "Got it?" She looked out at him, confused. As she backed up and sped down the road, her window still unrolled, Nick called up into the sky from the courtyard of the Minimum." *S'agapo, Maggakimu. S'agapo.*

~

Winding through the farm road towards the village, all Maggie could think of was "*S'agapo, Maggakimu. S'agapo.* I love you, my little Maggie, I love you." Stavro, his Greek inmate friend who was now in Medium Security must have taught him the words. She herself had picked up a teach-yourself book of Greek and knew what *s'agapo* meant. She stopped at a cow crossing and looked across the field at the lights of the penitentiary. He had been saving it. She put her head gently against the steering wheel and floated off into the dark.

Moccab at onze. What was he trying to tell her? Something he didn't want the guys in the patrol truck to pick up. She turned on the overhead light, scribbled it down on the back of an old parking ticket and wrote the first word backwards. She split up Moccab. Moc cab. Com bac. *Come back. At Onze. At eleven,* in French. The message was: *Come back at eleven.*

He wanted to do a "tool shed" tonight? At eleven? "Dear sweet Nick," she said out loud. The escape stories were never for real. But maybe this time he wasn't kidding. C'mon Maggie, she said to herself, be realistic. Get out of prison mode. But when she turned on her radio and picked up Crystal Gayle singing "I Want to Lose Me in You," she wavered. She crawled into the back seat and lay awash in the smell of his hair, the feel of his skin, the springiness of his body next to her. No one had ever kissed her like he had. Two hours later when she heard an announcer from Environment Canada, she sat up. The weather was going to be unseasonably warm. *S'agapo, Maggakimu,* she thought, and any resistance she had melted.

She stepped out of her car and walked slowly toward a cart in the pasture. In the distance, not far from the minimum security area, she glimpsed the penitentiary. Under the moonlight, the gun turrets with the spotlights rose up in a mist of fluorescent green as though poison gas were leaking up from the cellars. Nothing grew around the prison complex. Not even crab-grass in the cracks of the asphalt. She heard the barking of killer dogs prowling in the corridor between the chain link fences topped with razor wire where a friend of Nick's called Huddy had died trying to escape. But she wasn't afraid. Her whole body tingled. For the first time in a very long time she felt totally alive.

Anyway, she thought, an escape from the Minimum was different. There were no bars, no razor wire — only a little cow fence separating the building from a farmer's field. It wouldn't really be an escape. They could stay out until dawn and have the time of their lives. And no one would know. They could go back downtown in her car, maybe go up to the lookout on the mountain . . . It would be okay. He could sneak back in before his morning shift in the kitchen. Other people had taken off for a few hours and never been caught. Nick had told her it happened all the time.

A motorcycle roaring down the road broke the silence of the evening. She watched as a man in a black leather jacket with a girl on the back steered into the driveway of the house across the road. The pair unbuckled their helmets and put them on the handle bars. The man left the bike next to the fence in front of the house, and carrying a pizza box, stamped up the steps with his arm around the girl's shoulders.

Maggie walked up to the edge of the road, stood on tiptoe, and saw the bike was a Harley. Galloping wild horses racing through orange and blue flames adorned the tank. She hid behind a clump of bushes growing along the ditch in the road and through the window watched the two of them eating their take-home pizza. When they finished, the man gathered the girl in his arms and disappeared.

Maggie looked up at the stars and picked out the Corona Borealis that Dionysus hung for Ariadne on the Greek island of Naxos. All her fears and reservations were melting away. She raced over to the fence and looked at the Harley. The chain wasn't attached. They could "borrow" it for a few hours. Keys weren't necessary. Nick could hotwire it. She remembered her Aunt Philana telling her how her mother had wanted the adventure of being part of the world . . . "Well, Mum," she said aloud, "here goes!" She looked at her watch. 10:45. She turned around, looked off at the prison in the distance, and began running.

THIRTY-SIX

~

Full Moon

PICKING UP JOSÉ Carreras where he left off when they were kissing in the car, Maggie ran to the rhythm of the song in *West Side Story*. "Maria, Maria, I've just met a girl named Maria. And suddenly the name will never be the same to me . . ." It would be easy to spirit Nick out of the Minimum for a few hours. Only a month ago, they had gone through every detail of an escape scenario. She'd hide next to the tool shed just inside the fence until after the eleven o'clock count. After that, she'd whistle the music, and he would jump down to the ground.

Under the light of the full moon, she ran towards the immense prison compound as though the wind were carrying her. About a quarter of a mile from the minimum security building, she stopped. A silhouette on the field could alert the guards at the gun towers at the maximum security pen in the centre of the prison complex. She crouched close to the ground. Clouds were passing across the sky. As soon as they passed in front of the moon, she made a dash towards the three-storey minimum security unit.

She clambered over the cow fence that separated the courtyard of the Minimum from the farmer's field and curled herself up next to the tool shed. It was 11:05. The count could take twenty minutes, Nick had told her, longer if someone were missing. About once a month, at least one prisoner walked away. An escape from the place was easy, but a few days later the police usually found the inmate, and he was shipped off to Medium, sometimes Maximum, the hope of parole dashed. But theirs wouldn't be a real escape.

Minutes ticked by. A door slammed at the entry to Control. Boots with cleats on the heels echoed on a concrete walk into the court-yard. Rounds weren't supposed to happen until midnight! She didn't dare peer around the corner of the shed. She cocked her ear. All she could hear was the barking of dogs down at Maximum security. She pressed her hands to her chest to muffle the thump of her heart. She heard someone advancing towards the shed dragging something through the grass. He unlocked the door, threw in a shovel, cleared his throat, moved one step forward and stopped. Suddenly water arched out in front of her and splattered up like rain from an eaves. She didn't realize what it was until she heard him zip up his fly.

When she heard the door slam back at Control, she began to breathe normally again. 11:20. Second floor, second in, Nick had told her. She waited ten more minutes. Everything was quiet. She knew he was waiting. She dashed behind the bleachers of the baseball field, around the weights area, past the trailer for conjugal visits to the back of the residence until she was directly under his window. She hummed the tune from *West Side Story* and waited. Nothing. She put her hand in her pocket and curled her fingers around a small stone. His light was on. She let a few minutes tick by. 11:40. Where *was* he? She threw the stone up and cringed. The stone hit the third window in and she ran around the corner before anyone could see her. A window went up. *"Tabernac!"* an inmate hurled out into the night.

She crept back. Nick's window was open. Now she heard voices.

"Sure thing, Sandy." Oh my God, Maggie thought. Sandy was his case officer. "Talk to her in the morning," Nick was saying. The case officer sounded exasperated. "Everything's cool," Nick insisted. "Absolutely cool." The voices became inaudible.

A twig cracked under her foot. Every sound magnified in the night. A window jerked up about a foot from her on the first floor and a large head with a scar on it thrust out. "Stokie?" Maggie whispered, recognizing the scar. His room was directly below Nick's. Eight years ago Stokie had strangled his wife with an electric cord.

"Holy cow," he grinned and looked at her admiringly.

"Maggie," she reminded him in case he'd forgotten. She knew Nick had talked with him about her. She'd seen Stokie a few times on the other side of the visitors room. The man was all scars with a slash that went from the edge of his eye through his lip to his chin. "He's expecting me," she said breathlessly and pointed upwards. "His c.o. is up there," she mouthed the words.

"Don't worry," said Stokie. "Once Sandy leaves his room, he won't come back."

Maggie stood still as a statue, listening.

Stokie lit up a cigarette and put his foot up on the sill. "What's cookin'?" He had tiny eyes like a prize fighter and lots of tattoos on his arms.

"We're going for this motorcycle ride. Just for a few hours. Until his shift at 5:30," she whispered. "I've found a Harley we can sort of borrow."

"Yeah?" He scrutinized her even more. "Wait a minute," he said and took off. In three minutes he was back. "Sandy's back at Control. The coast is clear. At five o'clock, I'll make sure my window is open so he can get back in."

Nick's window shot up. When he saw her standing there, a smile spread across his face. He jumped up to the ledge in his green prison shirt and pants, threw his hips forward and beat his chest like Tarzan.

She rubbed her hands on her arms to show it was cold and he went back for more clothes. His jacket flying, confident as a cat, he leapt down. In three minutes they were over the cow fence, his hand curled in hers, running across the field.

He was amazed he was out here under the moon, running with her, the prison fading away. He never thought *she'd* have the nerve. Never thought *he'd* have the nerve. He smiled to himself, thinking of the look of envy on Stokie's face at the window as he watched the two of them dash away.

"Where we goin'?" Nick asked when they were far enough from the prison to stop.

"I have a plan," Maggie said trying to catch her breath. Under the brightness of the moon, she could pick up the shine of the chrome on the Harley against the fence. "You'll never believe it."

He picked her up in his arms, breathed in the perfume of her hair and imagined himself rolling with her in a field of wildflowers. He shook his head as though the whole thing were a dream. "You're fantastic, Maggie." He looked off in the distance and saw a small barn an inmate had told him about. "Now I've got a plan," and he grabbed her hand. "Let's fly."

As they opened the door of the barn, a bull calf stood up in a pen. The barn smelt of horses and fresh hay. A cat limped over to them and looked up expectantly. Nick looked quickly around. A ladder led up to a hay loft. "C'mon," he whispered, crawling up ahead of her.

When she got to the top, he threw down an old blanket, lifted her into the fragrant hay and they lost themselves in each other. Entwined as tightly as grape vines, they listened to the thump of their hearts. Slowly, with all the grace of a dancer, he peeled off her clothes and then quickly undressed himself. A wave of passion streamed up her body from her thighs as he lay on top of her. Hesitating only a second, he entered her. Lifting her like Dionysus' boat at the top of the tide, he moved back and forth to the music he was awakening within her, and when the wave crashed over them in a rapture of warmth, she imagined they were alone under the stars on a deserted beach in Naxos. Here, at last, after twenty years of confinement, she was breaking free.

"You okay?" Nick asked. Still in a wash of euphoria, she felt him squeeze her hand. Nick didn't know it, but this was only the second time she had ever made love. The first and only time had been with Andreas and then she had never seen him again. She snuggled in next to him, overwhelmed by the feel of his bare legs around her. Drifting off for a moment, she dreamed of white lilies in the dunes.

They sat up and Nick lightly stroked her breasts as though he had had an intimate connection with her body for a long time, then he lifted her chin and looked into her eyes. "You're beautiful, you know." He was the first man who had ever told her that. Until Nick, she had always kept her body wrapped up in prim suits and high-buttoned blouses. He ran his fingers over her hips and felt the small of her back. Now, as though he knew her body better than she did, he was showing it to her. Under the light of the moon shining into the loft, she looked with pride at the soft curve of her breasts and her long, slender legs.

She had always avoided her body. When they were at McGill together, her cousin Moira had accused her of being almost anorexic. She would never again see herself like that. Nick gently eased her down on the blanket and once again lay on top of her. A tide of warmth swirled over her and she felt flushed with fortune.

"Let me show you something," Nick said, suddenly sitting up. His olive-coloured body glistening with energy, he walked to the edge of the loft, coiled himself up, ran across the barn boards and leapt into a wide expanse of hay. He was sleek and sinewy, every muscle taut. A real Baryshnikov, she thought. Every night after weight lifting, he did fifty broad jumps in the gym. "C'mon," he yelled from the other side of the loft. "Let me see what you can do!"

She scrambled over to the starting point, ran as fast as she could, and jumped. Normally, nakedness embarrassed her but now all she felt was the excitement of the moment. "Not bad for a girl," he said. He took her hand and dragged her back to the edge of the loft. Laughing like children, they somersaulted in the hay. When the horses below whinnied like protesting neighbours, they buried themselves in a hay stack and imagined staying there forever. "Where's your red scarf?" he asked when they finally crawled out and looked around. "In my pants pocket," she said.

An oil lamp hung on a nail over a bench where he had flung their clothes. He felt around a window ledge until he found a box of matches. One leg up on the bench, he lit the lamp. Sweat shone on the dark hairs in the small of his back. He knelt behind her under the light of the lamp and braided her hair, winding the red scarf through the curls. When he was finished, she turned around and ran her fingers through his wavy chestnut-coloured hair. "Your turn," she said, and they sat cross-legged, his head over her lap, as she pulled out strands of hay.

Nick looked up at her, kissed her on the lips, and gently pulled her on top of him. "This time, let's try it with you on top," and he eased himself into her.

"Oh Nick," she said, amazed at the sensation of him suddenly inside her and the long length of his body beneath her.

"It's great for me too," he said after he felt her tense up and then relax into him . . .

Off in the distance, she heard a church bell ring once. It was one o'clock. If they were going on the bike, they had to get going. He had to be back a half hour before his 5:30 shift in the kitchen.

"Nick?" She sat up and hugged her knees. "How'd you like to go for a ride on a Harley?"

He locked his hands behind his head and looked at her. She had to be kidding. "Did I hear right? You've actually gone out and roughed off a Harley?" Just two days ago he'd picked up a manual for a Harley that was floating around the prison and was studying it in preparation for a motorcycle mechanics course he wanted to take.

"Let me show you," she said. They scampered down the ladder and out into the chilliness of the night. She pointed down the field to the house across the road. "See through those apple trees? We can borrow it for a few hours. It's not even locked."

A motorcycle ride at this hour of the night? Nick thought. November was no time for bike rides even though it was unusually warm. He was glad he had his fur-lined jacket.

"Shit, Maggie, you're something else," he said as they stamped back into the barn. He hadn't been on a bike for three years. He couldn't believe it. Back in the loft on his knees he grabbed her black leather pants and her angora sweater and pulled them on.

"If we're going for a ride, I'm wearing these." The pants went only to the tops of his boots, but otherwise they fit. From his prison pants pocket, he removed her butterfly pin, and without her noticing, slipped it into a pocket. "Here," he said, tossing her his green prison pants and shirt.

The zesty smell of Nick's green prison pants and shirt next to her skin excited her as she pulled them on, but then she imagined a guard at the surveillance tower thinking she was an escaping inmate and shooting her in the back. She sat down on the hay next to Nick and looked at him. What wild-eyed craziness in both *him* and *her* was she now about to unleash? "C'mon, Maggie," he said, excitement shining in his eyes. "You can't lose your nerve now. Let's get goin'."

~

"Oh my God, a Fat Boy!" Nick exclaimed as soon as he saw the huge and heavy Harley by the fence. It was built like a horse. "That's freedom on wheels," he breathed as he admired the galloping horses painted on the tank and touched the silver conch-shell studs on the leather saddle bags. He caressed the wide saddle. "It's a beaut."

Maggie held her breath as they pushed the Harley past the farm houses. Corrections Canada had an arrangement going with the residents along the road. The prison warden had given a reward to a farmer who spotted an inmate escaping a month ago.

Two more houses to pass. "Did you hear something?" she whispered to him when she thought she heard the slam of a back door. He shook his head. "Relax," he said. "We're doin' great." Just to be safe, they wheeled the Harley a quarter kilometre past the last farm house before they put on their helmets. She struck a match so Nick could see to hot-wire it, and in a minute the machine was rumbling.

"Okay, *now*," he said, and they jumped on. She felt a wave of exhilaration as he geared up in a series of little jerks that moved the machine in seconds up to a runaway roar. He crashed straight down the winding road toward the highway shrieking like a cowboy. She hung on tight, her body pasted to his back, her legs tight against his thighs. He was taking the corners so low she could smell the asphalt. She looked down and saw sparks. They stopped for a minute at the expressway. "I'll take you for a ride down the Richelieu. You'll love it." He'd taken the Richelieu before with Eileen on the ride back from Ile aux Coudres.

"Sure. Anything."

"Look. I can bring it up to 180. But I've got to concentrate like hell. Anything can cause an accident."

He went over the hump across the expressway and cruised steadily south toward the city, accelerating up. She looked over his shoulder at the speedometer — 100, 110, 120. After 120 km/h, she kept her head directly behind him under the protection of his back. The wind rushed past her. She held tight to him, petrified the wind might rip her away.

"You okay?" he hollered, bringing the bike down to 60. She looked up from the highway and off in the distance saw St. Joseph's Oratory.

"Great." She was afraid to talk. "Keep your mouth shut," Nick had counselled before they got on. "The wind can rip into the inside of your mouth and blow it up like a balloon." He cruised for a while and she wrapped her thighs tighter around him. Like a dancer she followed the rhythm of his body as he swung along the road.

Racing down an open road on a "borrowed" Harley with the perfume from their roll in the hay still on their skins made her feel she had entered another world. Now she was really living, she thought, really connecting.

At the turn for the Richelieu river, they stopped for gas at a twen-

ty-four-hour station and Nick took a few minutes to fix something
on the bike. "Gotta adjust the rear brake," and he tightened a nut with
an open end wrench from the Craftsman Socket Set under the seat.

Along the river they quietly sailed down a smooth road. Stretching into the solitude of the night, the clusters of street lights in faraway villages looked like islands, and Maggie imagined she was on a
boat with him in the Aegean en route to Naxos.

For an hour, up the Richelieu and back, they moved at a gentle
pace. The stars began to fade and she pictured the island of Naxos lifting out of the mist. In the harbour, chairs stood upside down on the
tables of the cafés. Behind the *tavernas*, steps wove up a hill of white-
washed houses and tiny chapels.

Nick slowed down and Maggie stopped dreaming. "I want a
smoke," he said jumping off the Harley. He stroked the long leather
seat and drew long and hard on his cigarette. "When I get out, maybe we'll get one like this." He threw his stub on the grass and lifted
her onto the seat.

Back in her imagination, the two of them sailed into the deserted
beach where Dionysus rescued the sleeping Ariadne after she was
abandoned by Theseus. Nick jerked the bike to a stop again. "You
okay?" He pulled a Coke out of the saddle bag at the back and gulped
it down. "Happy?" he asked and he ran his finger down the bridge of
her nose. "Another fifteen minutes and we'll be back at the highway
again."

"So soon?" she said. The lights of the faraway villages were still
blinking in the night. They took off and she picked up where she had
left off on the beach on the Greek island plucking fruits from the
famous Naxos strawberry tree which can create a delicious feeling of
intoxication if eaten on an empty stomach. Nick slipped off her
clothes and rolled her to the ground. Wrapped in his arms, they
rocked in and out of the water . . .

"Hey Maggie." They were back at the twenty-four-hour gas station at the Richelieu turn-off. "You fall asleep? Come on. We have
to warm up." After a coffee, she looked at her watch. Four o'clock.

They had an hour. Stokie had told him he'd watch for Nick at five.

Regret raced through her as she threw her leg over the seat of the bike. In an hour, it would all be over and she would be back to her uneventful life at the newspaper working as a copy editor on the Rim. He kept the bike up around 150 all the way back. Going down the hill just before their exit, he accelerated up. It was his last chance to rush into the eye of the wind. The machine gathered speed as though it were a Japanese war plane on a Kamikaze mission. They were shaking like an earthquake. There was a sharp turn at the bottom. A split second before she thought they were about to crash into a stand of trees, he eased off.

After he took the exit, he stopped. They were both quivering. "You okay?" he said, looking straight ahead. All his concentration went into steadying the bike. He turned around and smiled. "You didn't really think I was going to do it? Did you?"

She didn't answer for a few seconds.

"Did you?"

"I wasn't sure," she said. "You can go right over the top sometimes."

THIRTY-SEVEN

～

Jackrabbit Parole

NICK THREW HIMSELF on the grass by the side of the road and rolled a cigarette. "I need a few minutes," he said. Two hundred chickens floating in pools of slime waited for him in steel vats ten kilometres away at the prison. Hot chicken sandwiches — six hundred of them — were on the menu for lunch.

He shut his eyes. "It's a bitch to go back," he mumbled. "In forty-five minutes I'll be in the kitchen tearing slimy meat off those stinkin' chickens." He looked up at her leaning against the seat of the bike.

"You don't understand what it's like." The thought of his kitchen shift was already spoiling the excitement of the motorcycle ride he'd had up the Richelieu River. He sucked a second cigarette down until his fingers burned.

"That chicken smell in the kitchen always makes me feel like puking," he raised his voice but she acted as though she hadn't heard. "Just give me the slaughter room where all I have to do is slit their throats

342

and rip off all the feathers."

He lit up a third cigarette. A car whizzed through the underpass south toward the golden glow of the lights hanging in the sky over Montreal and he followed it until it rounded a corner in the distance.

Maggie leaned nervously against the motorcycle and waited for him to finish his cigarette. She couldn't think straight. He was inhaling slowly, his arms hanging down between his knees as though he had all the time in the world. Her stomach was in a knot. She glanced quickly at her watch. 4:55. He ground his cigarette butt into the earth and started to roll another.

"Nick."

"C'mere," he said.

She stiffened against the seat. "Nick."

"C'mon Maggie." When she didn't move, he jumped up and flipped her to the ground.

"Not now," she said. "Please Nick." She turned her head to the side and tried to force herself up on her elbows. "It's practically five," she begged. "We'll never make it back in time."

He suddenly leapt up, gathered her in his arms, and placed her on the seat. "Fast. We've got to go fast," she urged. Every minute now would count. He revved up the motor and circled around.

"You're going in the wrong direction," she screamed, banging his shoulder. "It's the wrong direction!" He raced over the ramp, taking the corner of the expressway toward Montreal at a forty-five degree angle. "Nick!" She hit his helmet.

At first she thought he was playing a trick on her. He would dash down to the next exit, then back to the country road toward St. Bartholomew, but no, he was aiming straight for Montreal. Her heart sank as they whizzed by more and more exits. She knew from the way he was hunched over the bars, they were on a jackrabbit parole.

In the distance she saw St. Joseph's Oratory and thought of all the crutches and misshapen shoes and braces leaning against the dark altars of the church. Sitting behind him on the bike, the minutes ripping by, she knew it was nearing zero hour when they would miss him in the kitchen.

"Nick, Nick," she said breathlessly when they came to a four-way stop and he slowed down. "Where are we going?"

"West," he looked right and left. "Up the Pacific Coast where they'll never find me."

"What about the Harley?"

"We'll put mud on the licence," he said and jerked quickly up to 120 kilometres an hour. "We have until the lunch-time count," he said at the next stop. "Stokie'll fix up everything in the kitchen."

"How can Stokie — ?" He pitched forward so quickly she nearly fell off. "And what about the Harley?" A call from the owner of the motorcycle to the prison could tip them off long before lunch. The sight of her car on the road across from the farm house flashed up at her. She had to get her car off that road. The keys, she suddenly realized, were still in the ignition.

When she saw a sign indicating a phone booth ahead, she pounded Nick's shoulder and he slowed down. "I've got to make a call. Someone has to pick up my car." He made a sign with his hand as if to say *not important* and went by.

Maybe Alphie was still at the press club. Sometimes he hung around there until dawn. She knew the number by heart. They had passed five more phone booths and were well into Ontario before Nick would let her call. The only reason he stopped was because he wanted to smear dirt on the licence and go into the bushes. "Three minutes," he warned.

She cringed after she charged the call to her Bell credit card. She was the only one on his visitors list, and the card is how they could trace her. Soon they would start to look for her.

"Alphie. Oh my God. Alphie. I'm so glad you're there. Look. I'm in a terrible jam. You've got to pick up my car. Yeah, yeah, I'm okay. Really. Listen. I don't have much time." She faced on-coming traffic, terrified she'd see the revolving red light of a provincial police car.

"It's eight kilometres along the farm road." She spoke quickly, the pieces impossibly out of order, about a village with a Pepsi sign out in front, farm houses, her broken tail light, and an open field. "You've got to go immediately, otherwise I'm in trouble. Look, call Michael Johannson at the refugee centre. He can go."

"Hold it, Maggie. Where exactly?" A trailer truck zoomed by. Hadn't she already told him. "St. Bartholomew," she screamed. "The prison! St. Bartholomew," she yelled louder. "If you have to, take a taxi. I'll pay."

Now he wanted to know what kind of car. She looked to the side and saw Nick beating his way up out of the bushes. Another truck rumbled by. The traffic was increasing. She looked at her watch. It was already six in the morning. Police on day shifts started at eight.

"A red Innocenti," she shouted. "Don't be ridiculous." He had asked her if she'd been taken hostage. Nick was banging at the door. She put a hand over her ear and ignored him.

"Something else. Can you hear me Alphie? Tell Foxy to tell — " The glass of the phone booth cracked as Nick delivered a judo punch at it. "I'm coming," she called out.

"I want a week out of my overtime bank starting now. Foxy will fix it up. Did you get that, Alphie? Tell them it's a family matter." Nick threw his leg over the seat of the Harley and revved it.

"Maggie, for Chrissake," Alphie yelled so she could hear. "What the hell is going on?"

"I've absolutely got to go," she said and hung up. Back on the bike, she thought about how Alphie liked playing godfather to her. What if he tried to trace her? He had good police contacts, guys he could enlist to do him a favour from his early days on the police desk. She shouldn't have used her Bell credit card.

A half hour later, they turned into an all-night gas station. "Where's that old lady's house?" Nick asked as he filled up. Maggie had told him during the summer that she often visited her mother's friend Elisabeth at a cabin in Ontario. He was getting nervous about travelling in the daylight on the stolen Harley with a Quebec licence. In half an hour the sun would be up.

"Near Kingston," she said. Elisabeth was a childhood friend of her

346 ■ *Jackrabbit Moon*

mother's. She had been a professor at the Curtis School of Music in the United States. Last summer, after a stroke that made it hard for her to walk, she had moved to a seniors' residence in Kingston. Maggie visited her every month, bringing her from the residence to the cabin where they listened to music and had a meal. Sometimes Elisabeth played something on the Steinway in the living room. The house was a kilometre off a remote dirt road, she had told Nick, the key on a nail under the porch.

"We'll go there," Nick said throwing his leg over the seat, "until I find a new licence plate for the Harley." She had to convince him to dump the Harley. She couldn't think straight. On the bike, they were totally exposed. He had no licence and no papers for it. If the police stopped them, everything was over. Every minute they were on the road in the daylight scared her. Elisabeth's house, she thought, was a good place to go. They had to hide somewhere. When she got there, maybe she'd be able to figure out what they should do. They took the scenic coastal road along the St. Lawrence river to avoid provincial police, but it was a lot slower than the expressway, and the sun came up about half an hour before they reached their destination.

~

The house was damp and needed a fire, but they were so worn-out they threw themselves on the four poster bed in the master bedroom without taking off their clothes. Just as she was drifting off, she thought of the Harley leaning against the porch. She shook his shoulder. "We've got to hide the Harley in the shed. The farmer down the road might come up here and see it." He rolled over. "Forget it," he said. She waited a couple of minutes, and then went outside and tried to wheel the vehicle into the shed but it was too heavy and after ten minutes she came back in and fell into a fitful sleep.

She woke to a loud voice on the radio from the living room. Nick was up. It was already three o'clock. By now, they would be looking for him. She raised herself on her elbows and listened intently. There was nothing on the national or local news. He jerked the dial from one station to the next until he found a heavy metal band and turned it up full blast. She looked out the window, saw it was a bleak day, and fell against the pillow. She put her legs to the floor and tried to stand. Suddenly she put her hands on her knees and screamed like the dwarf boy in *The Tin Drum* who made glasses break with his shrieks. Her head swimming, she wove into the living room toward the radio. Nick was busy making a fire and hadn't even heard her.

"Nick." She turned down the music. "I can't take it."

He whipped around and turned it up again.

"I need silence," she said. "My head hurts."

"Well, I need music."

She sat down on the edge of the sofa, her back humped over, her chest caved in, the way her mother used to sit toward the end of her illness. Now, with Nick dictating everything, she had no space of her own, no freedom.

"How about some food?" he said. She'd had thirty dollars, but they'd spent most of it on junk food, gas and cigarettes. She knew there was nothing in the fridge or the cupboards, but she looked anyway.

She steadied herself against the sink and stared out the kitchen window at the leafless trees. The emptiness of the gray sky reminded her of Saturday afternoons when she was in grade eleven and her father was in his study preparing his Sunday sermon and her mother was lying in bed with the blinds pulled down. Three o'clock was like a boat adrift, going nowhere. Off in the distance, she saw white caps on the lake where she had taken Elisabeth for a row last summer. Afterwards they'd had a picnic on the beach.

"We'll have to go to the village," she said. She had three dollars left in her pocket. They walked into the village in silence. It took half an hour and she felt so faint she never thought she'd make it.

"Like a coffee?" asked a man in a wide white apron inside the grocery store. She wondered if she looked that bad. She downed a coffee with milk and a lot of sugar while Nick busied himself at the back.

"Do you have a couple of cookies?" she asked. "On the house," he smiled, handing her a plate of oatmeal cookies.

"Oh thank you," she said. She heard the bell of the door ring as Nick walked out and she wondered what he'd taken. She sat down in a chair by the coffee machine and ate four cookies hoping they'd give her the strength to walk back. "How much is one apple?" she asked.

"Twenty five cents," he said. She walked around the store munching the apple and looking at country fresh bread, lemon pie, mushroom quiche, smoked salmon, blueberry muffins and local cheese but she had only enough money for milk and instant coffee. They didn't take credit cards. She took a second look at the quiche and the country fresh bread.

"Made fresh every day," the man called out from behind the cash.

"Looks lovely."

"You from around here?" he asked when she paid up.

"No," she said. "Just passing through." She was glad she had never shopped here when she visited Elisabeth. She bought everything from stores in Kingston. "Oh," she said, looking at her change. She had just enough for Nick's cigarettes. "Could I have a package of Export A?"

Nick waited for her around the corner, his jacket stuffed with wieners, buns, a beer and a package of Tang, but she said nothing. "C'mon, Maggie," he said, "try hangin' easy . . ." and he put his arm around her. "All that matters is that we're together."

When they got back, they listened to the six o'clock news. Still nothing. But that didn't mean they weren't looking. He had a cold wiener and went outside with a beer to fix something on the Harley. While he was outside she put "Horowitz in Moscow" on the video player. Elisabeth had a big collection of recordings, some of them irreplaceable tapes of her own playing. Horowitz was just finishing a Scarlatti sonata when Nick returned.

"We're not going to watch that shit are we?" She turned it down with a remote control. "It's Vladimir Horowitz," she said. "He's world famous. This was his famous concert in Moscow in 1986." She snapped the thing off entirely, and he turned on the television and went from station to station until he picked up Rambo rescuing some American from a fortress set up by the Russians in the middle of a desert in Afghanistan. When the film ended he went into the kitchen, found a screw driver, and said he was going out.

"Where?" she asked.

"We need some more food. I can do a couple of B&Es easy."

"We're okay," she said trying not to show her nervousness. "We can have hot dogs for dinner. Tomorrow I'll go to a bank machine in Kingston." The idea of him stealing food from Elisabeth's neighbours frightened her.

While he was gone she looked in the closets upstairs for something to replace the ugly prison greens she was wearing. She found a red flowered skirt and a black V-necked blouse she could tie around her waist so her midriff showed. In a jewel box she found some silver hoop earrings that belonged to Elisabeth's niece who visited regularly with her little girl. She wanted to look beautiful and sexy so that he'd be eager to make love to her as soon as he returned. Working as quickly as she could, she had a bath, washed her hair and fluffed it out. The earrings made her look Spanish like Carmen from the Bizet opera. She ran into the kitchen, made a jug of martinis, and put it in the refrigerator. The outside world didn't matter anymore, but she felt so drained of energy she could hardly move. There was some vermouth left over which she drank straight from the bottle and it buoyed her up.

"You look like a Gypsy," Nick called out as he came up the path. "You look great," he said and kissed her. "Hey. You been drinkin'?"

"Just a little vermouth I found," she said. He handed her a plastic bag with Chef Boyardee, cornflakes, Campbell's asparagus soup, beans, a tin of orange juice and a couple of beers.

"Here's what I was really looking for," and he produced a dusty Ontario motorcycle licence plate.

"Where'd you get that?" she asked. He had to have taken it from a permanent resident. None of the summer residents had motorcycles.

"I got it off a motorcycle in a garage just outside the town. The bike was covered with dust. Don't worry. No one'll notice. No one rides motorcycles now. It's too cold."

Still, she worried. What if the owner discovered someone had broken in and reported the stolen licence. "Did you leave the garage exactly the way you found it?"

He didn't reply.

She did her best for dinner and they ate by candle light at the French-Canadian refectory table. When they finished it was nine o'clock and the full moon was high in the sky.

After supper he built a fire and she sat at the table with a box of candle stubs she had found in a kitchen drawer and dripped wax into some chocolate mousse dishes. When the candles were in place, she turned off the lights, lit each one, and in another attempt at romance placed them around the room. Dried flowers in tall wicker baskets stood next to the sofas. She lifted them out and hung them on nails in the cross beams so the place looked like the barn the night before.

On the rug in front of the fire, Nick quietly waited. She went into the kitchen, poured herself a martini, and gulped it down. Then she placed an Indian incense stick on the ledge of the mirror next to the sink. Her hand wavered as she picked up a silver tray with a jug of vermouth and gin and two crystal glasses. She carried it into the living room and set it down in front of him. He had never had martinis. "I know you'd prefer a Labatt Blue," she said, "but this was all there was." When she brought Elisabeth to the house, they always had martinis or Harvey's Shooting Sherry.

He held a glass up to the fire, examined the diamond cuts in the crystal, and flicked his finger on it so it pinged. The silver tray was very shiny. "Premier Prix, Programme Rachmaninoff, Dec. 18, 1948, Paris," said an inscription on it.

Maggie was a classy woman, he realized, able to live in a world he had never seen before and couldn't help admiring, but he could never be part of it. Stokie and the guys from St. Bartholomew should see me now, he thought. The candles around the room reminded him of the time he played a shepherd in a Christmas play at the church in Pierrefonds the first year he was with the Evans. The radio was within reaching distance and he was dying for some heavy metal but he decided not to put it on.

Next to the fireplace Maggie settled herself on the floor and leafed through Elisabeth's CD collection, hoping she'd find something they'd both like. "I think I've found something." She snapped *The Best of Andrew Lloyd Webber* onto the CD tray and poured two drinks. "Well, here's to," and she clicked his glass and surprised herself with a vision of Archie and Mahitabel on one of their exploits. They downed the drinks and crawled into each other's arms. In a few minutes St. Bartholomew's, the *Tribune*, her apartment on St. Antoine Street, and her father's church seemed far away. She reached over and moved the selector button on the CD player to "All I Ask of You" from *The Phantom of the Opera*.

The music was slow and reassuring. Warmth floated into her. She listened to the words like a prayer. "Let me be your shelter. Let me be your light, you're safe, no one will find you, your fears are far behind you." She sank into him and tried to imagine they were two cubs in the forest in a cave where they could hibernate for the winter.

They sipped their drinks and she played the song over and over until the dread that had possessed her ever since five in the morning yesterday was almost gone. When the jug of martinis was drained, they undressed each other in front of the fire and he made lingering love to her, entering her slowly, but at the end she felt a tension in his body that disturbed her. The songs on the disc came to an end and the lonely silence of the November night returned. Wind keened through the windows. The candles burned down and the bleakness she had felt when she had woken up that morning returned.

He sat up. "Come," he said and dragged her across the hall to the child's room Elisabeth had specially decorated for the daughter of her niece. A mobile of animals hung from the ceiling. He threw himself on the bed. "Maggie," he said. Ignoring him, she lay back on the bed and rested her arm on her forehead but he pulled himself into her and began to suck strongly on her breast. Pain and fright tore at her. She wanted to curl up alone somewhere. She pulled away and lurched into the bathroom. Leaning against the wash basin with both hands, she tried to keep from fainting.

"Maggie," he called. "Start a bath. I want to play in the bath the way I did as a kid."

She limped back into the room. "Nick. I can't."

"Let me," he pleaded.

She went back to the bathroom, turned on the taps, threw in some Disney toys, and stood at the door. When he had had enough and stepped out of the water, she reached for some towels. In her mind, she saw herself in a braid at seventeen pick up the linen towel with the blue forget-me-nots in the bathroom of the manse. Her hands shook.

Nick put his arm around her. "Maggie," he said. "You okay?" He was suddenly the man he'd been the day he carried her up the steps of Notre Dame church. "Yes." She lay against him for a few minutes.

"I'll tuck you in now," she said wearily and walked with him to the big double bed in the other room. She waited patiently until he fell asleep but now she was afraid of Nick and even more afraid of herself. Her life, she recognized, was out of control. Nick was still desperately searching for a mother, while she needed a grown man and a life she could call her own. How had this happened to her? She was still too overwhelmed by Nick and the whirlwind of the last two days to be able to think clearly. For a long time she stood at the window and looked out into the dark.

THIRTY-EIGHT

~

Kingston

MAGGIE WOKE UP in the half light before dawn and saw mist rolling up the hill toward her window. She looked up at the gray ceiling and thought of the dead look in Barry Gillespie's eyes during a close-up shot at the end of the interview on American television the night before he was electrocuted. Until the end, all she had seen was his captivating smile and the boyish way he had of running his hands through his hair. The week before he died he had made the cover of *People* magazine where even the best photographers weren't able to pick up that final look she had seen on TV.

She had followed the case right up to the end because of what the psychiatrist at the Charbonneau Penal Hospital had said about him when she was doing research three years ago for the magazine piece. "He stabbed twenty-one young women in nine different states over five years but do you know that several women are still actually in love with Barry Gillespie?" the psychiatrist had said. The way he had said *women,* she knew he despised them.

That was just after Nick's trial before she even knew who Barry Gillespie was. The psychiatrist had been talking to her about the seductiveness of certain criminal personalities. She remembered how uncomfortable she had felt under the cold beam of his eyes as he pressed the tips of his fingers together. His face was round and pasty like a ten-year-old boy everyone knows will repel women when he grows up. "None of them believed he was capable of murder," he'd told her.

The mist was moving closer. Losing awareness, she felt herself descend into a shadowy place . . . From a gully at the foot of the hill black ducks rose up above the mist. A knife in hand, she watched from the window of the child's room as they approached. A foul smell hit her as the ducks swooped down in front of the windows and then up to the roof. She looked up to the skylight at webs of dirty yellow feet. Hard clicks hit the roof. Seconds later, through the window, she looked out into dead black eyes. From their beaks, thin as the razors on prison wire, she caught the shine of knives.

One by one, the knives jacked open and the ducks bombed through the screen into a tinkling mobile of multi-coloured bears and Chinese parasols. As they flailed at the tangle of wires, she stabbed at their bellies and watched their switch blade tongues curl like spent matches. They were coming fast as bullets. The teddy bear mobile dropped from the ceiling as a bird circled and a splat of shit hit her eye knocking her backward. Now they were bursting through the skylight. An arch of knives backed by a fan of black bodies hung in the air. The room was suddenly silent. A single flap and one swung down. She clutched the scarf at her neck, and tightened the grip on her knife . . .

Even inside the nightmare, she knew not to scream, but she shook like an earthquake. Behind the closed door of the child's room on the other side of the hall, she imagined a crimson puddle of blood. Her arm lay outstretched over the side of the bed. Feeling like a half-drowned child, she pulled away from the nightmare and opened her eyes . . .

She sat up and looked over at Nick's side of the bed. His head was not on the pillow! She saw her mother's eyes looking at her through the stained glass windows of Notre Dame church. She whipped back the covers. Nick was there, his head curled down. As he stirred she shut her eyes in relief. Slowly, like a blind person who must feel to know, she ran her hand down the long curve of his spine, pressed her palm into the small of his back, and listened like a mother to the rise and fall of his breath.

~

Later that morning, Nick munched on a cold hot dog over breakfast and switched the radio dial from one station to the next. "Nothin' yet." He stroked his chin. "But they're lookin'. They gotta be." He heeled back in his chair and rocked until a leg cracked. "And not just for me." He lit up a cigarette. Before she knew it, she'd have a criminal record just like him. He was no good for her, he thought. He swung back and forth as she silently sipped the Tang he had poured into the crystal glasses.

"Nick and Maggie. Maggie and Nick. Sounds kinda nice," he said pulling his chair up close. He spread his legs and put his feet on the rungs of her chair the way he always did when she visited him at the prison. He took her hand. "Ever see the movie *Bonnie and Clyde*?" He had seen it in the joint on late-night TV. His eyes swept her face.

"Faye Dunaway and Warren Beatty and C.W. Moss," she said without looking up. "Maggie?" He pulled up her chin. "Last night there? When I came up the path, and you were leaning against the door?" He glanced at her flowered skirt and shook his head. "Just like Bonnie." He smiled. "Just as beautiful anyways." He stroked her nose and tousled her hair the way he had done when they were in the barn.

"But Nick," she said. "This is . . ."

"I know what you're gonna say. This is different. Not when we get goin'," he said. "Listen. Later today, you'll go to Kingston. You'll get $300 from the bank machine. With the new licence on the Harley, we'll be in business."

~

On the way to Kingston, they stopped at a hardware store and he stole a Swiss army knife, then in the next village, he picked up a couple of May Wests even though she had begged him not to shoplift. What if he got caught? "Aren't you glad I did?" he said as he skirted along the dirt road toward the city. She had forced herself to eat the remaining hot dogs and the rest of the Tang for lunch, but she was still hungry and glad of the May West.

She needed energy to face Kingston. He banked the Harley off in the trees next to a side road near the highway. The plan was for her to hitchhike in, and he'd wait for her until she came back with the money. When it was dark, they'd take off for the West. The apprehensions of the night before were still with her but they appeared to have moved into another compartment of her mind. What seemed most pressing now was for her to get into Kingston.

She walked about a kilometre, too scared to hitch. Finally she faced the traffic and a car stopped. From the passenger seat, a man in a suit opened the back door. He had a nice smile.

"Going to Kingston?"

"Yes." There were a couple of squash rackets on the back seat. This was her chance to plead with them to take her to the police, to tell them she was the hostage of an escaped criminal, but she realized that would be a lie. This was as much her escape as Nick's.

The driver looked at her through the rear view mirror. "From around here?"

She hadn't thought up a story. Halifax popped into her head. That's where down-and-outers on the streets around McGill said they came from when they asked for money. "I'm from Halifax," she said. "I'm meeting my sister at the university."

"You hitched all the way from Halifax?

"Oh no. I was visiting a friend." She couldn't think of the names of any places except Holt. "Down the way," and she pointed out the back window.

The two men went back to talking about a ski vacation in February. They were sporty types. A *Toronto Sun* lay on the back seat. She picked it up and turned to page three. Nothing. Page four. There it was! Under Notes in Brief. The Greek ice monster from Montreal escaped from the minimum security prison at St. Bartholomew yesterday, the story said. Nicholas Mykonos was probably on a stolen Harley, possibly with an accomplice. She quickly shut the paper and put it back on the seat. A huge trailer truck rumbled by. They hadn't used her name. She looked out the other window at the lifeless grass by the side of the road. "I've got the Fraser parole this afternoon," the driver was saying.

They were from the Kingston penitentiary! Case officers, probably, guys who could smell out anything. The pen back in Montreal had her picture. By fax, her photo could now be everywhere. "It's his second try," he said. She had to stay calm. She touched the ends of her hair. Maybe they wouldn't recognize her. In the picture, her hair was pulled back.

The driver turned around. "We're going to King Street West. Where should we let you off?" The pen was on King Street West! She had to get out. The driver frowned at her through the rearview mirror.

"Ah . . ." She saw a sign for a book store. "Could you let me off at the book store?" She opened the door before the car came to a stop and jumped out. "Thanks a lot," she said without looking at them.

She stared woodenly at the books in the window without reading the titles, wondering now whether she'd read the entire story in the paper. Maybe they *had* used her name. She went into a magazine store next door and flipped through every paper she could find, including the *Toronto Sun*. Nothing. It must have been yesterday's paper. She hadn't looked at the date.

"You wouldn't have yesterday's *Toronto Sun*, would you?" she asked the man behind the counter.

"Don't you see the sign saying *Please Do Not Read the Magazines*? No," he said. "We carry only today's papers. The ones you've just read."

She walked out the door in a hurry. She knew it was virtually

impossible to track one down quickly. The *Whig Standard* newsroom
might have a yesterday's *Toronto Sun* but she couldn't go there. She
walked slowly along the street. If they'd used her name, surely she
would have noticed. Her thoughts went back to the case officers.

What if they suspected something? She looked at her hands. Her
finger prints were all over the back seat of that car. As a cub reporter
helping Alphie on the police desk her first summer at the paper, the
city editor asked her to obtain a police pass. Her finger prints were
permanently on record. She realized she was now caught between
her old law-abiding self and this chaos where stealing motorcycles,
shoplifting food, and escaping police had become a way of life, but
she didn't know what to do. She felt tied to Nick in ways she didn't
understand.

She went into a junk food place and sat in a booth by herself. Four
college kids were horsing around as though they didn't have a care in
the world. A colour photo showing a steaming cup of coffee hung on
the wall. Looking for change, she opened up her wallet and checked
every fold. Nothing. She pushed her empty wallet away and scrutinized the tips of her fingers.

Right forefinger. That was the finger they dipped in the gooey
black ink. The clerk had rolled it hard over the paper from one side
to the other, picking up every line so the print would be perfect.
"Every print different," he had said. The building was near the court
house. She had gone with Alphie and she remembered his laugh as
he said, "Now, you can never commit a crime!" He should see her
now, she thought. On the way out the restaurant, she spotted an un-
finished cup of coffee on a table near the door. She looked around to
make sure no one was looking and gulped it down.

~

She had her card in the automatic teller machine and was ready to
punch in her 4862, but her finger froze in the air. What if they had
traced her account? As soon as she punched in her number, they

would know exactly where she was.

She went outside and walked around the block. She looked into the window of a small grocery store. No one was at the cash. At the back, a kid in an apron was putting cans on a shelf. She looked down the street. No one was around but off in the distance she heard a police siren. She crossed the street to a park. A woman with a baby carriage parked next to a bench was pushing a three-year-old on a swing. Maggie walked up close to the carriage and pretended to admire the baby. A purse lay just inside. She looked over at the woman. The child on the swing laughed and waved his arms and the mother pushed him higher. She had on one of those cheap coats that look worn-out after a few wearings.

She walked quickly past them until she couldn't hear the sound of the child laughing. Leaves were gusting up around the naked trees. She plumped down on a bench. The last time she had wanted to steal was when she lost her gym bloomers in grade four and didn't dare tell her mother. She and a friend she knew from school gathered up broken alarm clocks, pencil cases, mitts that were too small and other paraphernalia their parents would never miss. Then they sold them at a "fish pond" at Girouard Park, where at five cents a fish, the kids took a wooden stick and fished for an item. The proceeds were supposed to be for the Red Cross. She never told anyone she used the proceeds for bloomers. Her father would have spanked her if he'd found out. Twenty fish and she was able to buy a pair of second-hand bloomers at a garage sale. Twenty-five fish now, and she could have a hot cup of coffee. She dug her hands into her pockets and stood up.

～

She was back at the bank machine. She had more than $500 in her account. How many times had she punched 4862 and never given it a second thought? She punched 4, 8, 6. All she had to do was punch 2. But her bank account was how they could track her. She imagined a Kingston police car with a siren pulling up. C'mon, Maggie, she said to herself. The real question was: Did she really want to go back to Nick with $300 so they could run away to the West Coast? Nick and the open road had for a short while felt like liberation but this was no better than the quick fix that accompanied a sensational page one story in the *Tribune*. She hit the cancel button, put the card in her wallet, and walked away.

∼

She didn't know which was worse, walking along the highway where she could easily be spotted or risking a hitch. She didn't want to take a lift with a man in a suit. He could be a case officer from one of the prisons.

After it grew dark, she hitched a ride with a trucker who looked like Mick Jagger. She was grateful he didn't ask questions. "Just a few kilometres down the road," she said. A kilometre before she got off, she took her bank card out of her wallet and stuck it under the insole of her shoe.

"You sure?" The trucker looked at her in a funny way when she said "here" at an unmarked road. He idled the truck and she took her time unclipping her seat belt.

"I'm going all the way to Montreal. You're welcome to come with me if you like." She let the seat belt slip slowly through her fingers. He put his foot on the accelerator and revved up a little, as if to say let's go.

"No, I can't," she said, but she was sorely tempted. This, she thought, would be her chance to run. But she couldn't. She would feel guilty leaving Nick all by himself in that lonely cabin. How could she just desert him?

After she climbed down, she watched the tail lights of the truck until they disappeared into the dark. Had she made a mistake? Maybe she had, but it was too late now. If she were on the ball, she would screw up her courage and tell Nick that they should give themselves up. The worst thing that could happen to them was to get caught.

Nick saw her climbing down and started walking toward her along the dirt road. "You sure took a fuckin' long time," he said. "Got the money?"

"The machine," she said, trying to sound as exasperated as possible, "ate my card."

"Ate your card? What do you mean, ate your card?"

"It just took my card and swallowed it. It happens."

"You go into the bank? Tell them what happened?"

"No, the bank was closed."

"Closed at two o'clock?"

"Well, it was three o'clock by the time I got there."

He looked at her as though he didn't believe her. She should have told him she tried and the manager had said there was nothing he could do.

"Well, you'll have to go in tomorrow."

"Look Nick, what we're up to is crazy. I think we should get on the bike, go back to Montreal, and give ourselves up. It's not going to work. Eventually we're going to get caught anyway."

"No way," he frowned and kicked the dirt. "Don't even mention it again. I've been cooped up too long to even consider it." She tugged at his arm as they pushed the bike silently through the trees.

"Get on the bike," he said when they reached the road. About a mile down the highway he spotted a tavern. "Got your Mastercard?" he asked as he pulled up.

"Gee. I don't know."

He threw up his hands. "You've got to have your Mastercard. Give me your wallet." He went through the folders. "Here it is." And he took it.

"Look Nick," she said. "It's dangerous going in here. The story's been in the papers."

He was damned if he was going to ask about the papers. It would just make him mad. "We're going in for some beers. I haven't been in a tavern for three years."

"So what did the stupid paper say?" he asked after he'd had a few beers.

"That you'd escaped."

"They name you?"

"No. All it said was that possibly there was an accomplice. They mentioned the Harley."

"Any picture?"

"No."

He drank his beer in total silence, but when a pretty young barmaid in a miniskirt came by to take another order he couldn't help flirting with her. Always the charmer, Maggie thought, but she worried about a tough-looking guy manning the cash who was giving them suspicious looks. After all, there were something like eighteen prisons around here. An hour and a half later, after Nick had had so many beers that he could hardly stand, they left.

Bumping up to Elisabeth's house on the bike, he veered off the road into some gravel, the back wheel cut loose, and as the machine crashed on a rock they both fell to the ground. Nick looked up with horror at the damage. The signals were smashed and the handle bars bent. As he hauled up the bike he saw a hole in the crankcase and a pool of oil on the ground. He stifled a sob. His precious Fat Boy now had a hole in its belly and was bleeding as though it had been mortally shot. He tried to start it but it was no use. In disgust he threw it against a tree and kicked it while Maggie lay on the ground feeling as though her wrist were broken.

As they laboured up to the house, he felt sick with anger and stopped at a tree to throw up. Just outside the door, he grabbed her shoulders. "I know you lied about the money," he slurred. "I always know when you're lyin'. Always. On the big things, the little things. Everything." He opened the door and fell to the living room floor in a heap.

A headache that came from an empty stomach was growing behind her eyes. It was cold and damp, and her clothes stuck to her the way they did when she went on a camping trip with a Sunday School group, and it rained.

"Let me start a fire," she said. He crawled across the floor after her and clutched each ankle as she moved around on her knees on the hearth piling the logs. Once she got the fire going, she led him to the sofa and swaddled him up tight to her in a blanket.

In the prison visiting room, with his broad shoulders and swaggering walk, he always appeared macho, as if he could do anything. But that was only one aspect of what had attracted her to him. He had a child-like side that also drew her.

"You won't ever leave me, will you?" he said. Even under the heat from the fire, he couldn't get warm. "S-say you'll never leave."

"I won't. I promise. C'mon. We have to sleep now." A half hour later, she felt him jiggling her arm.

"Maggie." He was lying on his side staring at her. "You weren't thinkin' of goin' on with him, were you?"

She propped her head up in her hand. She knew what he was referring to but didn't let on. "Going on with who?"

"With that guy in the truck. You were stopped there for the longest time."

"Oh," she forced a laugh. "I had trouble unbuckling the seat belt. That was all."

"Before we go to sleep I want you to say ten times, 'Nick, I will never leave you. Cross my heart and hope to die.'" She did it, but she didn't say it with heart, and he slept fitfully.

When they woke up, he announced he was leaving to find food. He went half way down the road and then came back and disappeared into the shed. A minute later, he came out with some rope coiled around his shoulder. "C'mere," he said when he came in.

"Hello!" Someone was calling from outside. Nick dropped the rope and went out to the porch. Maggie couldn't find her flowered skirt so she lifted his prison pants off a hook at the door and pulled them on. She could hear a short conversation and then Nick said, "Wait a minute," and came back in.

"There's a guy down at the bottom of the steps who says he lives up the road. Wants to talk to you. Looks like a farmer. Everything is normal," Nick said under his breath. "You understand?" And he ushered her outside to the porch.

At the foot of the steps, she saw Barny Baynes who lived two kilometres down the road past the store they had gone to the first day. He did body work on cars and served as a volunteer fire captain. Sometimes Elisabeth bought chickens from him.

"Oh hi," Maggie said running her fingers through her hair. She was aware she looked dishevelled.

"Saw some motorcycle tire marks down there, and . . ." He had probably seen the broken Harley, she thought and suspected something was wrong. "Everything okay?" Barney asked.

Maggie felt Nick standing right behind her and didn't dare let on anything was amiss. "Yeah, fine," she said. "We're here for just a couple of days."

"How's Elisabeth?"

"Oh fine."

"Okay," he said and he turned around, but the way he walked down the path, Maggie knew he didn't like what he saw.

~

"We gotta get outta here," Nick said. He went down the path ahead of her and she watched him pull the twisted Harley back from a tree. He punched the tank hard. "Broken! Finished! And it's all your fault. If you'd have got that money yesterday, we'd be five hundred kilometres from here, rather than stuck in this dump with nothin' to eat. I don't know why you didn't want to get it, but I know you could've, and you didn't," he said. "You think I'm dumb enough to believe the machine ate the card! Did you punch in the number?"

"Yes."

"I don't believe you. I bet you never even punched in the number. You were afraid that's how they'd trace you. That's why you were so nervous about that Mastercard. You think I didn't notice how nervous you were when I gave the bar-owner your Mastercard?"

He threw her down on the road and shook her so her head banged on the stones. She ground her fingers in the ground, looked up to the sky, and cried like an angry infant until the shrieks burned a hole in his head.

Her eyes shut, Maggie lay still on the ground and Nick stared at her, terrified. "Maggie, come back! I can't believe it. Oh Maggie. I'm no fuckin' good," he howled into the dark. "I never was any fuckin' good." He rolled to the side and pounded the earth.

After a few minutes, she opened her eyes and Nick hauled her up by the collar and dragged her to the house where he tossed her into an arm chair.

Nick watched Maggie's eyes roam the room the way Eileen's did before she took off to Magog. His sudden awareness of his powerlessness enraged him. "I can tell you want to run away."

Maggie said nothing. She felt spent and confused about what was happening to her but she knew what he'd said was true. She had reached an impasse with Nick and had no idea how to break through it.

"Look. I know where I can get another motorcycle, and then we can get out of here. We can use your Mastercard. I got it right here," he said, and he patted the back of her leather pants which he was still wearing.

He went behind the sofa, picked up the ropes and decided finally on the legs of the child's bed in the extra room. He knew he couldn't risk leaving her alone. He would have to tie her up. A feeling of doom hung over him as he tied the ropes around her legs. This was how he had lost Eileen. He despised himself for doing it but he didn't know what else to do.

Maggie looked down at the green prison pants she was wearing as he slowly bound her. "I'll put on one of those CDs you like so much, okay? I won't be long." He still smelled strongly of beer. As he talked, she heard her mother reading the passage from A Tale of Two Cities where Sydney Carton changed into the clothes of Charles Evremonde. In the wagon taking him to the guillotine, he held the hand of a young seamstress.

Her love of classical music, Nick recognized, was a sign that Maggie belonged to another world, but he was afraid to let her go. He could not imagine being without her. "I'm sorry I have to do this, Maggie, but I can't take a chance," he said.

Maybe she deserved this humiliation, this abuse, she thought. Everything had been her fault, starting with when she refused to see him on his first weekend out. But she had never felt so torn or so alone. The linen cloth with the blue forget-me-nots came into her mind. Lying on the floor, she listened to the faint beat of her heart. Out in the living room, Nick picked out a CD, put it on, and went out the door.

The sound of her mother's friend Elisabeth playing Beethoven's Waldstein Sonata out beyond the murkiness of everything that was happening to her quickened the beat of her heart. She had been about to give up, but the strong pulse of the music and the thought of her mother's friend slowly revived her. Through the Beethoven sonata, Elisabeth was urging her to find the courage to take some action. "Wake up, Maggie," she seemed to be telling her, "you can't just surrender like this. . . ." If she could find the strength, she knew now what she had to do.

THIRTY-NINE

~⁀

Flight

SCRAGGLY ROPES hanging from her wrists and ankles, Maggie ran down the stairs in her stockinged-feet and stood in the middle of the yard. Her eyes darted first to the tool shed, then to the crawl space under the porch, and finally to the path into the forest. If she was going to run through the woods, she had to have her boots. She ran back across the lawn and up the steps. Minutes later, still clad in the green prison pants, she came out the door with her boots in one hand and a quilted jacket in the other. Whether she had provoked it or not, he had slipped into violence, and she had to get out before she became a physically abused woman.

A few feet down the path into the woods, she untied the knots around her ankles, threw the ropes into the brush, pulled on her boots and ran, but after a few minutes, the trail petered out and she faced a dark forest of evergreens. She had to keep going. Sharp branches scraped her face and twigs cracked underfoot as she pushed

367

her way into the thicket of trees. She breathed more easily when she came to a marshy clearing of scarlet dogwood bushes and browning golden rod but the clearing quickly ended and once again she faced the thick forest. She dropped to her knees and crawled close to the ground with her head curled under.

Her heart beating hard in her ears, she raised her head. In front of her the roots of a mammoth pine twisted into the air like a testament to a mean land. She hadn't seen a single animal. In the summer, at the house with Elisabeth, there were always humming birds but here the land seemed dead. She peered through blighted trees that went on and on, and for the first time she was afraid she would never get out. Leaning against a tree with her hoop earrings and her scratched face, she knew she looked like a dirty Gypsy. How different was she now from some of the women she had written about in that series on child and wife abuse that she had done prior to Nick's trial?

The horror of her descent with Nick into hell where grievous behaviour had become normal filled her with despair. Back at the cabin, with a bent nail file she had found on the floor she had sawed the ropes free from the legs of the bed. Now she tried to loosen the knots on her wrists with her fingernails but they were locked in place. She put her head in her filthy palm and shut her eyes.

A few minutes later, she heard a chirp and looked up. A sparrow was so close she could stroke his head. Beyond the thicket she saw the light of another clearing. The bird flew ahead and she followed. The ground oozed with water. An uprooted cedar dripping with rot formed an impasse but the sparrow called her and she found a way across. Foliage reappeared and she walked quickly. The pines became tall as cathedrals and soft lichen formed a carpet. Suddenly bright sky appeared and she scrambled up through a stand of birch trees at the top of a hill. She watched the sparrow as he flew away.

She ran down the hill into an apple orchard where decaying fruit lay on the ground. She sat on the damp grass and stuffed the fermenting pulp into her mouth. Her wrists were red and chafing. A twig had punctured the thin membrane between her thumb and forefinger and blood trickled into the cracks of her palm. She tried once more to untie the muddy knots, but gave up. Stuffing another apple into her mouth, she stumbled down the hill toward a dirt road, the frayed ropes flapping against her legs.

At the side of the road, a bicycle with fluorescent yellow handle-bars leaned against a tree. What a miracle, she said to herself. She wheeled it down the ditch, up to the road, climbed on and peddled fast. It was a one-speed bike like the CCM she'd had as a child when bikes with gears were a novelty. But she could make good time on it. She peddled furiously for about a kilometre until her knees ached and the thought of Nick's rage when he found she was gone sent a pain through her. The way she looked, she couldn't hitchhike back to Montreal. She had to find a safe place to hide for the night. The wind swirled up yellow leaves from the side of the road. She'd head for Willow Wind.

Years before, when she was fresh out of journalism school, she had interviewed Mercedes Pedereweski, a tapestry artist who lived alone in a house of skylights and gardens in Willow Wind near Holt. She couldn't remember exactly where, but she knew it was in the region. Mercedes was a Polish Jew who had hid as a child during the war and survived. Maggie stopped on top of a knoll and looked across the vista of gently rolling hills. The sun was high in the sky. There was not a house in sight and for a second she felt the security of solitude. She had outgrown the need for the high that went with a page-one byline, she thought, and now she hoped she had put to rest the crav-ing for dark Dionysian trysts.

She let the bike career down an incline and around a corner past a clump of cedars. Beyond the turn, in the middle of the road, two mangy looking dogs with bald spots on their sides barked in front of a tar paper shack. The yard was strewn with garbage and cast-off fur-niture. She stopped the bike and stared at the dogs the way she'd been taught when she biked once with a cycling group in the Eastern Townships. The dogs never stopped barking. She took small steps, her head low, so they couldn't see the fear in her eyes. The door of the shack creaked open.

"Back here, Blackie." An unshaven man in smeared overalls and unlaced boots shambled to the edge of the road with a knotted rope over his shoulder and a can of beer in his hand. "Blackie! Drake!" He raised the rope and the dogs circled back into the yard and jumped on top of an overturned wood stove.

"I'm looking for Willow Wind," Maggie said as she bunched forward over her bike. Even from ten feet away the smell coming off him was foul. He threw his head back and took a swig of the beer. She quickly stuffed the ropes around her wrists up her sleeves.

"Willow Wind?" He put the beer on a tree stump and pulled out a pot of peanut butter from his pocket. He dipped a finger into the peanut butter and rubbed a sore on his neck. "A long way off," he said. "You gotta gash near yer eye." He took a step into the road, a gob of peanut butter on his finger. "Want some of this?"

"No." She stepped back. "How do I get to Willow Wind?" The dogs scratched restlessly on top of the stove. "Down!" he said. He swirled his beer, still not letting her pass. "You been in the forest?"

She stared down at the centre of her yellow handlebars. Her finger nails were ringed with black. "I been there," she muttered under her breath. Now she was talking as though she'd been brought up in the backwoods.

"I got to get to Willow Wind." She thought of bolting, but was afraid of the dogs.

He belched. "Bout forty Ks to Willow Wind. Past Sleepy Creek and Perkins Cove."

"Thanks very much." She peddled away quickly. Forty kilometres was a long way to go in this cold. Ten minutes later she spotted a caved-in barn. Thistles grew in the cracks at the entrance. From under some rusty fishing rods, she pulled out some mildewed grain sacks which she ripped into strips and wound around her hands. To keep her ears warm, she tied a piece around her head, knotting it at the top. From a ledge, she picked up a pack of matches and slipped them in her pocket.

Every house had a dog that barked as soon as she wheeled into view. They were all on ropes, but afraid of them breaking loose, she

sped by on the opposite side of the road. The only one that wasn't
tied up darted out into the road and followed her. He was a German
Shepherd puppy. His tail wagging, he scampered along beside her,
nipping at her boots. She longed to keep him with her, but when
they came to a crossroad, he went back, and she was left to her own
thoughts.

She thought of the dog who took the Polish tapestry artist through
the forest the night her parents were taken to the death camp. For the
article she had written, Maggie had asked Mercedes Pedereweski for
detail after detail about what had happened. Her mother had told her
to hide under some newspapers in a hope chest, then when night
came, to take the path over the mountain to a parish priest who
would hide her. The soldiers ransacked the house but they never
found her. The family had a dog who had fled when the soldiers
arrived. Beyond the back fence, at the edge of the woods, the dog
waited, and when Mercedes slipped out of the back door after dark,
they went over the mountain together.

Maggie loosened her quilted jacket. She was damp with sweat
from the push up the hills but her feet were cold and wet. Leaves flew
up from the shoulder of the road into the spokes of her wheels. A
chimney poked out of an empty hut on a hill. She stopped her bike
and clambered up through a patch of milk weed. If she could dry out
her boots, she might make it as far as Willow Wind.

She gathered up an armful of twigs and lit a fire. While her boots
dried, she ate acorns and thought about Mercedes running over the
mountain during the war. For three years, from the age of ten to thirteen, she had moved from house to house, living in attics, barn lofts
and basements. When the war ended a Catholic doctor helped her
find an aunt in France.

The acorns were bitter but Maggie forced herself to eat them. She
needed energy. During the war, when food was scarce, people mixed
them with corn. As she pulled on her boots, she remembered the
name of the road where the tapestry artist lived. Du Maurier, like the
British writer, Daphne du Maurier, who wrote about that murder in

the big house in the desolate English countryside. Maggie had spent only a couple of hours twelve years ago with Mercedes Pedereweski, but she was praying now for her to be in Willow Wind.

Back on the bike, the steady rhythm of the peddling was like a drug that allowed her mind to wander the way it had when she broke her arm in a car accident and a doctor gave her a painkiller. The fear and panic of the last three days were still with her and she couldn't stop thinking about Nick. She remembered his eyes as he held her hand in the visitors room at the penitentiary and asked, "Do you think the baby might have died of something else?" Had he shaken his baby, the way he had shaken her, in a fit of rage? Was that what he was afraid he'd done? She remembered a half-finished sentence of his the last night they'd met in the square.

She didn't know any more, not about him, or herself, or anything. She should have tried harder to persuade Nick at the cabin that the only sane thing for them to do was to go back and confess that it had all been a foolish mistake. When she had been a reporter in the thick of a story, she had known how to ask the critical questions, raise the unsettling issues, but she recognized that she had never been capable of doing that in her relationship with Nick.

She had to get to Willow Wind soon. The sun was fading and the temperature was dropping. She tried to go as fast as she could. The bike was making a worrisome noise at every revolution. Twice the chain came off. Around four-thirty in the afternoon as she was coming to Sleepy Creek, she heard the rumble of a motorcycle. She threw the bike behind a bush and then beat her way through some bull rushes where she hid until the motorcycle passed. Nick would patrol the roads close to the highway, probably on another stolen motorcycle. He'd expect her to look for a hitch on the 401 back to Montreal. When she didn't show up, he'd search the back roads. For fifteen minutes, she lay face down on the ground. If he suspected she was hiding, he would wait. She should have known he'd follow her. That's what he had done with Eileen. Why not with her?

Back on the bike, no matter how hard she peddled, she couldn't get warm. A half hour later, she again heard the sound of the motorcycle and scrambled behind some golden rod. After that, she lost her nerve and couldn't control the bike. In the dark, pot holes lurked everywhere. Going up the hills she wobbled from one side to the other. Finally, on the loose gravel of the shoulder, she lost control and pitched face-first into the ditch.

Back again on the bike, fighting bouts of nausea, she moved the peddles slowly. Everything ached, especially her wrist which she had sprained when she fell off the Harley. She longed to stride up to a clapboard house with a Tiffany lamp in the window and ask for help, but one look at her scratched face and muddy clothes and they'd slam the door in her face. It was completely dark by the time she got to Perkins Cove where she stopped a woman coming out of a grocery store. "Willow Wind?" she stammered. "Is it far from here?"

"You'll see a sign at the junction," the woman said.

"How far from there?"

"About ten kilometres."

Maggie pushed on until she reached the junction. After she crossed the road, the chain broke, and she left the bike in a twisted heap in the ditch.

A half hour later, on foot, she came across the neon lights of a bar across from a white church. Three motorcycles leaned against the front wall. A sign for Willow Wind said three kilometres. She sat down by the side of the road and stared at the thin despairing arms of a tree at the top of the hill. She wanted to slide down the ditch and fade away like an old Inuit woman left in the snow to die. How had she *ever* come to *this*? It was, she thought, because she hadn't had the courage to take charge of her emotional world. She had looked to Nick for everything that had been missing in her private life, expecting him to be her lover, her child, sometimes even a caring parent. Poor Nick. What a burden she had placed on him.

She took off her boots and tried to warm her feet with her hands. Her toes were stiff as icicles. She stood up and tried to walk. The pain made her whimper, but when she heard a car, in her stockinged feet, she hobbled into the centre of the road and put out her thumb. A tow truck with a flashing light stopped.

She could hardly step up to the seat. "I'm looking for Mercedes Pedereweski," she stammered. "She makes tapestries." Jammed up next to two men who smelled of beer, leather and tobacco, she moved in and out of a faint, her voice far away, as though it belonged to someone else.

"Mercedes who?"

"Du Maurier," she said. "Take me to Du Maurier Road."

~

In the dark at the top of the hill, Nick sat by the side of the road and bit into a rotten apple. He spat it out and pulled out a cigarette. He was sure she hadn't tried the 401. He would have seen her walking along the road. He laughed bitterly to himself. She thought she could fool him by going through the forest. He had checked every barn and abandoned shack on all the country roads around the forest and had found no trace of her, but he was convinced she wasn't far. He took two more puffs of the cigarette and ground it into the earth.

He would look until he found her but nothing would ever be the same. He could have taken anything, anything but that look of disgust he saw on her face when they were on the path. She knew he saw it because she turned away. "Ice monster! Punk! Scum!" Everything everyone had ever called him seemed to scream at him from that look. He hung his head between his legs. "Maggie, Maggie, Maggie," he said to himself. Now she was no different from all the others. The real reason he wanted to escape from the joint was to get away from those nasty looks. He'd believed he'd always be safe with her.

He thought about the fear he saw in her when he tied her up. Tears came to his eyes. If he really loved her, he would let her go. He was no good for her. Just like he was no good for Eileen. He had told her that more than once. The wind was cold and he pulled his jacket tight.

He got on the Yamaha Maxim he'd stolen from the house near the grocery store and drifted slowly down a sharp incline and around a corner past a clump of cedars. Beyond the turn he saw lights in the windows of a tar paper shack. He put the motorcycle in the yard next to a rusty wood stove standing on its side. He had to keep looking for her.

BEWARE OF DOGS was scrawled in red on a board tacked over a window. A dog barked from the back of the shack. He pulled his Swiss army knife out of his pocket and knocked. A filthy man in overalls and only a few teeth opened the door and he walked in. The shack stank of garbage and urine but when he found out that the man had actually seen her just a few hours ago, he forgot about it.

Nick figured he must have talked to her for quite a while because he could describe her in detail, including the little red spots on the top of her cheek bones when she was afraid. "The dogs terrified her," he said.

The old bugger knew too much about her. Nick eyed the poker lying next to the stove. If he found out he had so much as laid a finger on her, he'd waste him. The man must have read his mind because he suddenly said, "Ugly bitch. Wuddna touched her with a pole, she was so filthy." He threw back his head and laughed so that Nick could see all the brown stumps at the back of his mouth. "And so old. Old enough to be your bloomin' mother!"

The man patted the rump of one of the dogs lazing in front of the fire. "Wouldn't let her pass. Eh Drake? One word from me," he looked up at Nick, his eyes small slits, "and the dog wudda tore her up." The dog sat up, his ears erect, as though he'd heard something. "If they're on foot, no one passes this house unless I let 'em," the man said.

Nick leaned back against a one-legged stained easy chair with the stuffing oozing out of it and felt the Swiss army knife in his back pocket. If the dog so much as bared his teeth, he'd stab him between the eyes.

"Easy, boy." The man fondled the dog's ears and he lay down.

"Funny thing," he said. "She had these ropes hangin' down. Tried to stuff em up her sleeves, but they kept fallin' out." He heaved a log into the stove. The old man belched. Hungry?" Nick nodded. The man led him through a kitchen piled with plates that had fungus growing on them and took him out a back door. Two toppled trees lay at the edge of the woods. He gave him an axe. "If ya chop up them trees," he said, "I'll make ya a peanut butter sandwich." What a dump, Nick said to himself as he chopped the trees. If he didn't watch out, he'd end up like this ragbag with nothin' except a shack and some rabid dogs. He knew in his gut that it wasn't going to work out with Maggie but he couldn't just go to a police station and give himself up. He had to keep looking for her.

〜

Leaning against a tree near the mail box, her chin on her chest and her bare feet blue, Maggie heard a dog circling around her. A flashlight shone in her face and for a second she thought it was a prison guard. She lifted a bandaged hand up to her eyes and felt the rough rope brush against her bruised nose.

"Mer-ced-es?" She couldn't see her face.

"Yes."

"Maggie MacKinnan?" She found it hard even to say her name. "Montreal *Tribune*?"

Mercedes hoisted her up by an elbow, but Maggie crumpled to the ground. Finally Mercedes gathered her up and carried her to the house where she laid her on the couch and picked up the phone. "Don't call anyone," Maggie said when she heard her dialling. "Don't. Please. I'll be okay."

Mercedes sat next to her on the couch and held her hand. "I'm going to call a friend. A doctor. You're suffering from exposure."

"You mustn't." Maggie clutched her arm. "I know I look terrible." She hoped Mercedes didn't recognize the prison outfit. "I'm in trouble. But I, I . . ." She wanted to say she hadn't done anything criminal, but she *had* done something criminal; she had helped Nick escape, and that, she felt, was the least of it. She fell back against a pillow, shivering. What was most offensive was the pitiless side of her nature — the side that had impetuously desired Nick and then wantonly abandoned him. If she had not given into the temptation of the tryst and the fierce ride on the Harley they would not have plunged headlong into a chaos that she suspected was not yet over.

When she came to, the ropes were gone and Mercedes was lifting her into a warm bath. Afterwards she spread ointment on her bleeding wrists, made her sip a hot rum toddy, buttoned her into a warm nightgown, and packed her into a bed near the kitchen with hot water bottles and an eiderdown quilt. From time to time, Maggie woke up, and in her mind, thanked Mercedes for the comfort and the relief of this warm room away from everything. In the morning Mercedes washed her jacket, hung it on a line outside, and from her studio kept watch over the patio door to the room where Maggie slept.

～

Nick knew he was on the right path when he found the bicycle in the ditch. He would never have noticed it if it hadn't been for the yellow handle bars. "The bike had bright yellow handle bars," the old man had told him just before he left. "If you see a bike like that leaning against a house, you'll know she's inside." He started with the houses in the village but no one knew about a girl with hoop earrings and a quilted jacket until he got to a body repair shop. A man in jeans with his head under a hood stood up as soon as he heard Nick's description.

"Hoop earrings? Yeah. Me an' a buddy picked her up last night. She was in the middle of the road in her stockinged feet. Looked like she escaped from the loony bin. Your mother or somethin'?"

"No, my sister," Nick replied.

The mechanic couldn't remember exactly where they dropped her off. His buddy was driving. "He'll be back soon," he said. "He can tell ya."

It was 2:30 when Nick walked up the path to Mercedes' red brick house. Avoiding the front door, he circled around and looked in the windows. No one seemed at home. Curtains were drawn across a large patio door. He heard a voice and the sharp bark of a dog.

"Can I help you?"

He turned around. A woman in a long skirt hustled him toward the front of the house.

"I'm looking for my sister. She escaped from a nursing home near Kingston," Nick said. He was sure that Maggie was in the room behind the drawn curtains.

"She was wearing hoop earrings and a green and pink quilted jacket."

Accompanied by the dog, Mercedes walked him down the path. Nick could tell she knew something.

"I think you should go to the police," she said. "The station is six kilometres from here."

Nick's motorcycle stood next to the same tree where Maggie had been the night before. The licence plate, Mercedes noticed, was covered with mud.

"The police?"

"About ten o'clock last night, my neighbour called to tell me she found a woman half dead by the side of the road. She was suffering from exposure."

Mercedes saw Nick recoil when she said exposure. "She could hardly say her name. Ropes hung from her wrists as though someone had tied her up. The police took her away."

～

As soon as she got back to the house, Mercedes took Maggie's jacket off the line. Then she went into her room with a bowl of porridge and fed her with a small spoon.

"What's the time?" Maggie asked.

"Three o'clock," Mercedes said.

Maggie swallowed as though she were a stroke victim and couldn't eat. A dream filled her head . . . She was wearing the silver bracelet her mother gave her for her confirmation which meant she was seventeen because that was the last time she could remember wearing it. She was leaning over the railing of the Jacques Cartier Bridge . . .

She stayed in bed for three days and sat up only once when she heard Mercedes talking in a low voice to someone in the kitchen. It was her neighbour. "I'm sure he won't come back," Mercedes said to the woman. "But you never know."

He? Maggie lay back against the pillow and erased the idea. When the neighbour left, Mercedes came into Maggie's room with a hot chocolate. It reminded her of the Young Peoples Union after the Sunday evening church services at St. Ninian's when she was a teenager.

Maggie sipped the hot chocolate and remembered the frenzied look in her father's eyes when he banged his fist on the Bible during the sermon he gave against abortion. "Wrong," he had preached as he lifted up a series of pro-abortion articles which had appeared that week in the *Tribune*. He had gone into her room and found the articles she had cut out for her grade eleven current events class.

"Abortion," he said, "is against God's will." Looking directly at Maggie, he brought his fist down on the lectern. "Abortion is murder!" he had roared. The onion-thin pages of the open Bible ripped as he ground his fist into the leaves. In the church he looked from one girl to the next, then he raised his cloaked arms and said, "Let us pray."

During the prayer, Maggie vowed she'd get another copy of those articles. After school the next day she went down to the *Tribune* and found the back issues of the paper. In a restaurant opposite the paper, she cut them out all over again. Even then she was thinking of becoming a reporter. She'd been resolute when she was at the newspaper but when she got home she hid them at the top of her cupboard and never did bring them to class. Maggie placed the hot chocolate on the night table and put her head in her arms.

"Sleep," Mercedes said. "Just sleep." But Maggie couldn't sleep. She thought of how Mercedes dealt with the world, alone in the woods with her tapestries and her dog, shielding herself from the world by helping a stranger in trouble like Maggie, but not asking any questions. Perhaps she liked the solitude. But Maggie knew she couldn't hide herself away. She liked being part of the world, maybe now more than ever . . .

~

On the morning of the third day, Maggie was in the kitchen finishing a breakfast of pancakes and bacon, imagining what it would be like to stay in Willow Wind for a little longer, when Mercedes stubbed out her cigarette in a way that made her sit up in her chair.

"Maggie," she put her hand on her arm. "There's something I have to tell you." There was a long pause. "He knows where you are."

Maggie hadn't told Mercedes her story, but she responded as though Mercedes knew everything. "How can he know that," Maggie said. "I never once told him I knew anyone in Willow Wind." A sparrow pecked at the bird feeder in front of the window and she watched him fly into the trees.

"I saw him this morning in the bushes watching you when you were trying on the jeans and sweater." Mercedes had bought Maggie clothes to replace the prison pants and shirt she'd been wearing.

"He was right out *there*?" Maggie whispered.

Mercedes nodded. "He's gone now. You're safe for a while. I told him if I caught him again, I'd call the police."

"Again?"

"He came the day after you arrived. On a motorcycle. I said the police took you away the night before."

Maggie avoided looking at Mercedes. "Did you call the police?" she asked.

"No. Of course not and one of the things I learned a long time ago was to stay close to the truth when you lie." Maggie's new friend talked in the sad voice of the housekeeper in *Wuthering Heights* when she told the tale of Heathcliff and Cathy to the lodger in the house on the moors. Her eyes wide and dry, Maggie stared at a knot in the pine table as Mercedes tried to warm her icy hand.

"I told him a neighbour found a woman in bare feet by the road," Mercedes went on. "I said she called the police and that the woman was probably in the Kingston Hospital. He could never have checked," she said. "When he came, the neighbour was away."

Maggie looked off into the woods. "He didn't see my jacket on the line, did he?"

"I don't know. The first time he came I was in my studio. He walked right around the house before I saw him."

Maggie was afraid once again now that Nick knew where she was, but she also felt exhilarated. Nick was so much a part of her, the idea of him not needing her was almost unbearable. "I could fly to the middle of India and he'd trace me," she said. "Could you take me to the bus station? I have to go back to Montreal."

"You sure?" Mercedes asked. "You have someone to stay with?"

She could always stay at the refugee centre with Michael. "Yes," she said. Michael would help her out. If she was going to confide now in anyone, it would be him.

"You want to tell me what happened?"

Maggie felt too bewildered to talk. She had never revealed her feelings to anyone, she realized, least of all to herself. Her job as a reporter had always been to ask others the questions. Caught up in the tumultuous events of the last six days, she had sometimes felt like a reporter on a mad sprint for a story even though *she* was one of the subjects. "It's complicated," she said. "I sort of lost my mind."

"I know about those things," Mercedes said. "From the war."

"I think there's stuff I have to figure out by myself," Maggie added.

"Well," Mercedes said, pouring her another coffee. "If you ever want to talk, I'm always here."

Perhaps this woman who had so generously taken care of her was someone she wouldn't be afraid to open up to. Maybe she and Mercedes could become friends.

~

She was too numb to think as they drove towards the bus station in the city that Maggie could now only associate with penitentiaries. Outside Kingston, in a shopping mall, Mercedes stopped at an automatic teller, drew some money from a machine and handed Maggie five twenty-dollar bills. "I'll pay you back for everything," Maggie said after she bought her ticket. "As soon as I get back." And she stepped on the bus.

FORTY

～

Fire and Wind

NICK TOOK SOME sharp turns the way he had on the Harley Fat Boy with Maggie the night they went down the Richelieu, then he accelerated and settled into a steady pace about half a kilometre behind the bus. When he was on a high, he could do anything. How else could he have lifted the Yamaha out of the garage and walked off with it in broad daylight? The fire inside him was burning like a rocket. He hunched down over the handle bars and turned up the gas.

A freight train chugged along tracks next to the highway. A turn on the accelerator and he could be right under her window. Vroom, vrooommmmmmm. She'd hear the throb and look down. Fast as wind, he'd sweep up to the tracks, leap to the caboose, and wave to her from the top of the train like John Wayne. The train disappeared and to get away from the bus fumes he let the bike slip back.

A gray cliff moving in close from the side of the road reminded him of the prison complex at St. Bartholomew. Those bloated chick-

ens seemed years away. No matter what she said, he was never going
back. Minimum was better, but now, with the jackrabbit, it'd probably be right back to Maximum. Besides, Minimum, Medium, Maximum. What difference did it make? If he didn't have her, it was all
over.

The road widened and turned and for a moment he lost sight of
the green stripe on the back of the bus. He moved closer and kept
the bike at the same speed as the bus. He reached back and ran his
fingers over the back of her black leather pants until he felt the bump
at the bottom of the pocket. He had the cyanide pills in the sewn-in
patch on his underwear. When he came back and found her gone,
he'd thought about taking one. He had never told Maggie he had
them, but he did, and if he had to use them, he would. He wasn't
afraid to die. Die? he asked himself. Because he couldn't have her?
"Her, her, her," he screamed out at the wind. He hated feeling so
dependent upon her.

He slowed down to a cruise and thought back to those three days
with her at the log house where he had cracked the whip over her,
tried to control her. It was no way to live. He had to stop believing
she was the answer to all his problems. She was too different from him
and had too many ideas of her own to live the way he wanted.

The road climbed to the top of a hill. On the plateau, farms
stretched out in the distance. This Yamaha Maxim was better than
nothing but it had no balls, no blast. He thought of the rumble of the
Harley Fat Boy with Maggie on the back clinging to him. Two stolen
bikes in only one week. He'd lived a whole life in a week. But he was
a fool to be chasing after Maggie and trying to think up yet another
way to impress her. He was nearly twenty-four — far too old to be
trying to find a mother. He had to find another way to live his life . . .
He wondered what his friend Stavro would have thought about all
this. While Nick was learning Greek and they were making raisin-
jack together they had felt like blood brothers, but after Stavro had
been transferred to the medium security prison they had lost touch.
The sky was darkening. He was on a straight road now, the speed
steady.

The bus took an exit and he followed behind as it pulled into a gas station and everyone got off. After he watched her go into the restaurant, he pulled the bike into the woods and sat on a tree stump. He patted the front pocket of his leather jacket and pulled out her butterfly pin. It was all twisted, one wing hanging by a thread. Sitting on the stump, staring at it, he felt a wave of gloom as half-remembered things swirled up at him. Eileen crying, the baby shrieking. He put his hands over his ears and the butterfly dropped on the ground.

"He died of exposure," Maggie kept telling him. "Why do you keep asking whether he might have died of something else?" He took his hands off his ears and pounded his fist into the palm of his hand. A bird was chirping. "Only a Greek boy with roots that go back into eternity could have lashes like yours," she'd said. She was the one person who believed he could find a real job and live a normal life.

Maggie was right. He did not have to do crime to live on the outside, although he had to admit that since the Harley Davidson Special, all he'd done was steal bikes and do B&Es. Still . . . Some of that was to prove to her that he really *could* do it and that he wasn't a chicken heart.

He threw his leg over the seat of the Yamaha and squeezed his eyes shut for a second before he connected the wires to start up. As long as it had been a pretend escape, Maggie had loved everything they had done together. He knew he had given her the thrill of her life. He smiled to himself at the happy look in her eyes in the barn. But now. Now? He bumped the bike out of the woods and levered it through the gears. Maybe it was really all over, but no matter what, he was going to see her one more time.

FORTY-ONE

～⌒

Blue Forget-Me-Nots

THE SOUNDS OF the bus wheels on the asphalt drew Maggie into a trance that kept her from thinking of Montreal and what might lie ahead. She knew she had important decisions to make about her life but she wasn't yet sure what they should be. The row of trees flying past her were barren against the graying sky. She turned her head and saw a pair of laced hiking boots on the aisle floor. A tall man with thick black hair pulled down a pack sack from the luggage rack above. He threw it on the seat next to her and pulled out a sandwich and a book. "Sorry," he said when a beer rolled out and he had to scramble down around her ankles to retrieve it. The book had a McGill University stamp on the inside cover. He had a winsome smile when he looked up. "Got an exam tomorrow." On the little finger of his left hand he had a long nail, like Andreas. A tremor went through her, and she made herself think back to those events during her first year at McGill. She lay back against the seat and shut out the world around her . . .

After cross-country skiing up north, she had gone with him to a café where he had leaned across the table and kissed her. Then they went back to his apartment in the student ghetto. "Just for a drink," he had said. Afterward, she had waited for him to call but he never did. She knew his schedule and lingered around the architecture building near the crabapple trees hoping to run into him but when she eventually glimpsed his face at the front door, he turned away from her and went back into the building . . .

The hikers at the back of the bus were listening to music. Carly Simon was singing "Comin' Round Again." Everything came back, slowly, like a film that had been locked in a vault.

. . . After she missed her period, she had waited for him at the bus stop near his apartment, but he scowled when he saw her and she never tried again. The sound of the wheels on the highway reminded her she was on the bus. She looked out again at the trees and made the reel from her past slowly unwind.

Up in the medical library on Pine avenue she picked up a handbook on pregnancy with detailed anatomical pictures. It was called *Your Pregnancy Month by Month*. She looked around for a secluded spot. Finally, she stood at the entrance to the Osler Room with its wood panelling and stained glass windows. In a glass display case, a leather-bound book exhibited the Hippocratic Oath. The room was as quiet as a funeral home. She chose an alcove at the front and sat at a table with a brass lamp and read for an hour, oblivious to everyone. She consulted charts and drawings as though she were doing research for someone else.

Then she went upstairs to the "A" section and looked for two volumes on abortion. Carefully following the numbers, she read the titles along the shelf. *The Pathology of Infanticide, The Moment of Death, A Handbook for the Study of Suicide, The Criminal Mind, Make Mad the Guilty*. Chattering ladies were moving toward her. A McGill Red Wing guide in her white blazer stood ten feet from her with a group of middle-aged wives of out-of-town doctors attending a medical conference. Maggie circled quickly to another section and stared hard at a drawing of a diseased heart.

"Volumes on forensic medicine are in there, right where that young woman in the braid was standing," the Red Wing was saying. "Pathologists in coroner's offices often consult these books." Maggie stood still until she heard them go down the stairs. Both books she picked off the shelf back in the As were filled with statistics on prosecutions, jail sentences and deaths. The first one opened with a quote from the Criminal Code: "Every woman is guilty of an indictable offence and liable to seven years imprisonment who, whether with child or not, unlawfully administers to herself any drug or other noxious thing, or unlawfully uses in herself or permits to be used on her any instrument or other means whatsoever with intent to procure a miscarriage."

Sitting at a desk surrounded by the William Osler collection, she turned the pages as soundlessly as possible, as though anyone who wasn't a pathologist or a lawyer, and deigned read such a book, was already guilty of an "indictable offence." The case histories scared her, but she made herself read them. "More recently, a well-dressed young woman was found dead behind the wheel of her late model car," she read. "Investigation of the car revealed a partly filled bottle of vinegar, a douche bag, a rubber catheter and a fountain syringe. The fetus was of about four months gestation. There was air in the pelvic veins and the right side of the heart was distended with a bloody foam. Investigation indicated she had attempted to abort herself. Most probably with the help of a girlfriend and died by reason of the injection of air into the uterus." Maggie lifted her head and gripped the sides of the table. Staring down at her from a dark oil painting was Sir William Osler in a thick mustache.

After leaving the library, she walked slowly to the campus where she sat on a park bench and stared out into a sunny day. The campus was filled with picnickers on their lunch hour, children splashing in the fountain in the hollow, and soccer players idly kicking around a ball. A couple with a blanket settled under a tree a few feet from her.

While the Beatles sang "Yesterday" on their radio, the girl lay against her boyfriend's chest.

Coming up from Sherbrooke around the Roddick Gates, a young woman led a parade of four-year-olds wearing fluorescent-coloured beanies with small plastic windmills that turned in the breeze. Maggie stared at the children who held pastel loops attached to a rope and were licking ice cream cones. After a few minutes she stood up and began walking toward the Roddick Gates.

If she hadn't had those fake periods in April and May, she would have known something was wrong much earlier. She had counted on that spotting, believing her periods were back and she was safe. Only after she went through those books did she realize she had other tell-tale symptoms like nausea and heavy breasts. Her bra size had gone from A to B and she had never let herself make the connection. Now there was no mistaking it. That morning at breakfast when she had poured her father's coffee she felt stirrings in her womb. She leaned against a pillar at the gates.

At four and a half months, a doctor with his ear to the womb could hear the heart beat. She put her hands on her stomach. If she had caught it after one month, even two, she could have done it her-self with a catheter. For every catheter a druggist sold for bladders, she'd read, ten were sold to stop pregnancies. A little jiggling inside the womb, and the fetus could be jarred loose. Not that it would be easy to find the cervix — until she looked at the birth book with the anatomy drawings, she didn't even know it was *called* the cervix — but now at twenty weeks, that was out of the question. She couldn't do it herself.

She hesitated for a moment before she crossed the street and walked up four flights of stairs to the mathematics department to stand outside Professor Martin Ashbury's door. In October he had written an article in the *McGill Daily* criticizing the medical profession for not pushing the government to make abortion legal. She'd overheard a girl at the Danube Café talking about getting a name from him. She raised her hand, cocked her ear and knocked. The sound echoed out into the hall. The clack of a typewriter in the secretary's office two doors down stopped abruptly.

A woman with a gray bun came out into the hall. "Looking for Professor Ashbury, I suppose."

"Yes," Maggie said, flushing.

"Well, he's away," and she turned on her heel. Inside her office, she slammed the typewriter carriage and continued typing.

Maggie stood at the open door for a full minute before the woman raised her head. "Would you know when he's coming back?" Maggie asked.

"Absolutely no idea," she said, and went on typing.

Back on Sherbrooke street, aimlessly walking, she was plagued with doubts. Was she, or wasn't she? Maybe she wasn't. She sat on a bench near University street, locked her fingers over her belly, and pressed. Now she felt nothing. Some girls who tried to abort themselves turned out not to be pregnant. She had to do something. Anything.

She stood up and walked toward the statue of Queen Victoria and the Royal Victoria College walk-in infirmary. She would tell the receptionist she was Molly McNan. Once, when she ordered a text from the book store, the clerk listed her by mistake as Molly McNan rather than Maggie MacKinnan. She stepped into the middle of the traffic and jaywalked across. Cars were honking but she moved around them like a sleepwalker.

She mumbled the phoney name to the receptionist as she walked in the door of the infirmary. "You'll have to see the nurse first," the receptionist said. She hadn't realized she'd have to see the nurse. Two minutes later, when she was ushered into the nurse's office, she couldn't blurt it out. "It's sort of private." She paused. "Couldn't I just tell the doctor?"

The nurse held a case history card in her hand. "That isn't how we work," she said, her eyes narrowing. "But since we're not that busy..." She opened the door and waved her over to a row of stiff-backed chairs. "You'll have to wait your turn."

Two students were ahead of her. Panic twisted through her. The room was as bare as the anteroom of a police station. She suddenly wanted to leave but was afraid of attracting attention. She was looking out the window at the broad back of Queen Victoria holding her sceptre when the warden of the college stepped in the door of the infirmary. Dr. Baldwin, whose other title was Dean of Women, had a bust that looked hard as concrete. She spoke with a British accent that came from a long stay at Oxford doing post-graduate work in medieval English studies and moved through the halls of the women's residence like a Mother Superior.

"Tell the nurse to come to my office as soon as she's free," she told the receptionist. Maggie hoped Dr. Baldwin wouldn't recognize her from her interview at the beginning of the year. Every woman who came to McGill was interviewed by Dr. Baldwin or one of her assistants. "I'd like my daily report on the infirmary by three o'clock today," she said.

The warden was barely out the door when the doctor stepped into the anteroom. "Molly McNan," he called. Maggie stared down at her knees. At meat counters when the butcher called a number and no one answered he went on to the next. Three others were waiting. "Molly McNan?" He said the name louder.

Maggie felt the receptionist's eyes on her. "Aren't you Molly McNan?"

"Oh," Maggie said and strained forward towards the doctor's office.

The doctor was about the same age as her father. As she entered the office, he squinted at her the way the bus driver had done late the night before when he had asked her when she was expecting. The driver had said it in French, and she hadn't figured it out until she was on the bus that morning on the way to the library. She sat down and pulled in her belly. Even though she'd had to move a few buttons, all her skirts still fit.

"What can I do for you?" he asked.

"I've been suffering from . . ." Her heart pounded. She avoided the doctor's eyes and looked past the framed medical certificate to his examining room.

"When did you have your last period?"

"I think in February," she said, almost relieved she was finally admitting it to someone. For months the fear of what possibly lay inside her, growing, had prevented her from even going to a drug store and asking for a pregnancy test. She talked slowly. "In March and April I had this spotting, and then nothing in May. This morning, I . . ." She wanted to cry.

He told her to go into the examining room and get undressed. When he finished the examination, he pulled a white curtain around her and told her to put on her clothes. "You're five months pregnant," he said when she was back in the chair in front of his desk.

"So I really am," she whispered, *"pregnant?"* This was the first time she'd actually said the word pregnant out loud. She was embarrassed she'd asked, but she wanted a one hundred per cent confirmation.

"Yes," he said. "You're pregnant." She wished he'd speak softer. The warden might come by again and hear. He leaned back in his wide leather swivel chair. "What are your plans?"

Maggie put her hands under her thighs and said nothing. "What about the father of the baby? Are you going to get married?"

"No," she said. "That's not possible . . ."

Maggie pulled her eyes away from the rows of trees that reeled by the window of the bus travelling to Montreal. Marijuana was in the air. The student with the long fingernail had his pack sack again on the seat next to her, "Like one?" he asked, pulling out a couple of oranges. He had a beautiful smile. She didn't know which he meant, an orange or a toke on the joint in his hand.

"No," she said. "It's okay." A minute later, from the back of the bus, the sound of a heavy metal band hit like a stroke of lightning. An old man with blood-shot eyes and a bottle in a paper bag fell against the shoulder of her seat. "Turn that noise off," he bawled. The students looked back at him with no-damn-way smiles as the music thrashed on. Everyone watched. The old man stumbled back to his seat. A few minutes later, the students turned down the music and the bus went back to normal.

The sun was going down. Maggie tried to remember what happened in Andreas' apartment after the red candle wax dripped down to the rim of the Chianti bottle. Andreas was the first, and until Nick, the only man she'd ever slept with, but after a couple of months, he was like a ghost who had dreamt his way into her life and vanished. At first she wondered whether she'd just imagined he'd made love to her. For months prior to their date she had lain awake at night conjuring up romantic scenes that ended with passionate lovemaking in a forest under the stars. The details of what happened became inseparable from things she'd read and movies she'd seen. Perhaps that was why she had waited so long. In the Redpath library, studying, she would look up and think she saw Andreas standing in line with books to check out, but when she looked more closely, it was always someone else. Now, the events from that time more than twenty years ago were clear.

Her mind drifted back to the doctor's office that day at the Royal Victoria College infirmary. When she first sat down Dr. Roderick had a reproachful look in his eyes, like a disappointed father who thought he had a lovely girl and suddenly found out she was a slut. When she told him marriage was impossible, he pulled his chair up close to the desk and drummed his fingers on the blotter.

"You're not thinking of an abortion, are you?" He saw immediately that an abortion was what she wanted. "You know it's against the law?

"And at your stage," he added, "dangerous. I'll make an appointment for you with the head of the Mary Martha Centre in St. Henri," he said. "You can have your baby there and give it up for adoption."

Everyone knew about the Mary Martha Centre. It was a place where high school girls from poor families waited out their pregnancies in hiding. When it was over, most never returned to school but if they did everyone talked about them. In grade nine, a girl who lived below Sherbrooke street disappeared in the middle of the school year. She came back the following fall but stayed only a few months and then dropped out and took a job at Woolworth's selling lipsticks.

Sometimes it happened to girls who came from "better families" but their lives were almost always ruined. A girl from the church, a basketball star with the highest marks in grade ten, was sent to England. She took her grade eleven at a private school in the Eastern Townships, but afterwards she suffered a nervous breakdown and went to the Allan Memorial Institute where she received electric shock treatments.

Dr. Roderick called the Centre. When he got the director, he lifted an old-fashioned fountain pen from the black marble holder on his desk and scribbled her case history as he talked. "Very advanced," he said, as though it were a disease in its last stages. He had graying hair below his knuckles. He underlined her name, went over the M in indelible black ink. She thought of Madame Defarge in *A Tale of Two Cities* knitting names that could never be unravelled into a long incriminating scarf of people destined one day for the guillotine.

"Two o'clock? That'll be fine." He looked up. "They'd like your phone number and address."

She gave him the name of the subway station at the end of the line in the east end. "Honoré Beaugrand," she said, in French, "4821 Honoré Beaugrand."

"What's that again? And your phone number?" She used the first three numbers of her real phone number plus the year her mother died.

"Honoré Beaugrand?" he asked when he put the phone down.

"East end," she said and watched him pull his chin into the jowls of his neck. She sat ramrod straight, her hands firmly clawed into the arms of her chair. "I'm sharing with some students from the University of Montreal," she said, looking into his watery gray eyes. "I'm a student at the Centre for French Canadian Studies." None of it was true. Eastern Europe was her specialty, and she'd always lived at home.

"I see," he said.

He'd speculate about whether she'd carried a banner with the French university students in the demonstrations police had to break up. Perhaps he'd wonder whether the father of the baby was one of them.

She asked for directions on how to get to the Mary Martha Centre and then stood up. "Thank you very much, Dr. Roderick. I very much appreciate it," she said. Leaving his office, she shrunk down as small as she could, hoping he'd forget her.

Outside on Sherbrooke, just before she turned down for the Danube Café, she tore the piece of paper he gave her with the address of the Centre into pieces and threw it in a sewer.

No one was in the café but Lila, a waitress of forty-five with dyed black hair. She served as an information clearing house for Hungarians on all sorts of subjects, not necessarily legal.

"Hi Lila," Maggie said trying to sound casual.

"The usual?"

Maggie nodded. She always ordered a Hungarian cheese sandwich and two Viennese coffees, one with the sandwich, and a second one later. She had been dropping into the Danube Café, after class mostly because it was one of the few places where you could order a coffee and read or write without the waitress hovering over you with a bill.

"Haven't seen you for a while," Lila said when she brought the order. Maggie had to find some way of broaching the subject.

"Exams," Maggie said. She fingered the edge of her plate. "And ah . . ." She took a breath. "Could you?" She wanted her to sit down, but the phone rang, and Lila went behind the counter to answer it. She knew she could never finish the sandwich, and Lila wouldn't get off the phone and bring her the second coffee until her plate was empty. She opened her purse, slid half the sandwich into her purse, and rushed through the rest, forcing herself to swallow, afraid one of the chatty Hungarian regulars would come in and her chance would be gone.

"Lila?" she said when the second coffee finally arrived. She didn't have to say very much. She pressed her stomach with the inside of her arm, and leaned over the table. "I can't go through with it . . ."

"How many months?" Lila asked.

Maggie raised all five fingers.

"I'll do what I can," Lila said, but she looked worried. Maggie monitored her face as she made the calls, saw the long silences, the resigned looks. "You've left it too late," she said. Maggie's heart sank.

Frantic, determined to locate Martin Ashbury, wherever he was, she called the Mathematics Department from a phone booth on Sherbrooke Street. Speaking with all the authority she could muster, she said Professor Ashbury *told* her to call, it was *urgent*. The secretary, he had said, would give a forwarding number.

Clutching ten dollars in quarters from the nearest bank, she rang Toronto from a closed phone box in the lower level of the Ritz Carlton Hotel. After she explained her situation, Professor Ashbury gave her a phone number and warned her to say nothing about an abortion.

"Just ask for an appointment," he said. The doctor would ask for a code number when she arrived. Hers would be the third phone number down the ninth page of Rs in the Montreal telephone book. The doctor didn't like to do late pregnancies, he said, but he was a surgeon who could and would, even though the risk of complications was higher. The fee would be $500. Before she died, her mother had given Maggie $1,000. "For emergencies," her mother had said.

Three nights later, a car driven by a woman of about thirty picked her up at seven in front of a restaurant in Snowdon and brought her into a clean six-storey apartment house in New Bordeaux. Inside, a three-room apartment was fitted up like an operating room in a hospital. The doctor wore an operating mask which he never took off, so she could never identify him later, but he had a comforting voice and calming hands. After he had done the procedure, and she was still lying on the table in the white hospital gown, he explained that twelve to forty-eight hours later, she would expel the fetus in a mini-birth with labour pains at the beginning and the placenta at the end.

Once she left the apartment, she was on her own. He hoped she had a friend to help her. "If you haemorrhage," he said, "go to the hospital. You can't come here."

The bus from Kingston to Montreal sped across the bridge from Ile Perrot onto the island at St. Anne de Bellevue. She gazed down at the murky water. The bus was quiet, as though everyone were asleep. In half an hour she would be in Montreal. She lay back and called up that terrible day she had buried for so many years.

It happened very fast the following afternoon around three o'clock when her father was in his study playing possible wedding music for a couple preparing to be married. On the floor next to the tub in the bathroom she was ready with a pile of old beach towels. She planned to throw a towel over the whole thing quickly without looking while she was still lying on her back, and scoop it up into a green garbage bag, but it was painful and took more than two hours.

When it was over, her resolve vanished, and she couldn't help looking at the fetus. It was a boy, his face taut and twisted, as though he'd struggled a long time. She cut the cord and held him under the bath tub faucet and let a thin stream of water gently wash away the blood. He was covered with purple bruises. She stroked his eyelids. His wrinkled little body was prematurely old, the joints barely covered like an arthritic old woman. Trying to contain her feelings, she laid him on top of the white table her mother had used to paint her nails a few months before she died.

Outside in a park, fire crackers were going off. The festivities for the St. Jean Baptiste Day weekend were starting early. Blood was everywhere: on the bathroom floor, the toilet, the sides of the tub, the towel racks, the mirror. Using a hand towel and a plastic pail, she swabbed up the blood until every trace was gone. Tears poured down her face. From under the sink, she drew out a Kotex box, emptied it, and stuffed her blood-splattered skirt into it. Later, while she boiled the water for her father's tea, she put the blood-soaked towels into the garbage tin on the back step outside the solarium.

Too shocked to feel, she routinely showered, attended to her blood, and slipped into her dressing gown. "We're picking up the rings tomorrow," she heard the bride-to-be talking to her father downstairs in the hall. Maggie stood dead still. The front door shut, her father came back up the stairs, and put Fauré's *Requiem* on his record player.

Maggie reached into the back of the linen cupboard and lifted out embroidered guest towels of fine white linen. They hadn't been used since her mother died. The material was soft as flower petals. The rose and lavender perfume of her mother's sachet floated into the air. She held her baby to her and with her other hand laid out the towels in overlapping squares like the white crosses among the red poppies of Flanders Fields. The towels were embroidered around the edge in blue forget-me-not flowers. Neatly arranged, they made a little shawl trimmed with pale blue lace.

Her hand supporting the back of the baby's head, she put him gently down as though he were only sleeping and wrapped him up tightly, folding up the bottom, like a papoose. On his face she laid a thin cotton handkerchief embroidered by her grandmother with her mother's initials when she was still Eugenia Anne MacDonald and not Mrs. Eli Joseph MacKinnan.

She opened the bathroom door. Her father was pacing in his study. She heard him sharpen a pencil, pull the leather-backed chair up to the desk. The requiem was still playing. She slipped into her room, the bundle in her arms, put the catch on the door and lay with him until the music came to an end.

"Magdalena," her father called into the hall. "Could I have my tea." It was 4:30. She knew without looking. At exactly 4:30, he wanted his tea and shortbread.

"Coming," she said wearily.

"I won't be home for supper," she said when she put down the silver tea service with the Twining's Morning Breakfast tea, the hot water, the thinly sliced lemon, the cookies. "I'm going to a movie with a friend." Back in her room, she put on the black skirt she had worn to her mother's funeral. If she haemorrhaged, it wouldn't show a stain. A Bach Brandenburg concerto was now playing. Carefully, she rolled up the baby in a Swiss eyelet pillow case from her bottom drawer, slipped past her father's study, down the stairs, out the garden door, and into the back lane.

She walked down to the corner in a daze and stepped on the first bus. Sitting at the back, she rocked to the rhythm of the wheels as the bus pressed toward the centre of the city. The bus swelled with people who jostled against her, talking loudly, banging parcels against her legs. When a child with a hot dog dropped mustard on her leg, she stared down at the spot, but let it congeal in the June heat. She took in everything, but reacted to nothing.

Moving toward the east end and the river, she kept changing busses, until she was far from anything she had ever seen before. After St. Lawrence Boulevard, she passed into another world. She sometimes browsed for books on Eastern Europe in second-hand book stores beyond Union Street, but the east end was mostly foreign. Away from the familiar landmarks of Eaton's and Morgan's and Birks, St. Catherine Street deteriorated into a shabby street of five and tens, Go-Go bars and second-hand stores.

It was 1968. Off in the distance, at Lafontaine Park, history was about to be made when rioters overturned police cars, started fires and hurled broken bottles at Prime Minister Trudeau while he watched the St. Jean Baptiste Day festivities along with Mayor Drapeau in front of the municipal library. She found out about it months later in New York at her Aunt Philana's. The bus could have been attacked, and she would have looked straight ahead, conscious only of the small bundle in her arms.

The bus passed under the Jacques Cartier Bridge and proceeded toward the oil refineries by the river where the street coiled through a digestive tract of stinking factories, rusting scrap iron heaps, and dangling cranes. At a street across from a hydro sub-station filled with transformers, the bus stopped at a sprawling gray factory. Acrid smoke filled the air. Near a loading wharf, railway boxcars clanged. The bus passed a boarded-up convent with a cracked white plaster statue of the Virgin, her arms stretched out over a balding yard with weeds so starved for soil their necks bent forward.

She got off the bus at a small park filled with children in sandboxes, mothers pushing swings, and boys playing catch. She walked slowly down to the river. She wanted to place her baby in a stream that would carry him out to sea, but the current was weak and a dead fish washed up on a rock. Behind her, children laughed. Pretending she didn't notice, she walked in the other direction until she found a weeping willow tree far from everyone. She lay down on the ground and curled up with her white bundle. Newspaper photos of concentration camp babies and starving African children, their faces thin as skulls, passed before her eyes. A police car crawled along the road by the park, past the weeping willow tree, back up to Notre Dame Street. She looked back at the river. Off in the distance, around a bend in the island, the Jacques Cartier Bridge arched high over strong currents running to the sea.

~

Her hand on the bridge railing, she stared down into the beckoning water and moved in and out of a faint. The height from the centre of the bridge terrified her. Cars thundered past her like giant bugs. She held her dead child close and swung back and forth. Trying to stay upright, she looked into the evening sun that hung in the sky above Molson's Brewery. She kept her eyes high, picking out the silvery spires of the churches up the north side of the river toward the harbour. The clock tower said nine o'clock. In the distance, sirens wailed.

She stretched out her arms and held her baby over the water. The rays of the sun blinded her. From behind the light, her father appeared at the baptismal font. "In the name of the father." He dipped his fingers in the water, his long black sleeves waving slowly over the head of the child. "And of the son." He dipped again. "And of the holy ghost." She dropped her baby into the river and collapsed at the side of the bridge.

~

"Madame."

Maggie looked up.

"Nous sommes à Montréal," the bus driver said. "We're in Montreal. At the terminus."

She gazed back out the window into the night and the reel went on. On the Jacques Cartier Bridge, she felt a man shaking her shoulder, trying to wake her up.

"Mademoiselle, mademoiselle. Are you hurt?"

"Madame." The bus driver was insistent. She looked up at him. "It's the end of the line."

Maggie didn't know how long she had been staring out the window into the dirty panes of the neighbouring green-striped bus at the arrival port of the Berri-UQAM terminus. She stood up cautiously, steadying herself on the seat in front of her, easing her way into the aisle and off the bus.

In the bus station she sat on a bench until her eyes adjusted to the bright lights. A cleaner swept a stringy mop back and forth across the floor in front of her. She remembered the walk back on the bridge more than twenty years ago, and the interminable bus ride home to the manse. The cleaner squeezed the mop tight. When everything around her came into focus, she walked to the snack bar and ordered a coffee.

Now she finally understood what had tied her so tightly to Nick. The pictures of little Stevie looking like a napalmed child flashed before her. She took a deep breath.

The loudspeakers in the bus station barked out departures for far flung places and she ordered another coffee. All the tension in her limbs was gone, but she still kept thinking about Nick. The curtain she had lived behind for more than twenty years was no more. She felt completely exhausted but also relieved as she took the escalator down to the subway en route to her St. Antoine Street apartment.

FORTY-TWO

~~

St. Antoine Street

AT THE BERRI-UQAM subway terminus, Maggie took the escalator down to the tracks, sat on a bench and waited for her train. Outside a closed news-stand, a man with a violin was playing mournful music. Some young boys who looked like street urchins were smoking cigarettes and she couldn't help imagining Nick as a young foster-home boy, but now was not the time to think about that.

What, she asked herself, was she going to do now? Her head was still spinning. She stood up and pulled down hard on the sides of the sweater Mercedes had given her. When she arrived home, she would e-mail Max at the paper and tell him she was quitting. Her days at the Montreal *Tribune,* she knew, were finished. If she wanted to work again as a reporter she would have to leave Montreal.

The subway train pulled up and she settled herself in a single seat facing the subway map. She'd worked at the *Tribune* for thirteen years, she thought. It was a long time. When the doors of the train opened five stops later at Guy-Concordia, she stepped off. Outside, the street was dark and deserted. She walked down Guy to St. Catherine Street and reflected on the three years she'd worked the graveyard shift of the Rim copy-editing all those Eastern European pieces. While she had flung herself into the intensity of Nick's world, the Rim had offered her a routine that had kept her going. But now? The idea of embarking on something new frightened her.

She crossed the street to a second hand book store and peered into the window at the books, some of them written by journalists. She wandered in and leafed through a copy of Joan Didion's *Salvador*. Writing was still in her blood, but she had to be practical, she re-minded herself, a quality that she had tossed away after she became entwined with Nick.

Maybe she could try freelancing in Russia, perhaps for radio. She had always dreamed of living in Moscow or St. Petersburg. With her knowledge of the language and the people, she could do offbeat stories, something different that might interest the CBC or National Public Radio in the U.S. Later, she thought, she might try writing something literary.

She left the book store and walked down Guy to St. Antoine Street. When she reached the Green Pasture Mission, she saw the Irish terrier in the window. He barked excitedly when he saw her. For a little while he had been good company, but she hadn't been able to keep him. Any attachment, she thought, had made her nervous.

She turned down Georges Vanier Street and there at the end of the lane behind her house was her red Innocenti sitting in the parking space as though nothing had happened to it. Up close, however, she saw the telltale black paint from the Cadillac she had smashed into on Park Avenue. Her thoughts about a future in the land of Puskin and Dostoyevsky quickly paled. Now, in addition to everything else, she was a hit-and-run driver.

The doors of her car were locked but at the back under a brick was an envelope with her keys. "Call as soon as you return, love Michael," was scrawled on the outside. Michael had gone to St.

Bartholomew for her car. He had drawn a picture of Archie the cockroach with Mahitabel the cat sitting up on the carriage of his typewriter. One of the cat's ears was chewed off but she still looked game for anything.

Maggie stood at the base of the metal staircase and glanced up at the window Nick had slid open just a week ago. She walked slowly up the stairs to the platform and turned the key in the lock. In the kitchen, the tap dripped slowly in the sink. Wind blew through a hole in the window. Everything seemed to be waiting . . .

She picked her way through the debris in the living room and walked upstairs. Along her bedroom floor, the tall lamps from the street cast a gloomy shadow. "Oh no," she gasped when she saw a long figure lying on her four-poster bed under a draped sheet, the feet sticking up in a V the way they did at the morgue.

Suddenly, like the crack of a bullet in the night, a spring snapped in the mattress and the body slowly rose. She screamed and seized the sides of the door. "Bingo!" Nick yelled and she froze into silence, but she was not afraid.

"I knew you'd fall for it." Nick was shaking his head as though he couldn't believe he'd been able to pull it off. He leapt off the bed and grabbed her shoulders. "You thought you were finally rid of me, didn't you?" He smelled of beer. Maggie stared at three empty beer bottles on the floor next to her bureau.

He pulled a tablet out of his back pocket and with his thumb crushed the pill on her bedside table. "For whenever I decide we need it," he said, looking at her sideways. The smell of bitter almonds, of cyanide, filled the air. "Something I want to make clear. If I decide to die, you're going too." He forced a breezy smile. "Till death do us part," he slapped her back. "Till then, kiddo, you're with me."

She was now back in Nick's frenzied world, but for the first time she felt strangely removed from it. "Somethin' else," he said. "Will you look at me?" He gripped her chin. "No matter where you try to go, I'll always find you. So there's no point in tryin' to get away. I know the crazy roads of your head like no one else. You leave behind a million clues."

She pulled his hand off her chin, took a step back, and flicked back her hair. "Don't think you can scare me with all this stuff," she said, looking him square in the eye. "I'm not going to fall for it."

"We gotta get outta here," he said.

"Look Nick . . ."

"We're goin' West," he interrupted. "That was our original plan until you torpedoed it. We'll take your car. It's out there in the back. I saw it."

Not on your tintype, she said to herself remembering a favourite expression of her mother's. She had other things to ponder, other plans, and they couldn't include being on the lam as a gangster's moll.

"Nick," she said. "If we were smart, we'd call the police and give ourselves up."

"Call the screws?" he shouted, "You want me to actually *call* the headbeaters I've fought all my life? No way."

"Okay, okay," she said.

Nick grabbed a beer, wrenched off the cap with his teeth, took a couple of gulps, and leaned his hip against the wall. Ever so casual, everything under control, she thought, just like one of the Sharks in *West Side Story* singing "Cool," but she knew that underneath he was frightened. "Nick," she said. "We have to talk."

"Talk?" he raised his voice. "Talk — ? What we have to do is hit the road," and he dug his fingers into her arm and pulled her downstairs past the wreck he'd created in her living room to the kitchen.

"Listen," she said, shaking him off her arm. "There's no way I'm going out West or anywhere else with you." She had to work hard to be tough with him. Some part of her was tempted to give in to him. "I've got a life to live as a writer," she protested, "and you've got a life to . . ."

"What!" he grabbed her wrist before she could finish. "I bet you're planning to leave the country! Once again you're bailing out on me!"

"Get real. There's going to be hell to pay for *both* of us for this Harley Davidson Special, but when it's all over we can each move on and begin to live our real lives, do something useful . . ."

"Useful?" he snarled and whacked the wall hard with the back of his hand. "Useful to who? This goddamn society that never gave me a chance? I have no intention of bein' useful, especially not your friggin' idea of useful. Get a job, Nick, get your grade nine, Nick," he mimicked her in a singsong voice. "Always at me like an elementary school teacher who thinks she knows everything.

"You wanna know something?" and he raised his fist at her, "you know nothing, nothing about real life. I'll do what I damn well feel like and it won't be useful. My job in life is to do crime and I'm goin' to do it." He turned around and looked through the window of the door at her car in the alley.

"There's no way we're going anywhere," she said evenly, "so stop looking down at the car, and," she added, "you do not have to do crime."

"You're lucky I'm not goin' to drag you outta here by the hair," he said, deliberately ignoring her last comment. He threw his shoulders back and stood in front of her. "I could do it, you know."

"Sit down, will you?" and she stared him down.

"Maggie, will you quit tryin' to order me around." He frowned, but she saw a crack in his resistance.

"C'mon," she cajoled. "No matter what, we can't run away together. It's never going to work — as you saw back there at the cabin."

From next door he heard a piano playing and thought of the classical music she liked that drove him around the bend. A reminder that they didn't belong together, he thought bitterly, but she was still beautiful, and he still wanted her, even though she was always tryin' to control him.

He slumped down into a chair and looked around her cosy kitchen with a shiny table that wasn't scratched, new chairs that weren't broken, and no cockroaches crawling around on the floor. Would he ever be able to afford anything as nice as this? Would he ever be able to even hold down a job? To control his frustration, he dug his fingers into his thighs and stared at the floor.

"You know," he said, "all the time I've known you, you've always had some damn work plan you wanted me to obey, and they were all shit." He thought of how she had wanted him play hockey so he could work as a hockey coach, and what had happened as a result of that. "I should have committed suicide after the trial," he muttered.

"You were never going to commit suicide," she said, flinching at the memory of the smell of the cyanide upstairs and his suicide ideas. "You're a survivor." And what a survivor, she thought. Could she ever have endured what he had, starting with being abandoned at six weeks on a bus by his mother?

"The only reason I didn't was because you were hangin' around." He looked up into her green eyes and remembered those evenings with her during the trial when she had met him in the square with picnics and he had told her the story of his life with Eileen. He stretched out his legs. "I needed someone really bad and you were there . . ."

"Oh Nick," she said, and her old feelings of attachment to him welled up inside her. "You still need someone," she said, "but it can't be me."

Nick knew what she said was true, but it was hard to hear her say it. He needed a girl who would eventually settle down with him and have a family, he thought, someone who could really be his, but would he *ever* find such a girl?

Maggie leaned in close to him. She had to tell him how vital he'd been to her. "It wasn't just a one-way street, you know. I needed you too."

"I guess I always sort of knew that," he said. That's what had kept him going, he said to himself, the feeling that she had actually needed him.

"Most of the time, though, I was a pain in the ass," he said. "Well," he stroked her arm and smiled, "except for the Harley ride I gave you, and the roll in the hay at the barn." His blue eyes sparkled for a second and she felt him relax. "You liked that, didn't you?"

"You know I did," and she tossed back her hair. "Without you, I'd still be looking and acting like a *liberian*."

408 ■ *Jackrabbit Moon*

"You look nice in that sweater," he suddenly said. "And those jeans that lady gave you fit just right."

"Thanks, Nick," she said and smiled. Because of him, she had learned to feel normal in clothes that showed off her body and made her look like a real woman. "You know, until I met you, I never dared live my own life. You taught me to experience things for myself."

Nick could hardly believe what he was hearing. The idea that she thought he could teach her *anything* astonished him. Everything he knew how to do was illegal. "But when I first met you," he said, "you were a famous reporter . . ."

"Yes, but that was *all* I was, and it wasn't enough. All I did was work. I used to be really afraid of men. Now I'm different.

"Something else . . ." She took a deep breath. "When I was seventeen, about the same age as you were when Stevie was born, I had a baby boy that died." She couldn't believe she was telling him this.

"I knew it," Nick said. "I knew it. You were too ashamed to tell me, weren't you? I *knew* something like that had happened."

"I forced myself not to remember," she said slowly. "Working hard as a reporter allowed me to hide from what I did. You're the first person I've ever told, but when I was five months pregnant . . ."

There was a long silence as he searched her eyes. "You killed your baby before it was born? Was that it?"

"Yes . . ." Avoiding his eyes, she looked down at the table and took a second to absorb the sound of his words. "I was as guilty as you and Eileen, but I got away with it." The vivid memory of how the fetus had looked when she held him in her arms came back to her. She had no idea how close he would be to a real human being.

"Nobody knew," she swallowed, making herself tell him more. "If the baby had come to term and lived, he would now be twenty-three." She raised her eyes to his, "About the same age as you."

"Oh my God, Maggie . . ." He shuddered as he thought about it. Maybe that's what his own mother had wanted to do to him, too.

"Maggie, let's take off now, before it's too late," he pleaded with her even though he knew they should each go their own way. "I promise to treat you right."

"No, Nick, I can't." Nick breathed in hard. The keys to the car were right there on the kitchen counter. He was strong enough to overpower her. No, he said to himself, he would not do it.

Through the hole in the window of the kitchen, he smelled food cooking from next door. "God," he said, "I'm starving." There was so much to think about, so much to say, and no way that he knew how to say it.

"Why don't I cook some steaks," Maggie said. From the refrigerator, she drew out two T-bone steaks, a couple of potatoes, and slid them into the microwave. "I can make us a nice steak dinner in just a few minutes." She pulled down a box of soda crackers and opened a tin of oysters.

Nick dug his fingers into the tin and gulped them down before she had to a chance to drain off the oil. "I haven't had anything real to eat for two days. We should turn off the lights," he said, switching off the light on the table and pulling across the kitchen curtains. He spotted a candle and lit it. "God, it smells good," he said. "Just like Mum Evans.

"Maggie . . ." he said, bending in close to her. He wanted to tell her that it took guts for her to tell him about her baby, but instead he squeezed her hand. "How're the steaks?" he asked.

"Nearly ready." She pulled the steaks and two baked potatoes from the microwave, poured some garlic butter on top, and put them on the plates.

Nick carved into the meat and took a bite. "You know," he winked at her, showing her his old charm, "you're a really good cook."

"Let me get you a beer," she said. "Should we put on a little music?" Maggie asked as she poured a Labatt Blue for him. "I have a Crystal Gayle tape right here. We can play it softly."

For a few moments, they listened to the sound of upbeat Country and Western music. How many times had she stretched out in the dark on her living room couch and imagined herself in his arms while she listened to Crystal singing "Sweet Baby on My Mind."

"Maggie," Nick said when the song came to an end, "will you forgive me for the way I treated you back there at the cabin?"

"Look," she said. "I gave you a rough ride too."

"I want us to be friends," he said. "Do you think that's possible?"

"We can try, Nick," and she took his hand.

She looked out the window to the lane behind her apartment and spotted a police car. Telling Nick the secret she had refused to face all these years had drained her, but now she had to stay alert.

"I see a cop car out there," she said.

"Shit," he said and immediately thought of bolting out the front door, but he knew the pigs would probably be there too. He drummed his feet hard on the floor.

"We're going to need help," she said. "I'm going to call Michael, okay?" and she picked up the phone.

"Michael, it's Maggie and I'm here at my apartment with Nick."

"I'll be right over," he said and hung up.

Nick pressed his palms down hard on his knees. It was just a matter of time before the uniforms out in the lane called in the SWAT team.

She looked over at him and smiled uneasily. They were waiting for something to happen and they both knew that it would be hard.

Just as they were finishing their dinner she heard Purcell's *Trumpet Voluntary* out in the lane. The whistling continued. Purcell's *Trumpet Voluntary* was the last piece she had played for Michael on the pump organ at the refugee centre two days before Nick went to the halfway house. Michael was telling them he was there.

It was during Crystal Gayle's last song, "Before I'm Fool Enough to Give it One More Try," that both of them heard the vibrations of feet creeping up the metal steps to the kitchen door. There was nothing he could do now, Nick thought. Soon it would be all over. Through a crack in the curtains, he saw a crouched figure on the platform in a SWAT team cap and turned the back of his chair to face Maggie in order to shield her. He wanted to protect her. "This is it," he said through his teeth. "Stay cool." He knew Maggie had no idea what violence could be in store for them and he prayed to God he'd be up to it.

Suddenly, the slats of the back door splintered into pieces, a light came on, and five men in army fatigues burst into her kitchen. They took a step forward and pointed their guns at him.

"Don't!" Maggie stood up and screamed. "He's not dangerous!" Nick's eyes darted around the room as he stood up and balanced on his toes. He wanted to astound the SWAT team with a flying leap that would catch them off-guard and let him escape, but he knew they would stop him with a bullet.

Maggie stepped in front of him and tried to shield him, but they shoved her away and four of them rushed at him. One flipped him over, straddled him, and twisted his hands across his back. In a second, his wrists were in handcuffs. Upstairs, other uniforms kicked doors and moved furniture as though they suspected other fugitives.

Maggie stood at the kitchen counter, horrified. No matter how much she wanted her own life, separate from Nick, something inside her belonged to him.

Nick struggled against the SWAT team but there was a heel on his shoulder and two more over his calves. A boot pushed down his head. One of the men felt along the insides of his legs and from a pocket pulled out the Swiss army knife, her Mastercard, and the receipt from the bar they went to near Kingston. From his other pants pocket, one of them flipped out her broken butterfly pin. Finally they dragged him to his feet. A patch of wax from the candle stuck to his hair and he flung his head back like a wild horse trying to dislodge it.

Two plain-clothes men in gray coats with the collars turned up now stood by the back door silently watching. Maggie felt their contemptuous eyes going over her from neck to knees, trying to understand the nature of her connection to a man like Nick. How could any of them understand? One of them reached over to the kitchen table and gathered up the objects from Nick's pockets.

"This was my idea," Nick suddenly shouted at the two detectives at the door. "And she fuckin' screwed it up! You can't imagine how stupid she was!" The detectives gave him a strange look. "Don't think she could get away from me either. I'm not a black belt for nothing!" The black belt was a lie.

Maggie cringed as she listened to him take the blame for everything. "Don't listen to him!" she cried out. She wanted to tell them the truth. The ride on the Harley was *her* idea, damn it. She had *wanted* everything that happened that evening, needed it maybe even more than he had.

As the SWAT team lifted him down the stairs by his elbows, Nick turned around and gave Maggie a special look and then yelled out at the clot of people in the lane who were watching. "Read all about it in *Bonjour Police!*" he shouted.

Maggie looked down at the people standing around and saw Barbara Smith-Jones behind the police van furiously taking notes. The story would not only be in *Bonjour Police,* it would also be in tomorrow's *Tribune.* What did she care, she said to herself, she was moving on, even though she didn't know exactly where. That night, before she went to bed, and before they had a chance to fire her, she would e-mail in her resignation.

When Nick reached the van, he looked up and saw Michael. The night he'd slept at the refugee centre before the verdict, Michael had had a ponytail and an earring, but now he was wearing a collar like a priest. They'd had a really good talk that night. Just as the screws were about to shove him into the van, Michael stepped forward. "I'm his pastor," he said and put his hand on Nick's shoulder. "We'll be in touch," he smiled. "Hang in there."

∽

The next day, after Max had received her e-mail resignation, there was a full-blown story in the *Tribune* that led with the fact that Nick had been picked up at her apartment after a daring escape with her from the prison on a stolen Harley Davidson.

Using her police sources, Barbara had been able to dredge up nasty details about stolen beer and Chef Boyardee from the grocery store outside Holt near Kingston.

Nick's prison buddy Stokie was even quoted. "A prisoner who witnessed the escape scene at St. Bartholomew from his ground floor window, but did not want his name used, said 'the whole idea was that crazy journalist's.' However, police reported that Mykonos took the blame for everything."

The piece ended with a reminder that Maggie was the daughter of Eli Joseph MacKinnan, the minister of St. Ninian's Presbyterian church. Barbara really knew how to twist the knife, Maggie thought. Surely, she could have stopped at taking a shot at her poor father.

~

A few days after the story appeared Maggie decided to go to the manse. For a couple of nights she had stayed with Michael at the refugee centre where she had told him everything that had happened, and now she felt she would have to face her father.

"Father," she called out after she'd opened the door to the manse. It was nine in the morning and he was still in the solarium having his breakfast. He stood up as soon as she came in but said nothing.

This was going to be very difficult, she thought. "I'm so sorry you had to learn about it in the newspaper."

"Sit down," he said. "Let me get you a cup of coffee," and he got down one of her mother's blue Mikado cups and poured her one. After a long silence he said, "I had no idea until I read it in the paper that you'd been spending the last three years visiting that young man in the penitentiary."

"Well . . ." she hesitated, "I didn't talk about it because I wasn't sure anyone would understand. Knowing Nick sort of transformed the way I see the world."

Her father listened without saying a word and she wondered what he was thinking.

"I'm going to try my hand at freelance radio reporting in Russia," she went on. "I'm starting to work on a radio documentary for National Public Radio in the U.S., and as soon as I can, I want to go over there. You know how interested I've always been in Russia. I have some contacts in Moscow and a place to stay."

"I think that's a very good idea," her father said, to her surprise. For the first time, she thought, he wasn't complaining about her going somewhere else.

"If I can, I'd like to be more than just a journalist. All my life I've been standing on the sidelines reporting on other people. I'd like to help in a more personal way, giving something of myself, maybe working as a volunteer, perhaps through a church . . ."

After she had a few sips of her coffee, her father said, "You know, here at the church, people are talking, but many have been saying good things. It was your mother's friend, Alice, who summed it up best. Over the past few months she's been working at a food bank. 'Your daughter,' she said, 'befriended an outcast. She wasn't afraid to take a risk.'"

"Alice said that?"

"Yes." Her father put his hand on her shoulder and looked into her eyes. "And that's what I'm thinking too."

"Look Dad," she said, abandoning her usual habit of calling him father. "Maybe it's hard for you to understand this, but I really needed Nick. He helped me just as much as I helped him."

Her father looked out the window for a few minutes. Then, changing the subject, he said, "I think you'll do a fine job in Russia. Tell me more about what you'd like to do there."

"Things are desperate in Russia right now," she said, "especially for the women. Now that the system has broken down, a lot of them are out on the streets with their families, begging. Hardly anyone is writing about it, but I know from my contacts in Moscow and St. Petersburg that this is happening."

She hoped that eventually in Russia she would be able to do more than produce radio documentaries. She still wanted to try experimenting with literary journalism, maybe even fiction, but she was keeping that to herself.

"Maggie, my dear," he said as he poured her another cup of coffee, "You are one very gutsy girl, but you've always been such a loner, I guess a little like me. I wish I could have helped you more. Those years when your mother was sick took their toll, didn't they?"

She thought about that for a few minutes but it was such a painful subject she didn't want to broach it, at least not right now. "Look Dad," she said, "as soon as I get settled in Russia I want you to come to visit."

"I'd love to come," he said, showing pleasure at being asked. "You know how much I adore opera. I'd really like to see some of those big Russian operas in St. Petersburg.

"I've decided to ease my way into retirement. The elders are hiring a younger minister who will start to take over so I'll have a little more time." He stood up to go. "I have someone I have to see at the church in about ten minutes," he said, "but come back for dinner. One of the women from the auxiliary brought over a shepherd's pie." He smiled. "We can have that."

FORTY-THREE

~⌒

Send Off

AS MICHAEL DROVE her to the airport, Maggie thought about the radio documentary on the situation of women in Russia that she had produced a week before for National Public Radio in the U.S. She had been lucky it had been so well-received. Now she felt confident about going to Moscow to try working as a freelance radio reporter for CBC in Canada and NPR in the States. She was grateful that Katerina Petrovsky, who had stayed with her in Montreal three years before on a cultural exchange, would be meeting her at the other end in Moscow.

She had decided to broadcast under the name Catherine Mac-Donald, using the first name her mother had always wanted to call her along with her mother's maiden name. She had told her father about it and he thought it was a good idea. "Your mother would have liked that," he told her. Nick's escape and her part in it had been carried nationally by press and radio. For that reason, her old name, she thought, needed a rest, but she didn't tell him that.

Michael carried her suitcase and her tape-recorder into the air-port. As she swung through the revolving doors, her heart twisted at the thought of Nick back in prison. If he hadn't taken all the blame for everything, she probably would have been charged. "Michael," she said, suddenly out of breath, "you *will* continue to work with Nick, won't you?"

"All the time you were interviewing those women in Russia over the phone for your documentary, and talking to the CBC and NPR, I was working behind the scenes," he smiled. "I have some things to tell you but I wanted to wait until the last minute. I saw Nick for the first time this afternoon. Up until now, it's just been phone calls."

"So how did it go? Why didn't you tell me you were going?"

"I wanted to wait until I saw how it went," he said. "He's out of Stillpoint and in medium security over in St. Bartholomew in the same cellblock as Stavro, that Greek buddy of his."

"Oh," she said, "what a break."

"I told Nick not to get back into making raisin-jack with him or he'd never get out of the joint and I'd be visiting him for a very long time. Stavro is once again teaching him Greek and he has a sister of twenty-three that he wants Nick to meet." He waited a few seconds for her to take in that one.

"I'm okay with all that," she said. "Nothing would please me more." It was time Nick got a life with someone his own age.

"But the big news," he continued, "is that next week Nick's start-ing a course in motorcycle mechanics. I arranged for one of my ex-street kids who now runs a second-hand motorbike shop in LaSalle to come in for a one-on-one program."

"You have to be kidding! How did you pull off that one?"

"Brother St. John made a couple of phone calls. Remember him?"

"Oh yes. What kind of guy is this ex-street kid?" she asked, sud-denly feeling protective of Nick. "He's not in the business of stolen motorcycle parts or anything, I hope."

"Absolutely not," said Michael. "The guy has spent time in juvie like Nick but now he's completely straight. Don't worry. He's an upbeat guy who'll give Nick confidence," he smiled, "and later, maybe a job."

Amazing, she said to herself. Now there were all kinds of possibilities, but she couldn't help wondering how Nick was coping with the craziness of being back in the joint after being out "in the free" with her on the open road. "What's the atmosphere like in medium security over at St. Bartholomew?"

"Completely different from Stillpoint," Michael said. "Nick seems to have won the respect of the other inmates. In the visitors room I could see looks of admiration and envy."

Admiration and envy? Maggie thought. That was a change!

"Think of it," and Michael gave her a wide smile. "Here's an inmate who escapes in the middle of the night with a sexy dame who is dying for a roll in the hay with him. And then out of thin air she finds a Harley Fat Boy for him that he manages to hot-wire and steal. Later, after a vicious Swat team waving guns shows up at her house, he's gentleman enough to take the rap and let her entirely off the hook!"

"Put that way," she laughed, "it sounds better than the movies . . ."

Maggie leaned against her friend for a moment and remembered the feel of Nick's body next to hers during the wild motorcycle ride down the Richelieu river with the stars in the sky and the sparkling villages that made her think of the island of Naxos. Abandoning every vestige of control, she had to admit, had taken her to another planet.

"I spoke this afternoon with the prisoners' rights people," Michael went on, "and they told me that if Nick behaves, Corrections Canada will transfer him to Minimum and then after that, perhaps to a halfway house. But he'll still need a lot of prayers," he said. "All *he* has, when it comes right down to it, is his wits."

Maggie thought about that for a minute. People from the world she was part of, had, she suspected, saved her from the jaws of the justice system. Nick, however, had to depend mostly upon himself. How different in the end was she from most of the people in the media, the courts and the social welfare network whose workings she had condemned?

The prison system, though, was treating Nick better than she had expected, but that, she figured, was mostly because he had a pastor on his visitors list, even though Michael sometimes looked more like a rock musician than a minister.

"I told Nick you were leaving today for Russia, and he asked me to give you a hug goodbye and told me I should tell you thanks for everything. He made me promise to tell you about the motorcycle course."

"I'm the one that should be thanking *him*," she said. "When I get to Moscow, I'll send him a card."

The airport was busy, everyone with some sort of story to tell, Maggie thought. After she'd checked in and she was approaching the boarding gate, she felt touched when she sighted Alphie looking his usual sleek and worldly self along with Foxy in a coat so rumpled he could pass for a court house carrion crow. What an unexpected surprise! She hadn't seen either of them since she had come back from her escapade with Nick, though she had spoken with each of them on the phone.

"We have a little present for you," Alphie said, and he handed her a package wrapped in the old Soviet Union flag. "Don't forget to read the card."

Without him, she thought, where might she be now? "You didn't by any chance have a word with the police, did you?" Alphie had always kept up his police and court contacts. The fact that she had never been arrested puzzled her a little and she wondered if he was behind it.

Alphie rolled his eyes up and smiled. "Of course not. You know I'd never do a thing like that. The articles in the papers were punishment enough, my dear. Don't think of what happened as a calamity," he said. "Think of it as a story you'll be able to dine out on forty years from now. I wish I had one like it." He patted her affectionately on the back. "It'll make you a fabulous old lady!"

"Thanks guys. I couldn't have asked for a better send off," and after giving Michael a special wave she stepped through a door and into the line-up for the routine security check.

But she still had an important phone call to make before she boarded the plane. In the boarding lounge she picked up a pay phone, wondering if her father would be back from the funeral he had had to conduct, and he was.

"Dad," she said. "I'm at the airport. In just a few minutes I'll be taking off for Moscow."

"I'm so sorry I couldn't see you off myself, Maggie," he said, and she could feel warmth in his voice. "Write to me, okay? You're a writer. Write. And I haven't forgotten our plans to go to St. Petersburg together and take in some Russian opera. I'm counting on that."

"Oh Dad," she said. "I'm counting on it too. *A la prochaine.* Talk to you soon. Goodbye," and she hung up.

~

The aircraft lifted off into the cold January night and Maggie watched the familiar landmarks of the city disappear. After they had been airborne for more than an hour, she unwrapped the package from Alphie and Foxy. It contained two pair of jeans and a card with some impish-looking animals on the front. Inside it said, "In case of an emergency, here's two pairs of jeans you can exchange for whatever you need. Keep a pair for your exit out. Keep dancing." There was also a cassette of Russian folk music.

She had to smile at the way they wanted to paint her foray into Russia as a lark. If she acted like a real journalist and not just a reporter on the fly, it would be hard, slogging work. She was determined not to buy into all the stereotypes the West was peddling about how wonderful Russia's launch into capitalism would be.

The flight attendant was passing by asking people if they wanted drinks. Holding a vodka and tomato juice, she shut her eyes for a few minutes and wondered what Nick was doing. She had gotten off lightly. Prison was a nightmare, even if he had rediscovered a blood brother, whereas she was on a trip she had dreamed about. She wondered how Eileen was faring in Calgary with Colin, her new husband. Perhaps Esther Sykes at the Y would know. Halfway through her drink, when everything around her seemed to soften, she thought of the *Tribune* article that had appeared after the SWAT team burst into her apartment.

Her poor father, she thought, as she remembered the pointed reference in the piece to her father and the church. But he had taken it completely in stride. Just before she left he had talked about going to Venice on the McGill alumnae opera tour. Some day, he had promised, he would tell her about the Italian Magdalena she had been named after. She wondered what might have happened to this obviously sparkling woman he had known in his youth. Who knows? Maybe she was still alive.

She looked out the window of the plane into the black night and then decided to leaf through the newspapers that she had picked up in the airport. Toronto, she read, was now the new murder capital of Canada, surpassing Montreal for the first time, and unemployment across the country stood at one and a half million. The nation that a United Nations study deemed the best place in the world still had dark spots to answer for.

She flipped to the international news in a couple of papers, including the *New York Times* to see what she could pick up about life in the new country she was about to settle in. Gorbachev, who had at least tried to find a middle ground between socialism and capitalism, was out and the drunkard Yeltsin was in trouble. On American advice, she read, price controls in Russia were gone, and now hundreds of angry customers were smashing store windows in protest. Dog and cat meat was for sale, and in Moscow some wondered whether it might not be safer than a shipment of British beef, possibly rejected by the European Community because of mad cow disease. "Single Mothers Face Struggle to Survive," was the headline in one paper, and in another

"Street Children Call a Moscow Train Station Home." In still another it was, "Now It's Cadillacs, the Car for Discriminating Ex-Comrades."

Before she'd left Montreal, she'd spoken to an economist specializing in Russia and he had said that financiers from the West were pouring bundles of money into Russia, hoping to get rich, but that the money wasn't going into anything productive. "They did the same thing in Mexico and the Philippines," he'd said.

Maybe she would investigate that. "When the economy collapses," her contact had said, "the IMF always wants the money to go back to the lenders from the West and the poor end up suffering just so the financiers can recoup their losses."

Maggie sighed at the dimensions of the task that lay ahead. The mafia, Dickensian poverty, and the killing fields of nationalism. "These are tough stories that will require judgment," her Aunt Philana had told her when she had gone to New York to see her the weekend before to say goodbye. "But after everything you've been through, you'll be able to handle it."

She was glad she'd had the courage to tell her Aunt Philana about the darker side of her experience with Nick. There were some things, she felt, that she could tell only to a woman. She had thought of driving back to thank Mercedes personally, but instead she had phoned her and sent a cheque.

She thought some more about the work she would do in Russia. Community, she said to herself. She must never lose sight of the dream of community. "Write and broadcast about things that show how people can help one another build community," Michael had counselled her at the refugee centre the night before. She hoped that in Russia she would be able to make friends and let herself come close to people. Thank you, Nick, she said to herself, for helping me open that door. Without him, she would still be hiding behind a mask.

No matter where she lived, Nick would always be alive in her memories. She leafed through her pile of newspapers and in the

Tribune looked under the motorcycles for sale section at the Harley Davidson ads. Then she leaned back in the seat and finished off her vodka and tomato juice. The vibrations of the Harley as Nick revved up to take off with her on the jackrabbit parole filled her mind, but after a few minutes they faded and she looked out into the sky.

Off in the future, once he was out of a halfway house, she imagined Nick in a motorcycle shop repairing the engine of a Harley Davidson for a man in a business suit. Several motorcycles leaned against the wall, a greasy table was strewn with parts, and rock music filled the air. Nick screwed something onto the motor, patted the tank, and with a smile, proudly wheeled out the bike. In control, Maggie thought, maybe for the first time. She ordered another vodka and tomato juice and drifted off. Later, once she had established a life of her own in Russia, she would think about how to write about him.

About the Author

~∿

SHEILA MCLEOD ARNOPOULOS is the author of *Voices from French Ontario* (1982) and *The English Fact in Quebec* (1980), with Dominique Clift, which won a Governor-General's award in non-fiction for the original French version, *Le Fait Anglais au Québec.*

An investigative journalist for many years in Montreal, she has written about English/French relations, minority issues, and the problems of the working poor. She has received a National Newspaper Award, a Media Club of Canada Award, as well as a France/Quebec Intercultural Exchange Award to write about foreign workers in France. She was also given a special prize by the YWCA in Montreal for her writing about women and work.

Now at Concordia University in Montreal, she teaches in the Journalism Department and at Lonergan College where she gives an intercultural relations course that produces a book of short stories by students. She continues to write as a freelance journalist about contemporary social issues. This is her first novel.